Praise for the Blood & Ancient Scrolls Series

"Blood Ex Libris is a fast-paced, blood-soaked novel of passion, adventure, and vampire politics, as intimate as it is intense."

— Thomas Roche, Stoker Award Finalist

"Pick it up for the sexy, dangerous fun, devour it for the fast-moving storyline, and reflect on it for a long time to come for the genuine scholarship and creativity."

— Lars D. H. Hedbor, author of Tales From A Revolution series

"These books are simply the most fun. Raven Belasco brings much to the table: a lively writing style, a fascinating take on the undead, a great deal of discreetly hidden scholarship, and a sheer joy in creativity which can sweep the reader along pell-mell. Come to these books for the hot sexytimes; stay for the sheer quality; linger for the quiet intelligence that underlies it all."

— Chaz Brenchley, author of The Books of Outremer, and the Crater School series

By Raven Belasco

THE BLOOD & ANCIENT SCROLLS SERIES

Blood Ex Libris
Blood Sine Qua Non
Blood Ad Infinitum
Blood Triad (A Collection of Three Novellas)

ALSO

Adventures in Bodily Autonomy: Exploring Reproductive Rights in Science Fiction, Fantasy, & Horror
(Editor)

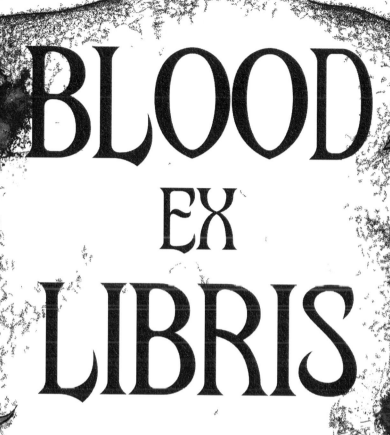

BLOOD EX LIBRIS

BOOK 1
IN THE
BLOOD & ANCIENT SCROLLS SERIES

RAVEN BELASCO

This is a work of fiction. Names, characters, places, and incidents are the products of the author's imagination or are used fictitiously. Any resemblance to actual events, locales, or persons, living, dead, or undead, is entirely coincidental.

Raven Belasco supports the right to free expression and the value of copyright. The scanning, uploading, and distribution of this book without permission is theft of the author's intellectual property. If you would like permission to use material from this book (other than for review purposes), please contact rb@ravenbelas.co Thank you for your support of author's rights.

Copyright © 2023 by Immoral Influence Publications

All Rights Reserved.

Originally published in a slightly different form in paperback and ebook in the United States by LMBPN in 2020.

Library of Congress Cataloguing-in-Publication Data

Belasco, Raven.

Blood Ex Libris / Raven Belasco

p.   cm.

ISBN: 978-1-960942-00-5

eISBN: 978-1-960942-01-2

1. Vampires—Historical Vampires—Vampire folklore—Fiction 2. Romanian History—Fiction 3. Djinn—Fiction 4. Librarians—Fiction 5. Journeys—Journeys of personal growth—Fiction

www.ravenbelas.co

This book is dedicated to my father. He never managed to finish *his* novel, although he worked on it his whole life. From him I inherited the problem of "I forgot to buy the damn milk because I'm in the fucking 18th century, that's why!" which is no doubt as frustrating to those around me *now* as it was to those around him.

It's also dedicated to Cairngorm McWomble the Terrible—who would much rather that I be walking him right now instead of faffing about writing this. He has no idea (nor, to be honest, does he care) how many plot problems have been resolved as I escort him on his walkies. He is the finest companion a writer could hope for.

Sometimes it's better to light a flamethrower than to curse the darkness.

— Sir Terry Pratchett, Men at Arms

Contents

Author's Note on Language	1
1. Prologue	2
2. Chapter One	5
3. Chapter Two	13
4. Chapter Three	24
5. Chapter Four	29
6. Chapter Five	38
7. Chapter Six	56
8. Chapter Seven	63
9. Chapter Eight	73
10. Chapter Nine	89
11. Chapter Ten	105
12. Chapter Eleven	129
13. Chapter Twelve	154
14. Chapter Thirteen	173

15.	Chapter Fourteen	185
16.	Chapter Fifteen	198
17.	Chapter Sixteen	226
18.	Chapter Seventeen	257
19.	Chapter Eighteen	285
20.	Chapter Nineteen	312
21.	Chapter Twenty	332
22.	Chapter Twenty-One	352
23.	Chapter Twenty-Two	378
24.	Epilogue	386
25.	Index of Non-English Phrases	390
	Glossary of the Am'r Language	397
	Acknowledgments	400
	About Raven Belasco	404

Author's Note on Language

This book has a bunch of words and phrases that are not in English. Some are in the am'r language, and some are in the languages from around the world, since the am'r get around and often speak the language of the country they grew up in, or the country they are in at the moment.

The am'r words are given definition when they are first used, but if you forget any of them, there is a glossary of the am'r language in the back of the book.

Likewise, there is an index of all the non-English words and phrases you will encounter along the way. If the meaning of those words is vital to the understanding of the story, I've made sure they get explained in the text. However, sometimes our protagonist doesn't understand what she is hearing. So you have a choice: you can experience the moment as she is experiencing it, or you can go to the index and look up the words if you don't like not knowing.

Whatever you choose, I hope you enjoy the journey!

Raven

Prologue

It's half-past-apocalypse, and I find myself sharing a weird bush-tree with this strange little rodent-thing for the same reason: we wanted to have a moment of privacy to do our business.

Well, I *think* it's a rodent. It seems to have more in common with a kangaroo, and it's mostly composed of outsized ears and a tail. But it, whatever it is, is kindly sharing this bush and this moment of solitary retreat with me. When you have shared the deeply vulnerable experience of *squatting* with any living creature, you tend thereafter to feel a commonality and respect for your fellow squatter, even if it *is* a ludicrous little bouncing thing. And since I now know what a ludicrous little thing *I* am compared to much more powerful things, I am doubly prepared to respect other living creatures. Even if they bounce and have extremely silly ears.

I can smell explosives and fire. I am covered in blood, and while I'd love to say it's mostly the blood of my enemies, I think it's half and half at best. OK, probably mostly mine.

My ears are ringing, and my vision is a bit funny. I keep seeing things out of the corners of my eyes, or even right in front of me. I blink and there is nothing there.

I think I'm in quite a lot of pain. My uncertainty about my pain level is due to the side effects of shock—something I appreciate for the first time in my life. Lately, I have been in shock so often, and so intensely, and now for such a sustained period of time, I'm amazed I haven't burned out my adrenal glands or nervous system.

But apparently I have not, and I'm grateful for the small mercy because when I look down and see all the blood—see the fabric of my trousers and the skin of my thighs slashed to ribbons, clotted into a ragged crusted mess between my legs, it hits me with a jolt, followed by a rush of nausea. It's good I can look at awful things and feel as upset as a person should. It proves I'm still a person, if not precisely a normal human. Not anymore. Not ever again.

Holding my squat, I try not to think about how my thighs feel. I look at the bouncy mouse-thing for distraction. It's done now and it rises up on impossibly tall hind legs to look at me. Its "arms" would make a Tyrannosaurus rex feel well-endowed. I combine that thought with its little pink whiskered nose twitching at me, and I find myself giggling. *Definitely shock.*

I have to go back down now. Underground. Back down into demolished caverns filled with murderous monsters. At least they're *my* monsters, which is a better situation than last time I was aboveground. I can't be certain the worse kind of monster isn't lurking about up here even now. I make such a tempting target for snatching; if they smell me, I don't think they could resist. And with all this blood, and the accumulated filth of everything I've just gone through, I don't see how even a normal human being could avoid smelling me.

The sun is coming up. I cannot handle the thought of the light-induced migraine, which will be added to my pains if I don't get back into the safety of darkness. Back to the protection of my monsters.

He's there waiting for me at the crack in the rock, which is one of the remaining openings not blown into smoking heaps of rocks and bodies. He is being polite—giving me a little space, a little privacy—but I know I need to hurry up and get back down there. I mean, I don't even *know* if the one person—albeit another monster—I can trust to always be truthful with me is all the way dead, so I need to go back down and help my blood-covered monster. My beloved.

Chapter One

I CAN VISUALIZE THE first time we met so clearly. The children's reading hour is every Friday at 4 PM during the school year. It was my favorite part of the job—because let's face it, I didn't get into librarianship for the money. The children's and young adults' section of the library is decorated in warm primary colors, brightly lit to chase away the ever-darkening days of November. Sitting in a semi-semi-circle around me were the restless five-year-olds up through the boredom-affecting twelve-year-olds, as usual. For once, they were all listening quietly as I read aloud *James and the Giant Peach*, although ten-year-olds Emma and Skylar were making each other friendship bracelets, and I thought six-year-old Noah was more or less asleep. I was just getting to the part where the Centipede tells off the Cloud-Men when I found myself losing my place, unable to focus.

He was on the other side of the children's area, sitting in the shadow of the empty puppet theatre behind Jessie and Avery, ages seven and eight—both of whom, along with the rest of the kids, were now staring at me, wondering why I'd stopped dealing them their Dahl-fix. He did not fit in this primary-colored world; his pale olive skin did not go well with crayon-yellow and construction-paper-green. His oval eyes were just nondescript dark eyes under the fluorescent lights, deep-set and shadowed in his face. The long black curls that fell around his shoulders did not reflect the brash reds or fluorescent blues in interesting highlights. His forehead was too wide, and his nose too aquiline and long. His clothes were more eye-pleasing: a black shirt that draped like silk from wide shoulders, and very nice black leather boots peeped from the bottom of well-tailored black trouser legs. The monochrome black made him protrude incompatibly with that warm, bright world. It also made him seem taller than he was.

He smiled at me and made a minuscule gesture indicating, "Please, do go on," and I abruptly remembered the over-sized peach and audience of confused children. I applied myself studiously to the telling of the tale, ignoring the sensation of his presence with painstaking effort. It worked; when I looked up at the end of the hour, he was gone.

For the next few days, I personified distraction. For example, I misfiled several new books, including a rather graphic adult fantasy novel, which did *not* belong in the children's section. My two co-workers, Andre and Zuzanna, each took me aside at different times, asking if I was OK. I assured them I was fine, went back to my desk, and stared off into space at the dark stranger whom only I saw.

He showed up next at Beowulf's. I wasn't surprised. In this small town, there aren't overly many options in the late-night-café-with-coffee-you-can-actually-drink department. We didn't even rate a Starbucks, so it was the only place to go in town. Luckily for me, it not only proudly produced both excellent food and beverages, but it was also only a block from the pint-sized public library where I spent much of my time. I would start my day with their dark chocolate mocha, and end it with their special-of-the-day for dinner, lingering over a cup of oolong tea and chatting with various book-minded locals. I even held a modestly successful monthly reading group there, which drew a varied crowd of rose-growing old ladies, students with body mods and trendy hairstyles, the local curmudgeon, and the local motorcycle club, which had only one member more than the curmudgeon club.

I would generally be at Beowulf's 'til it closed, whether or not it was reading group night. There was nothing to call me back to the in-law apartment over Mr. and Mrs. Muckenfuss's garage. Ma Muckenfuss had furnished and decorated it in finest "country grandma" style, and the only things there I really liked to look at were the brick-and-board bookshelves I'd stacked against almost every wall. There was also nothing to do except put in unpaid hours upgrading the library website, which was by now far grander than the Helen Abigail Winstringham-Fenstermacher Memorial Library truly required.

It's not that I was bored. It *is* important to keep small-town public libraries open and available to all, and I was hands-on with getting kids excited about reading and keeping the library as full of current and thought-provoking books as we could afford and shelve. But for one who'd dreamed of becoming an archivist, I'd fallen pretty far from my expectations. The only "old" books we had were the town council logs and birth records from 1853 onwards and the Helen Abigail Winstringham-Fenstermacher Collection, which was mostly recipe books, H-A-W-F's personal journals, the complete works of James Fenimore Cooper from 1896, and some turn-of-the-century Montgomery Ward and Sears Roebuck catalogs. Not exactly thrilling stuff.

The little dragon-shaped cast-iron teapot—Beowulf's was dedicated to the details—had been refilled once already, and I was considering going home and starting to read a new series of science fiction graphic novels as my weekend activity when Mr. Mysterious came in. The nighttime was kinder to him; his skin looked healthier in the amber-shaded light, and his all-black fashion statement seemed less ridiculous in a café-at-night setting. He still could have been taller.

Why should it matter to me, I had to ask myself. It was not like he was going to fall passionately in love with me,

I just stared at him. What do you say to that? I thought of describing "Sandu" in return, but all I could come up with was it sounded a bit like "Xanadu." Which I wisely did not share. I just kept my mouth shut, which usually makes people think I'm wiser than I am. Or at least not quite as socially inept.

"You work in the library, do you not, Anu—Noosh?"

Well, that started me off. I am passionate about my job, even if it's not quite the prestigious career I'd hoped for with the ink still damp on my Master of Library Science degree. Alexandru asked the right interested, sympathetic questions to keep me pouring my story out. I don't usually talk this much, and certainly not to somebody I've just met.

It was when the Beowulf's staff was starting to make the noises baristas make when they want to go home and wash off the smell of coffee grounds that I realized I'd monopolized the entire conversation and knew nothing about him except his name. Not only a terrible way to make a first impression, it was also more than a bit frustrating. What had come over me? I'm not usually *that* clueless.

"I'm *so* sorry for talking your ear off, Alexandru. I'd really like to get to know more about *you*," I apologized as I started gathering up my coat and bag. My glasses fell off as I bent over and I had to awkwardly shove them back onto my face, damning myself for not having gotten a better-fitting pair.

He smiled warmly, which made me feel all melty inside. Far too melty. "It is no problem, Noosh. I enjoyed hearing all of it. And I look forward to talking with you again."

And with that, he swept out of Beowulf's, his three-quarter-length leather jacket—having magically gone from being laid over the arm of the chair to on-and-fitting-snugly—a muted gleam under the streetlight. I stared after him. It'd been a prime night for staring. Indeed, including the recent days' bouts of staring into space, I might see if there was a world record I could break.

Chapter Two

HE WAS AT THE children's reading hour again the next week. I was going to have to talk to him. It's not that we're ageist at the Helen Abigail Winstringham-Fenstermacher Memorial Library, it's just parents generally don't like strange men—strange *foreign* men with long hair, dressed all in black—hanging out with their children. The kids didn't seem to mind or even notice him. Utter self-involvement for the win! I valiantly continued with *James and the Giant Peach*, despite being able to feel Alexandru Solin's presence.

After Skylar, Emma, Noah, Avery, Jessie, et al., were collected by their respective parents, I wandered as nonchalantly as possible over to him. He was leaning against a bookshelf, engrossed in *Bunnicula*. "If you apply for a library card, you can take it home with you," I said, feeling cool and smooth and in control, "although only if you are a resident of Centerville." There. That totally didn't sound like I was fishing for the answer.

"I am afraid I am living over in Blackacre," he said apologetically, and I had to stifle myself from asking, "So why aren't you in *their* public library?"

"Beowulf's has the best coffee I have found in the area," he said. I found it a doesn't-explain-half-enough explanation but was distracted when he added, "I was wondering if you would be dining there tonight?"

"Tonight and every night, unless I defrost something at home," I heard my mouth reveal without input from my brain. Shit! Why'd I tell him that? It makes me sound like a loser as well as being a librarian, which of course equals geek. Geek and loser. Way to go, Miss Cool, Smooth, and In Control.

"I myself never cook," he responded, winning my eternal gratitude.

"It's not much fun cooking only for oneself," I hazarded.

"It is not," he said solemnly. Well, there was another question answered. "So," he continued, "is that a yes? Will you dine with me this evening?"

I restrained myself from shoving my glasses up my nose. It was my nervous tic, but now was not the time for it. *Be cool, be smooth.* "Well..." I paused to make sure I remembered profoundly complicated things like, oh, my own library's hours of operation and the simple closing-up tasks I had done every night for years. "Um, I'm here until nine. I don't know how late you want to eat dinner?" Damn, damn,

damn! Could I not have phrased it in a way not guaranteed to end all possibility of a dinner date?

"Is it acceptable if I meet you there at 9:30 PM, and we share at least an after-dinner drink?" He smiled again, seeming pleased to have come up with this potentially workable solution.

I personally was beyond delighted with it. "That's perfect!" Did I sound too enthusiastic there?

"I will look forward to 9:30 and to seeing you…Noosh." A bit of extra warmth in his voice as he said my name? Oh, *he* was the cool, smooth, and in-control one here. I was just hanging on, trying not to make a fool of myself. And not particularly succeeding.

"Me too," I belatedly responded as he slid away. He moved like a cat. Maybe he was a professional dancer? It would explain his confidence, lithe movements, and sleek, exotic looks. But why would a professional dancer be in Centerville, or even Blackacre, which was no bigger a town, nor any more prominent as a center of the arts?

Needless to say, I did not pay too much attention to my last hours of work and went through the close-up checklist like an automaton.

External existence didn't start again until after 9 PM. He was there when I got to Beowulf's, an espresso to hand. Drinking espresso—how sophisticated and European of him. I knew no one who didn't get some variety of caffeinated beverage involving lots of milk and a flavored sugar syrup, possibly with whipped cream and things sprinkled on top as well. He was at the table with the cushiest chairs. I tried and failed not to think: Aww! It's "our table," and he remembered!

It was normally a happy discovery to come into the café and find it was filled with the warm, spicy scent of their award-winning Grendel's Mother's Black Bean Chili. This time I was too busy trying to eat neatly while enjoying making eye contact. Not a time to spill food down your shirt. And remember not to talk with your mouth full. I didn't eat much, and what I ate, I didn't taste.

Alexandru *nursed* that espresso. I managed to eat an entire meal—well, at least to move it around my salad plate and chili bowl as I talked and listened—and drink two pots of oolong tea in the time it took for him to not finish his wee cup of thick black coffee. Perhaps no one actually likes espresso?

Alexandru got more out of me about my life than I think I'd ever told anyone before. Not having any friends after second grade. Being called "bookworm" and "nerd" by everyone in the school, even the other geeks, and how books were my only friends for years. My discovery of computers, which made me even geekier but also helped me in making friends, which helped me care less about being a geek; my excitement about how computers were not the enemies of books and libraries but their best friend. How, while growing up, I'd *lived* at my local public library and had a schoolgirl-crush on Miss Evans, who was the archetypal "sexy librarian" and how she'd inspired me to get my Bachelor's in Computer Science and after that, my Master's in Library Science. About my wonderful years of college, where I finally blossomed socially. About my hopes of being a digital archivist someday, even though there were so few opportunities.

Alexandru did drop a few hints about himself. He would say things like, "Ah, I understand just how it is to feel alone amongst your peers," but before I could get more out of him, he would ask me another question, which would set me off again. I finally managed to nudge some information out of him: he had moved to the U.S. from Romania, had a house over in Blackacre, and had recently returned from some travel. When I inquired about his trip, he was pretty vague about details. He had been visiting family, who were pretty widely spread out around the world. *OK*. And he was independently wealthy, which didn't mean much to me but sounded nice.

I got much more out of him when the talk turned to music. He was a big Mahler fan too, leaving me in the dust. The passionate way he spoke about the great Gustav's music enthralled me. Given his knowledge and insight, I joked, he should write a book about Mahler. This brought the first smirk I'd seen to his face. He muttered something like, "Don't think Gustl would like that!" and promptly changed the subject. He got me talking about EDM, which I'd reservedly admitted liking, but he seemed honestly intrigued, and I found myself offering to make a playlist for him.

Beowulf's late-shift employees had to ask us to leave. I did get a wink from Mia-the-closing-shift-barista on the way out the door, so I didn't think I had to fear not being allowed back in the next day.

He walked me home. It was clear and the stars were bright. Since it had been an extremely warm winter, there were no distracting snowdrifts to lurch through. He strode beside me in the unusually balmy night. There was no one else out as, with the exception of Beowulf's, they roll up the sidewalks at nine around here. It was the deep quiet of late night, but the half-full moon gave us plenty of light once our eyes adjusted.

I can't say with any accuracy what we talked about, one of those "everything and nothing" conversations. More important than words was how his green-gold eyes gleamed in the moonlight. In fact, the moonlight did right by him; it brought out the planes of his face in high relief, making poetic the harsh curve of his strong nose. His hair fell so darkly that I could not see where it ended and his leather jacket began. He walked close to me, his eyes meeting mine in long looks. Is it any wonder I couldn't tell you what was said along the way?

It was like something out of a romance novel—certainly not out of the previous story of my life. I tried to savor every moment, notice every little detail. The night air still held a little of winter's bite. I'd forgotten my gloves; he noticed me rubbing my hands together for warmth. I'd been attempting to do this surreptitiously so my hands wouldn't be repellently cold if he just happened to want to hold one of them, but it gratifyingly ended up with him rubbing my hands to warm them. To do this, we had to stand quite close together, of course, me looking first down at my small hands being massaged by his larger ones, and, gathering my courage, up into his eyes. They were framed by thick black lashes that stood in sharp contrast to his skin, which in this light lost most of its olive tone and looked like alabaster.

When he didn't kiss me, I nearly died, but it was natural to stay hand in hand as we started walking again, speaking in low murmurs, quiet laughter. When we got to my little home, I didn't know what to do. Every part of my body and most of my brain wanted to invite him in, but I'd never invited someone I didn't know well up to my place for sex. Let's be clear: I wanted to.

Alexandru made up my mind for me. He leaned me against the doorframe and stroked his fingers down my hair. I shuddered. There was nowhere I could look *but* into those gold-green orbs. I now understood how someone could feel they were drowning in someone else's eyes.

He leaned forward. Stopped. Slowly leaned forward more. Stopped. Perhaps he was politely giving me time to back away if I wanted, but for me, it was a terrible tease.

I leaned forward the littlest bit to encourage him. Finally, *finally*, his lips brushed against mine in the gentlest of kisses: one, two, threeeee. When he pulled away, leaving me leaning foolishly towards him with my eyes still closed, frustration rushed hot through me.

It looked like he knew my feelings because he leaned into my neck and nuzzled it softly. I could hear and feel him breathing against my skin. My knees seriously considered turning into jelly.

He pulled back and looked into my eyes again. "Noosh, I must depart for some small while. I do not want to, *ei bine...*"—the last two words in the sentence sounded like "eh bee-ann-eh"—"to start things. Only then to leave. May I...will you let me resume this when I return?"

"Oh," I said, feeling like I'd just walked into a wall. This was not how I'd planned the next few minutes and hours to go. Not that I *had* a plan, but this wouldn't have been it. Still. He was being honest and considerate, which I had to respect even though what I wanted badly was for him to "start things." Right *now*.

I tried for an answer that walked the line between letting him off easy in recognition of his candor but also made clear that I'd been hoping for more and was disappointed to be losing out. "Alexandru. I-I would love to pick up right where we left off as soon as possible." Well, that was playing hard to get. No coy seductress, I.

Thankfully, my desperation did not seem to put him off. "I am not certain how long I shall be, but not more than a few weeks. I shall come into your library or Beowulf's as soon as I return."

Could women get blue balls? Blue walls? This achieved whole new levels of unfairness, in a life where I'd never experienced much romantic fairness anyway. "Do you have to go? Right now?"

Alexandru chuckled, a dark, rich sound like the best fudge you ever ate made audible. "Ah, *draga mea*," Romanian? Sexy! "I do not wish to go right now. I want what *you* want. But it is best this way, and when I get back, I will make up for every minute of waiting, I promise you this."

I think I sighed heavily. He was saying all the right things. Except for the clichéd bit about forgetting everything else in the world, he would now to take me upstairs, and spend the rest of the night, well, *actively*.

Alexandru looked down at me silently, eyes full of meanings I couldn't read. The look lasted a long, frustrating time. I was a moment away from looking down in confusion and unhappiness when he leaned down again and finally, *finally* properly kissed me.

His lips were this amazing mix of soft and firm. Like the topmost layer of skin was made of the softest microfiber, underneath which was titanium—warm, malleable titanium. So, not really titanium. I'm not cut out for this romance stuff. He kissed me chastely at first, and when I met him with enthusiasm, the kiss became passionate. No tongue, but meeting of lips after meeting of lips, like waves crashing on a beach.

I'd never been kissed like that before. Actually, I'm not sure how many people *get* kissed like that. It utterly wiped away all my doubts about myself, my doubts about this striking, mysterious person actually being interested in *me*, and replaced them with the warm knowledge of requited attraction.

I have no idea how long it lasted. While a few eternities *might* have flashed by, in the end, it didn't count because no matter how long it had lasted, it was over all too soon.

Alexandru withdrew slowly from the kiss, despite my hope that my lips' gravitational field might catch him again. He escaped enough to be able to look into my eyes. I was amazed my glasses hadn't fogged up. We had a meaningful conversation, just looking at each other. It was full of promises, assurances, and implications for the future. It could not be translated into mere words—and I am profoundly fond of unlimited multisyllabic words. I would be the last person in the world to talk about a "soul-to-soul connection," but if such a thing did exist, that's how it would be done. It was intoxicating.

He leaned in and kissed my forehead, then I was spun 'round and gently eased through my door. I sort of came to in the entryway at the bottom of the staircase, the door closed behind me, and a whisper echoed in Alexandru's wake: "I shall return to you soon, *draga mea*."

Chapter Three

Y OU CAN PROBABLY IMAGINE what I was like after that. Giddy. Singing to myself. Tripping over things. I was worse than any teen with their first crush. I waltzed around. *I could have danced all night, I could have daaaanced allllll niiiiiight!* Gooey love songs and some rather more explicit ones became the playlist of my life.

For the first week, I was manically energized. Never had the Helen Abigail Winstringham-Fenstermacher Memorial Library been more hoppin'. Returned books were back on their shelves almost before they were checked out. The children's reading hour ended up with everyone dancing—don't ask! The library website got a sexy new makeover and even more functionality, which possibly three people would ever actually use.

Dre and Zuzu went from worrying about me to teasing me mercilessly and asking when I'd introduce them to the mystery person. I bouncily traded quip for quip, when normally I'm the person who can't think of anything good in the moment, but has the perfect reply bubble up in her head three days later.

When the weekend came, I was cautiously careful not to expect Alexandru. He'd said "not more than a few weeks," so no matter how much I longed to see him, he wasn't going to be back yet, and that was that. I did the raking and other yard work for the Muckenfusses, who were happy to have someone on whom to foist such tasks since their free labor —i.e., their children—now all lived too far away. Mrs. M gifted me with one of her county-fair-winning Black Forest cakes, so I had the triple win of exercise, distraction, *and* cake.

Week two was a slightly more mellow version of week one. I couldn't keep up such bounciness, and anyway, what if I over-exerted myself and ended up with a cold or something right when Alexandru returned? I reined it in a bit and re-read all the Sherlock Holmes stories for comfort and pleasure, and after that, dug my teeth into some new science fiction that had been piling up on the "to read" pile. My kids were dismayed to discover there would be *no* dancing this week.

Week three I started getting antsy. He'd said, "Not more than a few weeks," which would seem to indicate I could expect his imminent return. By Wednesday, every day was full make-up and styled hair, just in case he got home a few days early.

He didn't get home early. He didn't get home at the end of the week, nor on the weekend.

No worries; it's fine, I told myself. He didn't say "three weeks," he said, "a few," and different people mean different things by such vague words as "a few." What with travel being what it is, he'd probably missed a flight. Really, there were a bazillion good reasons Alexandru might return any random number of days past a vague deadline.

So, I kept up my self-titivation if I was going to Beowulf's or the HAWFML (pronounced privately amongst us staff as, "Haw-Fuck-My-Life") which meant I had to do some shopping. Before Alexandru came into my life, I'd pretty much lived in Librarian Casual, which was not dramatically different from Slouchy Student. It was past time for a style makeover, and I thought I'd try Ready For Romance, which necessitated a different wardrobe. It was trips to the mall for me, although since it was during the holiday rush, it ended up being far worse than I'd remembered. Eventually, after much waiting in long lines and frustration with humanity, I ended up with trousers which more resembled leggings than anything else and pencil skirts—you simply cannot do the children's reading hour in a mini-skirt—and silky blouses, and sweaters that made miracles of my bust. Speaking of bust-related miracles, I made a dent in my savings in a lingerie shop where previously I'd bought only the no-underwire t-shirt bras. There was also the makeover, which cost more than all the clothing together but came home in a much smaller bag.

I went in for a well-overdue eye exam and found they made super-sexy spectacles nowadays, which really brought my look together. I got contact lenses for the first time, too, because kissing definitely worked better without glasses on.

The velocity created by the new wardrobe and wearing makeup lasted two weeks. I felt like I was playing dress-up every day and was a new person for it—bonuses were the ensuing compliments from Zuzu, Dre, and the whole reading group at Beowulf's, *including* our curmudgeon. What did me in were the weekends. I'd spent the first of the two weekends re-cleaning my rooms and attempting some cooking, just in case Alexandru happened to show up. By the third weekend, inertia and depression started to set in. Alexandru wasn't coming back to live up to his sexy promises. He obviously wasn't coming back *at all*. Maybe I'd hallucinated him in the first place. Since all I ever did was read, was it any surprise I'd gotten confused and thought I was living in a novel?

Still, I kept wearing my new wardrobe and my makeup. It was a combination of unconscious desperation mixed with a healthy enjoyment of discovering the art of attire and having fun with eyeliner and lipstick. I stopped thinking about Alexandru. The holidays were upon everyone, and I decorated the library, read holiday stories to the kids, and let the monthly reading group cancel because everyone was overwhelmed by all the shopping they had to do.

Really. I forgot all about him.

Christmas came and went. Gave presents to Dre and Zuzu, and the Muckenfusses and had a solo Christmas dinner in my apartment with some new graphic novels—no romance—to distract me.

Time stretched to two months. Three. My life was just as it had been before the brief moment of intense insanity where I imagined I'd somehow gotten swept up in a wild romance. I initiated a program of my kids sharing their favorite books, and my monthly reading group mutinied over *Gravity's Rainbow*.

Chapter Four

It had just turned to May, after a squelchy-wet April, which would have been very depressing if I'd allowed myself to think about hallucinatory men whose names sorta-kinda sounded like *Xanadu*. Which I didn't. So it wasn't. Honest.

I had settled into my old life, unchanged but for my new tendency toward tight skirts and red lips. I had given up on the contacts, however, and just wore the new sexy glasses. I'd always loved the Sexy Librarian look, ever since Miss Evans had shown me how it was done. I wasn't dressing up for anyone but *me*, dammit! Beowulf's had just opened up their covered back patio for the year, and I was sitting out on it, even though it was still too chilly in the evening for such things.

The café could get all too crowded in the winter months since there isn't much else to do on long winter evenings in Centerville. It was a refreshing change to have space to spread out in and not be breathing other people's air. I had spring lamb stew and oolong tea steaming in front of me and the newest *Library Resources & Technical Services* newsletter in my hand, when I heard the door to the patio open. All at once, my arm-hairs stood on end, and it *wasn't* the cold. I had my back to the door, and there was *no way* I could know his step. He walked so damn softly I could barely hear his feet on the flagstones. But I knew it was him.

Alexandru. Alexandru Solin. My hallucination.

Who, just possibly, was not a hallucination.

"Anushka," he said as he came around me. "Noosh," he murmured as he sat down. My first thought was to ignore him or even tell him to go away. I had a thankfully brief moment where I almost started crying. I'd wanted him to come back so terribly much, and then I'd given up. Now it was almost too much—and yet too little and too late. But I took a breath and got myself under control. It was stupid to pretend he wasn't there, and it was childish to be this angry at someone I hardly knew. Obviously, there wasn't anything between us. He was just someone I'd flirted with once.

Shit. I'm doing it again. Talk to the man, you fool.

Either he was good at reading my face or I was utterly transparent, but I could tell he'd followed my pathetic internal conflict. He'd looked serious when he sat down, happy to see me, but not pretending all was fine and dandy. Now he looked downright solemn.

"I do not have the right even to speak to you, *draga mea*, but I beg you to let me apologize." He looked like he wanted to take my hand, but I was still holding the newsletter. Would I have stopped him if he tried? I like to think so.

"Here I am, well past the time I said I should return, is it not? You would be within your rights not to speak to me again. I am a man of my word, and I broke the promise I made to you. If you will accept them, I owe you an apology and an explanation both."

Well, it was a fair start, I thought. I do enjoy a bit of groveling, particularly when it's due to me. I might as well let him continue. I nodded, attempting to look regal.

"Anushka Rossetti, *sincer îmi cer scuze*—I humbly and sincerely apologize. You did not deserve to be treated in such a manner. I have never wanted anything but to treat you in far better ways, I wanted only to share with you the happiness you have brought me."

Possibly a bit overboard, but in the right theme.

"As much as I wanted...as much as I *longed* to return to you, Noosh, I could not. There were good reasons for this, but to explain requires also some explanation which I think you will not find easy to hear, even if you believe me."

He looked intensely into my eyes. Since he looked intense even when he wasn't trying to with those magnetizing gold-shot green eyes, this look made my world stop for as long as the contact lasted. He positively *exuded* sincerity at me.

"Ohh-kay," I said, with possibly a weak-in-the-knees quaver. He had melted my resistance with a few sappy words and one long look. I was pathetic. But all at once, life was back to being thrilling, as it had not been for more than four dreary months. It did not bear thinking about how ready I was to jump back into the inexplicable whirlwind that was him.

I took a deep breath and said as nonchalantly as possible, "OK. Hit me."

"I am what you would call a 'vampire.'" His voice was soft, almost as calming as a classic therapist's voice. Hypnotizing, even. "Actually, I am *the* vampire, as you living humans see it. I am Wladislaus Drăculea, also known as Vlad Țepeș."

He waited for a response. I first had to hear the words, then make sure I'd heard them, then check them again. Process the information, and *then* think of something to reply that wouldn't sound idiotic.

"So. I'm sitting alone in a garden at night with Vlad the Impaler?" was what I came up with. I think I sounded reasonably cool since I could have responded in a number of other ways, ranging from laughing in his face to saying, "What? There really *are* vampires? Cool! Are you going to seduce me?"

He chuckled, which was as perfect a sound as any romance novel would have it: a dark vibration that caused all the blood in my body to start draining down to my lady-parts. *But wait! Do I believe this?* Why *should I believe this?*

CHAPTER FOUR

"That was many years, many lifetimes ago. It was a different world, and I a different man. I was a," he paused, "living human at that point, not a vampire. But, yes, I am," and here he hesitated, then said with dramatic humor, "Drahkcoolhyah..." letting the last syllable linger exotically and fade out.

I don't know if it was because he was, like, *mesmerizing* me, or because he was utterly matter-of-fact about it, but I could see no reason not to go along with it, at least for the time being. Of course, maybe reading too many vampire novels had made me all too eager to find myself in one.

"So, why are you telling *me*? Is this, like, you know, Louis telling the reporter in *Interview with the Vampire*?"

"There are many reasons, *dragă* Anushka, and the first is that I feel I must explain my breaking of the promise. But most importantly, I wish you to know me so that I can share more. With you."

For me, this was like finding gold at the end of a rainbow. We've all heard the myth, but no one expects it to come true. Probably not many people would stay to listen to any more of his nonsense.

But *I* filed the moment away to warm my future lonely nights. As much as I wished I could believe, I knew this was just a lovely dream bubble that would be popped by cruel reality all too soon. He was still sitting there, though, waiting for my response. "That's...lovely of you to say, Alexandru...or do I call you Vlad now?"

He laughed, and it was so infectious I felt myself smiling even though I couldn't see the joke. "*Nu, draga mea*, I'm afraid that name has been, *ei bine*, over-exposed. Too many people would have inconvenient questions. I am Alexandru in this time and place." He paused again, and I'm pretty sure he read my thoughts because he added, "And *never* was I the 'Count Dracula' of the novel."

This was slightly disconcerting. "So, um, you didn't inspire Bram Stoker or anything?"

"I never met him. I was elsewhere during that time." He considered for a moment. "Hmmm, the Victorian era in England, *da*. At least Mr. Stoker did *some* research since he got *parts* of my history right. There have been far worse recountings of me on either side of the grave."

I didn't say anything, because too many questions were jumbled up on the back of my tongue.

He cocked his head to the side and added, "Before you ask, I did *not* spend a summer with the Romantic poets. I did not give vampiric secrets to a Mr. Richard Matheson—or a fictional Daniel Molloy. I also have not met your Anne Rice. I do not think she would *like* me. I do not think she would care to share the term 'Christian' with such as me."

"Oh, uh, she renounced Christianity. Before she died. On her, um, her Facebook page..."

"Her Facebook page. I shall have to look it up. You look surprised. You were perfectly willing to see me as part of the modern world before you found out who I am."

CHAPTER FOUR

I tried to wipe the surprise and subsequent dismay off my face. Things were moving a bit too fast for me emotionally and conversationally. I was still trying to wrap my mind around a number of ideas, such as: I was sitting with Dracula, Dracula existed, and also vampires existed. If those things were *not* true, then I was sitting with someone who *thought* he was Dracula. That would be less world-reordering, but to be fair, it would still be an unexpected twist.

I tried to answer as if I believed him. "You're right. I'm sorry. It's just that finding out you're from the..." I tried to remember what I knew about Vlad the Impaler. "Fifteenth century? It does make me see you living around the time of the invention of the...of the printing press. And since my father was never able to use a computer as anything more than a glorified typewriter—which could get broken in ways typewriters never could, he said—and none of my grandparents even got on a computer, you can see it might give me a moment of, um, incorrect assumption."

He smiled at me. "One must keep with the times. I had a printed Bible in the 1400s, and I have a mobile phone and a computer now. I also keep up with the lingo of the times. It is easy; you simply follow what the young are saying and wait for it to become the common parlance. And I learn languages, although, I must keep relearning them as they change over time. Perhaps I should say 'change and grow,' but people call it 'decay,' which is just the ego of the old.

Next thing you know it is a couple hundred years later, and it has become almost a different language."

"A *Gutenberg Bible*?" I asked, getting to the most important part of what he'd just said. "Do you still have it? Is it a B42?"

"Ha! Leave it to the librarian! This is what attracts me to you: your mind. Although it is housed in a most diverting body."

This whole time, we'd been talking quietly in the back corner of Beowulf's patio. It had been about sundown when he arrived, but now it was full night. I'd not noticed because he was looking deeply into my eyes as he talked, and I could not help but return his gaze. Abruptly uncomfortable with the intimacy of the look and his words, I glanced away.

"*Nu, dragă* Noosh, *nu*, you must not get frightened now. I am not here to harm you. Come to my house, and I will show you some of my book collection. Most of it, including that Bible, is not in this country. It is on vellum if that helps you identify what it is. I will take you to see it someday if you like. You may read it cover to cover. It is in good condition, I think."

"It must be worth at least...thirty-five million, then!" I shook my head to wake myself up. Why was I such a geek? Dracula was here seducing me—or trying to—with sweet words and hot looks, and I was appraising books sight unseen and existence unproven in my head.

And, heh...Dracula, or someone who thinks he is Dracula, at any rate. But I still am a geek, even if he is a nutter.

He was laughing softly at me. "My Noosh is scared of nothing, not even being alone with vampires in the dark, so long as there are books to be cataloged. Come to my home and see some of them. We have a beautiful long night stretching out ahead of us."

When did I become his Noosh? I wondered. That's a bit much. No, scratch that. It would be stupid for me to pretend I *wasn't* going to let Dracula seduce me if he wanted to. I'd read Bram Stoker's "hack work" when I was twelve. I'd read *Interview* when I was fourteen. I'd binged on horror stories and followed the rise of the paranormal genre as a completist. The most fascinating man I'd ever met was telling me he was Dracula. Even if he was some pathetic vampire wannabe, I'd let this fantasy play out a little longer. It had been a while—to be honest, *years*—since I'd been with someone. Missing out on this vampiric—or at least kinky—booty call was simply not happening. For the time being, I supposed he could call me "his."

"All right," I said, "You've enticed me with books. Let's go."

Chapter Five

Dracula drove an Aston Martin DB4 GT Zagato—or at least, that's what he told me. I didn't know what all those letters and numbers meant. All I knew was even under the dim streetlights outside Beowulf's, I could see it was pure sex on wheels. He talked to me about the car for a while as we drove. It was such an amazing vehicle that I was able to listen without my eyes glazing over. I must have expensive taste.

It took some time to realize how fast we were going since it was dark out and I couldn't interpret the various levels of growl made by the DB4. It had sounded like it might be doing ninety when we were still at ten MPH, but eventually I noticed the trees on either side of the road seemed to be rushing by disturbingly fast. I felt a discomfiting mixture of terror and arousal. This was probably not inappropriate around a vampire, although it was mostly caused by the sense that I shouldn't look too closely at the speedometer.

To distract myself, I ever-so-subtly worked the conversation back around. "So, why do you call yourself 'Alexandru?'"

He was quiet for a moment, and I listened to the DB4 growling along. Like a tiger who was considering eating you, its beauty meant you'd find it a desirable way to go. Come to think of it, also perfect for a vampire.

"'Alexandru' means 'defender of mankind.' When I ruled Wallachia, I protected my people. They still remember me as a hero, and they are proud of me. That, *ei bine*, means a great deal to me.

"After I died, I could not go on calling myself Vlad. Looking like Vlad Dracula and *also* having his name was the sort of thing people would notice. The news of Vlad Dracula had spread far and wide since I was a crusader against the Turks and already known to a large part of the civilized world.

"I needed something common enough to not make me stand out, but also I wanted it to be meaningful. I looked first to my family, although most of the names were not, *ei bine*, particularly helpful. For example, take 'Vlad.' It was not just my name and the name of my father Vlad Dracul, but also of my half-brother Vlad Călugărul, who fought me for my throne, and it was the name of my son Vlad, who I called, 'Tepuluş.'" Here he chuckled, a darker sound than I'd yet heard him make, which gave me the shivers. "Tepuluş means 'Little Impaler,' you see.

"You could say my family did not waste names. Once we found one we liked, we kept it. Another example: I had a brother named Mircea, my father's father was Mircea cel Bătrân, and my other son I had named Mircea. And then there was Radu." Here he paused mid-sentence. Was this fascinating stream of information going to dry up?

I gently prompted him. "Radu?"

"Radu cel Frumos. That means 'the handsome.' He was…I heard an excellent phrase the other day: 'They put the fun in dysfunctional.' You could say that about my family." He shook his head as if to clear the memories like you would an Etch A Sketch.

"My father was fool enough to accept the 'invitation' of Sultan Murad—the second of that name, I note for your fact-loving mind, *dragă* Noosh. The Sultan was not pleased because he felt my father had not honored an agreement between them, so he took Radu and me as hostages to our father's loyalty, since he was trying to win back Wallachia at the time. This was not uncommon; the Ottomans called the practice of stealing sons '*devşirme*.' My people called it the '*tribut de sânge*'—the blood tax.

"Radu knew how to get along with people, and he took to the intricacies of the Ottoman ways with ease. With…pleasure. He became close to the Sultan's son, Mehmet. We did not have the terms 'homosexual' or 'bisexual' in those days. How I saw it then was that Radu became fully caught up in the indulgence of the Ottoman court. He also converted to Islam, which was for me far more unforgivable.

"I, on the other hand, did not know how to get along with people I considered my enemies. I did not care that my father had struck a deal with the Sultan. *Nu*, I did not get along well with anyone. No one thought I was 'the handsome.'"

"Well, that's stupid. You're gorgeous!" Oh, shit. That was my out-loud voice.

His chuckle continued to be dark and dangerous, making certain parts of me twitch. "Finally, *druga mea*, you let yourself say how you feel. I wish you would let yourself do so more often! In case I have not made myself quite clear, I feel the same way about you. You are gorgeous, beautiful, delightful, mouth-watering."

I was perfectly OK with the first three, but the last adjective made me shudder, although I didn't look too closely at whether it was alarm or…anticipation. Well, it was too late to worry, wasn't it? I wondered how close we were to his house.

His words brought me back from my musings. "My grandfather was an Alexandru. It is a proud name, so that was the name I took. It is also a common one among not just my own people, but in its various forms, it is the most universal of names."

Dracula—Alexandru—made a shockingly tight left turn into what seemed like dense woods. There was a loooong driveway, which curved at the end to deposit us in front of the house.

Drac—Alexandru pulled up and turned off the car. The lights and the sexy growl went away, the world immediately muted. Small car-cooling-down clicks and pings were the only things breaking the stillness. We sat there for a while, and I could tell he was watching me.

"Would you like to come in, *dragă* Noosh? Or shall we stay out here? You've made your admiration for this car apparent, but I assure you it's even more comfortable and interesting inside the house."

I didn't answer. I didn't know what to say. All the bravado I'd felt leaving the café with Alexandru was long gone. "Mouth-watering," he'd said. He reached over and took my hand, and his hand was the same temperature as mine. What did that mean? That he *wasn't* a vampire? That he *was* and had just fed? All the vampire myths I'd ever read crowded into my brain and made it impossible for me to think.

I felt unexpectedly bereft when he let go. Had I done something wrong already? No, he got out of the car and came around to open my door with sincere courtesy. This whole older man thing had some pros, obviously, although maybe there was an upper limit? If Alexandru was telling the truth and was indeed Vlad Dracula, he was over five hundred years old.

Just a *little* more than the usual age gap.

All this was running through my mind as he led me up the steps to the porch, but the ornate moonlit architecture—Dracula didn't have movement-sensing lighting around his house—distracted me from those thoughts. Everything was as fancifully carved as wood could get without breaking from an overdose of whimsy.

Looking up, I glimpsed pointed towers and more scrolls and decorative trim than seemed possible. Perhaps it was just the moonlight outlining all the edges that made it seem like we were stepping into an overwrought Victorian fantasy. I'd have liked the dress to go with it.

Once we were under the overhang of the porch, everything turned into amorphous shades of gray. We went through the front door, which didn't seem to have been locked. It did *not* open with a screeching protest of old hinges, which would have made me at least flinch, if not something even more twitchy and embarrassing.

And there I was, in the darkened entry hall of Dracula's house.

Nothing unusually dramatic happened immediately, although Alexandru did light a candelabrum and, turning to me with a wry grin, said, "I do of course have electricity. I even like it. But this is more romantic, isn't it, *draga mea*? Allow a man who has lived as many centuries as I a little eccentricity."

Since Dracula going home to a raised ranch and turning on the light switch to showcase a house full of neutral decor and Scandinavian home furnishings would have seriously killed a couple decades of vampire fantasies for me, I was willing to allow him such fitting eccentricity. The car and house were both making me feel somewhat vindicated in trusting that he was a vampire, or at least an extremely rich weirdo. Even if he *was* just an extremely rich weirdo, this was better than the living-in-his-parents'-basement type of weirdo.

He was a man—a vampire—of his word and led me through the dark house to the library. Where I promptly forgot about him. He might not have had the Gutenberg Bible, but he did have a first edition of the Gustav Dore illustrated one. Beside it was *Biblia de la București*, 1688, and the 1667 printing of *Paradise Lost* in pristine condition. And fascinating old maps. I could have poured over *Novissima Et Accuratissima Toti Regni Hungariae, Dalmatiae, Croatiae, Sclavoniae, Transylvaniae, Cum Adjacentib Regnis Et Provinciis Tabula* for the rest of the night. I didn't even get to the selection of books in what looked like it might be Arabic. I was distracted by thinking I saw a manuscript titled *Decameron* when Alexandru gently pulled me off the rolling ladder. "Come, *dragă* Anushka. There will be many other nights for you to read and reread all this. Come see my home. Come be with me."

He'd rudely awakened me from my Aladdin's-cave-of-books daze, and I turned on him. "What are you doing about preserving these rare...these *invalu-*

able works? I assume light isn't an issue, but temperature, humidity—what are you doing about those? Do you have a thermohygrometer? Have you checked for red rot or mold—or worms? Just one infected book could destroy this whole collection! And have you scanned them or archived them in any other way? Those *candles!* What if there was a fire? You could lose all of them! And—"

"Noosh! *Taci, micuţo*. That very question is one of the matters I needed to discuss with you and why I 'outed' myself to you. You shall fix everything and make it as perfect as only you can conceive, but the library will wait one night, *nu?*"

"Well, I guess."

"You overwhelm me with your enthusiasm for my humble company."

I had to laugh, and he joined in. He had the richest, most resonant laugh I'd ever heard. It made my happiness greater and prolonged the moment.

Alexandru led me, thankfully taking the dangerous candelabrum away from that astounding collection, down the hall and into a large study that looked properly lived-in: comfy chairs and an overstuffed and well-used leather sofa, all with reading lamps—electricity, finally!—and side tables, and a huge desk covered in piles of papers, old tomes, battered modern paperbacks, a laptop, and empty wine bottles with candles stuck in them. A little tacky, I thought, but there were no skull paperweights at least. Although one paperweight looked suspiciously like a real gun. *Eeep!*

Heavy velvet curtains hung down to the floor over what I assumed were windows. The walls were papered in velvet-flocked wallpaper, which, when Alexandru lit a fire in the fireplace, turned out to be dark red on gold. The curtains were a matching carmine.

The fire cheered me. The house was cold, and the heat made me realize how chilled I was. Drawn to the fireplace, I sat on a huge gold velvet well-padded ottoman and held my cold hands out to the flames. Alexandru installed himself in the chair to which the ottoman belonged. I stared into the fire.

"Noosh," he said in a gentle voice, "you have asked few questions. Your patience is admirable, but since I am more than willing to answer you, why not ask what you like?"

"To be honest, I'm afraid to learn too much. Is there a point when I know too many vampirish secrets and you have to kill me? Also, I don't understand why you're telling me in the first place, Alexandru-Solin-who-is-Vlad-Țepeș. Why *me?*"

Alexandru leaned forward and put his hand on my shoulder, which made me reluctantly stop staring into the fire and turn to look at him. His skin was a warmer olive in the light from the fire. Once I met his glowing gold-green eyes, I could not look away.

"*Ei bine!* You believe me! I sensed your doubt, but I thought the books might 'sell you,' as they say." At my lack of response, he added, "At least you are willing to go along with my unusual notion."

"Why me?" I asked again, not wanting to talk or think about whether I believed him or not. I was all too afraid I did.

"*Draga mea*, why not you? You are a keeper of knowledge and a student of history, yet open-minded about new things. That alone would make you a good person to tell if I was going to tell anyone. But why do you not hear that I wish to share not just information with you, but much more. How can I show you this? I do not wish to 'go too fast,' as the expression goes, but I'm not used to seducing women without using, how would you call them, my powers of persuasion. I find myself not knowing how to proceed. Please tell me how. End this uncertainty for me."

I stared at him in disbelief. "You *haven't* been using your...your powers of persuasion? If you haven't, I can't imagine why I'm here! I've never just gone to a guy's house for a booty call like this before!

"And I'm sorry, but I can't see the Prince of Darkness having trouble in matters of seduction. You've had five centuries of practice!" I belatedly realized I didn't sound overly understanding or empathic. I tried again: "Not that I think you're lying."

At least, I wasn't going to admit it if I did. "But again, why would you have the least bit of problem seducing me? I haven't been seduced in years. Hell, I don't think I've ever been properly seduced!"

I was still looking into his eyes, but small crinkles of laugh-lines appeared around them and a smile played around his mouth. "Ha. So far, only my books have seduced you. But, since you ask for it, I am not averse to seducing you properly!"

I just had time to think, "I've asked for it? What have I gotten myself into—?" before he leaned forward, swept me into his arms, and settled back with me sitting sideways across his lap. One arm was still around my back, and my legs hung over the other arm of the chair.

He reached up with the arm not holding me and ran a finger softly over my cheek. "You look like a proverbial deer caught in headlights." Then he chuckled, although I didn't find the statement particularly funny. "Ah, *da, draga mea*! Now I see the flash of lightning in your stormy eyes. Sexy!" He traced his fingers over my lips with such the lightest, most delicate touch that I found myself pressing them to his fingers, asking for more.

He tipped me at more of an angle towards him and brought his face as close as we could get and still look into each other's eyes. The glittering fire in his eyes became my world.

I had never felt this hot in my life, as if my whole body was on fire—not burning, but as part of the flames. "*Te rog, săruta-mă,*" he murmured. "Come to me, *draga mea*. Kiss me..."

Moving as someone bespelled, I brought my lips to his. My eyes closed against the golden firelight, to be replaced by the supple warmth of his lips against mine—at first just pressing lightly, building up from small teasing brushes and pressures to movements simultaneously insistent and yielding. Our mouths opened at the same time, and the hot, wet urgency of tongues brought intensity, depth.

He tasted of iron and salt. Not surprising, but surprisingly not off-putting. Certainly better than some people I'd kissed. It was a tingly sort of taste, the kind where you think, "Hmmm, I know that flavor, let me taste this again," although once you'd been kissing for a while, you didn't taste it anymore.

I don't remember the moment when my tongue brushed the sharp canines because my brain had melted into an organ capable only of considering the current and immediate next aspect of the kiss. As if I'd been kissing vampires for my whole life, I adjusted how I moved my lips and tongue to accommodate the additional toothiness and continued in blissful unconcern for anything except the best kiss of my life.

If I had been capable of it, I might well have thought, "He *is* a vampire!" But, to be honest, I had bought his line from...OK, OK, from the first time he said, "I am what you would call a vampire." Hasn't *everyone* been waiting their whole lives to hear someone say that?

Alexandru's hands were not idle, although he seemed to be putting his whole self into the kiss. Perhaps his hands were on autopilot as they traced curving caresses along my back and arms, down one leg to my knee and back up the other thigh, up my stomach to my breasts.

Feeling the sensation of his fingers through the fabric of my shirt and bra made me moan. That encouraged him to pull back from the kiss, lift me, and arrange me so I was straddling his lap facing him. He could lift me as if I were a doll, which only added to how turned on I was.

He pulled my head back down to his to continue the kiss, and this time my hands started moving of their own will, running over his arms and shoulders and chest. Under the black silk, he felt like warm stone carved into utterly masculine shapes. I desperately wanted to see what was under the shirt. Black silk was classically sexy and all, but I had a feeling just plain Alexandru was even better.

"Yes, take off my shirt," he whispered against my mouth, which might have startled me if I'd been capable of rational thought. At that moment, however, his knowing what I wanted made perfect sense.

It took me a while to get the buttons undone, because my focus was being engaged on so many other levels. His hands now had access to my back and my ass, which he was massaging in a way both relaxing and arousing.

The shirt I was wearing had cleavage well beyond risqué, so when he started kissing along my chin up to my ear, and down my neck, he encountered no fabric-based obstacle. He faced no obstacles at all—except for my whole body tensing abruptly. Which he caught at once, and murmured into my ear, "*Nu, nu.* You have nothing to be afraid of. I will not damage you. I will bring you joy. Relax." His hands kept massaging me, emphasizing the message: *trust me.*

In for a penny, in for a pound.

I let my head tilt back, let my chin turn away. True to his word, he kissed and licked and gently nibbled my neck, but did not immediately chomp his teeth into it. Those sharp canines simply teased and tantalized and teased some more, until I was actually longing for him to be a little rougher, bite a little harder.

At this point I discovered the entire front of my shirt had been unbuttoned, as he began sliding it off my shoulders. I shrugged backwards to help, and he suavely had my bra unfastened in one try. I was just conscious enough to wonder how many centuries *that* skill had taken him to acquire. But then my bra was gone and his lips and teasing teeth found my breasts. And conscious thought pretty much ended.

With my previous lovers, my breasts had been pretty useless. Literally: pretty and useless. They just weren't sensitive. Decorative, not functional. When a lover played with them, I encouraged them on the notion that future lovers of theirs would not much appreciate it if I discouraged them from any amount of foreplay.

Maybe my breasts had changed over the past (mumble) years, or maybe Alexandru was just especially good. I melted into a jelly-like puddle of girl, making incoherent noises and writhing around shamelessly on his lap. This encouraged him to amuse himself with them for a period of immeasurable pleasure. Just around the time those sensations became too frustrating, he started teasing the buttons of my fly open, only to discover my trousers were far too tight to allow him any access. He brushed his fingers up and down the inseam, and I could see him contemplating how best to remove the obstacle. I myself could not cogitate at all, and was consequently astonished when I found myself back on my feet, supported by one strong arm, as he forcibly tugged all the offending clothing off. At this time my glasses fell off. I'd been wondering when and how to get rid of them, anyway. I decided I profoundly did not care where they had gone—potential future *crunch* noises be damned! I helped not at all, as I was simply holding on to him with both arms and kissing whatever I could reach, namely the bicep and pectoralis muscles, which were moving agreeably under his unnaturally smooth skin.

When I nipped at his skin with my (much blunter) teeth, he made gasping noises, which really worked for me, so I experimented with nips and licks while he attempted to get his own trousers off. I probably doubled the amount of time it took, but I was having way too much fun to care. I felt tipsy: giddy and careless and mischievous. It was an almost forgotten sensation. I had no urge to speed things up.

I got my teeth around his nipple around the time he got his slacks to his ankles. This led to us falling over, and I am pretty sure only his vampiric agility saved us from ending up in a heap on the floor. *"Fir-ar să fie!"* he growled, but our chaotic tumble of arms and legs magically ended up with me straddling him again, knees on either side of him. While it was the same position, now something impressively hard was jutting into my lower stomach—uncomfortable, and probably not only for *me*.

He reached around the projecting obstruction, and began to explore a now rather damp bit of my anatomy with the pads of his fingers. I had become just as impatient as he obviously was. "More of that later," I murmured. I didn't want him to think I would *never* be interested in a future patient and thorough exploration—but there were more important things in my mind. I lifted up off his lap and tilted my hips forward. He was of the same mind, and grabbed my hips, eagerly guiding me towards him.

He was brushing against my labia. He was sliding inside me. Having not been warmed up by his fingers, I was just slightly too snug a fit. The small discomfort was in its own way a pleasure, making us go slower, making us work together to fit every millimeter of him inside me.

By the time I sat fully pressed against him, encompassing him, I was panting. His breath was more even, but his heart was pounding. Indeed, I could feel a strong pulse lower down.

Is that *truly* his cock throbbing with each heartbeat?

I'd closed my eyes while focusing on getting Tab A into Slot B. Now I opened them, and met his eyes, which flickered in the firelight like jewels in the face of the statue of a god. If he had been holding back from mesmerizing me, his control was gone now. I fell forward into the flickering iridescent depths, irretrievably lost to any world outside of him-and-me.

We started moving together slowly, and I felt an incredible orgasm start roiling up inside me, building with each movement. It came on like waves, and I don't know if each wave was its own "little death," or if they were all just part of one *grande petite mort*. Possibly they were both at the same time, in some kind of sex wave/particle duality thing.

While this was going on, Alexandru was getting ready for his big moment. My head was thrown back in utter abandon, which if I'd been thinking, I would have realized says, "Come on and bite me, big boy!" to a vampire. But when he *did* bite me, I was far too gone on an intense cocktail of brain chemicals to be frightened or even particularly concerned.

The bite became an integral part of the sex, the penetration of his fangs vital to the penetration of his cock, and vice versa. It took my ongoing orgasm up to the point where I couldn't even process the sensations. I saw stars, and got that shivery feeling you get when you're about to pass out. At some point in time, I heard him cry out, the sounds muffled because his mouth was full of my throat. We collapsed together like marionettes who, in the exact same instant, have their strings cut.

Chapter Six

Some while later, one of us stirred. It was hard to tell who, because we were thoroughly entangled. Like, when you're cuddled close with someone and a tummy grumbles, and you have to ask, "Was that you or me?"

I felt hungover, which was fair because I'd certainly been intoxicated. Movement made me remember I had a body and led me to do an all-over check. All over, I was sore. I think even my toes were sore. Especially sore were the places which had been penetrated. Those were not the almost-pleasing soreness of an intense workout, but the twinging ouchie which makes you wince.

Alexandru seemed to be in much better shape, but of course, he was a vampire.

He's a vampire. He's a vampire! He's not just a vampire, he's fucking *Dracula*. I just had sex with Vlad Dracula. Wow. Oh wow!

He was murmuring what I took to be Romanian expressions of tenderness, the *"mon petite chou"* sort of thing, as he picked up the rather useless me, and carried me over to the huge sofa on the other side of the fireplace. He settled me down in his arms, as tenderly as if I were as breakable as I felt. "*Draga mea*, I do not know what to say. You have made me deeply happy. I do not have the words for how magnificent you are, not in this clunky bastard language.

"You are quite weak now. I have drunk a good deal of your exquisite blood. You *could* recover on your own, but I should like you now to drink from me. It will make you stronger and help you heal faster. Also, I would enjoy sharing my blood with you." He'd paused several times as he spoke, sounding surprisingly shy, as if he feared rejection or expected me to run away screaming. Not that I could have run anywhere at that moment. "To feel you drink from me would mean a great deal to me."

How could I say no? After all the scary-wonderful things I'd just done and felt, I wasn't able to consider the greater ramifications of *anything*. I'd just gone through the best, most intense sensations of my life and felt more alive than I'd ever been. I was flooded with well-being and a wish for this goodness to go on forever and ever.

"Alexandru—"

He laughed. "Noosh, my Noosh. Maybe you should call me 'Sandu' now. I think we have reached a certain level of informality with each other."

I had to laugh, which hurt in places which I didn't know laughing could affect. The pain was not a problem, though.

It seemed far away, and happiness more than just near, it was all-encompassing.

"I think *possibly* we have become intimates." I interrupted myself to laugh again. "We know each other *biblically* now, and if that doesn't get me to the nickname stage, Sandu, I don't know what does!" I was still laughing at the ridiculousness of being naked in Dracula's arms in his vampirish lair after having had the best sex of my life and being used as a drinking vessel, albeit a happy one.

"Noosh, *micuţo*, you are perhaps in shock. I would rectify this. Will you drink?"

It was wonderfully polite of him to ask, I thought. Why not? *Whee!* Tonight, anything was possible. "Yes, yes, O Prince of Darkness! Pour your hot, hot immortal blood through my weak mortal lips!"

He scowled at me, which only made me laugh more. The sight of him biting his wrist open, however, abruptly stopped my laughter. Subsequently, as I'd laughingly requested, his hot, hot blood was indeed flooding into my mouth.

A whole new intensity was upon me. Having your mouth fill with blood is an experience like none other. It was thick, and the salt-copper taste got too intense very fast. I grabbed his arm to pull it away, but his muscles were like stone. I wouldn't be able to move his arm until he wanted me to, so I swallowed the viscous mouthful just to get it out of my mouth.

Once I'd swallowed the first mouthful, however, it became a great deal easier. I started trying to be less panicky, and more sensual. Or at least less awkward. He was moaning like I was sucking another part of his anatomy and started writhing against me. His erection had somehow returned with a vengeance. Oh, boy, was I in trouble!

He finally moved his wrist away. The wound was much smaller already. I grabbed his arm and watched for the few moments it took to close. "Oh. My. God. It's like the movies! I can't believe you heal so fast!" I refrained from asking him to chew himself open again just so I could watch him heal.

I'd been fucking a vampire for less than a full evening, and already I wanted to see flesh ripped open. Not a good sign.

While I had been distracted by his super-self-healing wounds, Sandu had not lost the thread. He slid on top of me and started slowly kissing my neck and shoulders and clavicle and breasts.

When I started to writhe in pleasure myself, I realized all my muscle aches were gone. My emotional well-being was now amplified by astounding physical well-being.

I also felt quite stoned. If I had been drunk before, now I felt all languid and opium-dreamy. Sandu's naked body moving on top of mine was delicious, and the sensations he drew from my breasts made me wonder if I was hallucinating—or if not yet hallucinating, if I shortly would be.

I also discovered I was impatiently ready for him to be back inside me. I wriggled around underneath him, and before long he got the hint, moving himself into a right position. He arched his back as he looked down into my face, and deliberately held himself just at the entrance. "Oh, yessss, now, now! Hard!" I commanded him, and he took me at my word.

He pounded himself into me, as desperately as if he and I had not just had astoundingly satisfying sex earlier, as if he'd been denied for years, for decades. This time, to be honest, I just held on for the ride. And screamed a lot. These orgasms were sharp, intense. I felt I was drowning in pleasure and coming back up for air and submerging yet again.

When he joined me in Orgasmville, his seemed not dissimilar to mine: he cried out and froze, every muscle straining, the veins showing under his skin. His gold-and-green eyes looked off into an unfathomable distance.

I passed out or fell asleep or something for a while. I don't remember anything until I felt him playing with my hair an unknown amount of time later. I opened my eyes sleepily, and he, propped on his elbow alongside me, smiled down at me. "My Noosh. It has been a long, lovely evening, more wonderful than I could ever have imagined. You must wake up now in time for sleep. It is almost daybreak. I prefer to rest now, and you need repose as well."

"I don't know that I do, Sandu. I feel...splendiferous! I've never felt so well. I want to go sort out your entire library right now!" I felt perfect. I didn't know how I could fall asleep since I was full of vim and vigor, a bit like I'd just drunk two double-caf mochas in a row. "Give me the tools of my trade, and I will organize *the world!*"

He did his low-chuckle thing, which didn't seem to have lost any of its effectiveness. "You just think you are wakeful, like a child who doesn't wish to go to bed. If you rest, I promise you will sleep deeply and feel even more wonderfully well when you wake. Trust me."

I didn't like the analogy but I realized I was pouting, so perhaps "Don't treat me like a child!" was not an optimal response.

I could follow it up with a foot-stomp, and wouldn't that be effective?

I clung to him. "Don't go just yet, please, Sandu. You've called me '*draga mea*,' for all this time, and, um *micu*-something. What do they mean?"

He leaned down and lightly kissed my forehead. Then kissed it again, just the barest pressure of lips, and again. In between feather-light kisses, he replied, "'*Draga mea*' means something like, 'my darling,' 'my sweetheart.' *Micuțo*' means 'little one.' It makes me happy to say these words from my native tongue to you. But now, you are indeed like a child who needs her sleep.

"This is your first taste of vampire blood, and you lost a lot of your own blood before I replaced it. Trust me, you must needs rest. Now."

"But why *me*, Sandu? What do you see in me? Why did you trust me enough to tell me who you are? Why have you shared your blood with me?"

"Is it not enough that I have fallen in love with you? Really, you have problems with your...your self-esteem. That is the phrase. I shall work on that with you, but not tonight. Now, we rest." He got up, and my body immediately missed the feel of him against me. He went only so far as to get a red-and-gold plush coverlet. He gently tucked it around me, then sat down beside me and went back to stroking my hair. He started to sing softly in Romanian, which sounded exotically like Italian spoken with a kinda-Russian accent.

Vlad the Impaler was singing me a lullaby. I'd just found out vampires exist, seen an "in my wildest dreams" collection of ancient texts, and not only that, fucked and shared blood with not just any vampire, but *muthafuckin-Dracula*. It also was The Best Sex Of My Life™. And now...now that same Dracula, whom I could call by his intimate nickname, was singing me to sleep. It must be real because not even I and my more-than-well-honed imagination could dream this up.

The unfamiliar words flowed over me. I almost felt I could understand them if I just listened hard enough, so I focused on them. He sang the song again and again, and gradually everything went out of focus. It was warm and it was safe, and I slept.

Chapter Seven

When I awoke, I stretched like a self-satisfied cat. Come to it, I *was* self-satisfied. I felt gloriously relaxed in every muscle and generally felt far better than it was decent to feel after staying up 'til dawn. The Best Sex Of My Life™ must be good for me.

I reached out for the reading light, found it, and turned it on. The room-darkening curtains were, unsurprisingly, exceedingly efficient at keeping out the least bit of light. I did want to find out what time of day it was—indeed, *what* day it was—and, well, get my bearings. I was buck naked and alone in a strange house, one that was not just unfamiliar but also somewhat bizarre and belonged to a man who could be described in the same terms. I was not even clear on its precise location.

First thing was to find my glasses. That was much harder to do since I was not wearing them, one of those terrible daily ironies. I slid my feet along the floor, so as not to inadvertently step on them. They were surprisingly easy to find, resting on top of my shirt, which was puddled on the floor between the chair and the ottoman. To feel somewhat less naked, I put both on.

Now that I could see, I went back to the sofa and folded the lush velvet cover. As I was doing that, I first noticed the feeling between my legs...and shortly thereafter, the related stain on both leather and velvet. *Gulp!* It was blood—*Gulp, gulp!*—and not a few drips, but sufficient to be called a puddle. Now a dried puddle. What was going on?! I knew I wasn't a virgin (not that losing my virginity had yielded even the slightest hint of blood) and I was quite sure it wasn't time for my period. Yet between my legs, and on the sofa, dried blood flaked under my touch. This produced a new level of anxiety and humiliation in me. The stain! I supposed a vampire would probably know the best bloodstain remover, but what if I'd broken some obscure vampiric protocol or something?

Looking around in my panic, I noticed a piece of paper that I was certain had not been there the night before. In a scrawl that looked like medieval handwriting it read, as best as I could make out:

> *My Noosh,*
> *Please feel free to explore the house. There is food in the kitchen. Eat—you will have much appetite. Please take as much as your body craves. I will return at sunset. Until then, I shall hunger for you.*
> *Your Sandu*

Thinking of sex reminded me of the blood situation, about which, sadly, he'd left no helpful information like: *Please note that after sex with vampires, there will be puddles of blood*. I'd have to muddle through this on my own.

I grabbed the rest of my clothes, which had ended up in truly impressive locations around the room, and set off to find the toilet, which, when I found it, was a pull-chain affair with a lovely handle instructing PULL in a Victorian script. The antiquarian in me appreciated the water closet, which had probably not been updated since it was put into the house. It had also, from the amount of dust, not been used in recent memory. I would have to ask Sandu if vampires peed.

Note to self: do not make that the *first* question when you see Sandu tonight. Try for something slightly more mature, like maybe, "ARGH! Why was there all that blood?" Hmm, no, maybe save that for after a calm and collected, "Good evening, my dear vampire. How did you sleep? Like the dead?"

Happily, there was a toilet roll. There was also a sink in the WC, so I was able to rinse my lady-bits and other vital wash-daily spots, to the point that I felt tolerably acceptable. If Sandu wanted a squeaky-clean lover, he ought to have put out soap and towels. The underpants were not wearable again until they'd had a wash, but the trousers, shirt, and bra were all fine, thankfully.

Those key issues resolved, I wandered farther down the hall, finding the barren kitchen, which was also filled with Antiques Roadshow dream finds. The icebox—I kid you not—held a bottle of orange juice concentrate, a few frozen meals, and a carton of vanilla ice cream. Obviously, Sandu didn't get much farther than the frozen foods aisle when shopping for guests. Looking around, I saw a small microwave, which was the only modern thing in the kitchen. Looking back down at the boxes, the Beef Stroganoff looked uninspiring, and the chicken and fish options were even less appealing. Stroganoff, it was. I found a flat of bottled water, which was far more satisfying than the gluey pseudo-food. I was thirsty!

Heh. Gosh, I wonder why!

It was upon entering the uncurtained kitchen that I finally got a sense of the time. It was afternoon, probably four-PM-ish. I hadn't yet seen any clocks. I wondered if the myths had gotten it all wrong, and it wasn't mirrors but *clocks* vampires couldn't abide.

I spent the next hour wandering the twisty halls and steep stairs and empty, dusty rooms of the house. Sandu seemed to have taken up residence in just the library and study. There were old chairs and bedframes covered in sheets in various rooms, and what promised to be—under an impressive amount of dust—a gorgeous dark-wood dining room table. And there was a large bathroom with an old clawfoot tub. The prospect of a bath was thrilling, but when

I tested the tap, the only thing to come out was first a rather horrifying tortured-pipe noise, followed by a gentle shower of rust flakes. So much, I thought sadly, for a bath. I would have to make do with my earlier French bath until I could demand proper facilities from my host, most importantly including a toothbrush.

I promptly forgot my complaints once I went back downstairs. I promised myself a good long time in the library, but first, I needed to do some research and could do it only on the internet. Back in Dracula's den, which sounded much better than "Sandu's live-work space," I settled with my phone on the comfy chair. While the search results loaded, I idly flipped through some of the paperbacks on his desk. Dracula had low taste in modern reading, no matter how many manuscripts and first editions of classics he had lying around. It was mostly thrillers and, I noted with amusement, a few of the most recent novels from two currently popular vampire-based series. I wondered what he got from them: a good laugh? Righteous indignation? Ego inflation?

I googled "Vlad Dracula" and followed various links, stuffing much information—of dubious veracity, to be sure, but better than nothing—into my brain. There was a lot of profoundly upsetting stuff in there that would require serious time to consider, along with all the other things to contemplate as soon as life slowed down a bit. In other words, when I got up the courage to think about what I had done the night before and whatever it was I was going to do next.

I pushed this daunting task aside and headed to the library, a place guaranteed to distract me entirely from thoughts that were too big and scary.

First thing I did, however, was to grab one of the reading lights from the den and carry it into the library. No candles around these priceless documents on *my* watch! Having set it up on a desk, I looked around the room, which also had those extremely efficient light-blocking curtains. Apparently my supposition of last night had been correct and sunlight was not a problem. At least that was taken care of. I'd have to go buy a thermohygrometer and lots of archival boxes to get damage prevention started as expeditiously as possible. Maybe I should just order them online and coordinate with Sandu to be here during the day when they were delivered?

One of the walls of curtains had a different drape from the rest of them, and I went over and cautiously peeked behind it. There was a huge home entertainment system hidden behind there. I pulled the curtains back to admire the largest flat-panel TV I'd ever seen. Shelves set in the wall underneath held DVDs. I saw the usual selection of blow-'em-up action movies and period pieces—I assumed Sandu was particularly finicky about costume and set design, having actually lived through it all. There was also a comprehensive selection of vampire films: *Nosferatu*, the

Hammer œuvre, every variation of Dracula movie through the years, and also shows like *Dark Shadows* and *Buffy* and *True Blood*. Obscure international B-grade horror films padded out the collection nicely.

Wow. Possibly the ol' Prince of Darkness was not the lady's man I'd assumed.

This was a collection worthy of serious geekhood, and if he'd watched all of these, he was spending his nights at home, not out seducing and imbibing. If this had been owned by a living person, I'd be worried about their emotional balance.

But wait, were vampires actually dead? Were they still human?

The amount of data I did *not* have in this situation was staggering. But, truth be told, I wasn't sure being a vampire was a good excuse for this film collection either. It pointed to deeper problems than a non-vampire would have.

Ah, well, Sandu's emotional stability was one of the least of the matters I needed to ponder right now. Since I didn't want to ponder *any* of them, I got well stuck into the waiting piles of leather-bound tomes and delicate manuscripts.

I have no idea how much later it was when I heard Sandu, abruptly right behind me, say, "*Dragă* Noosh, I came right to the library because I knew you would be here."

I yelped and almost dropped the 1370-1371 manuscript of the *Decameron*. "Sandu! Argh! Don't *do* that! This is so precious that if I destroyed it, I would *die!*"

He did his wicked-chuckle-thing. "You would not let it fall, I feel sure. And if you did, I would catch it. Do not fret, and give me a kiss if you would be so kind."

I was ready to fall into his arms when I remembered the unbrushed state of my teeth. "Oh, Sandu, I want to, but I have morning breath that's gone through afternoon breath and become night-and-day breath. I can't kiss you!"

"My sincerest apologies, Noosh. I have been the worst of hosts; forgive me. It is all here. I simply forgot to put it in the note. Come."

I tried not to snigger at the accented and imperious, "Come," which sounded just like all the cinematic vampires over on the other side of the room. I followed him down the hall. The candelabrum was lit again. Sigh. I was going to have to buy him some LED candles. We went past the kitchen to the back door. I'd glanced out to see an overgrown garden earlier in the day but had been far more interested in investigating the interior of the house. Now we stepped out into a yard thick with the exquisite scents of angel's trumpet and vanilla-scented white heart-shape-petaled flowers.

There were lots more flowers, but since I knew far more about books than botany, what most impressed me was that they were—of course—night-blooming flowers. Well, cheesy it might have been, but it *was* practical for a vampiric gardener. Dracula was a gardener? Or did he pay landscapers to come in during the day? The heady perfume of the mingling scents was almost as intoxicating as blood.

"Almost as intoxicating as blood." OK, WTF, Noosh? Have you habituated after only one night of vampiric delights?

Since it seemed another night of vampiric delights was on its way, the rational parts of my brain were ready to shut down again for as long as necessary. I'd never been like this before. *What the hell is happening to me?*

Internal conflict abruptly ended when we rounded a well-vegetated and vigorously blooming corner to find a large Japanese hot tub. *What?* There was also an adorable outdoor shower and a changing cabana, the sort of wee house you'd likely find on a beach at the turn of the century. I was floored.

"The amenities you need are in the cabana. Again, my sincerest apologies for disregarding your comforts and necessities as I did." Sandu was radiating sincerity and humbleness at me, which was quite nice. I could get used to it.

"Well, I think I can forgive you this one time," I joked, "but don't make a habit of it!"

"I assure you, *dragă* Noosh, I will endeavor to care for you with perfect scrupulousness from this moment forward. Any failure will devastate my heart." Sandu vampired himself away, having gotten in a perfect exit line that left me gaping. Even if he hadn't smoothly removed himself, I couldn't have come up with a timely and witty response.

No, it was better for my dignity that he'd already exited stage left.

Chapter Eight

The cabana, which was constructed of fragrant cedarwood like the hot tub and deck, was a perfect guest facility: sink, mirror—cancel *that* myth about vampires, apparently—piles of fluffy black towels. I found a toothbrush, a travel-sized tube of toothpaste, and a tiny bottle of mouthwash, little soaps for face and body, and mini bottles of shampoo, conditioner, and body lotion like you'd find in a hotel. There was a fluffy black robe, and the back of the room had a door to a toilet as modern as the one in the house was antiquated.

I made use of the mirror to check on two things: First, bite marks, and second, did I look as good as I felt?

Answers?

Nope, no bite marks. I was a little disappointed. All those love-bites should have left the classic two-holed vampire mark, at least for the sake of appearances. I'd been longing to sport such a mark since my pre-teens.

And, yep. My skin glowed healthily, even unwashed as I was, and the dark under-eye circles that usually plagued me were gone.

Oh, the money I've wasted on creams when the cure is free!

Despite the chilly air, I took my time with a hot shower and other ablutions. Once I was satisfied, I discovered that a pair of men's black silk pajama bottoms and a plain black t-shirt had been left for me. It was comforting Sandu didn't have clothing stored for his female guests since that would have implied there were a lot of them, or at least enough to warrant laying in supplies. Instead, everything seemed strangely half-planned, as if Sandu had thought out some aspects of hosting visitors but had been too lazy to follow them all the way through. For example, didn't he guess a guest might want to take a bath in the house? His was a bachelor's existence, what with him living in exactly two rooms of the house, but both those rooms were opulent and full of comforts and niceties.

I wandered back barefoot, the slightly-too-large men's wear making me feel naked-er underneath. There's something wonderful about wearing a lover's clothing. I found Sandu building up the fire in the den, which was lovely until the sight of the sofa hit me with the recollection of the upsetting bloodstain. Shit! I forgot about it entirely. A sideways glace revealed the absence of blood on the sofa. Oh, gods, he had to clean it up himself! I guess the shock of it had made me too stupid to think of useful ways of dealing with it. Now I felt sick with thoughtlessness and humiliation.

"Sandu, I'm so sorry! I forgot to tell you—I wanted to ask you—When I woke up, there was all that blood, and I didn't know what was going on, and then I got distracted. I am so sorry!" And not out-loud: Could I just sink down into the floor now, please?

He was at my side in an instant. "*Taci, micuțo, taci.* There is no problem. This is not unusual, and it was yet again my fault for failing to give you information. It is I who should be asking forgiveness."

"But, Sandu, if this isn't unusual, what *is* it?"

"Noosh. Anushka. It is...it was, *ei bine*..." He paused here, searching for the words. "Vampires, they, they ejaculate...blood. I do not produce semen. I have died. I cannot produce life. Blood is the fluid, the only fluid in my body. It is what my body runs upon. It is what my body produces. It was not *you*, not a problem from you. You woke up in—if you will permit me a little joke—in the wet spot."

"Ahhhhhh. Hmmm. Well, that makes sense. Sort of. But I have so many other questions! Do you sweat blood? Do you cry bloody tears? Do you, erm, *pee*?"

Sandu started laughing hard enough that he had to sit down. I was inclined to sulk about being laughed at, but I realized how ridiculous this whole situation was and joined in the laughter. Sandu pulled me down onto his lap, and we finished with a few of those moments where you catch the other person's eye and spasm back into laughter again. Then it falls off, you catch the other person's eye again, and...

Once we'd managed to get a grip on ourselves, he leaned forward, those glorious green-gold eyes still happily crinkled at the corners, and kissed me. I responded with enthusiasm, but as the kiss started deepening with intent to lead to further actions, I pulled back. "Sandu. Um. I do have some questions. Vampire stuff, and just *stuff*-stuff. Last night I had, um, unprotected sex with you without a second thought. I've never done that before. It's a bit late now, I know, but well, I should ask anyway if vampires can have STDs or anything? Can vampires get herpes? HIV? Something even more *deadly*? I'm using, um, birth control, so pregnancy wouldn't be an issue, even if you didn't, erm, come blood. That leads to even *more* questions, which you haven't answered yet, and...and...oh, I don't know where to start!"

Definitely not at: is safer sex even *possible* when you are drinking each other's blood?

"There is no problem. We have plenty of time for me to answer all your questions, although I wouldn't mind some breaks to do *other things* this evening. If you will not mind?"

"Oh? Oh! Yes! I mean, no, of course not, Sandu. I look forward to *some* breaks. After some answers."

"Yes, yes, my resolute lover. Answers you shall have. What would you like to ask first?"

Oh. Uh. Now that I had free rein to ask my myriad questions, my mind did this messed-up combination of tripping over itself with suggestions and at the same time, going completely blank. The afternoon's internet browsing came flooding back to me. "Ummm, Sandu. I have to ask about, you know, your *history*. All the people you supposedly, um, killed. In horrible ways."

He exhaled thoughtfully. "I understand what you are asking. You want to know if you are sitting upon the lap of a serial killer?"

Gulp. "Well, um, yes, actually. What is the difference between the historical Vlad Țepeș and the Sandu I'm with right now?"

Is there a difference? I wouldn't ask that aloud. Better to just assume there was!

"There are *many* differences. *Liniștește-te, te rog.* You sit so stiffly. You right now feel so far away from me.

"Listen to me, please. There is the factor of time. In more than one way, it is not only I who have changed but also the world. This world we live in right here and now is not like the one in which I was a prince and defender of Wallachia. That time, that world—as a modern person, you cannot understand it. The world was an ugly, fearful place. I am sure you know Breughel's *The Triumph of Death*?"

"Yes, Sandu. I discovered Breughel and Bosch back in high school."

"It is the best way to describe it to someone who lives now. Not that living skeletons were carrying people off, obviously, but yet it symbolizes with exceeding accuracy how much death was around us and with us. Look around the world at that time. Louis XI, *l'universelle araignée*, was hanging boys from trees for his amusement. The *Malleus Maleficarum*, as you undoubtedly know, was written then, and led to centuries of 'witches' being tortured and killed in uniquely cruel ways. In the New World, the Incas fattened up child sacrifices for months before drugging them and leaving them to die of exposure to the elements. In England, two young princes were walled up in the Tower of London for political reasons. In Italy, the House of Borgia had not yet *begun* its reign of poison and violence. The Renaissance might have started, but the age was still dark and cruel.

"I cannot say I look back on my life then without the pain of the clarity that comes with hindsight. You must understand, in my time, most of the violence I did was lauded by the people I protected, by the Church in which I strongly held my faith, and by both my allied peers and ruling superiors. You know I was held hostage by the Turks. They raised me from a tender age, and they taught me many things: to speak the Turkish language, mathematics and logic, court manners, and military history and skills. They taught me those for their elite Janissary corps. The Turks took the male children of their enemies and indoctrinated and trained them to be brilliant soldiers for Islam and the sultan. It was a most ingenious way of using their enemies' best resources against them.

"Radu, that handsome brother of mine, led the Janissaries against me, fighting against and killing his own people to serve our enemies. Is that not more evil than my deeds? You see our names through Western eyes; 'the Impaler' must be the bad guy and 'the Handsome' must be the good guy. But for Romanians, *Țepeș* was and is the good, strong hero, and *cel Frumos* the weak betrayer.

"It was in the hands of the Turks, or rather in the prison of the Turks, where I first saw impalement. I was to become all too accustomed to it in my time in the prisons of Egrigöz, Tokat, Edirne. Every day, right outside my window, I saw people tortured and killed in a variety of *creative* ways. I was whipped more than once in the same courtyards where I saw so many suffer, bleed, and die. Yes, the Turks taught me *many* things.

"After I died, the printing press invented by Gutenberg—the one that excites you so—was responsible for mass-producing the German anti-Drăculea pamphlets and vilifying my name. They relished and embellished the most horrific details, inflating numbers and inventing many stories *toată*—you would say 'out of whole cloth.' I became *știi*, the bogeyman. *Dracul* came to mean devil, not dragon."

Sandu spoke with building urgency, his eyes glowing with a mix of passion, sadness, and anger. Even if I could have thought of something useful to say, I would not have interrupted this torrent of words and emotions.

"When I tell you it is the factor of time, I mean more than just a passing of the ages and more than putting some kind of applicable context on my actions. I mean that as the world has changed, so have I changed, sometimes ahead of it, and sometimes I have lagged behind. I have been alive for over five centuries. This keeps coming up for you, and I admit it is with good reason. I am not the man I was all those long years ago. I have grown. I have learned from my actions, learned from observing the lives of men as they flashed past me. They take a little longer now since life expectancy has gotten longer.

"I *hope* I have evolved in the last five hundred years. Even if I have not moved forward, I have certainly not stayed the same. I died, after all. I am a changed being."

I couldn't help but interrupt. "Sandu, tell me about that. Tell me about being a vampire. All I know is conjecture and myth. Tell me the truth."

"The truth! *Draga mea*, there is a great deal to say, and I hope you allow us a 'break' sometime in the not-too-distant future! What do you wish to know?"

"Well, how can you have *died*, and yet here you are holding me in your arms and talking to me? After, well, last night, you were...um...full of life. You are warm—hah, you're *hot*—and I would not have guessed you were one of the undead."

"Ah, Noosh, thank you for your kind compliments. Any life, any heat I may possess is most certainly increased by your aliveness." He paused to kiss me, nearly distracting me and starting up our "break," but I caught it just in time and pulled back, trying to look adamant. He sighed.

"We do not call ourselves 'undead.' That is a cinematic term. It's so theatrical I must assume Stoker made it up.

"There is more than one kind of what you call vampire. There are the 'am'r,' which is what I am—what you think of as a vampire, what in Romania we call the *strigoi mort*. Am'r is what we call ourselves. And then there are, what in my homeland are called *strigoi viu*. We of the am'r call them 'am'r-nafsh,' and they are born when a vampire mixes their blood—which we call 'vhoon'—with a human's vhoon a certain number of times; they are not created by accident. Am'r-nafsh keep their mortality, but when they die, they rise again as am'r, the last fragment of living human gone. This happened to me. I died, killed by a rival, a Romanian traitor, who hired a Turkish assassin to do the job no man would otherwise dare. I am *still* angry at myself for being killed from behind like a coward!" He took a few breaths. It might have been centuries ago, but it obviously still held a sting.

"After a period of rest, I rose as am'r. You ask about our temperature. We are almost as warm as living humans, whom we call 'kee,' because the vhoon still flows in us. As in *Merchant of Venice*, 'If you prick us, do we not bleed?' Yes, we do, as you saw last night. We cannot create our own blood, however, without a, *ei bine*, an infusion."

I had to ask. "And the um, cum?"

"Ah, yes, the ejaculate that bothered you so. We still have a circulatory system, and we still have fluids within the body; it is just that the fluids are all blood, so if you cut us, we bleed.

"We do not, however, sweat or micturate vhoon. The way our bodies convert our food is more efficient than kee. We use everything. We have no waste matter."

"That's extremely convenient," I muttered. Imagine a life without having to use the toilet. I assumed it also meant no flatulence or indigestion, although perhaps blood-indigestion was even worse? Did vampires belch delicately after their tipple of blood? I hadn't noticed Sandu doing that, but, hell, you try not to burp obviously for at least the first few dates, no matter who you are. Look at me, calling them "dates." If this was my idea of a date, no wonder I'd had trouble with my social life.

I yanked my attention back as Sandu continued. "I breathe. You will have noticed this." Actually, I *hadn't*. I think I'd have noticed more if he *didn't*, but I kept my mouth shut. "We need oxygen still. Not as much as kee, I have noticed, but I do not know why. Some of us have been scientists, although I do not imagine there have been studies done about am'r respiration."

Labs full of white-coated vampire scientists. Or did they wear black lab coats? It wouldn't show the blood as much! And publications like the Am'r Journal of Medicine, and Popular Immortal Science, and Journal of the Am'r Dental Association—bet all vampires kept up with that one! That gave me the giggles, which I'd had more of in these past days than in the whole of my previous life. Was that a better response than running away screaming? It made Sandu demand an explanation. He took it quite seriously, however.

"We have had scientists, and there are still a few, but we are not used to, *ei bine*, working together for a common goal. There are no joint efforts like shared research or journals or conferences. It is something we need desperately if we are to move forward as a species."

"A species? You mean, a different species from *Homo sapiens*?"

"*Draga mea*, that is a long discussion which I promise we shall have in the future. For the moment, I want my promised break."

"Oh, yes, the break. I suppose it might be time for a break. Has all this talking made you, um, thirsty?"

"Yes, but not just for your piquant, ever-so drinkable vhoon." I didn't have time to contemplate that or ask further questions because Sandu stood, lifting me, and put me back down on the chair. I was thus at the level to ascertain that his black silk jammie bottoms were tenting flatteringly at the fly.

Well, nice to see that after yesterday's explorations, Vlad's Impaler was ready for more of me. I mentioned that to Sandu.

"My 'Impaler?'" He laughed.

I decided to take matters into my own hands, however. Literally. I reached up and stroked his cock through the silk. Since his cock already felt like silk, it was silk-on-silk, and I couldn't get enough of it. His response was immediate and gratifying, and it encouraged me to play more. You read about "straining fabric" in romance novels; I had my hands on a piece of silk set to split at the seams. I experimented with different ways of stroking it, swirling my fingers around it, tickling it with my fingertips. Basically, I was a girl with an exciting science experiment: "If I do *this*, what happens next...?"

He was making small non-verbal sounds, and had reached out to the back of another chair in an attempt to stay upright. I was totally in charge, and it was giddying. I was at this moment in full control of the most famous vampire in all of fact or fiction. It was delicious.

Speaking of delicious, I was getting tired of the teasing (although he showed no desire to rush me along) and so I tugged down his jammies, carefully negotiating around Vlad's Impaler, and enjoyed the sight of him erect and twitching. He made a strangled noise when I slid my mouth onto him. At first I focused on just enjoying the sensations for myself: the feel of the silky firmness of him, the satisfying sensation of fullness in my mouth, the pleasure of feeling him sliding in and out. After a while I thought to actually focus on *his* pleasure, and started teasing my tongue on the underside of his head. After *that* got a good response, I worked into a nice regular rhythm, trying to make sure not to scratch him with my teeth.

Although he *was* a vampire; must ask if he liked that sort of thing. Later.

After a while, he gasped, "If you don't stop..." I understood, but I kept going. I was pleased to bring him to that happy moment, and the sense of control I was enjoying was too good to stop without a proper conclusion. Besides, if last night was anything to go on, there were plenty more erections where that came from.

With a sound somewhere between a groan and growl, he erupted into my mouth. I had a moment of shock as I tasted blood. I had somehow forgotten I wouldn't be getting the usual fluid. But after the initial surprise, I swallowed with good grace: his blood was like it had tasted last night: viscous, salty, and a bit too metallic for comfort. Yet there was a depth to it I hadn't noticed last night, it was like a fine wine, with different notes on your palate at start and finish.

I came back to reality with his cock still in my mouth, suckling and licking him gently. When I opened my eyes, I saw his death-grip on the chair, and decided to be nice and let him sit down. I sat back, smugly self-satisfied, and he fluidly collapsed on the sofa alongside me. Somehow, he was wrapped around me before I could say or do anything, and I was trapped in a tangle of hot-fleshed arms and legs, being covered with kisses and little nibbles—sharp nibbles! I started laughing with delight, "I feel like I'm Calvin attacked by Hobbes!" This led me having to explain I did not mean the philosopher. There were some ways I desperately needed to bring Sandu into the modern world.

He divested me of my clothing (his clothing!) while I talked, and smoothly drew the glasses off my face. He went back to kissing me, and I started getting distracted by the contrasting sensations of delicate kisses and sharp nips. He hadn't drawn any blood yet, but I was most certainly getting a taste of vampiric foreplay. Well, I *had* teased him mercilessly for a while there: turnabout was fair play. Also, I was enjoying the flashes of pain stinging up my nerve endings, followed by his soothing attentions with lips and tongue.

We had been spooning, but he'd worked me 'round to get access to my breasts, and once there, he set-to in earnest. I was moaning and gasping in no time at all. I missed when he started drawing drops of blood and licking them up, but once I noticed it seemed a logical progression, and I was having that whole pain/pleasure confusion thing again, so I just lay back and enjoyed it. Well, perhaps I wriggled a bit, too.

Everything kept building and building, including, unsurprisingly, a new erection for the Impaler, which kept poking into my thigh. By this point in time I was aching to be penetrated.

"*Please*, Sandu!" He looked up and grinned.

"Please what?" He licked a few beads of blood off the skin right above my nipple. I was not usefully coherent: "Please...fuck me...now!"

Still moving far too deliberately slowly, he climbed on top, his knees separating my legs. I was soaking wet. He lined up his cock at the entrance. And proceeded to do this horrid tease where he lowered himself a micrometer at a time into me. "Ahhhh! More! *More!*" I kept moaning, almost crying in frustration.

His grin looked fit to split his face. His fangs were unnervingly prominent, but it didn't keep him from looking like a boy who'd just gotten the Official Red Ryder Carbine-Action Two Hundred Shot Range Model Air Rifle he'd wanted all his life.

This was my last thought for a good long while, because he was *finally* all-the-way inside me and was making up for his leisurely entry with pounding thrusts, leaving me unable to do more than occasionally gasp for air. It was astoundingly good. Every thrust was better than the last. I'd have sworn it couldn't get better with each one, but the next thrust would somehow be better yet.

There was no way I could have counted orgasms. They just rolled over and through my helpless body. Finally, he sank down onto me, hips still pumping away, and chomped down on my neck like it was a perfectly ripe peach. It was then I realized all the orgasms I'd had before were not *actually* orgasms, compared to what I was feeling *now*.

It's kind of hard to describe the nirvana you go to during orgasm. I think it's because your brain gets flooded with a rush of happy chemicals and it just sort of stops doing any of the stuff not quietly controlled by your autonomic nervous system. And for all I'm Ms. Cogito Ergo Sum, at the same time just having your brain shut off is, well, it's literally the definition of *nirvana*, isn't it?

A nice, quiet period of being held tightly in Sandu's arms followed, his cock still inside me, his lips nuzzling the tender place on my neck where he'd bitten me. It seemed the right side tasted better. I was the happiest I'd ever been, just lying there.

Eventually, of course, my brain started working again. Nirvana was snuffed out—at least until the next orgasm. I would become a sex addict at this rate. Although I couldn't see how being a sex addict was worse than never getting any.

"Sandu. The break's over. Tell me more."

Chapter Nine

Sandu chuckled softly. Probably due to centuries more wisdom, he seemed like he would've been perfectly happy not talking for the rest of the night, but I was being me. He liked me being me, so he was willing to indulge me. And I didn't mind being indulged.

"I feel like Scheherazade, *draga mea*, who must tell you a story to stave off your wrath! O my King, let your lowly handmaid tell her tale! But what shall I tell you?"

"Well, if you don't want me to cut off your head tomorrow, you'd better tell me more about being a vampire!" I teased. He got such an expression on his face, he almost looked his age. *Whoops.*

"If you wish to kill me, *dragă* Anushka, that is the way to do it. That and destroying my heart." He said it gently, and it tore at *my* heart.

"Of course, I don't plan to decapitate you tomorrow, Sandu. You started the joke! But...um...so the myths are true?

A stake to the heart, cut off the head, and put garlic in the mouth? And some holy water and a cross?"

His eyes gleamed again; the painful moment had passed. "You know not a small amount about the mythological methods of dispatching vampires, Noosh. Do you carry a vampire-slaying kit?"

"No! It's just, you know, you pick this stuff up." Here was the hardest thing to say. "Especially if you spend your formative years reading everything about vampires you can lay your hands on." There, it was out in the open. I was the girl in high school who'd sat in the corner reading every vampire novel ever published. It was humiliating. Up 'til now, I'd tried to play it cool, like it was a casual thing. Like any thorough researcher would know this stuff. I'm OK with being a geek. Hell, being a geek has become the ultimate cool. But having been a teenage girl who'd fantasized about vampires is still pathetic. And how much worse that I'd somehow ended up as Dracula's girlfriend? In any decent story, it'd be the person who'd never paid the least attention to the silly horror-movie creatures who'd end up dating a vampire. Then the author would have lots of excuses to explain things to the readers as the ignorant character found out about them for the first time.

Just my luck. I would probably have to unlearn *everything*.

Sandu went through the checklist. "No garlic needed, and the sign of the Order of the Dragon—which gave my family the name Drăculea—has a cross, a red cross like the flag of St. George. *O Quam Misericors est Deus, Pius et Justus*, it says. I could not have survived all these years if I did not have my seal. It, *ei bine*, holds me to my ideals. It keeps my spirit 'human' in a way that many of my kind have lost. Likewise with holy water. I could bathe in it if I liked."

"Or use it as cologne?" I grinned. And he grinned back, "*Da*, Dior's 'Scent of Sanctity'."

"Or 'Holy H2O by Calvin Klein'."

"*Nu, nu*, it would be Gucci."

At least five hundred years of some sort of life had not killed his enjoyment of witty banter. That was good since it made dealing with the details of this bizarre situation much more manageable. "So I could empty a bottle of '*Baptisme* by Chanel' over your head and all would be well, except you'd reek of righteous odor. So...brains and circulatory systems are vital to a vamp? Does that explain the head and heart thing?"

"We do not call ourselves 'vamps.' A vamp is an actress from the early years of cinema. As I have told you, we do not even call ourselves 'vampires.' That is a kee term." He saw me start to interrupt to pursue that fascinating line of discussion and headed me off. "It might well be because the head and heart contain vital systems, but I have always seen it simply as the damage factor. We heal from a great deal of injury; but annihilate the head and the heart, and we are too damaged. It is unlikely we could recover, even with just the one destroyed. But with am'r, it pays to be thorough. It is never regretted, taking time to pull out an enemy's heart after cutting off his head or vice versa. More preferable is burning it all."

"Ick," was my cool, unflappable response.

"This is my world, *draga mea*. You wanted to know about it."

"Yes, I did. *I do.* It's just that I'm used to it being fiction, not *reality*. But now, hearing you talk about it? It's all too real, too close."

"But you need to hear it. You will be entering this world." No one mentioned the option of me walking away. It didn't seem to occur to him, and no matter how weird things got, this was my first chance at a life even vaguely resembling my fantasies, in which—let's face it—I'd been living all this time. I wasn't stupid enough to think I'd ever get another chance like this again.

"But for now, enough of death, final or otherwise," Sandu continued, "Since you know all the myths, let me..."

"Bust them?"

"Yes. And I know of your reference."

"OK."

"Remember, I live in this time with you."

"I do. But sometimes you'll need to bring me up to date about something in the past I've missed, and you'll need me to update you about something in the present you've not been paying any attention to."

"Certainly. But now, ask me about whatever vampire myth you like."

"Um. Animals. Transformation? Special affinity? Tasty snack?"

"*Nu, da,* and not really. We do not have transformative powers. I cannot become a wolf, a colony of bats, or a pack of rats. And before you ask, not a vampire bat, either. Nor a vampire squid."

"Damn. I was hoping for tentacles."

"I'm afraid I must disappoint you there, my perverse lover. I must also disappoint in regards to any other transformation. No green fog for you. Also, my shadow does not act independently of me."

"You really are a buzz-kill, Sandu! Mirrors? Photographs?"

"Shall we go look in the mirror now? Your hair is a little messy. I think we shall see that mine is, too." I grinned and mussed his hair up further, to which he submitted with good grace. "But the matter of photographs is from ghost myths, not vampires. I can show you pictures of me over the centuries. I enjoyed the invention of *camera obscura* and its evolution over the ages. Ah, and the silver collodion process of early photography was no concern to me since silver is werewolves. Or would be, were there such things. However, being am'r meant I did not need to worry about the toxicity of the chemicals used in early photography.

"There are many benefits to being am'r or am'r-nafsh. We who have passed over into being fully am'r indeed have the superhuman strength of the myths, and increased agility and reflexes. We can see perfectly in the dark, and our vision in the light is greater than the kee 20/20 vision. Well, it would be if the light did not give us such bad headaches. We can see excellently during the day, yes, but we prefer not to.

"We have a profoundly increased sense of smell and taste, even touch." He paused. "And then there is the mind. The myth of our powers of persuasion is essentially correct. From the moment one becomes an am'r, one has the benefit of the powers you might call mesmerism, although in part it is only a greater understanding of how to influence thought and impel action. Some of us have a stronger talent for it, but It is a raw talent, so you need to learn how to use it. Am'r get more powerful as they survive the years, decades, centuries. All of our abilities become more controlled and formidable. It is as if we have the inverse of kee aging."

I'd been listening patiently, but I had to interrupt. "Tell me more about the mesmerism. You said you did *not* use it on me, but I've acted strangely since I met you. I have done things I'd've never thought I'd do."

"Ah, Noosh, you cannot blame me for your actions. Things will not go well for us if you distrust me and distrust your feelings for me. I have said I did not mesmerize you, and if you go around thinking I did, it will destroy our love."

That distracted me. Did I love Sandu? I was happy calling him my lover since it was an accurate description of our relationship so far, but *love?*

How could he have fallen in love with me this quickly? From all he'd said, it was a case of love at first sight, in which I did not believe. Shouldn't half a millennium of life in this cold, hard world have knocked such a romantic notion from his head?

Maybe some people just worked like that. I've had friends who claimed love at first sight with their partners, although those relationships didn't seem to have any greater chance of working out in the long run. But this was *different*. Sandu and I had drunk each other's blood. We had shared the deepest intimacies. Maybe blood was the fast track to love?

But wait! One had to assume Sandu had drunk lots of people's blood, so the whole blood-drinking thing didn't automatically confer intimacy on the act. Although thinking about it, he'd also given me his blood. Was that the normal way to do the deed?

He could see I was thinking, and he let me be. I was glad. After he had opened himself up to me as he had done, given me that much of himself, I didn't want to hurt him. I'd hate myself if I did. Also, these were my stupid issues. It was my problem, and I didn't have to make it his.

Vamp—uh, "am'r" were good at patience. I guess anyone could learn it eventually, and it probably helped to know you had all the time in the world. Wait, was that a myth too? "Sandu, are am'r immortal?"

"The final answers are not in, *dragă* Noosh. We have ancient ones among us, and those have not died yet of any 'natural causes.' When am'r die, so far, it has only been from violence or stupidity. Often a combination of both, but we do not seem to deteriorate as kee do through their lives. All evidence points to us getting better and stronger as the years go by. If that is not immortality, it is something just as good, or better."

"Is it comforting that you'll basically live forever and keep getting better?" It didn't seem unattractive to me. What I had was the certainty I would get old and wrinkly and infirm and addlepated and then die, possibly painfully or with a terrible lack of dignity. No other option available. Until now.

Sandu replied, "When one first becomes an am'r, the knowledge one has beaten death is intoxicating. That is, incidentally, the time when most am'r are killed. Changing from being kee to am'r, or the 'vistarascha' as it is called, is complex. First surviving a long period as being am'r-nafsh can help, but few manage it. If an am'r makes it through the recklessness and enthusiastic risk-taking period of one's early years, generally one settles down to a period of, how do you say...ah...'going to ground.' Being secretive and secluded. We do less of this in these modern times since building new identities is made trivial by modern electronics, by being able to be on the other side of the world after a plane flight."

"Wait, what? Identity theft is *easier* now than it was when you could just pick a new name and show up in a new town where they had almost no way to check up on you? Oh, hey, that must mean you can travel over water, right?"

Sandu sighed but not unhappily. As much as he was complaining about having to talk instead of fuck, I think he was enjoying explaining am'r to such an eager audience. I didn't think I could do any harm to his ego with all this attention. Either Dracula was already the world's biggest egotist, or he'd long ago given up on such things.

"You could travel through life incognito if you wanted to be a peasant, *draga mea*. I did a few times when it seemed like the best way to escape a situation. However, I am royalty, and I have been unwilling to become accustomed to a lesser existence. When there were few people in the world and even fewer noble-born, you could arrive at a castle and announce yourself, and be welcomed. If you had made yourself good letters of introduction, your rôle could be played for a while. You just needed to move on before someone who should have known of you, be it a fellow military officer or a family member, arrived to put shame to your tale—and possibly assist in your imprisonment and execution.

"Now, if one needs to, one can borrow or build from whole cloth an almost entirely foolproof identity, even to open a bank account or purchase a house." He swept his arm around, indicating his home.

"Crossing moving water is as quickly proven false as mirrors or holy water. It is pure myth, perhaps to make people feel safer in their beds at night. In the dark. When *I* roam." He gave a rather unholy chuckle there.

That led to a burning question, which I'd put off asking for too long. "Ah. Um. Yes. I guess the first thing is, are we...um...dating? And I guess the next question is, are we going to be...monogamous? Can you get enough, well, *sustenance* from just me, or are you going to need to...er...*dine out* sometimes?" How awkward was that? Especially since I was not sure how OK I'd be with any of the possible answers.

"*Dragă* Noosh, you ask such questions! I have never 'dated' anyone, but you can call this 'dating' if you like. I do not wish to frighten you off." He looked away. "What I hope for is something much, *much* longer term. I love—when I love—immediately and true. I have learned my life may be long, but love needs to be grasped tightly when it comes, and every moment treated as all-too-fleeting."

I thought about the stories I'd read about his wife, who'd supposedly thrown herself off a castle tower when she heard rumors he'd been killed in battle. I wondered how many times he'd "grasped" love since, but decided this wasn't a good time to discuss exes. One important question had been left unanswered, and it was a big one.

"How much blood do you need to drink? You seem to be giving quite a lot back to me. Can you sustain that? If you do need blood from others..." I finished the sentence in my head: how will I be able to cope?

"Those are important questions, *draga mea*, and I will answer you genuinely." He paused, and his thoughtful expression had me seriously worried.

"To start, I do not give you as much back as you give me. You would find that...excessive."

"'A dab'll do ya,'" I interjected, reaching for levity out of nervous tension.

"Just so. However, there is vhoon-drinking, and then there is sharing each other. In our language, we call this 'vhoon-vayon.' It is not a thing an am'r finds every day. It's like how kee have trouble finding true love and compatible sexual partners.

"If we do not...no, let me go back. As it has been, I have regularly needed to find—the word we use is 'izchhaish,' but let me call them 'donors'—for, let us call them 'blood infusions.' It can be that cold and clinical. If it would make you more comfortable, I can derive no more pleasure from drinking from an unknown kee than you would get from eating a satisfactory but not incredible meal."

Good, I thought, jealously and selfishly. "What about blood-borne diseases?" I had to ask. "Can you get sick? Can the blood you drink make *me* sick? Could you carry anything in your blood I could catch?" And why didn't I ask this before we exchanged blood? Or before the *next time* we exchanged blood?

"Am'r do not get diseases. That is for kee. As for you, *draga mea*, I would do nothing to harm you. The vhoon you get from me has been...transmogrified. It is no longer vhoon-kee, so it cannot harm you as things carried in vhoon-kee could."

"You are a good filtration system, is what you're saying."

"Ha! You have a special skill at rephrasing things, Noosh. But yes. I will be your personal filter."

"My own walking, talking Brita filter. I love it! What more could a girl ask for?"

"A walking, talking, fucking 'Brita filter,' I should think!" he countered. He had become uncoupled from me as we talked, something which I'd noted with great sadness at the time, but I was driven to learn more. However, it seemed it was now time to re-couple. I felt a brief pang of regret that I hadn't gotten more info from him, but it was drowned by arousal. There would be time to talk about everything else later.

This time he scrunched down the sofa, ending up between my legs. Ah. *Now* was the moment for him to spend some quality time down there. I settled into a position both comfy for me and which gave him plenty of access. But I realized—"Sandu! Um, I'm not cleaned up down there from last time!"

He had been running his eyes over my naked and spread body with a delight which made me feel there was no limit on how shameless I could be, but now he looked back up to my face with an even wider grin. "*Creatură senzuală*, I shall not mind drinking back that very vhoon I gave you in this most intimate way. I intend to drink all those sweetest fluids down there."

And he made good his promises. He laved the drying blood from the insides of my thighs. I wondered if flaked dried blood might be a gourmet vampire seasoning, like shaved chocolate? That thought made me giggle, which made him dig in even more enthusiastically. He licked and nuzzled at my labia, but what drove me mad for more were the little nibbles. I think both my inner and outer lips soon had little puncture marks in them, but I no longer cared; sensation was all. His teasing ensured that he had plenty of the local fluid when he got to the main point, a main point he licked in every speed, direction, and pressure until he'd figured out all of my favorite combinations.

When he had me up at the top of the cliff—the one you fall off of when you have the better sort of orgasm—he pulled back the slightest bit, changed the shape of his mouth, and went back down with fangs and tongue out. It meant my perceptions went from "Oh-god oh-god-almost-there" to "Wha—Yeeowch—Ohhhhhhh!" As before, the pain of his teeth sinking into my skin worked to intensify the pleasure and take it to a next level I'd never even imagined.

I screamed. I called out to random assorted deities. I think I even ululated. I most certainly bucked about like a bronco, but he held me down, and let only the smallest amount of hip-thrusting work in rhythm with what he was doing, to take me even higher yet again.

I came back down only partially, to notice he had climbed up my body, and was more than ready to get on with the impaling. *Oh no, I'm not sure I'm ready for*—was all I had time to think before he was sliding inside me.

It is amazing how the act of thrusting (and removing and thrusting again) a rigid extremity into a lubricated cavity can entirely fail to get old. The range of sensations can differ from stroke to stoke. I know I must have been high as a kite on happy brain chemicals, because I was actually thinking exactly that, oddly removed from the situation, as he fucked me with intense thoroughness and precision. And also: Maybe a vampire lover really is insatiable. I was looking forward to getting used to this.

He bit my neck, and again, thought stopped. I was becoming a real connoisseur of penetrations, because I swear the same things I'd just thought about his cock were true of his rigid incisors sliding into the other lubricated cavities even as he created them.

Afterward, I felt drained. My limbs felt heavy; even my eyelids did. I was oh-so-ready to drift to sleep, but Sandu wouldn't let me. I mumbled, "Lemme sleeeep..." and tried to ignore him.

"Anushka! You need not open your eyes, but you *must* open your mouth. Now—" A wristful of hot blood was spurting into my mouth. In my dreamy delirium, I compared it to drinking chocolate: rich, thick, coating your mouth and throat with flavor. And it seemed I'd acquired a taste for it; I was gulping the salty-metallic goodness down as if I'd had been tippling the ol' sanguinary all my life.

A new high came on. Fuck, but I was high more often than a wake-n-baker these days. The world seemed full of gold dust, sparkling in the air, gleaming along Sandu's skin, twinkling like galaxies in his eyes. He was patiently affectionate with the utterly stoned me, letting me caress him and wriggle around in lively cuddling as I relished the astonishing sensations of his skin on mine with the soft leather of the sofa underneath us. I babbled the whole time, sharing my every thought and feeling with the same innocence as a child who'd just learned to speak, assuming he'd *want* to hear it all. He smiled warmly at me and let me pour it all out to him.

A final gift, when he was ready to tuck in for the morning. "Lay back, *draga mea*, and I will soothe you to sleep while cleaning up after myself." As he spoke, he scrunched down in a fluid way, like a jaguar backing up, and slowly laved me clean, finishing as he had started, but in a soporific rather than arousing way. I faded out in a soothing, gently erotic cloud of being.

Chapter Ten

I AWOKE SOMETIME IN the late afternoon. I supposed I could fire up his computer to find the time, or dig out my mobile from wherever it had fallen since Sandu's antiques did not extend to clocks of any sort.

With a horrible start, I realized it must be Sunday, and I had to go back to work on Monday. It was a nasty intrusion of the real world into what had been the most incredible fantasy ever. I did not want this bubble to pop! Well, I had a day and I could enjoy it and then get Sandu to run me home after he woke up tonight.

After a nice juicy final round of amazing sex.

I did not want to go home. I did not want this dream to end. I just could not see myself shelving children's books, and how the hell could I chat with Dre and Zuzu about my weekend? "How was your weekend, guys? Me? Oh, not much. I just had a non-stop blood-drinking orgy and took the Real Vampires 101 hands-on course."

How the hell could I go back to normality after this?

Oh well, I didn't have to do anything about it until Sandu got up from wherever it was he bedded down for the day. It was past time for a proper cleanup out in the cabana. On the way to the shower, I rediscovered the huge wooden Japanese tub out there, surrounded by vine-hung trellised walls. Even during the day, with the flowers sleepily furled, this was an unexpectedly beautiful garden. It occurred to me to wonder if I needed to worry about a gardener showing up and finding me walking around naked in the late afternoon spring sun.

And is this me? Wandering around outdoors comfortably naked?

Today was a day for emotional jolts. As I became conscious of one kind of comfort, I also became aware that the nippy May air bothered me not in the slightest. I wondered if my inhibitions had gone to the same place as my body's concern for temperature.

Last night Sandu had not lit a fire. I'd been totally comfortable—and seen strangely well in the dark. And...wait a minute, my glasses! I didn't know where they were. Me, who scrambled blindly for them immediately upon opening my eyes in the morning. I hadn't even thought about them since I awoke.

I didn't need my glasses anymore.

My emotions jumped in all directions at once. My sense of what was good or what was bad was a wildly and uselessly spinning compass needle. A hot shower was the obvious resolver of all problems, for lack of anything better or more certain. As the scalding water pounded on my body, I was glad I could still appreciate the joy of heat, even if the lack of it wasn't a bother. The fluffy black robe was a sybaritic pleasure, tickling me where it touched my body.

I devoured three frozen meals one after another. They were as tasteless as ever, but once I started putting food in my mouth, I couldn't stop. Then I consumed the entire tub of ice cream. As I ate, I started composing a list of questions for Sandu: What the hell changes have been wrought in my body, and would this wear off or was it forever? What the hell would happen if I drink more of your blood? Could there be a problem with us continuing as lovers? After eating, I wandered into the library looking for pen and paper and immediately got distracted by the books. Seriously, when faced with what seemed like a first edition of Galland's *Les Mille Et Une Nuits, Contes Arabes Traduits En Français*, one had to have priorities.

Sandu found me there, hours having melted by. I caught a whisper of his movement this time, and when he swooped down on me and caught me up in his arms, I was able to lay the volume down gently.

Am'r didn't seem to have morning breath, or else they had special blood-toothpaste that left the mouth perfectly kissable with no minty scent.

"How was your day, *draga mea*? What texts have you devoured? Ah, that is a personal favorite, although I prefer the

Hazār Afsān." He interrupted himself and potentially me by kissing me some more. I was delighted he did not seem to be getting any less passionate.

But when the passion seemed to be heading in the direction of sex, I pulled away. "Sandu, there are things to talk about. I need to go home tonight, you know, and there are changes in—in *me*."

"Shhhh, *micuțo*, I understand, I understand. You must forgive me. It has been a long, lonely time since my heart has awakened. I just want to show you how I feel; I want to let go. But I am being thoughtless. Come, would you like to soak with me? I should have shared one with you last night, but you distract me, *dragă* Noosh. I think I shall blame everything on how delicious you are."

His special brand of flattery worked, and where better to have a potentially weird—well, weird was my new normal—discussion but in a long, hot soak? "I've seen the tub. It looks wonderful!"

"Then we shall be in it together, *draga mea*, and I shall faithfully answer any question you put to me."

He was leading me by hand as he said this, towing me along to the Japanese bath. He was an overgrown boy in some ways, no matter how many centuries he'd seen. It was funny to think about Dracula like this. It was not a side of him which I'd have anticipated, had you asked me a week ago what I thought Dracula'd be like. Not an adolescently-overeager horndog, although I guess most literary and cinematic vampires *did* have the whole "appetite" thing in common.

We went out to the tub, and he shed his pajama bottoms and I my robe. I looked at him as he swung himself into the steaming water. He had a wonderful body, with lean, wiry muscles moving under his smooth olive skin. I felt a rush of emotions just looking at him. Could I be in love with him, or was this a result of the chemicals of lust?

He was looking back at me; indeed, he positively smoldered at me. It was weird to be living in a romance novel, but there he was, ready to be on the cover, and either he was supremely exhibitionistic or supremely un-self-aware. Granted, he came from a time when nakedness was seen differently—and he was a guy, and it's always different for them—but I'd have to be pretty stupid to assume he'd lived all this time without realizing how well-built he was and the effect it could have on people who liked that sort of thing.

Likewise, I'd also have to be particularly stupid not to realize I was very susceptible to "that sort of thing." I'd never gone for his type before, but what type was it: hot, or vampire? I guess it sort of didn't matter *why* someone was looking all romance-novel hot for you if they were right there, doing so in the flesh.

"Come here, *draga mea*. You look like a hungry cat. I shall be a canary that does not fly away."

"Hah! Let's see—who's more like the cat here? And who did the *eating* last night?"

"I did not hear you complaining. Shall I not do it again...?"

"Well, if you *must*, I suppose I'll be gracious and let you, from time to time." I let myself be helped into the tub, although I had never felt more spry. Perhaps I was feeling a bit cat-like, myself, at least in terms of muscular litheness and an overall sense of being able to leap door-tops in a single bound.

I'd like to blame Sandu for starting things up again, but it was me this time. It was just too fascinating to touch his silky-smooth skin, the delicious firm muscles moving right under the surface. And of course, it was ever so tempting to press my lips to just where I'd been caressing, feeling his skin with my lips, smelling him.

Smells now meant a good deal more to me. It was like the scents were layered, with "outer" information about the skin and what it had come into contact with, and "inner" information coming up from underneath the surface. I could even smell the blood moving under his skin.

"There is something you need to know, *draga mea*, before we go any further." For a moment, the words were just the pleasurable sound of his voice, nothing more. The water lapped sultrily against us, its fluidity an erotic contrast to his solid body against mine. The scent of night flowers was as thick as incense in the air.

Finally, the meaning of his words penetrated my sensual trance. "What? Why? Um, what do you mean?"

He distanced himself, not physically but emotionally. It left me with an aching sense of loss and a desire to do anything to get back to the connected place we had just been and to do the things we had been just about to do. "You need to hear this, Anushka. I must tell you. Trust me that I do not welcome this interruption any more than do you."

I didn't know what to say. My brain was mostly shut down as surplus to requirements for the moment, and this did not sound like it was going to be good news. I felt a rush of realization of how stupid I had been, madly, repeatedly having the most unsafe sex of all time with a complete stranger who also was a vampire. What price would I now pay for the pleasure?

I think he could see the panic rising in my eyes, but we both needed him to press on. "There are rules to becoming am'r. Perhaps 'rules' is the wrong word. Facts, details, events...but none of those quite fit, either. Regardless, we have shared the most passionate gift twice now." He paused. "There are a few side effects, of which I have told you."

I nodded. Yes, I'd been hungry. Actually, there were side-effects he *hadn't* told me about: seeing in the dark, recovering 20/20 vision (something I'd not possessed since first grade), getting a major upgrade to my olfactory system, and no longer being bothered by the cold. They were obvious *perks* to drinking vampire blood, but, still, he hadn't warned me.

He continued, "If we never...loved each other this way again, I think you would eventually be as if this never happened. You would be as, *ei bine*, as unaltered as you were before you knew me. Or so I believe, Noosh; I do not know personally. I have never shared my vhoon with anyone who was not am'r or who did not become am'r-nafsh. It is not a thing done lightly."

Well, that was nice. He didn't do this with just anyone. But was this at the level of engagement-ring-rare? I felt frustrated at not knowing enough to even ask the right questions.

He had my full attention. What the hell would he say next? He looked almost uncertain. I'd stopped breathing and I would not breathe again until I heard his voice, his explanation.

"*Draga mea*, what I need to say is..." His voice trailed off here and then started again, "*is* if we perform vhoon-vayon, if we make love and exchange blood one more time, you would become am'r-nafsh. And it would be irreversible."

The world spun a bit, but not as much as I might have expected. I mean, this was the sort of thing you expected to hear from a vampire, right? They made those sorts of pronouncements. Consorting with vampires always led to a human being dead or, well, "undead, undead, undead."

And to think I'd been worried about STDs.

"Sandu. Vlad. Sandu. What does am'r-nafsh even *mean*?"

"The closest in English is 'immortal who is yet living'."

"Not the translation. I mean, what would it mean for me?"

He let out a deep sigh, and a part of him came back to me. I guessed I had passed some sort of "not running away screaming" test. My reward was the slight re-opening of his emotions. I was naked and soaking wet, and I wasn't even sure where I was, beyond "a creaky old Victorian well outside of Blackacre in some direction," so running off screaming was not a practical option, but I liked getting points for not having done it.

His hands started sliding up and down my back. It was comforting, but my body started reawakening and responding. Focus, foolish girl, focus!

"Ah, *dragă* Noosh, it would mean many things for you. For one, you would still be a living being. But when you died," he looked purposefully into my eyes, "you would come back as am'r. In a way, it would make you immortal without making you less alive. A 'life insurance policy,' if you like."

"While you remain alive, however," he added slowly, "there would be some changes. You would have more stamina, greater physical strength, your responses would be faster. You would see improvements in your vision, your hearing—all your senses. And your thinking would, over time, become faster, better. Never as rapid or powerful as am'r, but above kee abilities."

"Is there a downside to being am'r-nafsh?"

"*Ei bine*, for some, knowing they cannot die a normal death, that they would wake to the life of an am'r, is a real deterrent."

"Seriously? A lifetime of being, well, superhuman, followed by the promise of eternal life in which you are even *more* superhuman? That's a *problem* for people?"

"You are not being realistic. Once you are am'r, you must live on vhoon. And you would not prove immortal, if slain properly. Indeed, new am'r have a high mortality rate. Without guidance, a young am'r is more likely to be killed by an elder than to become one."

"If I become am'r-nafsh, would I sleep all day as you do? Could I eat food? Would I, uh, go to the bathroom?"

"Ah, *micuţo*, you have come to the true heart of the matter." He shot me a toothy grin. "To answer you in order, you could sleep with me through the day if you liked. You would tend to be nocturnal because the sun would be less of a pleasure for you, but you would not lose the ability to operate by day. You will not like the sun, but neither does any am'r. We do not turn into dust, to add to your pile of discarded myths."

"Are all am'r-nafsh, er, *partnered* with an am'r?"

"There may have been exceptions in the long river of history, but am'r do not vhoon-share with just anyone. It is a powerful thing. I love you. I wish to protect you, and give you the most precious gift such as I can give: to share my life. Hopefully a long, long life. In another way, it is a more profound gift, for having an am'r-nafsh makes an am'r more vulnerable to his enemies. It is a gift with a cost.

"As for food and, hmmm, digestive matters. You can, you *must,* eat food, kee food, but over time, you will become somewhat sensitive. You may lose the taste for certain foods. Vhoon, however, will never make you sick. The more you drink, the stronger you become, although it is a slow process, limited by your living flesh."

"And the, um, end result?"

"My ever-practical Noosh. If you eat, you must eliminate the waste matter, like any living creature. But vhoon is different, for both am'r and am'r-nafsh. As I said before, we process the vhoon completely. There is no waste matter."

As attractive as never having to go to the bathroom again might be, there were more important things to consider. Like, how do I feel about becoming half-vampire now, with a non-optional future of being a real, hundred-percent vampire?

Siren songs from years of reading vampire novels sang in my head: never growing old, staying perfect and beautiful forever, being basically superhuman. And what I had learned for myself in the last couple days; the sex—oh, the sex!

"Sandu! If I become am'r-nafsh, we will be able to keep, um, 'sharing the most passionate gift,' right? And, uh, what about after I become am'r?"

His eyes flamed hot enough to melt me. I had to hold onto him tighter so I'd not fall—well, float—off.

"Your question pleases me greatly, *draga mea*. You are thinking ahead to the future time when we as am'r will share ourselves completely for an eternity. It is a dream. It is the most beautiful my future has seemed since..." He looked off into a distant past. "For many long years."

He shook his head as if it were as full of romantic clouds as mine. I couldn't help smiling at his passion. He might not technically be a living being, but he was more alive than most people I'd known. He was more alive than I'd ever been. Well, up to now. Now, thanks to him, I was passionately alive as well.

Huh. And if *that* isn't a deciding factor—but no, I need to know more.

"There are, um, *changes* in me. You said there would be some, so I'm not surprised, but I need to know about what is happening to me. What is *going* to happen to me."

He gazed at me silently for a long moment, then got up and paced in the tub, which was just big enough to allow him a constrained back-and-forth.

"*Draga mea*, the first questions to answer are the immediacies, are they not? You have noted an increasing hunger, *nu?* Well, as long as I drink from you, you will need to replenish yourself, and I have not been feeding you as I should because food is such an," he looked a bit helpless, trying to find the right word, "an *inconvenience*. We should be feeding you meat and other foods that will make your vhoon strong, surging vitally inside you."

"Iron supplements, maybe?" I suggested.

He looked startled. "I do not know. I do not know anyone who has tried it. This is why I need your new thoughts and your fresh mind."

I teased, "And here I thought you only liked me for my blood and my body!" But he ignored me and continued, "You should now feel yourself glowing with vitality. At least, *draga mea*, you look as if you do.

"You will find yourself a little stronger, with more stamina. But you have not had any trouble sleeping, have you? Your body has been getting used to a different, *ei bine*, nutrient, and you need your sleep."

"But we have gotten off the point. I do not think you understand what I am trying to say, so I will tell you again. This would be the third time and it is like a fairytale; this time the magic happens, you might say. If you do not want this change to be unalterable, we cannot share blood ever again."

I didn't answer out loud. I didn't even answer in my head. He was right; I wasn't hearing him because, well, it was just *too much*. I was two-thirds of the way to being a partial vampire and one more bout of incredible sex would alter me forever.

I was *already* changed, too, and although so far I hadn't seen any downside to those changes, it did add to the overwhelmingness. To be honest, my most immediate concern was that we might not be able to have sex again.

I withdrew into my thoughts. Sandu left me to it, not staring at me, but silently letting me know he was willing to meet my eyes if I looked at him.

Now was the make-or-break moment. Here was this man who said he loved me. At any rate, he made me feel better about myself than anyone else had ever done. Sure, I didn't know enough about him in practical considerations of whether he'd be a good partner to live with or even to date long-term. However, I'd just had my first real taste of mad, passionate romance, and I didn't want to end or otherwise ruin it by overthinking. So far, my life had been shaped by being realistic, rational, and sensible.

The one time life offers me wild passion, don't I get to just *go with it?* If I let practical matters get in the way of a romantic dream come true, how much would I regret it for the rest of my boring life?

On the other hand, "living vampire." Condemning myself to a life of—well, I didn't even *know* what. I didn't have enough useful information. I'd been too busy fucking or being fucked to have gotten more than the merest hint of understanding.

I should get a list of all the changes that will occur in my body. All the pros and cons. All of it. Before having sex with him again.

Even as that sensible conclusion moved through my brain, part of me rebelled against it. In fact, the sensible section could claim not more than twenty percent of cerebral real estate. Maybe ten percent.

It was time to just fucking *live* for once. If I could only live by accepting a certain amount of, I don't know, "undeath," well, you gotta work with what you got. If I turned this down, if I ruined it with fearfulness, I deserved to go skulking back to my stacks, pull on shapeless "I've given up" sweats, hang unattractive spectacles off my nose, and devote myself to a life of celibate boredom.

Now was the moment where I could shake off the restraint and risk-avoidance that had so shaped my existence until now. Instead of reading about it, I could be the heroine of my own story. I was at the most important crossroads in my life: Do I become spontaneous, fearless, and free, or do I stick to the same-old and plod along, safe, responsible, boring ol' Noosh?

I knew the answer. It was time to throw my inhibitions to the wind. Bungee jump first, and find out how far down it was later. It was time for a new Noosh.

I swam over to him.

"I choose life. A new life," I told him, "and I choose *you*."

His eyes glowed. Not just metaphorically with emotion; they seemed incandescent, like an FX trick. Joy and delight radiated off him like heat. He did not move for a long moment, just gazed at me. I looked back at him, high on my dangerous decision.

"You do not do wrong, *draga mea*, *dragă* Noosh. We will have time later for me to answer your every question, but now, join me in this vitality. See the world as I see it; live and never die with me, *sufleţel*—my soul!"

As he spoke, he pulled me to him, my legs straddling his underwater. His cock was caught between our bodies, as tumescent and turgid and tumid as any romance heroine could ever hope for. I thought he would start there, since his need was obviously great—my own not far behind—but he ignored the great throbbing thing and kissed me.

It was pure passion: rough and intense. He bit my lips and tongue; sharp raw pangs of pain flashed through me, and he spread the blood around with his lips and tongue. I guess I was pretty used to the taste of blood by now; the viscosity and the salt and iron tang no longer made me feel sick or repulsed. It was part of sex, part of this new reality, part of decisively being alive.

The blood lubricated the kiss, our lips crashing against each other's, mashed by teeth and tongues thrust forcibly against each other. His hands moved on my back and ass and legs, rubbing, kneading, scratching, tugging the flesh into handfuls. I echoed his touch on everything I could reach on him, grabbing the muscle under the smooth skin, dragging my nails satisfyingly into his unnaturally smooth skin.

I suppose it could have been categorized as "just making out," but in the moment, it was sex enough for me. Genital demands forgotten, mouths and hands became the sex organs. And sex was more than pleasure, more than pain; it was trying to become one through violent physicality, cramming our separate selves into one whole.

I guess all good things must come to an end. But, for once, there were even better things to follow, which they could only do after our almost-devouring of each other had come to completion. But I did not feel complete; I was a thing made of hunger. And, looking into Sandu's eyes, I saw nothing but hunger: no love, no intelligence, only endless, bestial hunger.

I should have been scared, but what could I do? Run from the predator, thereby making myself into extra-tasty prey? Nor had I any desire to run, since my own needs felt equally predatory. There was no room for fear. Perhaps Sandu's eyes were the mirror of my own.

He stared into my eyes as if this was as much a part of the sex as the kissing had been. I met his gaze and held nothing back. I put everything in me into my eyes, pushed it at him—*take all of me now!*—as if vision could somehow be penetration.

He did not flinch away from me. Perhaps, he would never flinch away from me. But somehow it spurred him to take things to the next level: lifting me up and lowering me down and showing me he could indeed still be the Impaler.

I made something between a gasp and a scream, a pretty strangled sound, not worthy of the sensations I was feeling. Salt water is nice to soak in, but does not a good lubricant make. His hands forcing my hips downward while his cock pushed unrelentingly upwards could have been profoundly uncomfortable, if I'd been in a different state of mind. As it was, I helped along this impalement as best I could. The extra-buoyant salt water took away much of my work, but I did a useful wriggle *here*, held my hips in the most effective angle *there*. He had taken all of me into him—I could do no less.

When we had finally worked me down onto that which was impaling me, Sandu met my eyes again, giving me a meaningful look...except I did not know the meaning. He reached to the side of the tub, and picked up something I'd not noticed him putting there when he disrobed. It glinted in the moonlight: a short, sharp knife, more prettily curved than a scalpel, but obviously just as sharp. He held it to his neck, not hesitating, knowing just the right place from years of practice.

I was made of hunger, yes, but still not used to such things. It woke me up for a moment, back to the Noosh I used to be. For just a moment, I watched the blade slice horribly deeply through skin and muscle, until blood spurted out. *Holy crap!* was my main thought. But Sandu grabbed my hands in one of his, and put his other hand around the back of my neck, and pressed my mouth to the flow of the blood: I had no choice but to gulp down the rich redness.

Nectar, I thought, after the first (somewhat forced) swallow. The hunger had retaken me, and I was guzzling his blood as fast as my throat could work. His wound started closing, and I was working my tongue into the wound to keep it open, keep the flow of nectar from drying up.

I became aware of him moving under me, moving in me, moaning my name and "*Sufleţel, sufleţel!*" In the strangest way, I distantly became aware I was orgasming, the pleasure from drinking was in no way different from the spasms shaking the rest of me. It was a glorious pleasure, but I was far above it, enjoying the view from someplace superior to mere physical pleasure. I looked down to enjoy the tingling in every nerve ending in my body, the rush of pleasure through my arteries and veins. I felt a golden wave rush up my spinal column, and I swear I could feel it enter my brain and jump from synapse to synapse. I could feel chemicals changing resplendently: colors swarming, tastes dancing, scents spinning, sounds painting themselves in Post-Impressionist swirls I could reach out to, feel their flavor and frequencies.

Everything went black.

At first, it was an empty black. Sometime later, it became a rich black of all the colors combined. It became a velvet blackness. It became a warm, safe, soothing blackness. Eventually, I felt the hot water lapping my body and Sandu under me and in me, his arms wrapped around me and my arms wrapped around him.

I was alive, and the world around me was alive. The water teased my skin, as did the night air where my body was not underwater. My nerve endings tickled happily where I pressed against Sandu and where he pressed into me. I looked up and around and the night was full of color. The flowers were like gems, and their scents were jewels of fragrance. I could smell the saltwater and the cedar wood of the tub and the perfume of Sandu's skin and blood. It was not just smelling anymore; it was experiencing.

I brought Sandu's face back into focus and found him smiling fondly at me, contentment exuding from his pores. "*Draga mea, esti a mea,*" he said, and when I tilted my head at him, he explained, "You are mine."

I found that for once, I did not mind his possessiveness. "And you are mine," I replied. A witty rejoinder was not beyond me at this moment, but I felt the simple reply was best suited for the occasion.

"Yes," he agreed, "we are." He was fully healed. Maybe there was blood smeared all over my face, but if there was he didn't seem to mind. In a world so wide open and full of options, all I could do was ask, "What's next?"

Sandu started laughing. I would never get tired of hearing his laughter. The corresponding movement reminded me he was still inside me, and still as hard as if the most astounding sex ever in the history of the world had not just taken place. I laughed too, and started moving on him. "So next is—more?" I asked.

In answer he threw his head back and let me use my core muscles to ride him in the water. Lubrication was not wanting now, and it was a slick, satisfying trip up and down him. It was arousing, but just a pleasing, simple sensation. It could lead to orgasm eventually, but right now it was just an uncomplicated pleasure, enjoyed at its most basic level—although with my newly upgraded senses, even basic things were now enhanced and novel. After we did this for a nice pleasing while, he lifted his head up and looked at me, and his eyes were gleaming. "Hungry?" I asked him.

"*Da, ca un lup!*" he replied, and he rose up, pulling me off of him and disappointing me, as I'd been enjoying having him in there. Before I could complain, I was leaned back against the side of the tub. "You have given to me the greatest of gifts, *dragă* Noosh, even as you took from me my vhoon. Now, I will give you a little gift, and drink a little of the nectar flowing through your veins." He reached for my hand, and I was distracted for a moment, remembering my own perceptions of his blood as nectar just a little while ago.

I was brought back as he brought my palm up to his mouth and began kissing it. He kissed up to my wrist, licked with seductive promise. He continued up the delicate skin of my inner arm, to the inside of my elbow, and again he licked, sending shivers up my spine. When his questing tongue seemed to have found the right spot, he bit, and the pain made me cry out and arch my back. I might have pulled my arm away from him, but he held it fast. I decided to do the opposite and pushed my arm against his mouth. He moaned in appreciation, and dug his teeth in deeper, worrying the wound to let the blood flow. It hurt more than any other bite he'd given me. Thinking back, he'd always been distracting me with pleasure when he bit. But my feelings about pain were no longer as clear-cut as they used to be. I pressed my arm to him again; I needed to move it in *some* direction, any direction. He moaned again, and I felt his hips thrusting helplessly against my side under the water. I wished he was inside me still, and wondered what "gift" he thought he was giving me.

But the gift was still to come. As was I. His other arm slid down my body, pulling me up so I floated in the buoyant salt water. He curled his hand up from under me, his fingers playing up and down my labia. He eased off a bit on my poor arm, and I could take in the delicate sensations. After exploring the exterior with his fingers (the lapping water adding its own interesting sensations), he slid in one finger, two, and twisted his wrist to curl them at just-the-right curvature. He proceeded to move those two fingers ever so slowly. I started laughing in delight. Soon I was beyond the ability to make any sounds except moans and gasps. Meanwhile, Sandu went back to worrying the wound, but this time the sensations mingled perfectly: the pain adding zest to the pleasure, the pleasure adding an arousing depth of sweetness to the pain.

Orgasms. I'd had innumerable, multitudinous orgasms over the past nights. You'd think they would start to get boring. They never do.

As Sandu moved his fingers at different speeds and in different patterns of touch, the orgasms changed accordingly: from sharp punctuations of pleasure, to flowing falls down the well of bliss, to waves crashing and dragging me out to a sea of deeper satiation.

Some endless time later he'd subsided to moving his fingers almost-not-at-all inside me, his tongue gently flickering again over the now unbroken skin of my arm. The waves of pleasure slowed inside me, gentle now: little intertidal sighs. I was replete but still regretful when his fingers slid from inside me. Being caught up in his arms and cradled against his body, however, more than made up for it.

But still he was rock hard. Something had to be done about it. Languidly, I tilted my head up and kissed his lips, his face, his neck. He submitted to my attentions contentedly. I took a deep breath, let it fully out, took another deep breath, and another. And down I went into the water, pulling his hips into a position comfortable for both of us, taking his cock as far down my throat as I could in one fell swoop.

I had inadequate experience in the art of fellatio, so once I'd run through my limited repertoire, I just started making things up. But it didn't take long; I was feeling only the slightest strain on my lungs by the time he bucked wildly in my grasp, and I felt and tasted the blood come spurting out of his cock.

His hands reached for me, drew me back up. "*Sufleţel!*" he gasped, as I emerged, the saltwater running down my face, pulling my hair down heavy against my skin. I gasped in air and let him pull me into his arms.

Chapter Eleven

He was murmuring things in Romanian. It's a pretty language, but I wanted to understand what he was saying. I shifted my face a little from where it pressed into his neck and interrupted him.

"Sandu. English, please."

"Sorry, sorry! I was just saying that I am as happy as I have ever been. There has been much suffering in my life and much loneliness, but now I am blessed with the deepest connection, that of a patar and his frithaputhra."

"A what? And a what?" My questions were slightly muffled, my face being nuzzled back into that perfect place where his neck met his shoulders. Our arms were wrapped around each other, our bodies pressed tightly together. I guess am'r regulate temperature better because after all this time in the hot tub, I was not overheated. Nor was I all pruney, as I ought to have been. More changes in my body? If Sandu loved soaking as much as he seemed to, this was for the best.

"Ah, that is not Romanian; it is a language spoken only by the am'r. 'Frithaputhra' means 'beloved child.' It is the term for the one who is made am'r-nafsh, and still used after they transform into an am'r. A child and a parent do not stop being those things when the child is grown. And 'patar' means 'maker.' It is the term you will use for me."

"Oh, I will?" I asked lightly, but I was a bit shaken by the formality of it all and the realization of how little I knew of the world I'd just entered. The hot sex was real, but now it was over, and there was a metric fuckton of other realness I needed to know.

Sandu looked confused at my words, but he shook his head slightly and said, "Oh, you may still call me by name, but I am now your patar. I may call you 'frithaputhra' as a term of affection, but I have many other sobriquets for you as well. These are the terms of our relationship, like 'husband' and 'wife.'"

Gulp. So I had just *married* Sandu? No, I'd more than married him; we were tied together by blood. Random bits of vampire lore flooded my brain. I had to ask, "If you die, will I die too?"

Sandu stared at me, dismayed. "What you think you know of vampires will make it more difficult to impart to you what is real and true. *Nu*, my death would not cause your instant demise. Our connection is such that you would miss my vhoon, as I hope you would miss me as a person. And the more vhoon a patar can share with his frithaputhra, the more strength I can pass to you, the stronger you make me, and the greater our bond can become, but that is all. Forget the myths and the stories. I have much to teach you. But we must leave now for my home."

The last shocked me into the nasty remembrance of it being, well, technically Monday morning now. I had to go to work in six hours or so. "Sandu. I don't understand. We are at your home, aren't we? And I can't go anywhere but to *my* home. I don't have any clean clothes, and I have to open the library at 9 AM! I need you to drive me back to Centerville." I paused. "You said I still *can* go out in the sunlight. I'm...um...'am-ur-naffshhh,' is that how you say it? So I can still do the stuff normal humans do, right?"

Sandu's eyes betrayed his internal struggle in the pause before he answered. "I suppose you could live as a 'normal human' if it is what you truly want to do, Anushka. You *can* go into the sun, but you will now experience photosensitivity. You will crave the dark, and you will crave things you do not understand because I have not had time to teach them to you. It would be bad for you to be alone at this time. This is the most dangerous period for you, and you must stay with your patar so he may keep you safe, help you become stronger, and instill in you the knowledge you need to stay alive for many centuries to come."

"But, but...I guess I understand, maybe, but where do you want to go? Can't I just go to work during the day, and you can teach me at night right here?"

"*Draga mea*, you hardly begin to understand." This was said tenderly, and I could not take offense, despite feeling freaked out and bristly. "I *must* go, and you must come with me. This is a matter of life and death, important to many more than you. I am needed, *da*, but you also are needed for the future of the am'r. I promise to explain it all, but you must trust me now as you trusted me at the start of this night. As you trusted me when you left Beowulf's with me. You have done a great thing this night. You cannot go back to ordinary things, or you will do harm to yourself. To us both. You must go on with the great things, as strange or daunting as they might seem."

I sat there in shock for a while. To the minuscule extent that I'd considered my future with Sandu—my post-third-round-of-sex future—I'd thought this am'r stuff would come into my life in bits and pieces. It would add spice to my life, not *change* it. While my life could do with having a kinky bit of secret passion added to it, it was not the sort of life that included running off into the unknown. And this was not the general and distant sort of unknown. This was a specific and immediate unknown. The only thing I knew for certain about it was that I was not ready for it.

I moved my hands in the tub like I was treading water, enjoying the sensation of water flowing through my fingers. I lifted my head and used my new sense of smell on the night air, sorting through the amazing scents of earth and flowers and saltwater and cedar and Sandu. I looked up and saw the stars as I had never seen them before; they seemed sharper, blinking with every color of the rainbow. I'd made a choice, even if I'd done so with as much forethought as your average puppy gives to eating a dropped piece of meat. I'd told myself I wanted to be a new Noosh, to "be the heroine of my own story," to become spontaneous, fearless, and free!

OK. I can't flail about in terror because the story is starting to unfold around me.

So, we packed. Sandu packed a sleek tablet, requisite cords, and a selection of neatly folded black clothing into an expensive modern carry-on suitcase, while I hunted around the house for my clothes, some of which I put back on—not the unwashed panties—and my phone, which was dangerously low on charge. He locked up the house with the big old-fashioned key while I muttered about how criminal it was to leave his books in such a state. He promised me we'd come back and store them all safely and properly, exactly to my specifications.

We climbed in the Aston, and I found out how much better driving in a supercar is when you are am'r. Am'r-nafsh. Whatever. Sandu was no longer driving too fast; it was just right. I rolled down the window and the wind whipped insanely around me. We didn't talk at all on the way to my house. I needed the time to *not* think, to *not* plan, but to just enjoy the acuity of my new, improved senses, and my new sense of health and vitality and delight in life.

It was all go-go-go at my place. First, phone on the charger. I crammed as many pieces of clothing as I could into my old college duffel bag, and grabbed my laptop and a handful of battered old paperbacks—all comfort reading, and none involving vampires since I thought I might need some of that in the days to come.

I put on makeup at the same time as I packed it and got dressed in leggings and a flattering tunic-length sweatshirt that would be comfy for whatever kind of travel we were about to embark upon. Sandu, for his part, disapprovingly eyed my haphazardly-packed duffel and murmured about buying me suitable replacements. He also ascertained I had a passport. I had a strange feeling that if I hadn't, it wouldn't have been a problem for him. I wondered if being involved with the am'r was going to be a bit like being involved with organized crime.

The hardest, weirdest part came next. I picked up the still-charging phone and hit Zuzanna's icon on the main screen. Her muzzy, sleepy voice came on just before it went to voicemail. "Noosh. Fuck. What time is it?"

"Zuz. It's, oh, it's 4:30. Sorry, but I had to call now. Can you open the Haw-Fuck-My-Life for me?"

"Can I—What's going on?"

"I've got to go away. Right now. I need to take that vacation time I never take. I've got about two months accumulated. Anyway, I'm taking it *now*, I'm afraid. With no notice. I'll need you to take over for me. And...um...please put in the paperwork, too."

"Noosh, what the *actual* is going on?"

"If I tell you, you won't believe it. Just put 'long-distance family obligations' on the paperwork."

"You don't have any family. And you can't *not* tell me! I'm your best friend."

I took a breath. "I'm running off somewhere with a prince of an ancient lineage. Actually, *he's* ancient too, because he's a vampire. You might have heard of him—he's called Dracula. Anyway, we've been having an orgy all weekend, and now we're off to save the universe or something."

After a long pause she demanded, "Noosh. Are you high?"

"I wish I was. It'd all make more sense. That's all I've got for you, Zuz. Can you help me? Please?"

"Only if I get every detail of the full story when you come back from your—" there was a dubious pause here, *"vacation.* And I mean *every* detail, including which drugs are involved, because I think I'd like to try them."

"I'll bring you some drugs as a thank-you gift. Love you, Zuzu!"

"Love you, Noosh. Go have some fun, whatever it is. You seriously need it."

"Yeah, I know. I'm a big loser. Well, off to go do something 'bout that. Bye!"

Sandu hustled me out the door. We whooshed in the Aston's pure hedonistic pleasure to Blackacre Airport. There, I discovered that Sandu had already booked us tickets and set up a flight itinerary, ending up in Romania. I found this out as we checked in. He'd not told me directly where we were going, and I'd not asked since, by this point in time, our destination seemed superfluous. But I was not at all surprised; he said he was going home, after all.

Airports are even less fun with am'r-nafsh senses. Human blood…erm…"vhoon-kee" smells different than "vhoon-am'r," which was the first shock—or rather, the first shock was that I could *smell* the difference. Second shock: people who have been working all night *stink*. I could smell their sweat, could smell what each person had eaten that was now emitting from their pores.

And this was a nearly empty airport; a rush-hour scene would have killed me. And of course, there were the scents of the airport itself: decaying garbage, various oils, metals, and plastics, and the repugnant odor arising from the carpeted areas. One early-morning traveler in front of us in the security queue was a woman wearing an obscene amount of makeup, hairspray, and cheap perfume (at this hour of the day!) tottering on wedge heels she'd never learned to wear properly. The combined miasma of her products nearly did me in, and Sandu had to hold me up while the sweaty, onion-scented TSA worker checked her ID.

Ms. Vulgarity waved her hands about with impatience, mixing the stenches and wafting them into choking smog around me. "It will get more bearable, *dragă* Noosh," Sandu murmured to me. "You will learn how to manage the new sensations. See if you can smell the vhoon under it all." I practiced reaching under the unpleasant-ranging-to-downright-nasty top notes and looking for the base notes of the kee blood rushing through the veins of everyone as we passed them. It wasn't easy, but I could do it! It got even easier as I practiced, which was an excellent distraction for me. Everyone's blood smelled a bit different. Would I learn to differentiate blood types in the future? Of course, that meant I was contemplating a *weird* future. I was getting used to all this way too easily, but then, I'd been finding this whole thing far too easy ever since Sandu outed himself as Dracula.

Dracula traveled first class, in every way. We went through the shortest lines with the least hassle possible in modern air travel. We spent twenty-five minutes in an admiral's club—which at this hour smelled more of cleaning products than people, for which I was grateful, although it taught me astringency could be a painful nasal experience—before getting paged to be in the first group to board.

Once we were settled on our flight to JFK and I was looking out the window, I was able to enjoy another new, improved sense: vision. I watched in wonder as morning twilight turned the sky blue-gray, the first hint of pink surrounding a pale yellow glow where the sun would soon be, when abruptly sunrise became more than just a pretty visual to me. I slammed down the plastic window-shade and turned to Sandu in panic. He was opening the first-class travel kit and taking out the eye mask with a very determined manner. He looked weary, wearier than I'd ever seen him look. "Are you OK? The sun's coming up! Do we need to do *anything*?" I hissed at him.

A wan smile softened his face a little. "All will be fine. I can survive sunlight. It is painful, like a terrible migraine throughout my person, but I will not spontaneously combust or turn to ash or anything so dramatic. And have I not told you before? I can cross running water, too." He chuckled—not his melty-chocolate chuckle, but it still made me feel a little better. "Now, please let me sleep. It will make the pain more bearable. You could use the sleep as well, *micuţo*, for your body and mind have had much alteration and much transformation—as much change as anybody could stand. Rest will help bring some order to the chaos you now feel and bring you some stability and peace. *Somn uşor, vise plăcute*. Good night, sleep tight, you would say."

"You too, Sandu." I paused awkwardly. "My, um, patar. And my, um, my love." He turned, and his brilliant smile chased the gray exhaustion from his face, his eyes radiating happiness. He stroked my hair and whispered, "*Sufleţel!*" Still smiling, he settled the mask over his eyes and let his head fall back on the headrest. He seemed to be asleep, deeply asleep. If he was breathing, I couldn't tell.

I couldn't fall asleep quite as fast. I was like a five-year-old after too much birthday cake. My brain was whirring, but I couldn't concentrate on individual thoughts. I accepted the champagne and warmed nuts, but they made me realize I'd never been as thirsty in my entire life. I could barely make it until food service resumed, begging the flight attendants for water bottle after water bottle. I played with the travel kit and donned the earplugs and eye mask, wishing they had nose plugs as well. The recycled air just whooshed the scents of all the people and their food around, adding a nasty stale note to the already noisome atmosphere. I let back the seat and moved the pillow and blanket around to optimize my position, enjoying the opportunity to have more than two settings (miserable, and slightly less miserable) in a plane seat. The thrum of the engines finally lulled me to sleep.

I was awakened by a flight attendant telling me to put up my seat. I slowly put my earplugs and eye mask away, but after stretching all of that out, beside me, Sandu was still dead to the world. I was nervous about waking a sleeping vampire—"Am'r!" I could hear him correcting in my head—but it had to be done. I placed my hand on his shoulder hesitantly. His head immediately turned to me, and moving like an automaton, he pulled off his mask. If he did not exactly snarl at me, the look in his eyes was close enough. But immediately, the animal anger in his eyes was replaced by awareness, followed by warmth and affection, then wry humor. "Ahhhh, Noosh. I apologize for leaving you in such an uncomfortable position. In my country, we say, '*Hai să nu dezgropăm morţii*,' which means quite literally, 'Let's not disturb the dead.' My people understand such things well. But we have now between us the most intimate bond, and you need never fear any harm from me in any circumstance."

Something he had said over the past three days niggled. "Sandu, who are your people? Romanians or am'r? Can they *both* be your people?"

His expression changed to something almost forlorn. "The am'r are my people. I am one of them and I fight with them against all others. But I am Romanian as well; I love my birth-people and I will work to their benefit for as long as I exist." He gave a sad smile. "That they love me in return, that they still write poems and sing songs of me, keeps me more kee than most of the am'r. I have a connection to my first life and to the evolving kee world, which many am'r shrug off deliberately or lose over the passage of the years. I cherish it. When we go to the country which is still mine, I hope I can teach you to cherish it as well."

"So, the whole Impaler thing doesn't bother people anymore? I mean, I remember reading that you were constantly fighting with the…um…was it 'boyars?'"

"The 'whole Impaler thing,' as you put it, was a serious propaganda campaign against me. As I told you before, the invention of the printing press came at just the right time to allow the invention of international anti-Drăculea propaganda. They took stories of what I had done to protect my people and distorted them. Some things they made up with their own twisted imaginations. My people *know* what I did for them and they do not forget it. I can be both Romanian and am'r."

"It's just, when you talk about the kee and the am'r, you make it sound like they are two completely different things. Aren't am'r just people who live a long time? Well, after they have died, I mean; they start as people. Living human people. You know what I mean."

"I know you have a great deal to learn, *micuțo*, but you must be careful how you talk around us until you do. *Nu, nu*, do not take offense. You come from a different worldview, and now you must change how you see, and quickly. You are one of us, and you must get used to it. But until you do, do not speak unless we are alone. Am'r can have, *ei bine*, an attitude problem. Assume they do until proven otherwise or until I vouch for them.

"Remember, you are entering a new world, an utterly different and dangerous one. You will do best to stay back, be quiet, and learn. In time, you will be able to navigate on your own, but for now, it is my job as your patar to teach and guide you."

"And I just need to be a good little frithyputhy and keep my mouth shut and look pretty?" The direction this had taken was pissing me off.

"Frithaputhra. And yes, I recommend all those things. Do not worry. You are bright, so you will learn rapidly and soon be a strong feminist vampire!" He laughed. "Yes, I say 'vampire,' but it is because neither feminist nor vampire is a correct word. We do not need feminists among the am'r. You will find all the gender equality you could hope for. Where we are *not* equal is age. Am'r get stronger with age, not weaker, so you must respect your elders. Since you became am'r-nafsh only yesterday, everyone is your elder, what we call an 'aojysht.' You may feel like it sucks, but the only way to make it cease sucking is to live a long time and become an aojysht yourself. Then everyone around *you* must keep their mouths shut and look pretty."

I was a bit ashamed of my outburst, but I hadn't had enough sleep, and things were moving too fast for me to keep up. "Sorry, Sandu. I know all too well I have no idea what I'm going into. I get cranky when I'm nervous."

"You are speaking to someone who used to impale things when he was nervous." Sandu crinkled his eyes at me in that smile I loved. "Just try to ignore your nerves and take everything in—what is done, what is not done, what is said, what is not said. If you are polite and respectful, you will do just fine. But we now have landed. We must hasten to catch the next flight."

CHAPTER ELEVEN

Sandu led me unerringly through JFK. I breathed through my mouth and lurched after him since there was too much sensory information for me to effectively take in any. It worked reasonably effectively until he stopped in his tracks, leaving me to walk blindly into his back. He held me up and all but carried me back to a store, where he proceeded to try sunglasses on me. The salesgirl offered unnecessary advice until he found a pair he liked and purchased them.

I didn't want to take them off, even for them to be rung up. They not only blocked the brightness but somehow they also made me feel that I could kinda-sorta-maybe deal with *all* the sensory assaults. The price of those sunglasses—more than I had spent on my new wardrobe three months ago—flashed up on the register as they were rung up, but my sticker shock was muted by my deep and profound need for my brand-new security blanket. I focused on my breathing and vowed I would care for these glasses better than I had previously cared for anything in my life. I got a glimpse of me wearing them as we passed a mirrored bit of wall on the way out.

Oh, yes, I love them. No one's ever taking this blankie from me!

We got on the plane to LHR in good order, first class again. I could get used to this. I had never flown in any class but "cattle" before. I drank two glasses of champagne and requested extra of those little bowls of warmed mixed nuts. I spent the entire time before takeoff exulting in the sensations.

The complexity of the flavors was entrancing. The simple feel of the bubbles in my mouth would have been enough to get me drunk. However, I felt no tipsier after both glasses than if I'd stuck to the water. Since I hadn't eaten anything but a few handfuls of nuts all day, I should've felt *something*.

Sandu turned away all offers of drinks and nibbles, reclined his seat as soon as it was allowed, and with his sleep-mask donned—a signal to all and sundry that he was not to be disturbed—went right back to the sleep of the undead.

I decided to enjoy first class to the hilt this time, since I was stuck with my boring seatmate. I got my champagne refilled whenever the flight attendant came my way, and then switched to wine with dinner. I got the steak entrée after enjoying the smoked salmon appetizer. I got the ice cream sundae with every topping. I was hungry, but even more, the experience of taste was like a kid playing in a huge new playground. I relished every bite and tried not to moan too loudly in pleasure.

After dinner, I continued with a glass of port. Why the hell not? After that, because I could, whisky. I should by this time have been lurching up and down the aisle, telling everyone I loved them and serenading the plane with a medley of ill-chosen songs, but I felt nothing except less hungry.

CHAPTER ELEVEN

And ready for a nap, but not in the drunken exhaustion way—just still tired from not enough sleep and too much stimulation. At some future point, I was going to find out if I *could* get drunk anymore. But in the meantime, I dug out the eye mask and earplugs from my amenities kit and crashed out beside Sandu.

He was the one to wake me when we reached London. It was night, and Sandu looked healthy and happy again. I felt astoundingly well for someone who had no idea what time zone she was in. If being am'r-nafsh meant I did not get jetlag, I was not going to complain. Sandu navigated us smoothly through Customs—a thing I'd only previously experienced by watching TV—and we found ourselves with time on our hands before our next flight, to what was listed on the board as OTP, and which Sandu called "Aeroportul Internaţional Henri Coandă."

Sandu had threatened to buy me more clothing, and he was as good as his word. Next thing I knew, I was being escorted into shops with names on them I'd also only experienced through TV. Sandu scoured the racks with his eyes, lit on one or two items of which he approved, and next thing you know, I was in the dressing room being attentively waited on, likewise in a manner I'd never previously experienced. Not being given the option of choosing my own clothing might have been frustrating, but it turned out Sandu had exquisite taste. I couldn't have picked better clothes for my body type and personal taste. Anyway, since I was obviously not paying for any of it, the fact that I wasn't choosing the clothing shouldn't upset me. Well, that was what I repeatedly told myself.

"Does 'patar' also mean 'sugar daddy?'" I asked as we waited for the last bag of sexy new designer clothes to be rung up. Sandu laughed, and I marveled again how much I loved that warm, rich sound. "Ahhhh, *dragă* Noosh, *nu*, it is not a direct translation. However, you are my responsibility as I teach you, and it gives me a good excuse to spoil you as much as I like. Also, I am taking you to meet my people and my family. Old friends, and even old not-friends. I feel a desire to show you off. I sincerely hope you do not mind."

"Mind? Well, I'm not used to it, but I think I could get accustomed. Are you ri—will your bank account mind if I get used to it?"

"Very diplomatically put, *draga mea*. If you go on like that, I shall worry much less about you meeting your new people. To answer your question, I can and hope to spoil you unstintingly for decades to come, until you have all the money you could want, as well. Am'r do well with long-term investments. And we know where to find buried treasure since we were often there when it was buried. Indeed, it is the best sort of long-term investment, I have learned over the years."

I wanted to ask a great deal more about *that*, but the sale was rung up—on a boring old credit card sadly, not with ancient bags of gold doubloons. But that card had no discernable credit limit, I noted as our shopping progressed, so maybe it wasn't boring after all. I used the ladies' room in the next VIP lounge for the usual purposes—Sandu was right: if I ate, I must still eliminate. I also transferred the clothes from their various shopping bags into in my shiny new carry-on, which was from a designer whose name-brand bags I'd never thought I'd flaunt. Changing into the first of the new outfits was a joy, not just because of the shiny newness, but because I was ready to be in something clean that hadn't been worn for the past ten hours. I emerged into the lounge wearing black leather leggings and a midnight-blue cashmere tunic with silver stars all over it. Also, new leather ankle boots. I felt like a million dollars, although I didn't think the outfit had cost *quite* that much.

I spun to look for Sandu, and when I found him, his stare made me regret having on any clothing at all. We were both glancing around for a more private corner of the lounge when our flight was announced. I regretfully thought it was probably for the best since being thrown out of the airport for indecent behavior (or whatever the Brits would call it) was probably not effective in getting where we were going. And even with a complete lack of jetlag, I was ready to be out of the limbo of no-longer-*here*-but-not-yet-*there*. Travel to far-distant locales sounds romantic when you read about it, but getting there was turning out to be mostly tedious. Well, except for the shopping.

We boarded the final flight. In just over three hours, I told myself, I could hopefully *not* set foot on another airplane again for a while. The next round of champagne and nuts came at us and we both passed them up. "Oh, Sandu, I did want to ask you something." He looked at me and inclined his head, waiting for my question. "Can I get drunk? Tipsy, even? I tried to on the last flight, but it didn't work."

"Ah, *draga mea*, I am sorry I did not foresee that being a problem. I have not considered getting drunk in too many years to count. No, alcohol will no longer touch you, I am afraid. You can only get drunk by vhoon-drinking now. You might enjoy the *taste* of various spirits, though, while you are am'r-nafsh. Are you terribly unhappy about that?"

"Well, it's not a problem, to be honest. It's not like I ever drank much anyway. It just reminds me that I don't know, never mind *understand*, all the changes happening in me."

He looked grave. "I realize now there may be changes I shall not remember until you ask about them. Such a long time has passed since I was kee. You may have concerns about things I no longer recollect. Please be patient with me, and together we will, *ei bine*, muddle through."

The thought of the graceful, widely-experienced Sandu muddling in any way made me laugh. He took my laughter as a sign I was OK with *everything*, which was perhaps not perfectly accurate. However, he distracted me by pulling me to him and subvocalizing that I should go to the lavatory…and in a few minutes, open the lock on the door.

Seriously? He wanted to join the Mile-High Club? Now?

However, the thought of it aroused me to the point where I could barely walk the few feet to the tiny door. I didn't know how we would both fit inside *and* manage to do stuff. I also didn't know if we would get caught. I had never done anything like this. It was definitely *not* the old me. But the excitement of it mixed with the need of feeling Sandu inside me and I pushed all thoughts of how things could go terribly wrong out of my head. I shimmied out of those tight leather leggings on the idea that once Sandu was in this teeny room as well, it would become well-nigh impossible to extricate me.

Since it had taken me a good number of minutes to work my way out of the skin-tight and stiff-with-newness leggings, I gulped nervously and slid open the lock on the door. A moment later, Sandu entered, his eyes positively glowing with excitement. The lock clicked shut, and the light flickered back on.

Sandu kissed me and pressed himself against me. He was entirely ready to go, and probably a bit uncomfortable. I stifled laughter when I thought he might have had more trouble walking to the lav than I had. As if he knew I'd been laughing at him, he kissed me more roughly, leaving me breathless. He spun me around, and pulled my new panties (a sleek, sheer thong) to the side. He had his cock out and he rubbed himself against the outside of me. I moaned and rubbed right back against him, feeling the head sliding between my labia, back-and-forth over my clit. He nuzzled my neck, and I tilted my head to the left, to give him access to that other erogenous zone, loving the feeling of his lips and tongue running over my skin. He paused. "Which do you want in you, first?"

I paused, too. It was thoughtful of him to ask; if his cock was in me first, I'd feel the bite primarily as pleasure. If he bit first, I'd get pain before the pleasure rose up and it all mixed into one. For the old me, the obvious choice would have been the former. But the new me—well, she'd learned pain could be a seasoning to make pleasure all the better. I wondered if this made me any *more* deviant than just wanting to have sex with a vampire in the first place? But the new me quite liked the idea of being deviant for deviancy's sake. "Bite me," I told Sandu.

His cock jumped. I guessed, while there was no *wrong* answer in this moment, I'd still made the best choice. His tongue played over my skin in just the right spot, teasing both of us. He kissed my neck gently. I felt his lips draw back, and I tried not to wince or pull away in anticipation of pain. I felt the first hint of sharpness, and then the intense pinch of *that* penetration. The teeth pushed in deep to get to the jugular, the differently sharp sensation of sucking followed. It hurt, oh yes it did. But there was pleasure, too. Maybe I'd just learned to associate pleasure with being bitten, or maybe there was something special to an am'r bite—I wasn't going to untangle it all just now. Under the pain, a throbbing pleasure moved through me. I moaned again, and moved my hips urgently against him, pleading for more.

He was fine with the concept of "more," and pulled back his hips. I tilted my ass up for the best angle. There was no way to describe the sensation of him pushing himself into me: it was both local to where the action was happening, and yet, it seemed to thrum along all my nerve endings, turning all of me into a being made of sensation.

One thing got in the way: I could not cry out. I could not scream to release the intensity. I could not make a noise louder than a low moan. Sandu maybe sensed my situation, pulled his head away from my neck, and reached his wrist up to his mouth. He viciously tore it open—which would have seriously freaked me out a mere five days ago—and shoved the spurting wrist into my mouth. He lowered his head and returned smoothly to his own blood-drinking.

And thrusting into me. As I guzzled desperately, I felt like his blood was penetrating my mouth as well: that he was pushing all of himself into me. Mingling with the sensations and the blood rushing exhilaratingly down my throat, it was that thought that tossed me over the edge and I became a human-shaped wave of orgasm. It was all I was, all I ever had been, all I ever would be, now and forever.

I have no idea how long "now and forever" lasted. But we couldn't stay in the lavatory that long, and he finally could resist no longer. I felt his thrusts become erratic. He seemed to petrify, stone arms caged me, and I heard the muffled sounds he groaned into my neck.

We stayed that way for a long moment, but ultimately, Sandu detached himself. It became clear I was no good for anything, so he swiftly but with gentle affection leaned me against the sink and dabbed away some drips of blood from my sweater. With another damp paper towel, he spread my legs and gave a quick clean-up. He contorted himself and somehow got my leggings back onto me. A quick check to make sure we'd left no blood on any surfaces, and he opened the door and led me back to our seats, countering the annoyed looks of flight attendants and knowing looks of other passengers by murmuring, "Excuse us, she is not feeling at all well." I'm sure I was helpfully giving a pretty good impression of not being all right.

Screw booze. Blood was the way to go.

I felt like I was not just *in* a plane that was flying, but I had expanded my skin beyond the metal skin of the aircraft. I could feel the wind rushing around all of me, feel the wet droplets of clouds, and the separate layers of warmer and cooler air. I soared, powerful engines throbbing inside me, thrusting me into the night, thirty thousand feet above the Earth.

When we got back to our seats, Sandu buckled me back in and held my hand for the rest of the flight. I looked out the window—except of course, the window was in my skin, and I was looking out from where my face was at the nose of the plane.

We didn't talk for the rest of the flight, which was for the best since plane-shaped creatures cannot speak.

Chapter Twelve

I was sobered up by landing. I mean, the travel limbo was finally over, and now we were actually in Romania. Being here meant the next stage of my life—could I still call it that?—was now in progress. And since I had no idea what this next stage of my life would resemble or consist of—aside from "shutting up and looking pretty"—it was sobering. And speaking no Romanian grated at me. Yet one more important thing I did not know.

It turned out to be just after 5 AM Romanian time. Several flights had come in at the same time, and there were crowds milling around in barely organized queues. But Sandu had us through Customs in a remarkably short space of time. Everything was conducted in a language I could not understand, and I didn't see any money changing hands. Maybe he mesmerized the Customs people? Maybe it was just Sandu's experience at traveling, plus his citizenship, but shouldn't I, foreign citizen and neophyte traveler that I was, have slowed things down? But I never had to speak to anyone. I was getting used to things working super-smoothly when Sandu was running the show, and I couldn't complain about missing a chance to experience standing in the Customs line for hours.

Sandu collected all our bags, and we went out into a rain-damp sunrise. I would have found it chilly before I drank Sandu's blood, but now the wet, nippy air just tasted refreshing after stifling airports and the recycled air of airborne tin cans. We were in the utter chaos of the pick-up and drop-off area, and before I could get more than a lungful of the morning freshness it was destroyed by car fumes and honking and shouting. Despite the rain, I kept on my security-blankie sunglasses. Sandu was slightly gray-tinged again.

A nondescript black car pulled up and popped the trunk for us. Sandu tossed in the luggage and opened the back door for me. I crawled in across the back seat, and he slid in more gracefully beside me. The driver wore black leather and sunglasses. He had a pair ready for Sandu; he handed them back—and then outright stared at me. Even his sunglasses couldn't hide the fact. As he gawped, his nose twitched and twitched some more, making me wonder in embarrassment if I smelled nasty from all the hours of travel, or something.

"Noosh, this is Haralamb. Haralamb, *aceasta este* Noosh."

Haralamb turned to look at Sandu, then back at me, and asked, "...Noosh?"

"*Poreclă pentru* Anushka," Sandu replied. *Fuck*. My stupid nickname was still going to cause a problem with *every* person we met. My face flushed uncomfortably. It seemed am'r-nafsh could still blush, damn it.

Haralamb moved us out into the start-and-stop traffic. "*A trebuit să soseşti de dimineaţă, Voivode?*"

"In English, please. Noosh does not yet speak our elegant tongue. You know air travel is a thing of the kee world. *Nu*, do not again mention a private plane. I have told you before I prefer to travel incognito."

"The schedule would be more reasonable, you must admit."

"A little sunlight has never killed anyone. *Ce nu te omoară, te face mai puternic.*" Sandu turned to me. "'What does not kill you makes you stronger' is as common a phrase in Romanian as English. While you only feel overwhelmed, Haralamb and I are in some discomfort from the light. Him even more than me, because he is young, a baby am'r, you might say. You will go through this change yourself, in time, but you can learn to deal with sensitivity to light. And indeed, it makes you stronger to undergo such learning."

Haralamb asked quite urgently, "*De ce ai adus un* am'r-nafsh *aici?*"

Sandu looked pissed off. It was a scary-blank expression on his face; his color became an unattractive blanched-olive-gray. "This is not your business. Your business is to drive. Do so." The following uncomfortable silence stretched from Otopeni to București.

We moved off the highway to city streets which soon became twisty, narrow side roads, more like ever-contracting channels between buildings. Haralamb silently pulled the car to a stop in front of one building and popped the trunk. We got out without saying any sort of goodbye. Sandu grabbed the bags and led me to a most unprepossessing door. If *this* was Vampire Central, many of my favorite vampire fantasies, which had mostly been coming true up to this point, were in for a serious bubble-busting. As we waited for Sandu's knock to be answered, I tried to squash depressing visions of a gaggle of greasy, unkempt vampires hanging out in a dirty basement, plotting improbable world domination. Would it all come down to that, after all?

The door was answered by another guy in all black, which I started to guess was the am'r dress code. Who knew that the goth kids were right, all along? He had a broad forehead and wide-set green eyes. Not green like Sandu's, but a pale gray-green that popped distractingly from his much darker olive skin. He had tousled walnut-brown hair. He had very full, beautifully shaped lips, and cheekbones to die for. He looked like he'd just wandered off a runway or out of a fashion shoot, and that did wonders for my fears of finding a basement full of socially ill-adjusted freaks. No matter what Sandu had told me, it would not have surprised me too terribly much to discover that this was just a group of kinky maniacs who all shared some blood disorder for which they refused to get treatment. That was far more likely an explanation, if I was honest with myself.

The male model smiled broadly and welcomed us with expansive arm gestures and rolling Romanian, "*Intră! Fii binevent! Bine ai venit! Intră, tatăl meu, și tu, și tu, noua mea prietenă!*"

Sandu, laughing, leaned in and kissed him warmly on either side of the face, and stepping back, put his arm around me to herd me forward. "*Dragă* Noosh, meet Dragomir Pricolici. Dragoș, meet Anushka. 'Noosh' to her friends."

"And we shall indeed be the greatest of friends, Noosh," Dragomir said, "for I have long waited for old Țepeș here to fall in love again. It is clear that he has—and seeing you, the reasons are obvious!" He leaned forward with the intent of giving me a Euro-kiss such as he'd exchanged with Sandu but abruptly froze, his nostrils flaring. He turned to Sandu, "But she is only am'r-nafsh! And you brought her *here?* How fascinating!"

"Yes, as you see, I have, and I need your help in taking care of her in the time to come, *da, fiul meu?*"

Dragomir smiled down at me. "I will guard her with my body and soul, of course. You did not have to ask me. *Voivode, domnul meu Drăculea, tatăl meu iubit!*"

Sandu snorted. "None of that now, *domnule Pricolici—prostuțule!* Shall we move on, and I will tell you more as we go?"

We went from the front hall through an obviously abandoned house: torn wallpaper, walls with gaping holes, dangerous floorboards (which the men courteously warned me about as we went), wrecked furniture, broken bottles and other rubbish strewn about the place. To get down one hallway, they had to actually move a table missing a leg and ruined chairs out of our way. After that, we went down a set of stairs I was extremely dubious about and into the basement, which managed to be even more disgusting than the main house had been. Further piles of smashed furniture were tugged aside…revealing a hidden trapdoor. I would have been even more dubious about going down it, except for the part of me—either a painful romantic or a thirteen-year-old kid—that was cheering. Hidden trapdoors. This was getting good.

We came out in a long, dark, hot corridor that smelled dank and vile, yet somehow not as overpowering as an airport full of people. The smells were interesting to me, and I tried to tease them apart: dusty stone, wet stone, dirt, mold, stagnant water, decaying animals, rats (alive), and a *soupçon* of sewage. I blinked, realizing it was pitch-dark down here, yet I could see. Well, not fully, but I wasn't utterly blind, which was not nothing. I could make out shapes, at least. Dragomir courteously guided me. "At the fifth step, reach to the right. You will find a handhold. Step far to the right, and walk holding on until it ends." He went first, I went second, and Sandu brought up the rear.

My heart pounded (probably audibly) as I took the five steps. Should I take big steps or small ones? Are there booby-traps involved? At the fifth step, I reached out to the right, and a sort of banister I'd never have noticed if I was not looking for it was carved into the stone of the wall. I clung to it and desperately stepped as far as I could to the right. I did not explode, nor get shot with daggers or poison darts. Or lasers. It seemed watching *Indiana Jones* had not fully prepared me for am'r adventures. I would have to ask Sandu later what would have happened to me if I had stepped wrong, but in the meantime, I was exceptionally focused on following the banister precisely forward.

It was hot in the corridor, and we went along it long enough for it to start to get boring, or at least for my heart to stop pounding. Dragomir stopped and said, "Now we go down again, *domnișoara*. Just sit down and edge forward, like so..."

We climbed down metal rungs driven into the living rock. The air that came up to meet us was cooler and cleaner. When we got down, I looked around a world composed of shades of gray and saw we were in a much larger tunnel. It felt, not decrepit, as the house above had been, but impressively ancient. When I looked behind me, however, I saw something that clashed with that perception: an ugly mini car, squarish and battered and scraped all to hell. Sandu laughed when he saw it. "Inimioară still runs? She looks as lovely as ever."

Dragomir laughed as well. "You be kind to her, Țepeș! She has a far more beautiful soul than you!" He turned to me. "Her name is 'Sweetheart.' She is a 1985 Oltcit Special. She may not be much to look at, but she is my sweet little ride. Will you get in, *domnișoara?*"

I didn't know what "*domnișoara*" meant, but it felt formal. "She is charming. And please, call me Noosh." I climbed into the back seat while he courteously held the front seat down for me. Sandu got in the front with Dragomir, but I did not feel unhappy about it. They were clearly old friends who had not seen each other in some time. With am'r life expectancies being what they were, who knew what "some time" meant?

Meanwhile, the car named Inimioară had started right up, with a healthy engine sound despite her appearance, and we took off rather too recklessly down the passageway. It was a surreal journey, careening down an ancient tunnel deep under Bucharest in a beat-up micro-car, listening to two vampires making in-jokes and teasing each other. Fellini could not have directed anything more bizarre.

In the front seat, Dragomir turned to Sandu. "I am glad you are back home. There are rumors, and I have a bad feeling in my blood. Can you tell me what has been going on? What do you know about the incidents which have occurred?"

"I have much to tell you, Dragoș, but it should wait until we meet with . It will save time if I only tell my part of the story once. I know of some incidents, although perhaps not all of them, and I have my own tale to tell you. I think we might again be cursed with living in interesting times."

"*Da*, I think you are right. It will be a pleasure to fight alongside you once more. It has been too long."

I must have drifted to sleep after a while, since the view was just a monotonous rush of bare stone tunnel. I jolted awake when Sweetheart was brought to a lurching stop. Sandu and I exited with some difficulty—the tunnel here was a good deal narrower, and there was *just* clearance—and Dragomir waved us on. "Go on without me. I must turn Inimioară around." He took off at the same careless speed and shot around a corner in the passage ahead. Sandu and I were at the bottom of a flight of stairs that led up to a round entrance. No light came down the steps. I wondered if everything in the am'r world was in the dark, which basically meant I'd be seeing only in murky shades of gray the whole time.

We went up the stairs, turned left, up more stairs, and came out into a hallway with a simple but pleasing geometric pattern carved along the walls. It was a pretty long corridor and the carving ran all the way down it, with doors opening at intervals on both sides along it. The doorways all looked the same.

How did anyone find anything around here? Sniff it out like a bloodhound? *Bloodhound, hmmm.* Or just centuries of memorizing, "the sixth door on the right when you're coming from X direction leads to Y room."

Everything smelled of stone, old stale air, and the faint powderiness of dust, although, of course, I was just a newbie. Perhaps after a few centuries, one could follow scent-trails of people who'd passed along a hallway a decade ago?

The corridor ended at a pair of large double doors, quite medieval-looking. We stood before them for a moment, not saying anything. I found myself deeply unwilling to go through the doors because I had a feeling there were a lot of vampires on the other side of them. I was just not ready. I was not sure what Sandu was thinking, yet also not sure I wanted to ask.

He looked at me and smiled wanly. "*Draga mea*, shall we get up our courage and go in?" I smiled back at him and wondered what could make a five-hundred-plus-year-old nervous. Was bringing a new "girlfriend" home to meet the family always this uncomfortable for everyone? "There is a side door there." Sandu pointed, and I saw a smaller door to the left of the imposing double doors. "We shall usually go through there. But I think now we make an entrance. Stay right where you are." He walked over to the wall and pressed an area of the carving that looked no different to me than the stone around it and was back at my side before I could blink.

The double doors groaned as if they were being tortured and swung ponderously forward. "This is why we do not often use them," Sandu whispered to me, and he straightened up as if by instinct. I imitated him, but he abruptly and deliberately slouched into an "I don't care what anyone thinks" posture of the sort fifteen-year-olds adopt instinctively.

The doors finally stopped groaning in torment. I realized I was standing there looking ridiculously nervous and belatedly tried to imitate Sandu's posture. That probably left me looking like I was having some sort of seizure—and you never get a second chance to make a first impression! Sandu glided unhurriedly forward and I tried to swagger like I wasn't about to find out if am'r-nafsh could throw up.

We walked into perfect silence. Kee can't be truly quiet. Someone is always whispering, chewing, sneezing at the wrong moment, mouth-breathing, shifting in a noisy sort of fabric, et cetera. But am'r are, well, *deathly* quiet. It could have been a room full of corpses, except that they were standing up. And all watching us.

I could smell them. The smell of am'r blood washed over me: a combination of many individual scents, each a unique note. And "note" was right—it was like an orchestra of fragrance. A blood orchestra. I had not yet learned how to separate out the flute and clarinet and different violins, but the differences tantalized me, playing over the underlying

CHAPTER TWELVE

scents of age and stone and ancient wood and other things to which I couldn't put a name.

They were all wearing black, from leather to suits. Or jeans and slouchy shirts. A few traditional outfits, various types of robes and other garb for which I did not know the correct names. But still, all black. Except for one of them. He was in the center of it all, standing in front of a long table, wearing a cheery golden-yellow caftan-robe-thingie with lots of colorful embroidery on it. He looked as cheery as his clothing, with a warm olive-gold complexion and a mustache just like Freddie Mercury's. He had long hair, much longer than Freddie had ever worn it, pulled back tightly in a thick ponytail. He was smiling at us warmly enough to make all my nerves fall away. His dark eyes twinkled like he was always laughing.

With this glowing presence guiding us to the center of the room, the rest of the am'r seemed like ignorable shadows. Maybe it was foolishness on my part, but I felt utterly safe once I had seen the smile sparkling at us from Mister Sunshine.

It was still completely silent, however. The tone of our footsteps had changed, and I realized we were now walking on marble. Also, I finally paid attention to a rather vital detail: I could see in full color again. Around the walls of the room were great globes gleaming with an even, somewhat greenish light, which provided enough illumination for me to see as well as I could in daylight. I spared a moment to wonder about what was creating that unnatural light. The scale of the globes was on par with the height of the walls. I hoped it had started as a natural cavern, or else it would have taken a colony of Tolkienish dwarves a long, long time to carve it all out. My ability to believe six impossible things before breakfast—or whatever mealtime it was, I had no idea—was getting a bit stretched. I desperately quashed a strong desire to giggle.

I heard Sandu greeting each am'r in a low but friendly voice and decided to pay attention, but the names rushed past me faster than I could take them in: Neplach, Vulferam, Dubhghall, Atanase, Cătălin, Daciana, Gilles, Astryiah, Eben, Cyrus, Hisao, Răzvan, Maxym, Melesse, Chepkirui, Nthanda, Mahtab, Azar, Monserrate, Tecla, Apolinar, Anoub.

I tried to note at whom Sandu nodded, but it was all too fast and the names too strange. I was happy to finally see women in those all-black uniforms, but I wasn't sure am'r women were less or *more* terrifying than am'r men. Men might be kind out of a comfortable chauvinistic assumption of superiority, but women could be cruel to a new female in their midst.

Don't think about that. Focus on Mister Sunshine.

We finally reached Mister Sunshine, and his smile somehow grew even more welcoming. Sandu dropped to one knee, head bowed. I looked down at him in dismay since he hadn't cued me what to do. I belatedly dropped down likewise and looked at Mister Sunshine's feet, which were bare and a bit dirty.

"*Domnul și Stăpinul meu,*" said Sandu and added, "My patar, here I am." Shocked, I whipped my head around to look at Sandu's face, but he was peering at the grubby toes as I had done. "Aojysht, meet Anushka Rossetti, my frithaputhra. I bring her here to be our archivist and information scientist, the keeper of our knowledge. The one who will help us consolidate our history and our potential and move forward as a united culture. Noosh, meet Bagamil. You could call him your 'grandfather.'"

My head swam. I wondered if I could still pass out because the black curtain was definitely coming down behind my eyes. I felt far away from everything, sort of swimming in space, weightless.

I next found myself sitting down in a chair with Mister Sunshine—Bagamil—kneeling in front of me, chafing my hands between his. "Really, Sandu, *dragonul meu*, that was most unfair to Miss Anushka." He looked kindly into my eyes. "Let me guess, that came as a complete surprise to you, little one?"

"Um, m-my *lord*," I stammered, and remembered a few comments Sandu had previously made. "Not a *complete* surprise, but a pretty thorough one, yes. But please, call me Noosh."

"And you call me Bagamil." He paused, the way everyone did right before saying my nickname for the first time, "Noosh. Despite my frithaputhra's somewhat dramatic display, I do not stand upon formality." Bagamil put word into action by pulling up a chair—an impressive high-backed medieval number, not particularly comfortable, per se, but just what you'd hope to find in a vampire lair—and plunking himself down into it. "Our Sandu is very enthusiastic, and he sometimes forgets to tell other people the details he has worked out in his busy, labyrinthine mind. Let me endeavor to bring you up to speed. But first—" He raised his voice and addressed the room. "This is not a formal meeting, not today. Greet each other and reunite. For many of you, it has been a while, no? There are still more of us expected, so the formal assembly will be tomorrow. *Aojasc' am'ratv!*"

The roomful of vampires echoed, "*Aojasc' am'ratv!*"

That seemed to be the end of his announcement, for Bagamil turned back to me. "I look forward to speaking with you more privately in the future, Noosh, but let me respond to some pressing issues now. Sandu, it appears, may not have asked you if you *wish* to be our, how did he put it, 'archivist and information scientist,' so let me inquire now if you might like the job? We need you most urgently. Our kind tend to be solitary, individual types who don't often want to work—or even play—together, nor has there been much tendency to work collectively for the benefit of our people.

"We have been thus for as long as I remember—which is far longer than you can imagine—isolated, secluded, self-contained. We would likely have continued to go on this way for as long again, perhaps, except there seems to be a—well, let us call it a force—gathering together like a gang or faction, but with far too much power and growing influence. I do not like the direction in which this is going, and neither does your patar, nor others of our kind. It seems we must also gather to counter this threat."

Listening to this, my imagination had pretty well failed in the face of a vastly weirder reality. "What do you need me for, then? I mean, I can't imagine *I* bring much to the party."

"Ah, do not doubt yourself! We have no one trained as you have been, and, as Sandu has told me, with the passion you bring to your art. As you may imagine, we have many documents—histories, monographia, philosophical works—which deal with the am'r and how we began, how we have evolved, and who we are as a race. We need these items collected, sorted, safely stored, and made digitally available to all the am'r, so we can move forward with correct thought and right order. It seems to me you are uniquely perfect for this task. Thus, you 'bring much to the party.' We also would receive the benefit of your new points of view. You could shake us up where we are stuck in old ways."

He paused, and smiled but asked seriously, "that said, frithaputhra-of-my-frithaputhra, will you consider sharing with us your skills and your knowledge and your fresh views? Will you help us fight chaos with order?"

How could I refuse? It was nothing more than the goal of my life, the organizational and methodological idealism that is the keystone of every librarian's soul. How often outside a librarian's wildest fantasies are we called in like superheroes to save the day? Indeed, part of our job, part of our very selves, is our thankless toil, quietly saving culture and society from the barbarians at our doors. Although nowadays, "barbarians" are lowest-common-denominator shows and social media influencers, a society in which educating kids comes dead last in priorities, science and history are seen as the enemy, and whacked-out ideologues and fanatics want to ban knowledge and burn books. We are the invisible organizers who quietly save the stacks of human knowledge while the past, present, and future Romes burn. We do not get capes or costumes of spandex. We do not find ourselves starring in the sorts of novels we usually shelve under "fiction."

So I could not say no as a librarian, nor could I say no as plain ol' me. I mean, if a bunch of vampires comes along and says, "Oh, our hero, save us!", I ask you: whose ego is such that they could wave a hand and say, "Oh, 'fraid not, sorry. I'm too busy with more important stuff just now. Good luck, buh-bye!" Whoever that person might be, well, it was *not* me.

But then again, I'd already made one huge life choice without any input except from my hindbrain, as it were. I was still caught up in the ridiculous consequences of that decision, so maybe this next one warranted a moment's consideration?

But when I thought about it, what they were offering me was just the sort of promotion I had been longing for—and telling myself I was *not* longing for, no, not even a little—back at the Helen Abigail Winstringham-Fenstermacher Memorial Library. It was not like I was going to go out and fight bad guys on the front line or whatever. I was going to simply be sorting scrolls and copying codexes, scanning and cataloging, in some back room.

Or back cavern, if current surroundings were anything to go by, so at least temperature and light wouldn't a problem, and conditions would be stable, but I was going to have to insist on getting in hardcore measures to deal with humidity and air quality, immediately dealing with deteriorating leather, never mind papyrus, parchment, wood, and silk, with red rot, and with pest management...

Once I started thinking about the details, I felt better. I could do triage and set up the right preservation environment, then scan or otherwise transfer to digital each item as I cataloged it. I could figure out the organizational system as I went along, seeing what we had, and work up the digital archive based on that. Of course, while it all took but a moment to list, I'd be needing my new longer life—existence, whatever—if I was to see such a job through to completion.

So, really, what was the difference to my life—except now it seemed I'd be doing it all underground? And what was the difference between a cave and the basement of some of the library buildings I'd worked in? Not much. If I was to be stuck in front of a computer for endless hours day in and day out, it didn't matter if I was above or belowground.

I wasn't disappointed. Sure, I'd chosen to be the New Noosh™. But hey, I was in another country, surrounded by vampires, and all this alarming, high-speed reality had knocked some sense into me. It seemed that despite my impetuous choice, I'd be landing on my feet and doing the job I'd trained to do, not starring in some crazy novel after all. I was relieved, to be honest. And of course, I'd be around Sandu, which meant plenty of amazing sex, and other luxuries to which I'd like to become accustomed. It looked like I might well be able to have my cake and eat it, too. I'd never wanted to leave the world of books, just the world of *boring*.

This was an adventure perfectly made to fit me: not too big, not too small. Just right.

I looked up and saw Bagamil watching me. Sandu was hovering over his shoulder, looking more anxious and uncertain than I'd ever seen him. It didn't look right on him. I wanted to wipe that worried look off his face and never see it again, so I smiled at both of them and said, "All right, boys, I'm on board! Show me to the books!"

Chapter Thirteen

Of course, it's never that easy. I didn't get to see my new charges that night, or day, or whatever it was aboveground. First, Sandu had to schmooze with old friends. Random am'r wandered over to us in singles or groups. All in all, it was a bit like any cocktail party I'd ever attended, only without the cocktails, and with too many tongue-twister names I had to try not to mangle.

The first ones up were what I could only think of as "Vlad's Romanian Crew." They came over in a group of six, Haralamb and Dragomir having joined the party in the intervening time. I got to meet Daciana, my first female am'r. I looked her over carefully, which was fine since she was doing the same to me. As with the other am'r I'd met, she took a long sniff, and I wondered if that was a standard thing. She had gorgeous wavy chocolate-brown hair and green eyes that were shockingly beautiful in her pale, heart-shaped face. I liked her right away and hoped she'd like me.

"Hello," she said, her thick Romanian accent shaping the English words in a velvety way. "It is truly a pleasure to meet you...Noosh?"

"Yes, 'Noosh' is right! It is a pleasure to meet you, as well," I tried to say her name just as Sandu had said it, "Dah-chee-ahn-ah."

"I am sure you must have many questions," she said to me. "I would be happy to answer any you would like to ask."

"Oh, yes!" I said, too eager and grateful to be embarrassed by my gushing. "I'd like that very much, please!" But I didn't get to ask her anything because Cătălin and Atanase and Răzvan were all introducing themselves with the stereotypical eagerness of a guy's male buddies to meet the new girlfriend, and Haralamb and Dragomir were acting cool because they already knew me. It made meeting everyone much easier because it was just like any other human gathering.

And since I'm not particularly socially ept at the best of times, I'd take all the help I could get.

I liked all the Romanian am'r. They were approachable, with real smiles that showed as much in their eyes as the curves of their lips, and they all welcomed me enthusiastically and congratulated Sandu—some called him "Voivode" and some were on a first-name basis—as if he and I had gotten married. Well, I guess we had, in the am'r way, although it was something I still wasn't letting myself contemplate too deeply.

Next up was Neplach, who, in black robes, with a shaved head and a long beard, managed to look like a monk or something, and to whom Sandu was warm and genuinely respectful. I figured he must be an aojysht or whatever the word was. He was politely formal in return and greeted me with a deep bow.

Gilles followed, with whom Sandu was cool and careful. I was almost anxious about what correct greeting I should give him, but he just sniffed a bit, then bowed a bare inch in my direction and said, "*Enchanté, ma belle mad'moiselle.*" He turned to Sandu and spoke low in rapid French, ignoring me. I was fine with that.

A beautiful woman came up next. Her skin was a warm dark brown, perfect to the point of looking photoshopped. She wore her hair in thick fishtail braids, with two narrower ones that came forward and around her forehead like a thin band, wrapping back to overlay the ends of the other braids at the back of her head. The rest of the length of hair whooshed out into a cloud of blackness that caught the light in strange and fascinating ways. Her features were delicate and her face heart-shaped, her eyes perfect almonds lined dramatically with kohl. Sandu introduced her as Melesse, and her greetings were made in a flowingly accented soft voice and with a graceful bow. There was a burning confidence in her dark eyes that contrasted with the soft speech and elegant manners. She was subtle with her sniffing, but I could sense her curiosity about me.

There was no time to consider that because a trio of variously Hispanic and Latin sorts came up. Apolinar, whose flowing black hair made him look like a hidalgo of old, and Monserrate, the quintessential Eurotrash, more fashionable than I would ever be, made much of me, sketching elaborate bows. It was fun. Tecla was tall and sturdily built, wearing battered old motorcycle leathers and boots. She had hair that was dark and curly with bleached streaks on top and shaved sides. She managed to bow to me while thoroughly checking me out with her eyes and nose the whole time. It didn't feel skeezy like it would have if a man had done it, but I did find myself blushing and even shyer.

Next up was a tall am'r with faded tan skin and a marvelously beaky nose. His shiny black hair, which would have curled if it had not been cut so short, was outdone only by his eyes, which were an even shinier black. Anoub was gravely polite to me, with a serious and precise incline of his head and barely a twitch of his nostrils. He somberly asked Sandu if he could speak with him later. Sandu gravely replied in the affirmative.

Next up was an odd duo. Wulferam was one of those huge Northern men with thick reddish-blond hair and bright blue eyes. Dubhghall was slimmer and shorter, with black hair and twinkly cobalt blue eyes. They spoke in big voices, laughed loudly and frequently. Sandu was honestly pleased to see them. Both bowed formally to me but grinned widely and informally as they did it. They made no bones about sniffing my scent appreciatively, either. "So you're the wee lass who has at last woken Sandu up from his long dry spell," Dubhghall teased, "When was the last quine to drive ye bampot, Vladie? The Victorian era?"

Sandu mimed boxing his ear. "I will not have you telling tales about me, Pict."

Wulferam joined in. "What was her name? Minnie? Wilma? Such a fool you made of yourself over her. But this one, she is *vakker*. And smart, too! *Frøken* Noosha, you are a perfect distraction for a man! Thank you for making our brother so happy. He was a sour old man, and we were tired of him! Now he is young again, thanks to you!"

I side-eyed Sandu and he hustled his troublemaker friends along. I would have to ask him about "Minnie from the Victorian era." I could have sworn he'd said he was not in England at that time.

Two other am'r came up to us, and Sandu turned to them with evident relief. "Eben. Cyrus. So good to see you both here. Noosh, here you have some fellow countrymen."

"Good t'meet an American lady abroad," said Eben in what sounded to me like an English accent. He bowed with easy grace and inhaled very politely. The second accent I recognized as Cyrus dipped his head, sniffed quickly, then chimed in, "It sure is a pleasure, Miz Noosh. How you findin' things? It was a real shock for me comin' here the first time. If I hadn'ta had Eben here, I don't know what I'd'a done."

Sandu chimed in, "You will find this quite romantic, *draga mea*. Eben is from the North, from around the time of your War of Independence. Cyrus is a Southerner from the start of the twentieth century, *nu*, Cyrus?" "Yessir. I became am'r thanks to Eben in 1906, and I stuck 'round him ever since. He just can't get rid of me, po' man." Eben smiled warmly at his frithaputhra, and Cyrus slid an arm around his patar. Eben had sepia-toned skin and huge, liquid brown eyes behind ridiculously long eyelashes. A low, wide nose, and his smile flashed brilliantly from lush, full lips. And sideburns. No, more than sideburns—full, luxurious muttonchops. That made me realize how few am'r I'd seen with any facial hair. So far, only Neplach had a beard, and Mister Sunshine sported the Freddie-stache. Without stretching my imagination, I could see Eben in a painting in the style of the period, standing formally in a waistcoat and powered hair.

Cyrus had eyes that were somewhere between green and brown—it was hard to tell in this greeny light—and fawn brown skin under a mop of loose brown curls. His face was chiseled under the am'r smooth skin so that all that softness didn't make him look youthful.

They made a gorgeous couple. I wondered if the percentage of gay am'r relationships was similar to the kee world. Or maybe, as Anne Rice imagined, if most of the am'r I'd met tonight were queerer than three-dollar bills? Am'r show tune sing-alongs later tonight? This cavernous space would make a great place for a rave. I had to stop myself from giggling.

Sadly, Eben and Cyrus moved on, and Mahtab and Azar were next in line. They bowed with warm formality, and both were ridiculously handsome, with liquid dark-brown eyes, lightest olive skin, and thick, wavy black-brown hair. They greeted me with gentility and kindness and a certain amount of nostril gymnastics, but they quickly maneuvered it such that Sandu ended up turned aside, talking with them in low, urgent tones. Two more am'r joined them—Chepkirui and Nthanda, who made silent bows to me during perfunctory introductions and immediately stepped into the hushed confab. With nothing left to do, I admired them. One was tall and slender as a reed, with skin so richly dark that the greenish light became purplish on her skin, and her umber eyes flashed intriguingly in a beautiful round face. The other, also tall, had dark, reddish-brown skin. His was a heart-shaped face, with round eyes under arched brows and a broad triangle of a nose. When introduced, his smile accentuated high cheekbones and squinted his eyes into deep slits.

This gave another female am'r a chance to come over and bow to me sinuously, as if her spine had extra vertebra. "*Shalom!* Is it 'Noosh?'" she asked. She was shorter than most of the other am'r but had glorious honey-warm skin. Her thick, curling hair was practically the same color, with hypnotically warm golden-brown eyes. She was deliciously curvaceous and wore a black dress that demonstrated she knew how to work those curves.

"Yes, just 'Noosh.' Really."

"I am called Astryiah. Welcome to the am'r. This must be overwhelming for you, and you are doing very well. I remember my introduction many, many years ago. I am glad never to have to go through it again!"

"You are too kind, Astryiah. It is pretty intense, to be honest. But as you see," and here I gestured to Sandu and the absorbed knot, "not too much is expected of me."

"Do not be too certain of that, Noosh. You are being observed. Our kind look for weakness in prey, as any predator does. They contrast your strengths with their strengths. They sniff out your emotions and fears." As if this were not disconcerting enough, she was very obviously sniffing me, her nostrils moving minutely but appreciably. She saw me notice this and said quickly, "Excuse me, but it is rare to meet another's am'r-nafsh. Even rarer, I would say, to meet Vlad's. You give off a most exotic perfume, so there will be many sniffing around you. I mean this figuratively and literally."

"Why would you not often, um, *sniff* am'r-nafsh?" I asked, perplexed. "Don't they normally live with the am'r?"

"You do not know?" Amazement was on her face and in her voice. "Can he have not told you?"

"*Shalom*, Astryiah," Sandu interjected. "It is excellent to see you again. It has been a very long time, has it not?"

"Indeed, Vlad. Perhaps we shall have time to speak together and catch up on some of those years?" Sandu inclined his head to her, she inclined hers to him and to me, and moved off with that unworldly am'r grace.

I wanted time to speak with Sandu rather urgently myself. What had he neglected to tell me *this time?* But Hisao—gorgeous in his own way, with pearl-like skin and beautifully upturned dark eyes—introduced himself to me. His black hair was cut in an improbable jagged style that ignored gravity. He bowed to us both with knife-like precision. "*Konbanwa*, Dracula-san. We meet at an interesting time."

"Indeed, Hisao-san. I am pleased you were able to make it. There will be much for us to discuss."

"And perhaps time for us to...reminisce together, as old friends?"

"Certainly. The *onsen* is still in good order. I will make time for *hadaka no tsukiai*. Tomorrow?"

They nodded at each other, and Hisao wandered away without saying another word. I had always thought courtly intrigue—all this whispering and planning in obscure ways could be nothing *but* intrigue—would be exciting, but it was just *tedious*. Maybe it was more exciting if you had some idea of what was going on and were not being kept on the sidelines. I was going to have to talk to Sandu about catching me up and involving me, at least to the extent to which I could be helpful. I wasn't going to just stand around gormlessly, if I could help it.

Next up was an am'r I disliked on sight. While his black hair *was* greased back, that feeling of unctuousness came from the deviousness oozing from his pores. His black eyes squinted. The rest of his face was classically handsome, but I couldn't find him attractive. Sandu was tense again. "Maxym. *Dobryj vyechyer*."

"Vlad." He lowered his head a fraction and turned to me, "And Vlad's frithaputhra." His bow to me kept an intense eye-contact that was physically nauseating. "And she is still only am'r-nafsh. How, ah, *refreshing*." His nose quivered. I had not known you could use the movement of nostrils both offensively and threateningly, but Maxym accomplished both with his pointed intake of air. Also, he still was keeping my eyes in that slimy, uncomfortable contact. I realized he was trying to fascinate me, to see if he could get me under his control.

Sandu replied, with anger clear in his voice, "And as my frithaputhra and am'r-nafsh, Noosh is very much under my protection and the protection of all my friends. Which of course you are, Maxym, *da?*"

"Oh, *da*, *da*, of course I am. You can count me as Noosh's *bodyguard*, friend Vlad. Oh, I will guard her body, most certainly."

I managed by sheer force of will to tear my eyes from Maxym's. He covered his surprise with a second small bow, complete with an ironic flourish of his hand, as his exit.

I was alarmed by all of this and furious with Sandu because obviously, there was such a vast amount of stuff I hadn't been told that I didn't even know where to start with the questions. Wait, yes, I did.

"Why is my being an am'r-nafsh exciting so much comment, *Sandu?*" I hissed, making his name almost a swear word. "Or shall I go back to calling you 'Vlad' like everyone else? Or maybe... *Voivode?*"

He turned me around to face him, and to my utter and complete surprise, gave me a hug. I didn't know if PDAs were acceptable in am'r etiquette, but it was decidedly the right thing to do for me at that moment. He spoke softly in my ear, "*Draga mea*, please continue to call me Sandu. As I have told you, I am a different man now. We am'r take so many names over the years, it can become confusing what to call an old friend. Or old enemy. But this is not the moment for me to explain all. Please give me time to get us alone, *dragă* Noosh, and I will endeavor to make you happy with me again."

Well, I couldn't argue the sense of that. Pissed as I was, I understood intellectually that this wasn't the place to get into a lover's quarrel, nor to demand detailed explanations. I nodded my head against his shoulder, and he kissed my ear, then my cheek, and followed with a quick peck on the lips. Were we scandalizing the am'r, I wondered? I had not seen anything much in the way of any physical contact. It was all bows or polite inclinations of the head from outside the boundary of generous personal space. Were am'r more puritanical than Anne Rice and so many other writers fantasized? I'd not have guessed it from my three days of kinky heaven with Sandu, but obviously, there was a great deal I had not and *could not* have begun to have guessed. I would have to "shut up and look pretty," dammit, and wait for the answers I deserved.

Chapter Fourteen

THE GUESTS HAD THINNED out, although there were still some small groups talking amongst themselves. All the Romanian gang was gathered around Neplach. Vulferam and Dubhghall were huddled (albeit loudly) with Cyrus and Eben, and the rest were variously bunched. Bagamil was bouncing around all of them, but every time I looked one or more had slipped out of the room, to transfer allegiances or shore up their support base or whatever shifty politicking needing doing. I might not have known what the hell was going on tonight, but I wasn't stupid. That this had been the opening night of the Am'r U.N. was clear.

What problem was causing the am'r to organize to "promote international cooperation?" Sandu seemed to know at least some of it, and he hadn't seen fit to share any of it with me on the way over. But then again, at this point, the overarching am'r issues that had come up tonight were a pretty distant second to my own personal and immediate issues. Sandu was going to have to talk until his throat was sore to make me "happy" with him again.

Sandu did a raised-hand half-salute-half-wave-thing to the remaining am'r, and led me out through a door opposite where we'd entered the room. We went down one corridor, turned left, went upstairs, turned left again, then right, and after that up some more stairs. I despaired of ever finding my way around this warren without an escort. Would I have to keep notes on how to get from point A to point B for the next few decades? Do they maybe have some kind of useful GPS device for newbies? Or even just a map?

At the end of the last corridor was our destination. The door had a carved design centered in it: what I made out to be a dragon, curved into a circle, its tail coiled around its neck. Running the length of the dragon's back was a cross, painted blood-red. Sandu opened the door, then swept a bow to usher me in. There were more of the gently glowing green lights, but these were tiny and ran about the room like fairy lights. The ceiling was much lower and the room was room-shaped, not just raw cave, although one couldn't go so far as to call the walls even by any means. Most of the wall space was taken up by tapestries, except for one wall, which showcased a long, straight sword, in a black scabbard with a little worked metal at various points along it, particularly the tip. It obviously had the place of honor, but it seemed a plain, workaday sword, with a cross-guard with flared tips and hilt decorated solely with what I would have called a Maltese cross. Other bladed weapons fanned out around it, from swords to knives of many shapes, some with fancy pommels, et cetera, but they obviously were not as, well, *central*. The furniture continued in the heavy medieval theme: thick dark wood with wrought iron both decorative and functional. There were fleeces strewn on the floor; it looked like an entire flock of black sheep had died in the name of underfoot comfort.

This was the receiving room of Sandu's suite. It had a few chairs, side tables, and lots of tapestries. The next chamber was monopolized by a huge four-poster bed with heavy tapestry curtains, wardrobes, and more tapestries covering the surrounding walls. The third and obviously most private room had a huge, heavy desk, so covered with papers and other detritus as to be operationally useless. What made it clear the space was Sandu's were the precious old tomes, hardcover classics of the ages, and cheap paperbacks piled willy-nilly on tables and floor.

This room had no tapestries; large exhibition-quality photographs lined the walls. From the invention of the camera to obviously current artists, the common theme was decidedly "Romania: its landscapes and culture." Other than that, it was just *books everywhere*. Books in shelves, under the art. Piles of books growing around the shelves, which had evolved over time into looming stacks of books. It made me both fall a bit more in love with him *and* also want to smack him silly because of his lack of care for the inestimably valuable books he casually left on the floor or in unstable towers on the desk. I mean, a messy stack of paperbacks is one thing, and there were plenty of those around the place. But other books, as tantalizingly ancient and irreplaceable as the ones in his library back in Blackacre, were haphazardly shoved in those piles as well.

Blackacre. Wow. The thought of my life back in Centerville hit me hard. It seemed a million years ago, and the life of some other person. But it had been days—mere days—since I'd left there.

Sandu found me in his office, staring into space, quietly freaking out. "Before we talk, *draga mea*, give me your mobile." It was an odd request, but I dug my phone out of my bag and handed it over. He plugged it in to charge, along with his phone, in a socket in the rock wall. I was bemused. "We have *electricity* down here?"

"We have our own electric generator, and many of the private rooms have outlets where computers and other electrics can be plugged in. But we do not yet have antennae for mobile service. This is just to keep it charged—you cannot use the phone or its network down here. However, you can access the internet through the computer. You may use mine," a sweep of the hand to indicate his tablet, now on the floor beside his desk, "or there is an extra cable for your laptop. But there will be time for such things later."

"Yeah. We have some *stuff* to talk about." I said this kind of flatly. There was still more than a little annoyance pinging through me. I plunked myself down on a threadbare Persian rug. The only chair in this room was behind the desk, and was already taken up with a stack of what looked to be a leather-bound collection of Milton's greatest hits admixed with battered mid-1900s crime novels. Thus I demonstrated—or at least attempted to demonstrate—that I wasn't going anywhere until we had indeed talked about *stuff*.

Sandu melted down into a comfortable squat beside me. "*Dragă* Noosh, let me start by apologizing to you. I have meant to impart numerous details to you, but somehow I never did. Matters have moved precipitously, and they needed to—I wanted them to—but I did not expect, *ei bine*, the distractions to be quite as *distracting*. Since I have met you, time has rushed in such a way that I feel I cannot keep up, when for many years, it has moved so very tediously. I am not used to the pace since we came together."

Well, it was a good start. But Sandu still owed me some massive explanations, and I was not going to let him off the hook by telling him I knew exactly how he felt. "So. This am'r-nafsh thing. Why is everyone so damn shocked I am here? I thought being an am'r-nafsh was a natural part of the process?"

"And it is, *draga mea,* it is. However, we am'r tend to keep our am'r-nafsh out of the am'r world. We hide them, one could say. Am'r do not tend to congregate, and certainly we seldom dwell together. It has been tried, and when it did not succeed, we did not try again, for it is not in our natures. We are best when we spread apart. Most especially when we have an am'r-nafsh in our protection, we stay away from the other am'r. Once a frithaputhra has crossed over into being full am'r, then, well, they eventually go their own way in life. Very few stay together as Eben and Cyrus have done. As I hope you and I will do."

"But *why* do you keep the am'r-nafsh apart?" I asked, frustration leaking into my voice.

"*Ei bine*, as you know, am'r-nafsh do not have the full strength of am'r. They are vulnerable, almost as much as kee. But more than that. It is in love we make our frithaputhraish: for companionship and for saving them from their mortality. Well, you could say that our frithaputhraish are our main weakness, and while they are am'r-nafsh, they are almost our Achilles heel.

"And then there is the vhoon-am'r-nafsh." Sandu paused and seemed unwilling to start again. "It is...more fragrant, more delectable than any vhoon-kee. It is more...more *nourishing* to an am'r than vhoon-kee. This makes the bond between patar and frithaputhra all the stronger and sweeter because each is giving the other a most special gift. The longer the am'r and the am'r-nafsh vhoon-share, the stronger they can both become. As I give you strength through my blood, the blood you give back to me, mixed kee and am'r, makes me stronger yet. And, as I have told you, strength is *all* with the am'r.

"Thus, the am'r are surprised because I brought you here when this many of us are gathering. Some will reckon I have handed them my Achilles heel. They do not understand why I have endangered myself like this."

"I'm more concerned with why you have endangered *me* like this."

"Ah. But you do not see. You are not *really* in danger, not when *I* am here to protect you. And what is more, you are also under Bagamil's protection. You have met more am'r tonight who will fight for you as well since many have given their allegiance to Bagamil and to me. We will not let any harm come to you. Those am'r who have, ah, *issues* about why I brought you do not think that through. I will make it even more clear tomorrow. They *will* all know you are not to be touched, that Bagamil will destroy anyone who threatens you—if I do not get there first—and that many strong am'r will also stand between you and any threat."

"And you *knew* Bagamil would approve of me? And your friends?"

"Yes. Of course. That was one reason I was late in returning to you. Before I came back to you, I went to Bagamil and spoke with him. I told him I had found someone who could solve the problem of our lack of tangible history, of organizing our past and telling our story to the am'r alive today and those to come. And I told him that I loved you and that I wanted to bring you back as one of us."

"But ... but how could you have known you *loved* me? I mean, we'd only had two dates, if you even could go so far as to call them that! How could you have decided to make me your frithaputhra, with all you tell me that means, on the basis of two dates and one kiss?"

"Have you never heard of love at first sight, *micuțo?*"

"Well, of course, but I don't *believe* in it!"

"*Ei bine*, then I do not know how to answer you. I have loved you since I saw you reading to those children in your library: your voice, animated with the story and sharing the love of reading. The sight of you, with your unruly black hair and storm-gray eyes, and those kissable lips. The scent of you reaching out, tantalizing me. You were mouthwatering to me before you became my am'r-nafsh, *dragă* Noosh. Now you are unbearably delectable."

"Well, thank you. I think." I could understand things a little better from an am'r perspective now, but there was still an am'r tendency to mix the language of romance and the language of gastronomy which disconcerted me. Does he look at me as a human-shaped buffet or the love of his life? I guessed the answer was *both*, for the am'r, and I wasn't sure when I'd get used to it. That made me realize I was all-over uncomfortable, and not at all sure when—or if—I'd ever be comfortable again. Too much had happened in too short a time, and I still hadn't processed either the fact I was now *not really human* anymore, or that I'd somehow signed up for a relationship more intense than marriage.

Nevermind I was now on the other side of the world, underground somewhere in a cave-system full of vampires, an unknown number of which were of the opinion I was tastier than a cheese burger *and* that they could use me to get back at Vlad Dracula for centuries' worth of unspecified vengeance.

And to top it all off, I'd taken a new job without even giving notice at the Haw-Fuck-My-Life.

I felt tired, lost, and homesick. Being at Sandu's place in Blackacre was at least recognizably familiar and near-enough to my home, but where I was *now* was wholly alien. Even with Sandu there beside me, I felt alone.

There was a knock on the door, which made me start like a small, terrified woodland creature. Sandu, however, was expecting it, since he got up to answer it, saying, "Ah, finally." I did not see who was outside, but Sandu said, "*Mulțumesc,*" and came back with a tray of food. "*Pălincă, ciorbă de burtă, papricaș de pește, mămăligă, sarmale, plăcintă cu mere, cafea.*" He pointed out each item. "I cannot share these beloved dishes with you, but the aromas bring back such memories. Eat them, please. I am happy that this way of sharing my love of my country is yet open to you."

The food was hot and all of it was delicious. The aromas Sandu spoke of had made me realize I was starving. I ate as he directed: first, a shot of strong plum brandy. A small bowl of sweet and sour soup was followed by an amazing fish stew, thick cornmeal bread, delicious stuffed cabbage leaves, a delectable apple pie, strong coffee, and more of the plum brandy to finish. I kept going until my stomach hurt. I wondered about the catering facilities in a vampire den but decided I felt too good to care.

"Are you feeling any better, *dragă* Noosh?" Sandu asked, and I heard the anxiety in his voice. "I have said I would care for you, but I keep forgetting to feed you. It is a habit—and a pleasure—I lost long ago."

"That's OK," I said and was surprised to find I meant it, that I'd not added it to my list of complaints. "I don't really *feel* hungry these days until I remember that food exists."

"But you still need to eat, and more often. You are not feeding just yourself, but your patar as well. Even when you take vhoon back from me—as I so relish you doing—still, my drinking drains you far deeper, and you need other fuel to replenish what you've lost. I must help you remember to eat. And you must remind me to remind you."

At this point, I yawned. I couldn't help it. Blame the full belly. And maybe the killer brandy—even if alcohol wasn't supposed to affect me anymore, that stuff was no joke.

"And now I remind you to sleep. It has been a long, wearying time for you. You needed sustenance. Now you need rest."

I couldn't disagree with him. *Still.* "And then more answers."

"*Da, draga mea,*" he said as he pulled me into the bedroom. "As many answers as you like. A lifetime of answers. Many lifetimes of answers."

I looked into the other room at the bed, which was profoundly inviting. But *first*..."Um, do am'r digs include bathrooms?"

"Always my practical Noosh! Yes. For all the fuss that has been made, this is not the first time an am'r-nafsh or even a kee has been on these premises. I have invited am'r and their frithaputhraish here before, just not when I have had so many other guests."

"*You* invited? *Your* guests? Is this place your...house? Or, like, palace? This is all yours?"

Sandu laughed. I pretended it was not *at* me. "Yes. This is mine. It is a work in progress. A 'fixer-upper' you might call it. I started it when I was still am'r-nafsh. There were tunnels already in București when I got there. We have never stopped making them, to deal with the Turk and with other enemies through the ages. But *these* tunnels, this hidden stronghold—the urban cavers cannot find us. The pitiable homeless *Bucureștenii*, crammed wretchedly into the city's tunnels, will not stumble upon us. The scientists and television crews have not found us. They will never find us. I have spent the centuries since I built București into a capital, spent them down here, making it safe and secure. I do not need to sleep in my 'native soil,' but when I sleep here, I truly rest."

"Why didn't you tell me I was in the *real* Dracula's castle? That's so cool!"

Sandu gave me that look. "There are times I feel I know you as I know my own soul, *dragă* Noosh...and there are times I feel I shall never understand you. *Ei bine*, you asked for the lavatory. Follow me."

We went back out of his rooms and down a corridor for a bit. There was a door in the right wall, which, when I poked my head in, turned out to be an extremely primitive privy: a cold stone seat over a long, deep drop. "Well," I said, disheartened, "this continues the medieval theme all too faithfully."

"I am sorry. There has not been much reason to update it. Now that you are here, we can of course renovate to suit you. I will see you back in the bedroom."

I cannot recommend medieval jakes. When I got back to the room, the traces of dinner had vanished, and Sandu was turning down the bedcovers. Dracula, my own personal ladies' maid.

"Let me tuck you in, *micuțo*. It is a pleasure for me."

"Uh, you're not going to sleep with me? This *is* your bedroom, right?"

"It is, and I will sleep with you later—and all the rest of our days. But I must meet with some people. We must speak hurriedly, without time for explanation, and while we all speak English, it is faster and more private for some of us to speak in our native languages. It would only be tedious for you. Sleep now, and I will join you in a while."

I didn't want him to go. Didn't want him to go out for clandestine meetings into who knew what sorts of danger from which he might never come back, leaving me alone in the midst of a danger I could hardly begin to understand. But sleep was irresistible. I couldn't stop myself from being pulled down into it. The bed was soft and hugged me into it and pulled me down further. I was mostly asleep when Sandu tucked the covers over my shoulders, and I didn't notice him leaving the room.

Chapter Fifteen

I was buried deep under rock and dirt. But I was warm, held securely in the dark, and safe from the cruel, sharp light. It was like the earth was my mother, embracing me and keeping me protected and secure. It was never stifling, never confining. I could never feel claustrophobic again and would from now on long for such snug enfolding in the rich earth.

I was there for an eternity, warm and safe, safe and warm, down in the darkest center, and I never wanted to leave. But I was called back, and with each layer up, it became bearable, and even comfortable not to be in that safe darkness. Each layer brought a new sense of freedom and space that made the light tolerable, acceptable, worthwhile. By the time I came up to the point where I was aware of myself as a person sleeping in a bed under covers, it did not seem a bad thing to be, and I could no longer remember where and how I had been.

I realized there was a presence in the bed with me, snugged up under the covers. I was still in a warm sleepy place, but he was not. Or at least, parts of him were not. I felt Vlad's Impaler poking demandingly between my legs, his hands questing around on my body and his lips and teeth making a tentative exploration of my neck. It wasn't that I was *against* the idea of another bout of The World's Best Sex™, but I was having a hard time pulling myself up into wakefulness. Indeed, sex was all very well, but sleeping was so niiiice, too...

I must have drifted off into deeper sleep, but I slowly came to the realization that Sandu had worked his way inside me, and was moving slowly in and-out, creating the most marvelous gentle waves of pleasure. I moaned as the pleasure built up along with my increasing consciousness, and this inspired him to reach around and play with my nipples, making sleep recede even faster on the building tide of bliss. I started moving my hips against his, making the motion and the intensity greater.

His lips and tongue were doing their usual foreplay on my neck, but also moving over my shoulder and the back of my neck. It was still sleepy-fuzzy and lovely, not quite real. It felt like I was still dreaming, and that was part of the pleasure.

It went on in a marvelously timeless way before I felt Sandu's teeth slide gently through the skin and muscle of my neck, pushing me into a new kind of orgasm: soft, smooth ripples across all of me, not pushing me to all the intensity of the universe, but perfectly sustainable for a long ride of sheer delight. As he had the last time we had fucked, he took a break from suckling at my neck to rip open his wrist and shove it in my mouth. This "66" was perfect: our bodies pressed together, his Impaler fully inside me and moving just enough to provide wonderful friction, and his salty blood gushing silkily down my throat as he drank from me. I gulped and gulped, and felt the high come on that took my fuzzy sleepiness to full waking dream, all synesthesia and ecstasy.

After we were done, and my lips rested against his perfectly healed wrist, he held me and we lay together, not wanting to move again, ever.

A quiet knock on the door woke us and Sandu slipped away, leaving a vacuum at my back. I sat up slightly and watched as he found a black silk robe in a wardrobe, and another tray was delivered for me. "I must admit," Sandu said as he served me breakfast in bed, "it is easier to remember to feed you when there are other people to be told to remember it for me." I found myself inhaling cups of strong black tea, more mămăligă with sour cream and cheese, and sausages.

I've always liked saying—to myself, anyway—that after my morning caffeine and a good breakfast, I felt "almost human" again. But nowadays I felt better, stronger than I ever had in my life, even when I forgot to eat, and caffeinated beverages were simply to be drunk for the pleasure of the taste, as they also no longer had any effect on me. It seemed every time Sandu and I had epic sex—or at least the blood exchange, but I didn't see the sex as *optional*—I would find myself feeling just a bit more...more...well, *more*. My blood gushed contentedly through my veins, well-being rippled through my nervous system, my muscles moved smoothly and never knotted from fatigue or strain, and my skin glowed with health and was pretty much poreless. Drinking the blood of the undead (or whatever the am'r were) made me more alive.

Except that I still had to use that damned indoor outhouse.

I stopped and stared at Sandu when I got back from the so-called bathroom. He was garbed—that was the only way to describe it—in what looked like a museum piece or a costume from a film on his life. It was a black...well, not a *dress*, but I had no idea what to call it. The lovely fitted item was made of fine black wool, with a double row of silver buttons to the waist, after which it was open to the knee. When he moved, black wool hose were exposed, showing off his well-muscled legs. His black leather boots came to mid-calf, fitting him tightly.

At his neck was the only thing *not* black: a white silk mandarin-collared shirt peeked out from the black wool. A golden chain ran diagonally across his chest, down to where it was attached to a sword. I was not surprised to see it was the sword from the place of honor in his front room. Over all of that, a wide belt of tartan-like fabric wrapped around his waist. Finally, but most eye-catching, a thicker gold chain went around his shoulders and held on his chest a dragon curved into the form of a circle, its tail strangling it, divided along the middle of its back from the top of its head to the tip of its tail by a blood-red cross. It was the same symbol as I'd seen on the door, and I realized it must be the Order of the Dragon.

Since he was dressed to impress and ready to go, I felt pressure not to dawdle. Two pitchers of hot water and a pile of towels had come in with the food, which was enough for me to have a French bath and change into the outfit he'd picked out.

I wondered if I'd ever have control of my wardrobe again. But at least this did remove the guesswork of what to wear to the vampire U.N. Council.

Sandu had chosen an outfit of medium-gray silky wide-leg trousers, which looked like a skirt until I walked, and a tight, darker gray knit top that clung from a mock-turtleneck through fashionably long sleeves with thumb-holes. I figured the turtleneck was an excellent idea. It sent a subtle message of, "Don't even think about my neck!" My black leather ankle boots peeked perfectly from under the swishy wide trouser-legs as I moved.

There was a mirror inside the wardrobe. I was glad because I liked what I saw outfit-wise, but my hair was a *disaster*. Curls need attention and pampering, and mine had been sorely neglected as of late. They were more frizz than curl by this point. I dampened the unruly mass, found the leave-in conditioner in my suitcase, and pulled it all severely back into a chignon, which was my default Librarian-style, and which I could do perfectly even in rushed situations like this.

Sandu was making the movements and small noises of impatience, but I felt eyeliner, mascara, and lipstick were called for. He obviously didn't disagree, so he did not verbally hurry me along. He was edgy and impatient, however. *That* made me feel nervous, and when I'm nervous, I tend to look for extra things to do to avoid the inevitable. But I was dressed and styled and could find no more ways to put off going down into a conclave of am'r, not knowing who would be friend or foe—nor how much actual difference there was between the former and the latter.

As we went down the twists and turns of the hallways back to the Rave Cave, Sandu doled out information. "We shall arrive there a bit early to greet the am'r as they enter. I have gathered them here in *my* stronghold, but they need to see that Bagamil fully supports this and believes as strongly as I do that it is the only way forward for the am'r. And they need to be made aware of you, *dragă* Noosh, and understand you are under powerful protection."

"What you're saying is that we are stuck in the receiving line."

"Yes, 'receiving line' is the right phrase. I am the host, and now I have you as my hostess. We cannot get out of this duty, as much as we both would prefer it. This is an exceedingly important gathering for the am'r. Tonight will change the course of our culture, and it might even change us as a people."

"No pressure, then."

Sandu laughed. "No pressure at all."

When we arrived at the vast, cavern-y room, Bagamil—in his Mister Sunshine outfit—was already there, alone, in the same place as last night. He nodded at us. We nodded to him and kept walking. No last-minute advice or game-changing directives or anything.

Damn. I'd have liked the comfort of his nearness, even for a few moments.

It seemed the big front doors would be used again tonight. Sandu found another otherwise-impossible-to-locate button to press to open them from this side, and they swung open with their grumbly stone complaint.

Would he ever give me a guide to all the ridiculous and overly-complicated shit I need to learn to live in this vampire warren? He couldn't personally lead me around forever. But that was a problem for another night; we had enough more immediate problems to deal with. Once we'd survived this event of life and death importance, we'd get around to the mundane problem of how to find the door, never mind my way from point A to point B.

The Romanian Crew was waiting on the other side of the doors, obviously the cheerleaders for Team Bagamil. Was there another team? And if so, who was on it? They came past one-by-one and Meet-N-Greet Round Two: Vampiric Boogaloo began. Everyone in the Romanian Crew had warm smiles for both of us, and said, *"Noroc!"* which seemed to mean something between "Good luck" and "More power to you"—an am'r sentiment if ever there was one—to Sandu and me. Daciana added in a discreet aside to me: "Do not worry. You will do fine."

After we'd greeted the Romanian Crew, the real work began. Down the winding stone corridor stretched the clustered and disordered queue of vampires, some conversing *sotto voce*, some standing alone and watching us impassively.

This was going to be the receiving line from hell.

I cringed as I watched even more am'r coming down the hall to add to the group waiting to be welcomed in. There were am'r I met last night, and more to meet for the first time. Sandu and I had managed to get "married" without all the usual fuss, but it seemed we still had to do time in painful social ritual as if to make up for the early bit having been so easy and enjoyable.

I met Llorenç, a saturnine Catalan, Violante, a strangely blonde Italian, with amazing amethyst-colored eyes, Tryphena, on the arm of Zopyros, who was another example of patar-frithaputhra bonding which had withstood the test of time, and Jiang Lili, whom Sandu was obviously quite surprised to see. He introduced me to her with almost painfully careful courtesy. She was breathtakingly gorgeous, with eyes like black jewels, the palest skin of any am'r I'd met so far, and perfectly straight black hair that fell thick to her knees. She was also the farthest from human-seeming of all the am'r I'd met. Her beauty and her utterly expressionless face made her seem "vampire" in a way none of the other am'r had done. Indeed, many of them had seemed *all too human* in their character and actions.

There were more, but they blurred together, and after a while, I couldn't remember the current impossible name by the time the next outlandish or unpronounceable one came along. The am'r trickled in one by painful one, needing to be greeted from across a formal and not insignificant personal space.

Sandu made significant eye contact and subvocalized a few urgent words with one or another of them, and I tried to mark those. They are all some variation of attractive, I thought, although the luminous good health of their skin, hair, and eyes that marked an am'r—And now me as well!—might have a lot to do with my perception. Basically, am'r all looked photoshopped into inhuman perfection. It made it hard for me to read them, because even the ones who set Sandu's spine uncomfortably straight just looked unreadably, inhumanly gorgeous to me.

It all lasted too long. Way too long. It couldn't have taken *years*, but it felt like it did, and, who knows, am'r might not care about the passage of time. Maybe it was like entering a fairy mound and eventually stepping back into the real world to find hundreds of years had passed. No. Stop it, silly girl. Obviously I was getting slap-happy, fatigued by the stress of it all.

Abruptly, a change—a charge, actually, like an electrical one—filled the atmosphere. I could sense that Sandu was quivering with tension, although outwardly he was perfectly relaxed—almost *too* relaxed, and back in his affected teenage slouch. A party of seriously be-suited am'r had reached us. The rest of the am'r had walked up singly or in pairs, but this group of am'r was even more of a unit than the Romanian crew.

In that first instant of seeing them, they could have been clones, there was such a similar quality among them all. Gorgeous clones, all dressed in aggressively modern-cut suits like GQ models. Or maybe male strippers. They were too studied, too perfectly creased, their black patent shoes shined too mirror-like. They made the rest of the am'r before them seem human, unaffected, and even a bit *untidy*, which was a real feat.

Who the fuck are these guys?

I didn't have to wait long to find out. He who was obviously—painfully obviously—the leader led his clique right up to Sandu. It was as they got closer, I realized they did *not* all look the same; their hair ranged from light brown to glossy black to the leader's shade of...not brown, but almost a dark orange. Almost all had dark eyes, but the kingpin had eyes that seemed brown at first, but upon closer inspection were oddly metallic, catching the greenish light like they were mercury. While face and nose shapes showed no commonalities, their leader stood out with a Pontian nose that distracted my attention even from his eyes.

Anyone who's heard jokes about a correlation between nose and penis length will eye this man with consideration.

Under his impressive beak was a well-manscaped goatee with extra-long mustaches. It made me realize what set this group of am'r apart: facial hair. Almost none of the am'r had any worth noticing, beyond Neplach's beard, Eben's impressive muttonchops, and Bagamil's Freddie-stache. But all of this gang had proper facial hair, from trim mustaches to perfectly-shaped goatees. None more so than this guy, however. Obviously, he made sure to be the leader in *everything*.

I noticed he had the same teenage slouch as Sandu: uncaringly loose, indifferent, insouciant, perfectly "I don't give a fuck, I don't even care that I'm here, and I'm *really bored* right now." His body language mirrored Sandu's so perfectly I thought maybe he was mocking him, but when I saw his eyes—those strange metallic eyes—I saw no humor there. If I hadn't seen the look in his eyes, I might have been taken in by his easy smile and casual, "Vlad Drăculea. Good to see you, *old friend*. It has been too long. We must catch up, yes?" Then he turned his head to me...and the nostrils in his long, aquiline nose whiffled my scent, and whiffled some more.

Obviously, the news about me had gotten around since last night.

Did you hear the news? Vlad's brought in not only a new frithaputhra, but an am'r-nafsh one at that! Gasp! Shock!

You'd never believe that beings who had centuries under their belts would gossip like teenagers, but it seemed there are some things people never grew out of.

Anyway, news had clearly gone around about me, because tonight all the am'r I met for the first time were obviously prepared to meet me, and upon introduction, clearly and obviously did *not* point out that I was a deelish am'r-nafsh. There *were* various nostril reactions, which I'd come to be rather sensitive about, but they ranged from "utterly expressionless face with the barest olfactory tremble" to "keenly interested but trying for subtle deep inhalations."

Wriggling your sniffer like a pig scenting truffles must be just as impolite as conversationally bringing up my "scrumptious snack" status would be. So if I'm right, it means he's being deliberately rude before he's even said word one to me. Nice.

"And this must be the one who has swept you off your feet, old friend." Twitch, twitch went the nostrils. "I can...*see* why. Truly, *Kazıklı bey*, you will make us all *jealous*."

Sandu ignored this, which made me proud of him.

Although he's probably been practiced at diplomatically ignoring things since five centuries before I was born, and doesn't need me being proud of him.

"Noosh, may I introduce *el-Fātiḥ, Meḥmed-i s[]ānī, Kayser-i Rûm, Turcarum Imperator*, otherwise known as the Grand Turk. Fātiḥ Sultan Mehmet Han, this is my fritha-puthra, Anushka."

I decided if there was at least one person in the world who could and *should* call me by my full name, it was this guy. I never wanted to achieve any level of informality with him. I mean, it was impossible to have learned anything about Sandu—about *Vlad*—and not have read *his* name. This piece of work was the asshole who'd seduced Vlad's brother Radu and turned him against Vlad, and who'd fought against him many times during their lives. They had been mortal enemies, back when they were mortal.

Did this mean they are *immortal* enemies now? I'm guessing yes from body language alone, although the rest could just be Mehmet's charming personality.

"Anushka, *sevgili*, this is truly a pleasure." He bowed deeply, and on the way back up, he *winked* at me. *Seriously?* "It is good to meet the lady who has become so dear to my *old friend*. I hope we shall become friends as well. *Good friends*."

Oh, ick. I just stared at him in disbelief.

"And this is Yiğit bey," Sandu interrupted tonelessly, moving my attention along to the next of Mehmet's posse.

I was eager enough not to be interacting with Mehmet that I bowed overenthusiastically to a startled Yiğit, who returned the bow while so faintly mumbling a greeting I couldn't make out even what language it was.

I exchanged nods with each member of the posse as they came through. They all had their variations on the themes of facial hair and too-sharp suits, and their names were all more tongue-twisters I had to try to get right the first time: Demirkan, Ertuğrul, Oğuzhan, Cüneyt, Karadağ, Zeynel.

Finally, there was no one left to meet, watch their nostrils wriggle, and attempt not to mangle their name. Sandu and I went back through the throng of am'r, who'd gathered in a rough crescent around Bagamil and the long table. Bagamil was standing at the head, not yet seated. Various am'r had already settled themselves in the available chairs. Everyone else crowded around, looking like they were totally fine with *not* being seated at the table. I wondered for how many this was true.

Sandu took a seat to Bagamil's right, with Neplach on his other side. I stood behind his tall-backed chair. In another life, I might have had an issue with standing behind a seated man. Today, there was no flame of feminism in my heart because *not* being directly in view of all these assembled am'r was totally fine with me. Hiding behind Sandu's chair, to be painfully honest, seemed seriously the better part of valor, right at this moment.

Bagamil did all the talking. It might be Sandu's underground castle—or lair, or even *warren*—but Bagamil was obviously the one in charge, and Sandu, in his function as The Notorious V-L-A-D, The Impaler, Infamous Ruler Of Story And Song, was obviously supposed to just sit there and look pretty.

A nice turnaround. *Pleasing.*

Bagamil laid out the background premise: the am'r were too isolated, so to take the best advantage of science and technology in this age, they needed to learn how to work together and share information.

He'd avoided the dread buzzword "community," which was undoubtedly wise on his part.

Horrifyingly, at this point, he brought *me* into the picture—although no one made me come forward and do a PowerPoint, thank everything!—explaining the idea for an am'r historical archive, and how they now had an "archivist and information scientist among our number." Never had these titles been given such weight and importance. While my fellow librarians would never know about it, I swelled with pride for our whole profession: the science and the art!

When Bagamil paused before his next line of reasoning, a voice came across the table. One I already knew and disliked: Mehmet's.

"If I may ask, 'Bagamil,'" he said the name with obvious air quotes, "why do we need this 'archive?' What purpose does it serve? We know who and what we are, surely.

There is nothing in old manuscripts to teach us how to be am'r—unless there is an am'r *Kama Sutra*, perhaps? I think *I* know all the ways to sup from," here he looked knowingly and disgustingly at me, "a sweet girl...or a plump boy. Still, I would be willing to have a look and see if there is some thrilling technique lost back in the mists of time."

There was an obliging chuckle from many throats.

He's *acting*, I realized. He's just acting this crude to mock and disparage Sandu and Bagamil's ideas. Did the ones who laughed *get* that? These creatures are all supposed to have superior brains than I. Or did they laugh to show they support Mehmet's side? This was all too complicated for me. I'd just signed up for some good sex, not all this political drama.

"A good question, my dear Fātiḥ." Bagamil was obviously prepared for hecklers in the audience. "And it brings me to my next point, and the main reason I gathered us here this night. A number of am'r—I will not list all of them, but if it is not you yourself, it could well be one sitting next to you—have come to me with grave stories of being approached, and in some cases attacked, by other am'r recently. There seems to be a faction that has come to associate themselves with the myth of the jinn and seem to think they themselves have taken on the powers and characteristics of these 'genie' spirits from kee legend and fable.

"These misguided young am'r are looking for a sense of belonging, for a powerful history, for pride in their culture and inheritance. Do they get that from the am'r as we are now? No. We have an extraordinary heritage indeed, but we do not have any *resources* for them. And how many of you aojyshtaish would be willing to teach history classes or do seminars on the history of am'r culture which you have personally experienced...? None? So I thought.

"This is why building an archive is so vital for us now. And why we needed to gather together this day: so that we could plan a response to those misidentified neophyte am'r. No penalty need apply, and none need come forward and reveal themselves or their intimates. No, we start simply by providing resources for them. They can educate themselves privately from their own computers and mobiles, and I myself, along with a number of aojyshtaish, are willing to share from our own long experience and rebuild—perhaps build for the first time—pride in our kind. In our history, our unique qualities and abilities, and in ourselves. Not just as individual am'r, but in our undying heritage, which is as poetic and *legendary* as the one they have latched onto, and all the more so for being tangibly *real*."

The snarky tones of Mehmet's otherwise beautifully accented voice insinuated themselves as soon as Bagamil had finished speaking. "Well, how *nicely* tied up, with a little ribbon. How lucky for us all that you have identified and solved it all by yourself, or at any rate, with your little group of sycophants and hangers-on. I cannot see why you felt the need to haul in the rest of us by crying 'Emergency!'

since you have single-handedly fixed this little problem. You, who are so fond of technology—why not just email us the minutes of this meeting, which we did not need to attend?"

"I have not tied this problem up, as well you understand," replied Bagamil lightly, as if Mehmet had not just abrasively mocked and otherwise verbally attacked him. "There are many aspects that need further dialogue from *all* of us to decide the best plans with which to move forward."

"'Dialogue,' is it? Or will it just be The Great Bagamil telling us what to believe and what to do? Orders we can scurry to follow in our efforts to impress?" The venom now dripped from Mehmet's voice. The am'r were looking from one to the other like they were following a tennis match. Or like a litter of kittens following a laser pointer with their furry little faces. The thought would have been funny except for the nasty undercurrent of storm-like tension building.

"I have never asked for those things you insinuate, Fātiḥ Mehmet." Bagamil was unblinking, his voice still gentle, but with unyielding strength right under the surface. He was still Mister Sunshine, but now that sun was the inescapable, scorching, midday-in-the-desert sort of thing. "If you have an issue with me, be open about it. Tell me what problems you are having, and we will resolve them here and now."

"Oh, you would like that, Aojysht of aojyshtaish, wouldn't you? You, powerful in your age, will put me in my place in front of all—another problem neatly tied up in a ribbon. But I do not intend to let you try to tie me up in your fastidious bonds."

Mehmet stood and swept an arm around to address all the am'r as he spoke. "And you would all do as well to think for yourselves and not just fall into line—fall into the pretty stories of our 'great am'r heritage' solving all problems, which Our Great Leader here would have you believe. There is more out there than just *his* point of view.

"Go find it for yourselves! You are powerful creatures, with minds of your own. Will you *naïvely* follow this one who sets himself up as your leader, who gives you no respect, does not allow you the rewards which are surely due to such formidable beings as we? He would have you hiding in the shadowy corners of history, not reaching out and taking what the world *owes* the likes of such mighty immortals. Yet even *he* must fall back on the truth; must admit this to be all about power when he challenges me, as you saw just now.

"Think for yourselves! Do not be mindless puppets in his hands. Stand up and *demand* what should be yours!"

Proclamation proclaimed, Mehmet made a dramatic, sweeping exit. The am'r did not exactly clear him a path, but there was somehow—conveniently—no one in his way as he and his besuited followers exited.

There was profound silence for a moment. The am'r would never do anything as sophomoric as to start whispering to each other, but there were plenty of silent reactions. Some gave meaningful glances to a friend or ally, some stared straight at Bagamil—or Sandu, I noticed—*carefully* looking in no other direction.

The latter are the better poker players, one must assume.

Sandu swept his glance over the am'r faces, doing his own count of who was looking where. Neplach was looking off into a middle distance of his own. I'd never presume I knew what was going on in *his* ancient head. As for Bagamil, he had a sad smile on his face, the look of a man who is not surprised by anything because he has seen it all before.

His smile became more upbeat and spread across his face. "My am'r," he said in a voice that carried across the room without his seeming to speak above normal conversational tones, "I agree with Mehmet."

There was a visible start on even the most blank-faced am'r. "You *should* think for yourselves. And I would never want any less, not from any of you. I am not asking you to follow me slavishly. I only stand here speaking because I am, as Mehmet said, the Aojysht of aojyshtaish, the eldest among us, and it is our tradition that the most senior, the most powerful of us should do this.

"We *do* believe in power since we are a powerful species, proud and singular. I expect nothing less than strong self-governance from each of you. If I was to try to control you as Mehmet suggests, would you stand for it a minute? No! We are not a people who allow ourselves to be controlled. If we are in any danger, it will be from clinging blindly to self-sufficiency, not from being herded like sheep."

I'd been under enough stress from all this Am'r U.N. nonsense, and this struck me as hilarious. Vampire sheep! That would be baaad!

I must have giggled a little too loudly because Sandu let me know he was displeased. He didn't say anything, or turn and look at me, or anything so vulgarly *observable*. A subtle shift in how he was sitting made me sober right up. What further sobered me was the idea I was connected strongly enough to someone to know what they were thinking, what they wanted from me, with only the barest hint of body-language. Sometimes I didn't *like* this bond we had. It was lovely during sex and all, but the strength of it, the intensity of it, was disconcerting at the best of times and alarming the rest of the time.

Bagamil provided a timely distraction from such thoughts. Whatever relationship issues I might have, there were waaaay bigger issues immediately surrounding me. "Does anyone wish to criticize me further, or may I get on with sharing information with all of you?" No one spoke. Bagamil continued, "I will let Vlad tell the story, for it is his to tell."

Sandu rose and gave a small bow. "First, I tell you all: although Bagamil is my patar, and I owe him my respect and my devotion and my obedience"—I saw Bagamil from the corner of my eye make a miniscule, rapidly suppressed shift in his own body language and recognized it as stifled laughter—"he has never asked me to follow him blindly, never discouraged me from thinking for myself. And neither has he asked such a thing of *any* am'r, at any time. We follow him—as much as we follow *anyone*—because of his wisdom and his strength. I say he is *indeed* Aojysht-of-aojyshtaish, and we could look to no one else for better guidance at this time.

"This is just *my* opinion, of course. But now, let me tell you now of what befell me in January of this year." Hearing this, shock coursed through my body. I hadn't realized anything had "befallen" him. I'd just assumed he had gotten distracted and blown me off for all those months.

I didn't wonder what had happened to him in the slightest, just had the world's biggest pity party. *Shit*.

"I went in December to Bagamil's citadel. It was in leaving, after we had agreed I would bring back our new archivist and information scientist as one of us..." Here he gestured to me and I wished for the mutant superpower of invisibility as all am'r eyes flickered over to me.

Sandu'd said that going to check in with Bagamil was "one of" the reasons he was late in returning. Well, here come the other reasons!

I had to force myself to stop thinking and focus on what Sandu was now saying.

"—in Ashgabat where I was captured. I had stopped to feed, and all too late discovered my izchha had been dosed with maadak." There was not a proper kee gasp or anything, but an almost noiseless intake of breath like a silent flapping of bat wings. While I had no idea what he was going on about, the listening am'r were clearly shaken up. "I woke up in a basement, which I later found to be in a small town outside Mashhad. I was kept there for months, given the choice of maadakyo izchhaish or starvation. Each time, after I fed, they tried to question me. The first time, they tried torture as well, but they did not, *ei bine*, have the experience with such things as I do." Sandu's voice was flat, emotionless. It gave me the shudders. I did not like the emptiness in his voice *at all*. "But they only tried that once. I believe they were told to cease because their attitude was different the next time. They tried to pretend they were treating me with respect, and to trick the information they wanted out of me."

"And what information *did* they want?" A woman's voice. I looked and saw Jiang Lili at the far left of the table. Her face was a polite, mildly curious mask, no more.

"Information about Bagamil. And me. And many of you, your formidable self included, Jiang *fūrén*." He did a small bow to her, and she inclined her head slightly. "I am afraid I disappointed them. They did not get much useful information from me." His voice was still quite hollow, but I could sense the pride in him. I could not pretend it was a surprise Vlad the Impaler would be used to torture and interrogation, nor that he also would be proud of his experience at overcoming it. Indeed, if he'd gathered any particular skill set while he was mortal, "professionally experienced at torture, knowledgeable in all related fields" would probably have place of pride on his CV. It was never going to be my favorite thing to contemplate, but it was something I most likely was going to have to get over.

"Eventually, there was one izchha who had obviously not drunk much of the maadak, for her vhoon was relatively free from the poison. I drank just enough to convince them I would be incapacitated again. In a stroke of luck, my captors became distracted with turmoil from the kee world while they were waiting for the maadak to fully afflict me. I used the external confusion to aid my escape and made my way back to Bagamil to report the situation."

"Who were your captors? Why have they not been brought here before us?" This was from Maxym, at the other end of the table. I still didn't like him. He was not as dismissive as Mehmet, but he sounded dubious of the whole thing and doubt oozed into your brain from his oily voice.

"That was the only part of their plan that was ingenious. They were all newly am'r, of a patar I have never met—although I will know him when I *do* meet him." It was perfectly clear Sandu was looking forward to this meeting, and this unknown am'r should *not* be. "I have not found their scents since, although I have not yet done a concerted search. It was deemed more important to assemble us all together first and to make known that some am'r, some unknown number of us, are planning something quite *stupid*, which we need to frustrate and terminate."

"What do you suggest is the next step?" This was from across the table, one of the am'r Sandu knew and respected.

"A good question, Hisao-san." Small bow. "I shall let Bagamil answer." Sandu sat down. I wanted to reach out and take his hand, where it lay on the arm of the chair. He'd been tortured! Put in real danger because he'd gone to get permission to bring me home to meet the family, and I hadn't known or cared! Just felt sorry for myself the whole damn time.

However, I was pretty sure Sandu would not thank me since that public gesture of comfort would probably be perceived as a sign of weakness among the am'r. I silently promised both Sandu and myself I'd more than make up for any lack of empathy later when we were out of the vampiric public eye.

Bagamil stood, and he was relaxed, at ease as always. "My suggestions are manifold. First, we shall send Sandu and a few he chooses out to find his temporary captors. We shall obtain more information from them than they received from *my* frithaputhra," he added with a dark flash I was surprised to see from Mister Sunshine. "In the meantime, the rest of you should warn your associates, your companions, and frithaputhraish. Move any am'r-nafsh you may have to the safest locations. And keep careful yourselves! Do not feed from unknown izchhaish. We will share the information with you as we acquire it."

"How will you share the information with us?" Mahtab asked.

Sandu responded, "This is where the new technology comes in. Our goal is to set up a private 'intranet,' into which you would 'VPN.' Anushka—Noosh and I will organize this and send you the information you need to connect into it. Sharing data after that will be trivial."

Bagamil brought things to a conclusion, "But these are all *my* suggestions. And I have one more: I suggest we recess for you to consider matters and to consult with one another. I will hear *your* suggestions for *me* when we reconvene in three hours. *Aojasc' am'ratv!*"

Three hours was the longest intermission or bathroom break I'd ever heard of. Of course, am'r didn't go to the bathroom—obviously they needed all that time for gossip and machinations. I, however, *did* need to go to the bathroom and had no idea how to find my way back to the indoor outhouse up by Sandu's suite.

Sandu stood up and turned to me. "*Drugŭ* Noosh, again, there are many people I must speak with. I would appreciate having you at my side, although I fear this will be tiresome for you."

Astryiah appeared beside us. "Daciana and I are having a bathe during this kibitz. Daciana stands with you, of course, and does not need her mind made up further. I already have my own opinions and no one can change them."

"Of course not!" Sandu replied with a real smile.

Astryiah smiled with affection and amusement back at him. "We shall take your Noosh with us because otherwise, she will be *so* bored and *so* offended by all the sniffing nudniks that she will run away from all of us and go back to the kee."

Sandu looked at me. Astryiah looked at me. I certainly felt ready to run away from the am'r, and possibly from this scary intense relationship I'd found myself in as well. But at the same time, I also wasn't sure I wanted—or to be honest, *dared*—to even be separated from Sandu. And I'd never been alone with another am'r before. There were also some conversations which I wanted to have with Sandu *alone*—but getting any alone-time seemed highly improbable.

Well, what the hell, a hot bath would be nice, and better than staying here, desperately wanting to talk to Sandu and unable to, all the while being a delicious nosegay to a crowd of scheming vampires, most of whom I didn't know and some of whom I didn't need to know any better to know I did not like. I gave a slight nod to Sandu. Damn, I was doing those am'r micro-expressions now, too.

"Very good, very good! Come with me!" Astryiah peremptorily grabbed my hand—I felt a jolt of how strange it was to be touched by a non-Sandu am'r—and yanked me away. I looked back at Sandu helplessly. "Don't worry, Vlad the Heart-Impaled," she tossed back over her shoulder, "I will bring her back clean and safe. And with all the vhoon she left with!" Sandu looked not remotely comforted by that. Neither was I.

Chapter Sixteen

As we got to a doorway, I remembered my call of nature, and, profoundly embarrassed, mentioned it to Astryiah. "Oh, that." She laughed. "You won't miss that when you become am'r, chamuda. Mmmmm, where did you 'go' last?"

"It was a room off Sandu's suite. I'm afraid I don't remember where it is."

"Never fear, *chamuda*, I know how to get there. We take this way." This left me uncharitably wondering how she knew where Sandu's rooms were.

We found the nasty little latrine, and Astryiah waited well down the hall from where I was doing my business.

It was humiliating, being the only person who needed to, well, excrete, in a group of people who were beyond such things. Centuries beyond. There were some real downsides to being am'r-nafsh. On the other hand, to get to the next stage, I was pretty sure I would have to, well, to kick the bucket, and I was not prepared to look into that option just yet.

We met Daciana in a hallway on the way back, and we walked together in the direction I assumed was the onsen Sandu had mentioned the night before. It was not a comfortable thing to be following two vampires I hardly knew. Underground, disoriented, and lost to all sense of direction, I was taking it on faith we were going where I thought we were going. It might be a final, fatal assumption.

Am'r didn't go in for small talk, it seemed. My companions didn't chat with me on the way. Which was fine. I had a lot to process. They walked fast. I've always liked women who walk fast. I happily kept up the speed and the silence.

After turning down one passageway, it started to get muggier and smelled of minerals and steam. I wasn't surprised when we turned a final corner and were in a series of rooms decorated in the "unfinished cave" style, thermal pools steaming gently within. There were columns made by stalagmites that had grown up to meet stalactites, and more of each that were planning to become columns when they grew up. The green lighting came from under the water in this room, the curving ceiling and walls and columns decorated by the swaying reflected light.

Astryiah and Daciana had their clothes off before I looked back at them. I decided modesty was superfluous here and shucked mine with relief. Even with my reduced sensitivity to temperature, the humidity was making wearing clothing annoying.

I climbed awkwardly into the same pool into which they'd slid splashlessly. I had thoughts about choosing a different pool and keeping my am'r-nafsh perfume out of temptation distance, but that probably would have been ungracious, if not downright rude. This was supposed to be a friendly bathe, all of us girls together.

The water was almost too hot—that is, just perfect. We all made little sounds of pleasure as we settled into it, and I almost forgot I was around vampires and just felt like I was around people who were on the same page as me. Astryiah slid close to Daciana, and they murmured unintelligibly over the water sounds. Here and there I caught the names of am'r who'd been at the Very Important Conclave just now, especially "Mehmet," but I didn't try too hard to make out what they were saying because the water was luxuriously warm, and it was turning my body and brain into melty butter. I watched them talking, and they looked like pre-Raphaelite sirens in a living painting. Both had wavy hair: one a dark chocolate, which was now essentially a warm, glistening darkness, and the other's honey-colored hair, now that it was wet, a darker honey than her gilded skin.

Since I had time to think, my thoughts went back to am'r sexuality. Aside from knowing that Sandu was into me, and from being introduced to Ebon and Cyrus as a couple, I had no way of figuring out if this world I'd joined was very queer, or very straight, or what. Every am'r was huffing me with equal enthusiasm. And I knew from Sandu that for the am'r, the act of blood-drinking was intrinsically tied to sex. So was everyone all just pansexual once they became am'r, no matter what their preferences in kee life had been? That would make at least one way that I would fit in easily, although I had to admit that the gal I'd dated in college had been in no way like these am'r women. Men, well, honestly am'r men didn't seem that dramatically different from kee men. That thought made me grin down into the steaming water in front of me.

After a while, I was barely capable of holding myself up in a sitting position. My body just wanted to float in the mineral-thick water. The gals were still gossiping or plotting world domination or whatever in velvet-accented whispers and ignoring me, so I gave in, let my head fall back, and floated, watching the play of light on the rough ceiling and variously-sized stalactites in almost a dream state.

Indeed, maybe I even nodded off because what seemed like the next moment, they were both on either side of me and far too far inside my personal comfort zone. They were silently staring at me with hunger naked on their faces, their mouths open slightly, showing a bit of fang. I splashed upright in ungainly surprise and burgeoning terror.

"Hush, *chamuda*, we will not bite you." Astryiah put out a hand to my arm to calm my clumsy movements, but her touch, while it froze me, did not soothe me in any way. She left her hand there regardless of my living rigor mortis, and after a while, as she talked, she absent-mindedly stroked her fingers up and down.

"*Nu, nu*, do not worry, Noosh," Daciana added. I looked back and forth between their earnest but not particularly comforting faces. They were flushed. Which, to be fair, could be from the hot water, but their eyes were glittering and they looked aroused.

I'd probably reverted to my deer-in-headlights look, which was almost certainly the wrong look to wear around predators.

My mind now racing, I realized I'd made the mistake of relaxing around them because they were *girls*, fellow females. Yet another of those "could be your last" mistakes I'd recently been exploring. *They are fucking vampires*, I belatedly admonished myself. Just because they are women doesn't mean they can't and won't tear your carotid artery out and suck on it like a Pixy Stix.

Astryiah was still stroking me. "You are the most delicious thing I have smelt in a long time. Vlad's 'vhoon-anghyaa'—that's bloodline, in our language—mixed with yours is a powerful...mmmmm...I should like a better word than 'aphrodisiac,' but I'm afraid that's what it *is*, to us. You cannot blame Daciana and me for enjoying an innocent lungful of you. We both promise not to go any further. Please?"

Her voice was entreating and seemed sincere. Or maybe she'd zapped me with vampire mesmerism, and everything she said would sound reasonable and valid. What should a rabbit say to the two foxes eyeing it?

"Just don't bite me, not even a little," I choked out. "It'd make me feel like I'd cheated on Sandu. Or something." They took this as permission to slide closer to me, and their arms slipped around me in the water, around my back, encouraging my legs up so I was floating again. I closed my eyes and tried not to shudder. Uneasiness flared and flickered in my mind, along with such thoughts as *How do I keep ending up in situations like this?* and *I need to find out if am'r can smell fear!* After a while, the heat and the sensuality of the situation combined to melt my tension, and I just floated there, feeling their bodies pressed to mine, their fingers intertwined with mine, listening to their deep, slow, meditative inhalations. Their faces were close, moving around in the area of my neck and shoulders. No one spoke. It was the most intimate non-sex I'd ever had.

They were truly reveling in my essence, totally focused on me. How often in life did one experience that? Well, in my limited experience, only with vampires. But it seemed they didn't even need to be actively having sex with you to make you feel this way. It was heady. I didn't want it to stop, but I was afraid of what would happen if it went on. Not in the "fear of something bad" way, but in the "fear of doing something that feels good at the time, but that you know is wrong."

After an immeasurable stretch of time, Astryiah sighed—a profoundly regretful sound—and pulled a little bit away from me. A few seconds went by and Daciana did the same. Like a child forced to leave a favorite toy. Or dessert. A few more seconds and I belatedly realized it was all over, opened my eyes, and looked from one to the other.

"We are close now, *chamuda*. We may not have vhoon-shared—" and here Astryiah gave another lamentful sigh, "but you have given us a gift, nonetheless. Your trust is as beautiful as the rest of you." Daciana was nodding in solemn agreement. "We were your protectors for Vlad's sake before. Now, we are your friends, your allies, for your own sake.

"We return now. We have skipped the trivial tittle-tattle and intriguing, but there are a few with whom I *do* need to speak, and Daciana should be visibly supporting Vlad—a show of numbers, as it were. But you—I do not know if Vlad wants you back in the Great Hall for this next part. I will take you to his rooms, and let him know you are safely there. He can decide what he wishes from there."

I genuinely wanted to get back to the relative safety of Sandu's side, but Astryiah was impossible to argue with. She simply ceased to perceive me as she pulled on her clothing. Neither am'r seemed bothered by damp clothes or by their still-wet hair. Did am'r drip-dry better than the rest of us? My curls were going to need proper attention imminently, but I was more bothered about forcing my wet limbs into now-clingy sleeves and pant-legs.

We returned by hallways that seemed familiar enough—except that all stone corridors look more or less like other stone corridors. There were no pictures or signs to help guide the way.

Of all the ways in which I was in over my head, why was it not being able to find my way around the lair that bothered me the most?

Daciana peeled off shortly after we left the onsen with a smile to me and a meaningful nod to Astryiah. After more obscure turnings, I was back at Sandu's door.

Astryiah turned before she left. "It was well you trusted us," she told me, with a sober mien. "But do not *trust* others in the same way. It would not be good for you." I had about a million replies to that, ranging from "Well, DUH!" to some really sarcastic zingers, all trying to rush out of my mouth, but for once, I had the good sense not to say any of them. I just nodded, possibly a bit curtly, because her assumption of my utter naïveté left my ego rubbed raw and smarting. And then she was gone, and I was alone in Sandu's suite.

I wandered around the rooms. Too many things to think about. Would Sandu think I'd cheated on him? I mean, we'd had this really intense naked thing, but, hey, we were in the baths, and they only sniffed me! "Only sniffed me." Was this my new normal? Splashing around in hot springs in vampire-gnawed caves with lesbian (or at least bisexual) creatures of the night who had an overwhelming desire to slurp my blood as soon as look at—or, rather—sniff me? It was all just too weird.

Anyway, how could I even know what was considered cheating in a patar/frithaputhra relationship? It's not like Sandu actually ever told me anything I needed to know before I was literally in hot water, so fuck him if he didn't like what I'd done! He could damn well tell me the rules before getting pissed at me for breaking them!

I was flushed and sweating with anger, not pacing so much as stomping around the medieval-chic rooms. I passed my purse and grabbed it, found a packet of tissues, and dabbed the sweat from my face. And did a double-take. There was the lightest diluted red on the tissue. I was now literally sweating blood. *Fucking great.*

I resumed stomping. I didn't think I'd had this many mood swings in the worst of my teen years, but then my teen years hadn't seen half as many changes as I was going through now.

The next target of my anger was—well, it was still Sandu. How could he just leave me here to go through this all alone? Wait, what if he didn't even know I was here?

Astryiah might be older and more powerful than I could imagine, but for that very reason, her concerns might be on a totally different level than updating Sandu on where she parked his girlfriend. She might have stopped for a profound gossip session with some other ancient and powerful being and not have even seen Sandu yet.

He might even now be wondering where I was and worrying.

And what if he needed me? Three hours were definitely up by now: the big dramatic Convocation of Doom was almost certainly back in session. Both Sandu and Bagamil had stressed my importance to them. I didn't get why I was important, really, but what if Sandu *needed me* right now, and I was off sulking in the bedroom, pouting in am'r-nafsh angst?

I could find my way back to the Rave Cave by now, surely. My fears of not knowing my way around were obviously just projections of my fears about the uncertainty of my situation. I was positive that I just went down the hall to the right, and then two lefts, and there were the first stairs and then it was all very easy from there.

OK. Maybe not quite so easy.

I felt really good about the first four turns and a staircase or two. It felt like I was a Big Girl Am'r-nafsh who could *totally* find her way around a vampire warren. Then I got uncertain, and I made some bad guesses. I'd tried to go back and correct them...and then I'd realized I was completely, *perfectly* lost.

I leaned on a wall and tried not to cry. That ended with the thought: *I've just totally failed.* I slid lifelessly down the wall, and ended up in what was as close to fetal position as you could get while still sitting upright and having a *thorough* cry.

Blood-tinged tears, which I discovered as I tried to wipe them on my sleeve. *Of course.*

My glorious cry-out eventually wound down. I mean, I was as scared and as confused and as lost as a person could hope to be, but I'd also been living my wildest fantasies and having glorious sex (and whatever that literally and figuratively steamy session in the onsen was) at regular intervals. Even with all the reasonable frustration and distress, I could only keep my self-indulgence up for so long.

My tears *did* show up on the knit gray top I was wearing. I had a real appreciation for why am'r might want to wear black all the time. I mean, with all the blood that got shed, wearing clothes on which bloodstains did not show was a fine plan when getting dressed in the morning. Or rather, evening.

My equanimity had returned, but how was I going to find my way to either the great hall or back to Sandu's suite?

Now that I was thinking about it more clearly, I realized *he* probably could find me—once he realized I was lost—by sniffing me out like a bloodhound.

I'd probably left a distinctive scent-trail; what with being am'r-nafsh-delicious and all, and he'd be hyper-attuned to it.

Of course, the next immediate idea was a realization that if Sandu could sniff me out, probably *all* the am'r could follow me as easily as if I were dropping breadcrumbs along behind me. (Would that I had been, because then even I could follow my own path.) The thought that any am'r who wanted to follow me could—and could probably also tell I was *alone*—was a thought I abruptly started worrying about.

When you were lost, the accepted wisdom was to stay put until someone came to find you, right?

But I wasn't sure I could handle the utter humiliation of Sandu having to scent-hound me because I was incapable of remembering how to get from Point A to Point B. Also, there was the all too real threat of an am'r less trustworthy than Astryiah or Daciana coming across me in this random stretch of hallway.

How far was I from the Rave Cave? I could be right next to it, or I could be on entirely the other side of the vampire warren by now.

I was still engaged in internal debate—i.e., too terrified to make a damn decision—when I heard footsteps coming down the hall to the right. They were am'r-soft footsteps, which meant I more sensed someone was coming than heard them, but it gave me time to stand and look as nonchalant as possible, hopefully like I'd *not* been a crying mess of girl just a moment ago.

It was Mehmet. *Well, fuck.* I composed myself. *He* didn't need to compose himself, he just glided over. "Anushka, *sevgili*! How *lucky* to run across you here! I wished to speak to you, but despaired of a moment alone with you, as I know how busy my friend Vlad is keeping you with the tedious social duties of being his consort."

I nearly laughed because most recently, my "tedious social duties" had consisted of nearly having a lesbian threesome in a hot spring, which, despite being more than a little nerve-wracking, could not in any way be categorized as *tedious*. But I didn't want to laugh around Sultan Schmuck because he might take it as evidence of pleasure in his company, so I just inclined my head and said, "Well, I *am* in a hurry to rejoin Vlad."

"Ahhh." He sighed. And glided closer. I tried to move as smoothly away. "My female frithaputhraish I do not send running about to do my errands, always in a busy hurry. I give them respect and honor them in luxury, with servants and other attendants to do their will. But perhaps as a modern American woman, you are unused to such attention and generosity in your partner?"

I wouldn't have known where to begin to respond, but he flowed on, obviously not in the slightest bit worried about my busy schedule or my clear desire to be elsewhere. "It saddens me to see such a special woman as yourself not appreciated and pampered as she ought to be. But my concern is much deeper. I fear my friend Vlad has perhaps not told always told you the truth, or not all of the truth, all the time? Did I not observe such a thing last night? You were quite dismayed when he announced you to us all, and rightly so!

"Obviously, a woman such as you, using your feminine perception and natural instincts, must surely feel how wrong it is to endanger your precious self so recklessly. I wonder at my old friend, that he would heedlessly risk such a jewel in the company of thieves, as many of our number could be named, I am sorry to say. Yes, I am offended on *your* behalf, *sevgili*, and I do not wonder at your own wounded feelings. No, no—no need to protest, no need to say a word. I understand all!

"I am afraid there is more which my dear old friend—I say *friend* despite his failures in this and other matters—there is *more* he has not disclosed to you, and of a darker and more dangerous nature. I know your immediate safety may be compromised, and yes, you are right, of course, but I must ask you to consider how well you *know* Kazıklı bey and know his history? Both his history with you—and how often *has* he failed you, I wonder?—and his history as Vlad Drăculea, stretching back through many dark years?

"Come, I would not be so forward with you if I was not deeply afraid for your *safety*, for your very *life!* I know you know in your soul you have been treated shamefully—*villainously*, I would say, if Vlad was not such a dear old friend! But don't just listen to my words. Who am *I*, after all, whom you have just met? Speak to others. Ask them the questions in your heart. Ask them about the man who has tied you to him in such an indecent hurry. But hurry, *sevgili*; danger is all around you! Of course, of course, I have kept you too long, I am sure, and my *old friend* is not one whom it is good to anger, as so many of us have learned to our cost.

"*Sevgili kızım*, come speak to me whenever you want true answers. My door is always open to you. Any of my men will lead you to me. I offer you a safe haven in any storm. Remember this: if you need me, I am here!" With that, he slid away down the corridor, leaving me speechless and dazzled by his free-flowing bullshit.

I started walking in sheer bemusement, not choosing a direction, my feet just going on autopilot. Where the *hell* did he get off, puffing His Nosy Self up, and worse, implying all that shit about Sandu? I mean, all his fancy words about "pampering" me probably meant he'd stash me away in a harem, given that he had literally had a harem when he was kee and apparently still did. Respect? He already had invaded my space, made assumptions which nauseated me, and just generally insulted my intelligence.

Obviously, Sandu had his odd notions, like taking charge of my wardrobe. But he'd always chosen stylish and sexy—and surprisingly comfortable—clothes, pieces I'd have chosen for myself if I'd ever have had the budget.

On the other hand, he *did* make some valid points about Sandu, points which I couldn't deny and needed to consider. Sandu had explained more than once that he came from a time I couldn't understand, and he'd said he'd changed over the centuries. But in the recent past—well, since I'd known him—he'd certainly demonstrated some serious failures to communicate.

I needed to make a list of things I needed to know and demand the answers without digression, no matter how interesting or distracting.

I had asked him stuff and he'd always seemed like he was giving me answers, but I kept being caught short on matters I could and should have known at least a little bit about. He didn't do well with volunteering stuff before I needed it, either.

That would have to change. Sandu wasn't actively lying to me. Of course not. But...if he was, how would I know?

And Mehmet wasn't the first am'r to warn me that I didn't know enough and was in more danger than I understood.

My wildly vacillating thoughts and the unfamiliar corridors I wandered were equally confusing, and that increased the intensity of each. I stopped and looked around. I hadn't miraculously walked right to the big front doors or even the back entrance of the Rave Cave, although I had to admit I'd been hoping just the teensiest bit I might do just that. I was simply *somewhere* in who-knew-how-many miles of vampire-hewn underground passages.

I could be across the border of Romania by now and never even know it. And speaking of "who knew," what was going on back at the big dramatic council session? Had they chosen who'd take the Ring to Mordor yet?

Damn, I was getting slap-happy now, along with figuratively and literally getting nowhere. My whole self was jangling with distress and I did not know what to do. Maybe the best thing really was to just sit down and wait for Sandu to come to my rescue.

That thought was humiliating enough that I started walking again, taking a random left because I felt the Rave Cave was *definitely* in that direction.

I heard—or felt, or something—the barest hint of someone coming towards me, out of sight because the corridor curved ahead of me. Consternation flooded me. While it couldn't get much worse than His Nosiness Mehmet, and I'd bumped into him already, there was still an all-too-high percentage of am'r I did not wish to meet while lost in a lonely passageway.

I looked around, belatedly desperate for a hiding place. There were no nearby right or left turns to take, nor an alcove to hide in.

Alcoves were among those missing useful landmarks that might help a person find her way through miles and miles of tunnels, dammit. But, nope, couldn't have those!

Old-fashioned black robes came into view, and I made out Neplach's face. I felt my distress melt. My only reason to trust him was Sandu's and Bagamil's obvious like and trust of him, but my gut feeling was that Neplach was a good guy, or at least someone who wasn't out to devour or otherwise do something bad to me. By this point, that was good enough.

"Anushka! Glad am I to find you. Sandu has been getting more and more unquiet about your continuing absence. We who know him feel it, even though he is well-schooled in hiding emotion. Still, it began to trouble me as well, and I came away to see if I could find you. Why are you," Neplach indicated the corridor with eyes and hands, *"here?"* He looked at me with all-too-shrewd eyes and I felt myself squirm like a naughty schoolgirl who'd been caught smoking cigarettes. Did he think I was meeting someone for an assignation? Or running away? From the beginning, I'd felt respect for Neplach, and I wanted him to respect me as much as an aojysht *could* respect the rawest am'r-nafsh.

So I told him the truth. "I have to admit that I'm a bit lost, sir." I could call Bagamil by his name—or "Mister Sunshine," in my head—but Neplach was not the sort with whom I felt I could be on a first-name basis. "I was trying to get to the Rave—errr—Great Hall, but I couldn't find it." So much for gaining his respect.

He produced the very first smile I'd seen on his face. So far, his expression had been set in a coolly detached, fixed reserve. He wasn't the youngest-looking am'r, but I realized that when he smiled, he looked to be maybe in his thirties. It was when he wore his impassive, emotionless, not-so-much-cold-as-closed expression that it became obvious he was an aojysht. Or showed me what aojyshtaish *should be*, at any rate. "*Moje dcera*, you have my sympathies. You are in a hard situation right now, and everything must seem like it is *too* hard, like it is stacking hard-upon-hard. We shall not say 'lost,' but say 'exploring.' No, 'reconnoitering.' Is it the better word?"

"Yes, sir. Yes, it's much better. 'Reconnoitering,' that's it. Thank you, sir!" I was touched and close to tears—my emotions were too fucking close to the surface these days—that this imposing elder with plenty of concerns of his own would take the time to show compassion about my lil' sense of pride.

Neplach indicated the way to go. I tried not to wince, as it was the direction I had been walking away from when he found me. I followed him and he continued, "It *does* take some time to learn this place. You will become used to having time. It is one of the significant things about becoming am'r: you have the time to learn patience. Although," he scowled, which was a daunting expression on him, "your patar is perhaps not the best am'r to teach you. He seems never to have learnt it himself." He paused, then added, "If you ever wish to talk, you may come to me. I would be pleased to be of assistance to you. However, you also have Bagamil as a teacher and guide. You could not ask a better exemplar, thus you will not also need my meager knowledge."

"Oh, *no*! I would be honored to learn from you! Please, there's so much I need to learn, and I always feel lost—not just in the hallways, but in understanding—now that I am here." In this am'r world, I meant.

"Well. Then it shall be so," was all he said, but I could tell he was pleased. I was pleased too because not only did I now have an additional resource for how to live the life vampiric, but also because Neplach seemed to like me. To me, that felt like a pretty big deal.

We went back. We went right. We went left. We went down. We went up. Not in that order, but don't ask me what order it was because I certainly couldn't remember. In a surprisingly short time, we were passing through the back door of the Rave Cave. "Look as if we have been in serious discussion," Neplach said in such a soft voice I wondered whether I'd heard him right. But I had no time to question, so I turned my head to him and said, in normal speaking tones, which was pretty much shouting to a roomful of am'r, "Yes, I think so, too."

"Your concurrence pleases me. It has been beneficial speaking with you, Anushka, frithaputhra of Țepeș. Thank you for your time."

"Oh, no problem, sir! It was an honor for me to...um...be of assistance to you."

"And think about what I have said. Remember it."

"I promise I will, sir. Thank you." I put as much emphasis on my thanks as I could without making it sound like I was thanking him for rescuing me from a deserted hallway and other fates worse than death.

He escorted me over to Sandu, who did not in any way externally exhibit having been worried about me. He merely smiled warmly, as if I'd only been away for a moment. Neplach inclined his head and said, "Thank you for allowing me time with your frithaputhra, Drăculea. She has imparted much to me about this fascinating 'information science' and I look forward to seeing our archives put in place. Indeed, I hope you will call upon me for any aid I can provide? And I may have some documents for Anushka to...is it 'scan?'" He turned to me, and I *swear* there was a hint of a naughty twinkle in his dark eyes.

"Yes, you *know* it's 'scanning,' sir," I tossed back playfully, giddy with relief at being in Sandu's presence again. I turned to him. "He understands it all, Sandu. He's as tech-savvy as anyone, so don't let him pretend he doesn't get all this strange new lingo."

Sandu slid his arm around me, which nearly had me in tears of relief. I leaned against him gratefully. "Ah, no, *draga mea*, I have too much respect for Neplach's knowledge to believe he does not understand everything of which he speaks. And does *not* speak. He is a man of deep understanding, and I owe much of my own to him. Thank you, *opat*." He reached out his hand, and Neplach took it, and I, being closest to them, saw them communicate by look and touch alone.

Neplach took both my hands in his and pressed them avuncularly. I wanted to give him a hug, but one just didn't do that sort of thing with Neplach. His barrier of distance and dignity was back up in force, and it repelled indecorous gestures like hugs.

After Neplach was out of sight in the crowd, I realized I'd been leaning on him more than I knew. I abruptly felt less safe, and I realized in my time away from Sandu, some of my unthinking faith and trust in him had been shaken. I'd wanted nothing more than to be back at his side...but now that I was, I wasn't sure I *did* want to be here after all.

Maybe I should have stayed in the damn suite. *His* suite, of course—I had nothing of my own here. Everything was his, including me. Would I trade all the sex and excitement and travel and being Super-Librarian, Savior of the Universe, for being my own person again, in my own home, where there was no one around who wanted anything from me—particularly not chugging all the blood out of my body?

There was a crabby part of me, which possibly overlapped with the piss-your-pants scared part of me, that said: Yes, yes, yes! Get out of here, find the airport, and get back to Centerville. Get your ass out of being in over your head!

While I was working through this, another am'r had come up to Sandu, who casually kept his arm around me while they talked. I am pretty sure I was introduced to said am'r and responded in a reasonable manner, but the second it was over, I could remember not one part of the interaction.

"Noosh," Sandu said, *sotto voce* even for an am'r, "did anything happen to you? I smell your tears, and I see them on your shirt. Are you well?" I didn't know how to respond. All the doubts I'd ever had about Sandu crowded into my mind. I could see him standing there, handsome as hell, his wavy black hair loose around the face I thought I'd grown to love. But did I know him? I mean, beyond what he liked during sex, did I truly know him?

And if I didn't know him, could I love him? And could I trust him?

I could probably trust him to take care of me because he'd made it plain that an am'r-nafsh was a valuable thing...but could I trust him to tell me the truth? Or tell me anything in a timely manner? Doubt swirled around in my head. I pulled away from him.

"What. Is. Wrong?" Sandu subvocalized at me out of the corner of his mouth, his eyes traveling around the rest of the room, watching people. I didn't know how to answer him. I had willingly given him all my trust when he first bit me, and when he'd shared blood with me the critical third time, and again when he'd told me to pack a bag and run off with him, and yet again when he'd brought me into an underground vampire warren. But now, my trust felt broken.

But why? Because of the stuff his immortal enemy had said about him?

That was neither information nor advice I could trust. But it was more than that. He had *earned* my distrust more than my trust by not telling me things I needed to know, or only telling me after I'd needed to know—or only five seconds before, which was almost as bad. He had pressured me. He had manipulated me by insisting I make choices when my ability to think was compromised by sex hormones and having drunk a vampire's intoxicating blood. A cold emptiness flowed through me, replacing my love and lust for him with stiff wariness. I could see him standing there, but it was like a filter was over my sight, removing all colors in the range of love.

"I don't...feel well," I said. A not-dishonest, if not an accurate explanation. But then, I'd learned how to do that from him. "I want to go back to the suite, please."

"Voivode?" It was Haralamb, dressed in leathers like he was in an am'r motorcycle club. "You are needed. A matter has arisen."

Sandu looked at me and I could see emotion roiling in his eyes, but his face was blank, and anyway, I had my new filter on. I looked blankly back at him.

"Take her to my rooms," he told Haralamb. "See her safely there, and return immediately."

Haralamb escorted me sullenly from the Rave Cave via the back door. I could tell that if he missed out on any action because of me, I'd never be forgiven. Right, left, stairs, blah, blah, and we were at the door with the twice-dead dragon on it. Had he been strangled with his own tail, or had carving a cross down the length of the poor beast done the job? Haralamb opened the door, glared me into the room, and slammed the door shut. If he'd not been am'r, he'd have stomped loudly down the hall. As it was, he stomped off silently.

Haralamb's pissiness had rubbed off. Now I felt pissy too, as well as numb and confused. I stomped as loudly as a still-living creature could around the rooms, glaring at everything, even the tempting piles of books.

Which, let's face it, had thus far been used only to help seduce me. Diamonds for some gals, ancient and obscure books for me.

I wondered what was happening down there. Haralamb clearly thought shit was about to go down. Should I have been at Vlad's side for this—or maybe fighting back-to-back? I mean, this was obviously the point in the movie when I discovered my hidden vampire-slaying skills and did a fabulously choreographed fight scene to a throbbing beat. Was I going to be missing all that, sulking here in the bedroom? But I didn't *want* to be fighting back-to-back right now. I wanted to be talking to Sandu *tête-à-tête*, and he wasn't going to have time for such things until his Vampire: The Gathering LARP in the Rave Cave was over. It wasn't about me, anyway. It was about obscure am'r politics, which had been going on since well before I was born. And no one, especially not Sandu, had bothered to bring me up to date on any of it.

Not my monkeys, not my circus. I can have a nap.

But first, a visit to that nasty medieval toilet. At least I could get there and back without getting humiliatingly lost.

On my return, a shadow detached itself from the wall and became a female am'r in a black robe and headscarf. They made her movements bat-like, in that way am'r have of living up to their stereotypes. The scarf made her face more striking, emphasizing her dramatically peaked eyebrows and gray eyes—strangely like the ones which I saw when I looked in the mirror, only even more almond-shaped—and making them pop dramatically from her soft brown skin. "Annooshkhaa," she said, the syllables rolling off her tongue strangely. It took a moment for me to realize it was my name.

"Uh, yes? Who are you?"

"Call me Shaqîqah," she said sibilantly, smiling as if she had made a joke. If joke it was, then it was—of course—lost on me.

"OK, Shah-KEE-kah," I tried to pronounce her name right. "Nice to meet you. The Rave—I mean, the Great Hall—is that direction. I'm pretty sure. Maybe we'll get a chance to talk there." I assumed the attitude of a person who was in a hurry to get where I was going. I was getting a not-great vibe off of her, and I wanted someone else:

Bagamil, Neplach, Astryiah—even Sandu—to be nearby before I had to spend any time interacting with her.

"Anushka, you will wish to hear what I have to say. There are things, many things, you have not been told by Kazıklı bey, whom you call—what is it? Sandu? Hah! He has as good as lied to you by omitting so much essential information."

Well, *that* had my attention. She wasn't the first to tell me about Sandu's lies of omission. Even Bagamil was unimpressed with his frithaputhra in that regard, and it was precisely what I was so annoyed about right now. "How do *you* know what he has and has not told me?" I asked her, still suspicious but unable to pass up a chance to find out more.

"You know you are mated to him for the rest of your life? As his special swill? He will not let you leave him, and if somehow you did, you would not be safe from any...from *all* am'r, who would use you to get to him, and who would devour you for your irresistible blood. You know this?"

"I know all that. I'm still getting used to it."

"Did he tell you before he irrevocably changed you?"

"Yes. Sorta. Well, he told me I would become am'r-nafsh, but he didn't explain fully what it meant." Why was I telling her all this?

"Did he tell you that am'r-nafsh are never revealed to full am'r? That those of your kind are kept safe, guarded. Not brought to a dangerously large gathering of our kind?"

"Well, not until we got here. Things have been a bit rushed."

"And did he tell you that you can never rejoin the kee world? Or such facts as now you can never bear a child?"

"Huh? Wait, what?"

"He could not sire one on you, of course. But if you could leave him—if he let you—and you made your life back among the kee, your body has been changed too far. You are not a functioning woman anymore. You are not a fully living being. You can never go back, even if he would let you. Even if he had not made it too dangerous for you to even attempt, with all the enemies you now have."

Well, *that* was a lot to process. I wasn't sure I'd ever wanted to have kids, but it was not one of the permanent changes he'd listed in the hot tub. In fact, he'd said he wasn't sure what would happen if I wanted to go back to trying to live a normal life, which would have been a prime moment to bring up that going back to a normal life wasn't actually an option. Little details like those might have given me more pause and possibly kept me from just saying, "Take me now, big boy!"

I know no one gets anywhere with what-ifs, but a person *does* have to be able to look back and reevaluate decisions. What if Sandu had committed the sin of omission—combined with criminal distraction—past a place where I could forgive him? Bagamil must be able to do some kind of am'r divorce proceedings or something? Sandu *had* said most am'r did not stay forever in their intimate couple relationships. Or maybe Bagamil might know if there was some way to go back to my old life. There was no guarantee either Sandu or this bat-like stranger was telling me the full truth. And, even if there was no way to go back, maybe I could shop around for a new am'r—um, *companion*—who would place more value on things like truthfulness and telling your partner all the stuff they need to know in a timely manner. It certainly seemed like there would be no lack of willing am'r to partner up with me.

I didn't know what to think about any of this. Shaqîqah watched my face as I tried to order my thoughts. My gut was telling me she was not someone I'd ever be close friends with, but plenty of the am'r gave me uncomfy vibes.

I needed to go back to Sandu's rooms and have my nap, after all. It would clear my head a bit, and at least help me get started ordering my questions for when Sandu had finished with the am'r summit meeting. I could even ask—*insist*—to speak with Bagamil, and maybe Neplach, and get the answers I needed from someone who seemed more responsible and trustworthy.

I was just opening my mouth to thank Shaqîqah for her thought-provoking information and to excuse myself from our hallway conversation when she moved faster than I could see. Her hand blurred up and then down hard against my neck, where I felt a sharp *pinch*. "Owww! Hey!" I rubbed my neck and backed away from her. "What the fuck? I'm going to..."

Neither Shaqîqah nor I found out what I was going to do, because darkness swam up over my vision, along with a nausea-vertigo combination that encompassed my entire being. And I was gone.

Chapter Seventeen

At some point came the nightmares. My blood was on fire. It burned through me and left me a charred wreck. My blood was filled with broken glass. It sliced through every artery and vein and capillary and arteriole and venule. My blood was a black nothingness. It ate through me with fangs of pitiless obliteration and left an aching hole where once I had been.

But I ached, so I existed. I hurt, therefore I am. The unfunny joke ran through my brain, and I felt too shitty to laugh.

I heard a language I didn't know being spoken around me. It was a mushy flow of "sh" and soft "juh" but also unexpected hard syllables. I felt like I should recognize it and almost like I should be able to understand it, but it flowed and thumped around me, and I floated helplessly in it.

I cracked aching eyelids open. I couldn't see. *I can't see!* But I realized the air I breathed was close and stale, so there must be something over my head. This was not a comfortable realization, although it was better than blindness. Probably.

I realized I recognized Mehmet's voice, and that bitch Shaqîqah. Shit, piss, and damnation—I'd been kidnapped. Am'r-nafsh-napped. It did not bode well for my future, which I assumed now looked more or less like "Be a tasty snack for some quantity of vampires, immediately or soonish: TBD. Die in process, certainly unpleasantly."

It's funny, I mused in the darkness of my sack, imminent death sure puts a whole new perspective on things. Sandu seemed entirely forgivable at this moment. Sure, he'd been imperfect at telling me the things I needed to know, but life had been moving pretty fast, and it *was* hard to talk with your mouth full, as it had often been when we were alone together. Oh, how I wished to be alone with Sandu now. Or in a room full of people along with Sandu. Just *not* with the Sultan Schmuck and the nasty Bat-Bitch!

I wondered if I'd be dying shortly because they were getting back at Sandu for some ages-old drama, or if it was just for my piquant bouquet. A gal likes to be wanted for her own qualities. Would I get to say any last words? I'd at least probably get a final sight since they probably wouldn't drink my blood with this bag rucked around my neck, what with necks being the canonically popular spot for a vampire to enjoy a nip.

"She is awake," Shaqîqah said. How did captors always seem to know this? Was it breathing patterns? A special bond with their captive? What?

The sack was tugged roughly off my face by Bat-Bitch. I was sprawled on the floor. Mehmet stood in front of me and offered his hands to help me to my feet. I refused his help and forced my body upward on its own, stifling moans and gasps as the last bits of fire, glass, and darkness shot through my nerve endings, making passing out again seem all too possible. My legs hardly got me up and, once I was standing, I realized they were not capable of keeping me up. I looked around in a hurry and saw a place to the left where I could sit, a bench built out from the wall and covered in carpet. I managed to make it over there and collapse gracelessly onto it. Shaqîqah snorted. I bit back everything I desired to say to her.

Not inciting vampires to kill you is the better part of valor.

Sultan Schmuck was still standing with his hands outstretched to me. "*Sevgili*, my apologies for your treatment on the way to being with us. It was felt you would not come on your own and we needed you to join us without delay."

"Join you?"

"*Peki*...let us start over. Even from the introductions. Do not think of me as Mehmet. It is a name I left behind when I realized what I am become. *Merhaba, benim adım Iblis*. That is, 'Hello, my name is Iblis.' My sister here is the Qarînah. And you...we cannot call you such an uncouth name as

'Noosh,' but in my native tongue '*naz*' means 'coy.' I rename you Naz *hanım*, Lady Naz, and you will become jinn like us after you transit from being mere mortal clay to the eternal smokeless fire." As he said this, he'd grabbed my hands with both of his and leaned in and kissed me ceremonially on both cheeks. It was a fast movement, but I still had time to freeze in terror, thinking he was going for my neck *already*. But he did not. He let go of my hands and smiled delightedly down at me.

I just looked at him. What do you say when you discover your abductor is batshit crazy? Not just Sultan Schmuck but *Sultan Psycho*. "Back away slowly" was the best advice I could think of, but I had a stone wall to my back, and as I looked around helplessly, I realized I was in a dungeon. Specifically, three walls were stone, one was metal bars. Sultan Psycho saw me looking. "Apologies for the temporary lodging, *sevgili*, but we must keep you safe. Our enemies will be searching for you."

I was still floored. My tendency in uncertain situations is to babble, and seldom before had I ever been at a loss for words. However, this was such an unexpected turn of events—not that I understood how events had turned—that it seemed not-unreasonable I should have a whole new type of response to them. I just looked mutely at the Vampire Formerly Known As Mehmet.

He was uncomfortable with my staring silence. "We have much to discuss, Naz hanım, and there is much for me to teach you." Bat-Bitch snorted again, and Sultan Psycho gave her a sharp glance. "You may leave us. I am sure you thirst. Take care of your needs. And see to the others. Let them know to be on guard."

After a muttered, "*Hader, ya Sultan*," Bat-Bitch swished out, obviously in a temper. Good riddance. At least this left me with only one insane vampire to keep an eye on.

Not that I could handle even one if it came down to it, but at least I only had to try to look in one direction at a time.

Said insane vampire sat down beside me on the carpet-covered bench and I immediately started trying to inch away as unnoticeably as I could.

"Yes, there is much to teach you, *sevgili kızım*. What my old friend Kazıklı bey and his patar, whom we call the *Gavur*, have told you are *lies*. We are not am'r, but '*cinler*,' or as you might say, jinn. Do not be surprised!

"I have prayed and studied for many years, and it has been revealed to me that we are indeed *other*, but we are *not* godless, forsaken beings. There is a place for us under Allah, who created all. We fit in an order, not as some revenant of mankind, but of a different plane, with more powers than the beings of inferior clay. It is good you are but newly brought to the am'r world. You do not need to unlearn too many lies but can begin with a true understanding, something that eludes not only most am'r, but also the ignorant kee, who cannot begin to guess at these hidden truths. You will join the jinn I have personally created, who have known no other way but the truth. You come at the time of revelation and revolution when a world of lies is torn aside. We can begin anew, with a rightful leader who shall lead us out of shadow and shame into the light of Allah, with a scorching wind!"

I could guess who this "rightful leader" was. He was the nutjob gesticulating frenetically by my side. Everything back at the underground Castle Dracula abruptly seemed reasonable and homey. All the am'r stuff that had seemed overwhelmingly alien was, in the face of these rantings, perfectly rational and practically *ordinary*. "Iblis" here had rewritten the entire Islamic faith to suit his particular flavor of narcissistic insanity. Sandu, even in his most bloodiest Vlad history, couldn't top *that*.

I realized that he had asked me a question and was waiting for an answer, but I had no idea what either of those things might be. "I...I'm sorry. I'm dizzy and weak. I think I need bl—food." I'd been all too close to saying I needed blood, but since the only blood I wanted was Sandu's, it was vital to ask for another sort of sustenance.

"Of course!" he cried, actually slapping his forehead. "You are still of clay, and clay must have clay!" He went and shouted at the door to my cell. Another am'r showed up, and they said things in the mushy language, which I was figuring was probably Turkish. Mehmet's jinn were definitely polyglot, as they all spoke what was probably Arabic just as frequently, and then English as well. It would be nicer to be impressed by the skills of my allies than my abductors. The other am'r went away. Sultan Psycho turned to me. "Naz hanım, I must leave you for a while. I will return and speak with you more after you have rested and fed. There is much to teach you!" He was utterly thrilled by all of this. Dismay was the main emotion I could muster.

I must have fallen asleep waiting for the food. It was there on a tray when I woke: a cold vegetable dish made with beans and chard, a still-slightly-warm dish of what seemed to be cornmeal with cheese, and tea in a funny two-pot system I wasn't sure I figured out correctly. There was a pot on top with tea leaves in, and a pot on the bottom with hot water. I poured the water from the bottom into the top and let it steep, then drank it from a little glass teacup. I ate and drank voraciously, and it seemed to knock the last of the drugs out of my system. Without thinking, I checked my pockets, but my phone was not in them. Of course not. I'd left it on the charger back in Sandu's room. Undoubtedly, even if I had not left it behind, they would have taken it. I tried to use my now-undrugged brain to come up with a magical solution to being locked in a cage by evil vampires who thought they were genies. Vampires who think they are genies! How is this my life? For fuck's sake!

No magical solutions came to me. I waited around for something to happen, but nothing did, so I rolled a bit of carpet into a pillow and went back to sleep on my stone bench.

When I awoke, the dirty dishes had been removed. Disposable hand wipes and a strange bucket had been left in its place. It had a lid. When I lifted it, there was another lid underneath, with a hole in the center. I eventually realized it was a seat and the bucket was my...toilet.

Just kill me now. Even the medieval jakes were better than this.

But I used it, terrified someone who *no longer needed to shit* would show up while I was in what was an even *more* awkward and humiliating position than defecation usually was, just because I was this lesser being who still had to do such disgusting things.

There were few ways to make one's imminent unpleasant death look kind of attractive, but this bucket was one of them.

I waited. I meditated on the patterns of the various carpets in the room. Whoever had prepared this cell for me had clearly thought the way to make a dungeon a home was to "just add carpets." Since I no longer had to worry about the kee issue of muscle soreness after sleeping on a slab of rock, I would have traded those carpets for their weight in books in a heartbeat since "home" for me is "just add books." Being a captive, I would not have felt at home even in the Vatican library, though.

Wait, no. Honestly, if Sultan Psycho held me captive *there*, I might not even notice my lack of liberty.

CHAPTER SEVENTEEN

I was, for lack of anything else, still pondering what might be hidden in the Vatican library when the Psycho Sultan himself arrived and joined me in my cell. While this could mean my painful death at any moment, I was bored enough that any diversion was welcome. At least he was easy on the eyes. Today he wore a black-on-black-on-black three-piece suit; the suit was matte black, the shirt glossy black, and the tie a textured matte. His shoes, I could see my reflection in. It made his dark-red hair and metallic eyes look even more pronounced, more surprising. He was not unhandsome, but it was not a comfortable attractiveness.

"Naz hanım, *tatlım*! I have so many things to say to you. Where do I begin? But first, I must ask myself, are you missing Kazıklı bey? For you must have believed you loved him to have made such a commitment to him. I understand such a connection cannot be broken so very easily. It is known that he was not forthcoming with you, and no one was surprised. He is a distant, secretive man. You would say 'damaged,' *öyle değil mi?*" He waited impatiently for my response, so I nodded, not trusting what would come out if I opened my mouth even a little.

"So, let me tell you about the man called Impaler. He is damaged indeed. Has he said to you that he is misunderstood? That he did what he had to do in order to survive? That those times have changed, and those living now can surely not understand him? I have heard just such excuses from him...but *I am his age*. He was born—born to his living mother, that is—just one year before me, did you know? We all change over time—indeed, I am most changed myself, being now a creature of smokeless fire, hehehe!" He again impatiently waited, this time for me to laugh with him. I managed a strangled chuckle.

"But you do not hear me making excuses for my past because I do not have such things to account for. Listen to me: Kazıklı bey might say times have changed, but he did such things as horrified us all back in those 'bad old days,' as he would tell them.

"*Dinle!* He had a castle called…what was it, eh? Cetatea Poenari, that was it. He built it just as he wanted it. He built the dungeon right under his bedroom so he could listen to the screams of those he ordered tortured to death. This is true! He was no stranger to captivity, but when Mátyás—he was King of Hungary and Croatia, and we all fought each other, oh, many times—when Corvin Mátyás had imprisoned him, he impaled insects and rodents to relieve his boredom. That is also true! And when he had people, not just small helpless things to torture, he did this: he would skin the feet of the person and pour salt onto them, but that was not enough. He would bring in goats to lick the salt from the skinned feet! Can you imagine? But it also is true! And he roasted children. Not bad enough? Then he fed them to the mothers! And the mothers—he cut off their breasts and forced their husbands to eat them! And after all that, he had those husbands impaled! Yes, those things are true, but they are not *all*. When he ruled the Wallachians, those you would now call Romanians, he got rid of the poor and weak by burning them alive. Does that shock you? It is true! In only seven years of rule, for, *tatlım*, he did not rule very long, he killed at least one hundred thousand, many of which were his own people! And what have I seen with my own eyes? After he failed to assassinate me in a most cowardly effort, I marched to Târgovişte to fight him on his own ground. But when I got there, I found twenty thousand of my men impaled in a forest of death before me. And this *after* he had invaded Bulgaria and impaled even more of my people, men and women. I tell you these things are true since I saw them with my own eyes. I can still see them..."

I sat through this, mute. Sultan Psycho had that effect on me. I'd known the bare facts of Sandu's history, "When He Was Vlad," as it were. I had read explanations that the impalement of the twenty thousand Turks had ended a war and saved his people, but at the time, it hadn't borne thinking about, not in detail. Being forced to hear it from someone who'd been there, well, it was horrific. Beyond horrific. I couldn't imagine ordering the deaths of twenty thousand people, not even to end a war and save more lives in the long run. And impalement is a most gruesome death: the greased spike sliding up through your body, puncturing its way through muscle and organs, to come out your chest or your neck. You might die at any time along the way or survive for days. I could not do it to even one person, nevermind twenty thousand at one go.

I'd told myself I'd accepted that history. That this was not just in the past, but *deep* in the past. He was Sandu now, and the Sandu I was with in the here and now was *real*. The Vlad of the past was shrouded in myth and the worst sort of legend.

He'd told me about the propaganda machine that was used against him.

How much of what Sultan Psycho had just told me was pure misinformation? Would I let him keep those lies alive? Should I judge Sandu on them?

It was strange, but when I was safely near Sandu, it was all too easy to doubt him. But far away from him—stolen away from him—all I could feel was trust in him, belief in the person I thought he was. Sultan Psycho was trying to wedge us apart and had been doing so even before he'd abducted me. It was backfiring, however. Now, in my head, I sprang to Sandu's defense. This asshole who was hallucinating that he was a genie was not going to lure me to the Dark Side by repeating centuries-old slanders about my...well, my *love*, dammit, and my patar, which turned out to mean something to me, after all.

I realized with a start that I needed to respond to the scheming, insane vampire sitting beside me. How to play this? "Yes," I said slowly, thinking fast. "Those were terrible things. I don't know how anyone could do them."

Mehmet the Mad Genie fought to keep the triumph from showing on his face. It did, however, glow out of his metallic eyes while he looked solemnly at me. "I am sorry, Naz hanım, to have to tell you those things, those true but painful things. You needed to know them. Do you understand?"

"Yes..." *What to call him? Oh!* "Yes, my Sultan." It felt icky to say that, but I forced all the sincerity I could muster into it. "You have...you have helped me understand."

"*Peki!* Now we go on with your teaching!" And so we did. Sultan Psycho had apparently blocked a far too generous number of hours into his schedule to devote to lil' ol' me, although thankfully he also left to attend to his own business for long stretches of time. The cranky minion whom Sultan Psycho called "Ṭīr" dropped off food about once a day, or what I assumed was a twenty-four-hour-ish period, not having a watch or any other way to tell time, and replaced the bucket with a new one. I think they just tossed them away after one use, which was neither environmentally nor fiscally responsible of them, but I wasn't going to complain.

Most of my hours I spent sleeping, thankfully. Am'r-nafsh don't seem to have much problem with insomnia. I was finding I could just drop off and sleep deeply whenever I wanted, which was quite handy for a prisoner.

On the second "day," along with the food came a washbasin, a towel, and a change of clothing: a black kaftan heavy with embroidery. I washed and changed gratefully. The kaftan was pretty comfortable, actually.

Every day, the Mad Genie Formerly Known As Mehmet came in to instruct me on how the am'r were *really* jinn. Laying out his reasoning—if you could go so far as to call it that—gave him pleasure, and more than just pleasure. It was as if every person he convinced strengthened his belief in his own narrative.

First, he explained how the am'r had been terribly confused for ever so long, thinking they were vampires—he called them that as a sort of insult, which was a disturbing echo of the fact *I* had already taken to doing so—when they were *really* jinn.

"It was an easy misunderstanding, Naz hanım, for the stories of the vampires and the aspects of al-jinn have many commonalities. Jinn and vampires can live secretly in the society of the people of clay. The tales of jinn and myths of vampires both include shape-changing, invisibility, and the power to fly. Even the word 'jinn' comes from 'covered by darkness,' as vampires must live, and both are associated with the madness that comes from poetry. Both are rumored by mortals to live in ruins or burial sites, and both are attracted by blood and drink blood, nor can they eat other food. As well, both are associated with the sickness or death of mortals, no surprise! One of the Faith reading *Dracula* knows what those symptoms of the girls mean from the start; no need for a vampire-hunter to explain!

"As I studied and prayed, I realized how misled we were, calling ourselves 'am'r.' It was a *Frenk* concept. It never felt true to me. In my upbringing, there was a better explanation for all I have become. Indeed, there is no better way to explain my immortality, for does it not say in the *Kur'an*: 'Shall I lead thee to the Tree of Eternity and to a Kingdom that never decays?' It was my own self, do you not see? I know the way to Eternity, and it is not apples, no, but the smokeless fire that runs through my very veins as blood which will transport and transform you. *Of course,* I would not bow down before Adam! 'Thou didst create me from fire, and him from clay.' Why should I kneel before mortal clay when my immortal fire is obviously superior in every way?"

Aside from such confusing, narcissistic gibberish, which I had to pretend was enthralling and enlightening, he also expounded on his political agenda. His political opinions were probably as insulting to his fellow Turks as his religious "inspirations" would be to fellow Muslims. It seemed he had a personal grudge against the founder and first President of the Republic of Turkey, Mustafa Kemal Atatürk; am'r have the opportunity of holding on to *long* grudges. Lucky me, I got to hear all about it.

"I killed him, you know. I had to. He had done much damage already. His illness was no illness—unless you can say he came down with *me*, hehehe! I drained him, and I gave him blood poisoned with maadak. Ah, but if I had known then of my true heritage, of my true destiny, it would have been different! I would have set up a court! *Biz cinler*—us jinn—are strong believers in justice, *sevgili*, and when we had found him guilty of his myriad crimes against the Ottoman Empire—*my* empire—I would have pulled out his heart with my own hand and squeezed all the blood from it down my throat! But I still thought I was an unclean creature, and I kept to the shadows, killed him like a coward, drained him and poisoned him, and they thought it was "cirrhosis of the liver." I never got the credit for killing the one who had displaced my namesake Meḥmed-i sâdis, Vahideddin

!

"He destroyed what was left of my empire and made it a secular nation-state. What does this mean but a godless, directionless disarray? 'Democracy,' 'civil rights.' He abolished the caliphate! He dedicated his life to dismantling the legal and scholastic institutions that had been key pillars of power amongst the Ottomans! I will shoot him with his 'six arrows!' Six arrows straight to the seven gates!

"But now I can correct it. No longer are we creatures unclean. As pure as smokeless fire, I and my jinn will step forward. We are meant to be the rulers of clay since we are above them in body and spirit. We shall rebuild my empire. No longer just The Two Lands and The Two Seas, but the whole world shall finally follow the right path, the clay serving the fire. Do you see how beautiful and *right* it will be, my Naz hanım? But of course you do; how could you not? You will be by my side with the rest of your brothers and sisters of the fire as we scorch the world clean. The world-empire of Jinnestan will be ours to rule!"

After Sultan Psycho had pontificated enough, he would leave me "to think and pray upon it." I'm not sure who he thought I might pray to. Indeed, the whole thing left me more than a little confused about who *he* prayed to, although narcissism being what it was, even when he addressed "Allah" he was probably really talking to himself. After he left and the relief wore off, there would be boredom leading into a nap, waking to find food and a replaced bucket, washbasin, towel, and a new kaftan, which killed time before more napping. It turned out that being a prisoner was more about boredom than terror.

After some days had passed, I was shocked awake from yet another boredom-induced-nap to find Ṭīr right over me, sniffing hungrily. If I'd not awakened just then, I'm certain he'd have lost control and had at least a sip, if not drained me dry. I was at one of those junctures where I had to guess what to do right the first time. There would be no second chances.

"Iblis!" I shouted. "My Sultan! Defend me, Iblis, leader of the Jinn!"

Ṭīr rocked backward with such speed he was nearly clumsy. He looked terrified. "You do not...there is no need to tell Fātiḥ. I apologize. It was just—*your smell!*" He left, and the door slammed shut behind him.

I found that am'r-nafsh *could* have insomnia after all, or at least, I felt no desire for sleep again until after Sultan Psycho's next visit. He came in, looking severe. "I know of the transgression, *tatlım*. There is no more need to worry. The offender has been dealt with. You are safe in my care, and when you are ready, I shall make you safer still."

I knew better than to inquire further, but curiosity overcame me. "Safer?"

"You are only one of us in *potential*, shall we say. The blood of my enemy runs yet in your veins, *güzelim*, and I will clean it away for you and build our own connection stronger yet."

I seriously did not like where this was going, but I had to know. "How, my Sultan?"

"We will replicate the ritual that made you into what you thought was 'am'r-nafsh.'" Three times we will share our blood, and it will wash you clean of the tainted blood of Kazıklı bey, then I will become your father-in-fire. All my people will scent the connection on you, and you will be perfectly safe with any of them. And when you pass from your state of clay, you will finally be one of us completely."

He paused, and his eyes gleamed in a way that was just as recognizable as normal kee lust, "But *that* will not be for some time. We will be able to share the joy and strength-giving ritual *many* times before that day."

Ah. I *had* wondered why Mehmet hadn't just drained me dry and lobbed my empty carcass at Sandu, and why he was taking all this time to "educate" me.

I'm being wooed. This was ridiculous. I'd already been wooed by one vampire. Now another was going well out of his way to do the same.

I felt dangerously close to a fit of giggles. But while Sandu could handle my giggles, if impatiently, I knew the Mad Genie took this all far too seriously. I needed to restrain myself.

"And," he added, "you will do for al-jinn as you were to do for the 'am'r.' You will use your skills to catalog the many documents that prove we are the people of fire, *not* of clay from the sepulcher. I have of course proven it to many, but there are still more who need to see the truth. You will make these texts available to those who wish to learn. You have come to me just at the time when I needed you most, Naz hanım! Your abilities will be crucial to our task, and the loss of you crushes our adversaries at the very time when they most need to consolidate their strength! Seeing you at my side will be a blow for Kazıklı bey, and all those who ally themselves with him will see who has the truth and the *real* power!"

Ah. He doesn't love me, he just loves my Librarian-style.

If I gave in to my overwhelming need to giggle now, it would end with me rolling on the floor, howling with laughter caused by the preposterousness of it all, combined with not being able to remember the last time I'd relaxed.

Oh, right, it was while I was being girl-sniffed in Dracula's spa. I had to bite the inside of my cheek to control myself and accidentally bit so hard I tasted blood. Shit! Now I had to keep my mouth shut! What would happen if Sultan Psycho smelled fresh blood?

Happily, he was more than ready to fill in any conversational gaps. Indeed, his fondness for his own voice probably meant that not only did he not see me as lacking in social skills, but I was just the sort of person he liked talking to best of all.

Maybe the barest whiff of the blood did get picked up by his well-endowed sniffer since he leaned close and stroked the bitten cheek. Or maybe it was just him feeling comradely from all the talk of our amazing strategic alliance and certain victory. That talk was entirely one-sided; obviously, he was taking my muteness as implicit agreement. I swallowed, an unconscious nervous reaction backed up by a conscious desire to get the blood out of my mouth. He said, "*Sevgili*, when you are ready—when the hurts caused by the Wallachian monster who has caused so many such pain have healed—call out to me as you have called out once already, and I will come and share the fire in my blood with you. The scorching wind will cleanse you, and you will become one with us. With *me*."

The fire of zealotry raged in his metallic eyes. For a moment, he seemed a creature of fire, his flame-colored hair burning in my peripheral vision. He was feeling lust. I felt nothing but terror.

The moment was happily broken by Bat-Bitch sweeping into the cell, glaring at me. Her, I had not missed. "*Fātiḥ, gel! Yanlış bir şey!*" He looked at her, looked back at me, and with vampiric speed—that is, genie speed—they were gone.

They did not, however, forget to close the door.

I had a lot to work through. It was a pretty heavy trip the Mad Genie had just laid on me. Sadly, once it was safe to roll hysterically on the floor, I no longer found anything to laugh about. I tried not to think about the hopelessness of me making it out of this situation alive, since I sure as shit wasn't going to let Mehmet do *any* of the things he wanted to do with me. I remembered the wonderful ways Sandu and I had shared blood. I was aroused by the memories and sickened by the thought of defiling them with Mehmet. Bouncing between those two extremes, I uneasily drifted off.

I was wakened by whispering. Sandu whispering. *Sandu!* I looked around wildly, and there he was, on the other side of the bars. I was up and over to him as fast as any am'r or jinn. I reached through as he did, and we grasped each other in a desperate, full-body hug. It probably looked pathetic, but I have never been happier to see anyone in my life.

It was everything a reunited lovers' embrace should be. Except for the cold metal bars. At first they were no distraction at all, but after a while, they became bothersome since we could not get any closer with such a barrier in our way. I pulled back a little to look at his face. Sandu's eyes glowed passionately gold-green at me. "I have missed every aspect of you, *draga mea*. I cannot stand to be separated from you. It has been torment. My anxiety for you has known no bounds, my frithaputhra."

"Sandu. *Sandu!* You're here! Finally! Hey, what took you so long? I don't even know how much time I've been here, but it's been way too long. Mehmet is insane! Hey, what about the guard? He's crazy too, and I think he really hates me now. We need to get out of here!"

"Don't worry about guards or anyone for a little while. I left them a distraction. Tell me what has gone on with you. Has he...has he...*offended* you? I smell his presence, but not..." Sandu's voice trailed off, not sure how to phrase his question. I decided to let him off the hook.

I knew who "he" was. I had no idea how many male genies were in this place, but for Sandu, there was only *one* to be worried about. "He hasn't bitten me. He hasn't tried. He says I must *ask* him, which is *so* never going to happen." I summed up the Madness of King Genie in as short a description as possible for something so labyrinthine and abstruse. "And his hatred of *you* is shot all through this. He wants my turning to him—have I mentioned 'never gonna happen?'—to be part of his destruction of you, although I don't fully understand the details."

"Mehmet has become more irrational over the years since his vistarascha. He has never since been the enemy I once knew, but for many decades we have avoided each other, and I did not apprehend how things went with him. He was no danger to me, thus I did not care. But now he is a danger to us all."

"So why are we standing here? Get me out of here and away from these crazy-eyed genies!"

"Oh, *sufleţel*, I am sorry. Bagamil thinks—and I agree—it would be best if they do not realize we are aware of their plans. I am only here to tell you what is going on, to keep you from despair, and in hopes that perhaps you can work with us from this side. And...I wanted to see you, to assure myself of your well-being, even though we were reasonably certain they would not harm you, at least not right away."

I did *not* like the "reasonably certain" or "at least not right away" bits, but there were bigger fish to fry. "You're going to *leave me here?* What the fuck, Sandu? Why is *that* a good idea?"

"If you are removed from this cell, Mehmet will know we know his plans—all he has told you, which you have just told me. It is important that he believes we are ignorant of them."

"Well, *I* think getting me out of here is just as important. Can't we make it look like I escaped on my own?"

Sandu looked unhappy. "*Dragă* Noosh, I am afraid it would not be believable. Can you tear these bars apart? Or, if you could find some other way to escape the cell, do you think you could escape without one of Mehmet's followers finding you? If Mehmet came looking for you, do you think you could escape to me before he tracked you down by scent? No. You by yourself do not have the skills to elude capture, nor the strength of a full am'r. If I took you from here, it would be clear that an am'r has done so. And who the am'r was. Even if I was not leaving the spoor of my scent as we speak, they would know it was me who came for you."

I didn't say anything. I thought my hero had come to rescue me, but it turned out he'd just come to say hi and then leave me in the lair of an insane vampire who thought he was a fucking genie and who wanted to use me in disgusting and evil ways.

"Noosh," Sandu said, in a soft, gentle tone that tugged at my heart even through my rush of resentment, "please, will you stay here and help us? If you say you cannot, I will take you from here, even if it destroys all our plans. But please consider before you choose."

Well, fuck. If he puts it like *that*, I have to stay. Da-da-da-DAH-DAHDAH: Super-Librarian to the rescue!

"OK. I won't be the one to ruin all your plans. I guess I have to stay." I could say no more without bursting into tears. I snapped my lips together and tried to freeze my face.

Sandu pulled me as close to him as far as the bars would allow and slid his arms warmly around me, giving me a sense of security I knew was false. I leaned in desperately, regardless.

He spoke, low and urgent into my ear. "I feel certain Mehmet will move against us immediately. It is like him to take the offensive. He remembers when he was a brave and incisive warlord, and some part of him is *still* that man. Stay with him and keep learning his plans, and I will come for you at the most fitting time. After that, we will never be separated again, *sufleţel*. But do not let him bite you, and do not share his vhoon, no matter what. I do not know if his madness would flow into you...but do not risk it."

"You *don't* have to warn me," I murmured. "I will avoid sharing his blood with every bit of strength in me." I paused, then added, "Speaking of blood, are you OK? Do you need...some?"

"I did not want to ask," he said faintly. I had to replay his words in my head to make sure I'd heard him correctly.

"Look, they've been feeding me. Um, *food*, that is. I'm doing fine. But you'll need blood for stamina in what's to come, won't you?"

He paused, and I visually examined him: he was *glowing*. Full of health. Full of blood. What the...? I tried to put aside all thoughts that tried to crash into my mind and just wait for an answer.

"I just, *ei bine*, drained an am'r. He was recently woken from his vistarascha, one of the same vhoon-anghyaa as the ones who captured me. I needed to kill him since he was the guard of the ingress I used, and when one is on an errand where one's best and fastest reactions are called for, it is foolish to pass up a chance to enhance one's abilities. To—how to say it—fuel up.

"However, your vhoon would indeed be best for me, *draga mea*. It would sustain me far better, make me stronger, and last longer. Vhoon-kee is better for me than vhoon-am'r, and vhoon-am'r-nfash, especially my own am'r-nafsh, is best of all. It would be optimal for me to drink from you now, and I want to. Oh, how I desire it! But I am not certain how you feel."

His eyes had a trapped animal look to them. He needed me to get it, but was being careful of my fragile modern Western kee mores.

I took a deep breath. "We haven't talked about you drinking from anyone else and what it all *means*." I added grimly, "There is too much we have not talked about!" I sighed and continued, "But I get it. It's more than just sex or just food for you. And of course, you need to do what you need to do to keep you safest. That is the highest priority. But please, once we get out of this..." My voice trailed off because I honestly didn't know how I wanted to finish the sentence.

He looked relieved. "Do not worry, *micuțo*. I would rather your vhoon than anyone's. And after this is over, we will have time to speak about everything—as much as you desire and need."

"Don't make rash promises, Sandu! You don't know how much I can and will want to talk about things! 'Endless' will be just a start!" He chuckled softly and I added, "But seriously, let me…sustain you before you go."

He pulled back to look into my eyes again. "You are the only one with whom I have ever had such a connection. We are not just lovers, not just patar and frithaputhra, but true partners. You nourish me with more than your vhoon, *sufleţel*."

He had said many marvelously romantic things to me, but this took the cake. Tears started down my face, and he reached out a finger and scooped up each, then licked them from his fingers. I turned my head, angling it to give him the best space to bite. His hand slid down, cupping my butt and pulling my whole body against him through the bars. His teeth slid into my skin, and there was the tang of pain, but under it was the deep throb of pleasure, as always. I couldn't properly tell the two apart anymore, at least not with him. I pressed my neck to him, urged him on to more. I could feel the blood rushing out of me, and I wanted to feel every swallow he took. Who knew when we would have this again? I threw myself into savoring every sensation, cherishing the pain as I would cherish the pleasure.

I could feel his cock hard against me, pressing into me much like the iron bars on either side. There was no time for such things right now, but it was good to know he was aching for it the way I was. I know an erection is not proof of love, but it was a comfort to my ego, considering I was only as well-washed as I could be from a bowl and wearing a shapeless sack of a kaftan.

I don't know how long he drank from me, but it seemed all too short a time when he stopped, tearing himself away with a growl. He tore a shallow cut on his wrist and applied a few drops of blood to my neck. "Vhoon-vaa: blood healing. Rub it in well." He took his hand away, and I almost reached out after it. "I will come for you soon, *dragă* Noosh. It does not matter where—I will find you and I will come for you as soon as I can."

He was gone so fast I could hardly see him leave, even with my enhanced senses. I put my fingers to what had been unusually large holes in my neck to finish rubbing in his blood and felt the wounds close. I felt a pang of sadness when my skin was smooth and unbroken again, with no tacky drying blood, as if it had just soaked in.

The walls of my cell were pretty thick, but I heard muffled shouts and a crash. I hoped Sandu got away safely. I didn't think he wouldn't, but I could still worry, just for something to do.

Chapter Eighteen

I'd just sat down, awaiting the next development, when Sultan Psycho arrived, obviously in a hurry. One minute he wasn't there and the next minute he was, looking intently through the bars of the cell at me. I took one look at his face and decided I needed to lead this mad horse to the right choice of water and fast.

"Vlad came to steal me from you," I told him.

"*Biliyorum.* I would recognize his scent anywhere. He and some companions, all of whom I *will* recognize again," he said in such a way as to make me shudder, "have made...have made a...commotion. We ended it. They got away with their lives, unfortunately, but I realized what Kazıklı bey wanted. He was here for *you,* of course. Did I not tell you that you are my best weapon against him?"

Boy golly, this fella knew how to make a gal feel loved for her own virtues and thus totally want to throw herself into helping his bizarre plans. Squashing such thoughts, I said, "I told him I would not go with him. A woman cannot serve two masters. I know who *I* wish to serve." I bowed before him. Nauseating and possibly a tidge overdramatic, but Iblis ate it up, because narcissism.

"You are as wise as you are beautiful, *güzelim*. Seeing you at my side will convince many confused am'r to let go of hiding in the shadows and join us. And with your skills, we will build towers of knowledge such as we had back when I was Sultan and Caliph. I shall gather artists and scientists and build al-jinn universities and mosques that recognize our place between Allah and clay. I will be a patron again, sharing knowledge with my people. I will be *Avni* again, and you will collect my works. Naz hanım, your library will be in my main palace, and our palaces shall never be underground again!"

His eyes glowed with triumph. He was celebrating the victory before his war had even properly begun. Well, all the easier for the am'r to take him down before he caused real damage, then. I tried to imagine the response of international human governments when faced with a terrorist who claimed to be a genie and who drank blood—and shuddered. When the scientists got their hands on this am'r *jinnī*, the *real* war would begin. What mortal human would be able to stomach *not* being top of the food chain? It hit me with a pang.

I had just found this world, just joined this fantastic underground species or family—or order or phylum, or whatever the am'r were—and now this batshit megalomaniac was going to destroy it all, starting with the one I was just starting to love. *No, it's too unfair! I'll fight it tooth and claw, and since my teeth and claws aren't sharp enough yet, I'll fight with, I dunno, with wits and spying and disinformation, and anything and everything my feeble little am'r-nafsh self can pull off. Don't piss off this librarian!*

"What would you like me to do, my Sultan? Start the library for you? I could start cataloging documents right away and making a list of what we will need for proper conservation and digital storage, and al-jinn computer network." I had taken off in full omniscient librarian mode, which could usually intimidate even chemically-altered teenagers, but Sultan Psycho had other ideas. He interrupted me with a hand movement, swatting away my uninteresting words.

"There will be time for such things later. Now it is time for you to share yourself with me, Naz hanım. Time for you to become one of the people of the fire."

Oh. Shit. This was happening a lot faster than I thought. I was going to need all my fighting-with-wits skills now.

"But my Sultan, as you know deep in your heart, I am just as much a distraction as your library. In your wisdom, you know the time for that is not *now*, but at the moment when you celebrate your great victory. When you become Sultan and Caliph again! Until then, not only am I a distraction, but I haven't proven myself *worthy* of the fire in your blood." I was betting the farm that there was no limit on how thick I could butter him up.

This had better work, or I don't know what I'm gonna do.

I could see him considering my words. He was looking for an excuse to have a vampiric booty call, but I'd made some points that were pretty compelling to an egomaniacal, delusional narcissist. I pushed on.

"In the highest moment of your victory, you will take your worst enemy's frithaputhra to be yours, after she has proven herself by aiding your cause in every way and showing your jinn adherents and subordinates that she has truly allied herself to you. Our enemies can only fail in the face of the scorching truth you bring the world."

I paused. Blarney was not my natural medium, but I had to make this good.

"In that final moment, you will seize it all, and we will drink from each other to toast your new world!" I ended my flow of bullshit and found myself panting, my heart pounding, and blushing from the embarrassment of saying those simpering, ego-massaging words out loud. But this was a moment where there was a choice of dying of embarrassment or dying of much worse things.

He stared at me, his strange eyes filled with the flames of madness and power lust and just plain *lust*-lust. I decided the best thing to do was kneel before him, and in bowing my head, keep my neck out of his view. Once down on my knees, I thought: This could totally fail. Even backfire. Sultan Psycho was irrational and unpredictable. Although I thought I had a certain understanding of the direction of his fanaticism by this point in time, I still truly had no idea what I was doing. I was playing with smokeless fire.

He left me down there for a few minutes. After I had become certain I'd failed utterly, he reached down to me, saying, "Rise, *güzel danışman*. Your wisdom may exceed even your beauty." He pressed his lips to my palm, taking an extra moment to sniff it and to slowly lick his tongue up my hand, pulling away right before the wrist—and right before I broke and tried to snatch my hand away. "But you are right, Naz hanım. Our consummation is for the future, for the...*fullfillment* of all our efforts, hehehe!"

He still had my hand and he led me from the cell. I'd never been happier to leave any place in my life. We went down corridors very different than in Sandu's warren. Some areas were still raw stone, but as we got farther away from my cell, Ottoman ornateness began to show up, carved into the walls with exotically curved doorways. I wondered if having a taste for blood also meant that you became a master stonemason, or if that was not the case, where they were finding people to carve these places. Probably better not to find out, considering what I knew from Vlad's history. He had worked rival boyars to death to build a fortress after their families had all been impaled. Of course, Mehmet came from the same brutal time, and Vlad had learned plenty about violence in the court in which he had done a certain amount of growing up with Mehmet. Ugh. Best not to think too closely about the Health and Safety practices on any of these underground citadels.

We finally came out in a counterpart to the Rave Cave in Dracula's underground lair. It was a domed chamber, although this one had lots of colorful tilework and amazing hanging metal lamps. It also had the same design idea of "just add rugs," and here, patterned throw pillows as well. Those were spread generously over sprawling sofas along the walls.

These might be the bad guys, but I had to admit to liking the décor.

Some of the male jinn were still in those perfect suits they had shown off at the am'r U.N., but others, in the comfort of lair-sweet-lair, were in robes or drapey trousers and vests. Most were bareheaded, but some wore embroidered caps. The suits were all in the basic black scheme, but those wearing traditional garb didn't seem to feel any need to dress like an am'r. I guess being a jinnī opened up fashion choices to those who had long felt stifled by more gothic fashion dictates.

There were female jinn here, too. They wore a variety of outfits, from tunics with wide trousers to kaftans. I did note that none were wearing headscarves or other coverings, but they were all otherwise quite modestly attired.

"Naz hanım, these are my family, the ones who first understood we are the people of fire, not the night." He turned from me and spread his arms wide. "*Cinlerim*, my jinn! This is your sister Naz hanım. You can tell she is not yet fully one of us, but you will accord her perfect respect. Anyone who fails shall answer to me. She will be our *kütüphaneci*, our storyteller and record keeper, who will give us back our stolen heritage and make it accessible to all who would learn the truth."

I wondered how crazy the rest of them were. That is, if there were any saner people in the room, for whom bringing the girlfriend and blood donor of their leader's biggest enemy into their secret hideaway and telling her their secret plans would be an *issue*. As the Mad Genie talked, I looked at their faces, but no one seemed the least bothered, and they gazed at me with curiosity and interest. Quite a bit of interest, in some cases—I made a mental note to avoid alone time with any of them.

"And as you know, she *was* the chosen of Kazıklı bey. She has denied him—turned him away to join with us—and even now he is breaking, losing the faith of the *gulyabani* he leads for the Gavur. Both Kazıklı bey and the Gavur are weakening, and when we hit them with the final blow, those who once followed their lies will come to us eagerly and readily. Prepare yourselves; we are in the final stages to our magnificent conquest!"

They cheered him loudly, a few ululating. Either they *all* had drunk the Kool-Aid—Blood-Aid?—or else it was simply that anyone who wasn't entirely sure about this plan was at least sure they were *not* going to be the one who cheered the least. After Sultan Psycho had soaked up enough of their applause and praise, he gestured to a female jinnī, who came gracefully over to us. "Obizuth, prepare Naz hanım for our travel."

Thus far, my experiences of female jinn had not been overwhelmingly positive. But Obizuth had kind liquid brown eyes under lovely brown hair with golden highlights. "Come with me, sister," she said, her accented English as thick and sweet as Turkish Delight. She led me out of the main room to a smaller version of the same thing, this one including a delightfully tinkling fountain.

The women had all exited behind us from the main hall, so it was just us ladies now. I was introduced to Umaya, Bghilt, Haraja, Tab'a, Ferij, and Nadilla, all of whom seemed friendly enough, although they were all rather invade-y of personal space. Observation of their noses proved they were enjoying my special am'r-nafsh perfume. Apparently even jinn, despite *definitely not* being Children of the Night, enjoyed a good huff of am'r-nafsh. As long as they restricted themselves to wuffling the air, it was acceptable.

It seemed they wanted my clothes off, too. I wasn't sure if everyone stripping down was a direction in which I desired to go, but I had little control over the situation. But as they crowded with me into the hammam, it all became clear.

There was no relaxing for me in the steam room as I had done with Astryiah and Daciana—oh, ages ago, it now felt like. Remembering it almost felt like remembering my childhood, and thinking about life pre-Sandu was like trying to remember being in the womb. I sat in a room full of naked apex predators, all of whom gazed with gleaming eyes through the steamy air at their deliciously-scented prey. The hot steam was wonderful on my skin and muscles, but I was overly aware that my sweat in this steam room was like a drug in a vaporizer—not a comfortable thought. I tried to appreciate the varied beauty of their shapes, glistening with sweat and steam, but I was far too jittery.

The thing which finally relaxed me a little came after conversation had finally, shyly, started up. "At least the Qarînah is not here!" said Nadilla, who was tiny with huge eyes, like a little brown deer. The gals all snickered, and I carefully mentioned, "I must admit, she and I got off to...um...a not-great start." Everyone laughed, and I laughed with them. "Oh, there is no good start, middle, or finish with the Qarînah!" snickered Haraja, who looked like I always imagined the goddess Hera would look: cool ivory skin, heavy black coils of hair, roundly maternal curves. "Not as much Qarînah as *Qybah*!" spat Nadilla, and the laughter died nervously. Everyone tried to be casual, like they weren't worried the Qarînah was hiding in a steamy corner. I had no idea what *that* meant, but at least I was around people who held roughly the same feelings about Bat-Bitch as I did, which was a comfort. A very small comfort, but I'd take what I could get.

"What does Qarînah mean?" I dared to enquire. "She told me her name was Shaqîqah..."

There was a pause, then Haraja snorted. "You do not know any name for her, then. Shaqîqah means 'sister.' It is a way to refer to the Qarînah without saying what she is."

I waited. Finally, I asked, "Well, what *is* she."

"The kee called her a—what do you call it?—a 'succubus?' The way they called jinn 'demons.' But she is just the same as us. Only more famous." Haraja rolled her eyes eloquently.

Nadilla spoke up. "She says she is his, ehhh, *kumandan muavini*...?"

"Second-in-command," Haraja informed her.

"Second-in-command, *evet*, because she is an elder, what we once called an aojysht. But I think it's because they tell stories to scare children about her."

Ferij, who'd said little before, spoke up. "She scares children—and everyone who spends more than a few minutes in her company." This time, the worried looks that the Qarînah might be hiding in a dark corner were undeniable, and the topic was definitively dropped.

Conversation restarted with discussions of packing and what everyone was going to wear. Since their outfits had all looked roughly similar to me, I would not have thought it would take terribly long to sort out, but it seemed the topic was virtually inexhaustible. It started in English, but soon was a cacophony of languages I couldn't begin to understand—a moveable Babel that took us from the steam room to a room with another fountain and a cold plunge, and followed us to a shared dressing room with a huge walk-in closet. The clothes were organized by sections, although how one could tell one section of black robe-y outfits from another was beyond me.

The underclothing, however, was entirely individualistic, Some wore teensy bits of sheerness that would have made Victoria's Secret models blush. Others wore sports bras and practical boyshorts. Everyone had their own sense of style, and what worked best for their bodies. It was a smack upside the head to me, a reminder that women who cover do not lose themselves underneath, and that it could be a choice of showing pride in one's heritage, resistance to standards of feminine beauty, or a thousand other reasons.

I didn't know how to reconcile that with their choosing to follow Sultan Psycho. Everyone is free to make their choices in life, from the fashions you follow to the leader you follow. But these women—I wanted to respect them. After being allowed into their world, I wanted to be free to admire their strength. And I couldn't, not with their choice to tie their lives to this loony-tunes monomaniac. But I didn't have the time right now to square that circle, as it was time to dress *me*.

It turned out I'd been borrowing kaftans from everyone without knowing it. Now, I was turned over to Obizuth for wardrobe, and she loaned me her sheer hot-pink underwire bra and matching thong. Bghilt was prevailed upon to loan me a long black-on-black embroidered sack-dress, which went over matching trousers. My boots were deemed clean enough for me to wear them; I was oddly but profoundly grateful to be wearing *something* which was mine and which fit me; not likely with someone else's shoes.

Sweet little Nadilla, who seemed, from the reactions of gals around her to have the wickedest wit and dirtiest mouth, fell on my hair with cries of delight and took great pleasure in conditioning it and arranging my curls into perfection. She cooed over them and told me in English how jealous she was of my hair, then snapped a comeback in Arabic to another gal without missing a beat.

After that, I sat around and waited and watched while the girls chose outfits, rejected them, chose new ones, gossiped and laughed, and packed small bags with a couple of days' changes of clothes and styling products. They seemed to be a happy and kind and generous bunch. Remembering they were my enemies was difficult, and what did it even mean—enemy—in this context? I knew for sure Mehmet wanted only bad things for Sandu and Bagamil and everyone who followed them, but would these women fight for "Iblis?" Did they really buy into his shit, heart and soul? Would they fight the am'r for it? I couldn't tell. I thought about asking them but felt too shy and scared and stupid to do so. I was finally having a moment of relative comfort, and I didn't want to do anything to mess it up.

I had to remind myself that it was nice to have this safer-feeling moment, but I didn't dare bond with my captors. I couldn't forget that Mehmet/Iblis was in the next room, and he wanted to kill Sandu and add me to his harem.

As things drew to a close, my tummy growled embarrassingly loudly. I'd been aware of weakness and hunger ever since Sandu had snacked on me, and while adrenalin had made the weakness ignorable, the hunger was getting less so. To my horror, everyone in the room stopped, turned their heads to me, and stared at me as if I had made some astonishing noise comparable to whale song or a discharging canon.

"Oh!" Nadilla giggled. "She needs *food*!" They all laughed, which made me grow hot with awkward discomfit. "We have some for you! Do not worry!" she said and ran off. She came back with a tray, and while I ate, she taught me about the cheese-filled pastry, *"börek,"* I was eating and *"aşure,"* a cold pudding of spiced grains, fruits, and nuts. And tea. The gals all looked a bit wistful about the tea, which they called *"çay,"* which sounded like but was not what I thought of as "chai." They did, however, finally show me the correct way of using the two pots: you steeped the top pot nice and strong, filled the pretty glass cup as full as you liked tea-strength-wise, and finished by diluting it with the hot water in the bottom pot. And they had sugar cubes, which had been missing in the previous haphazard service. I think they had fun showing the clueless Westerner how it was done, and I was sure they missed drinking their çay. They kept sniffing it as appreciatively as they sniffed me.

It never stops being weird. I was as much a drink to them as a cup of tea. Seriously, I was having the strangest captivity in the hands of an enemy ever.

Finally, things were all packed. And the one who needed to eat food had been fed. If the ones who needed to drink blood had been fed, well, I didn't know about it, nor did I want to. We all donned head-scarves—I was taught a few styles of wearing them, and it was decided which worked best on me—after which we could finally go.

We walked through passage after hallway after corridor. Some halls were finished in tiles and carvings, others cut out of the living rock, awaiting decoration. As we went, our ranks swelled with male jinn joining us with various bags and packages of their own. I finally started to wonder where we were going.

We came out into a huge parking-lot cavern with an entrance big enough for a bus, filled with all sorts of cars from battered vans and utility vehicles to a wide variety of sports cars. Many of the cars were being loaded as we got there, and the group we had been for a short while dispersed to the different vehicles. I stood looking lost and useless until Sultan Psycho came up to me. "Naz hanım, *güzelim*, your radiance makes it clear you belong with us. You bloom with the happiness that comes only from being with your own people. Come now. You ride with me!"

He led me over to a typical sports car—rounded corners, low to the ground, spoiler, fancy lights—which he said was an Etox Zafer. He described it in reverent terms, which, since I knew nothing about cars, went right over my head. I made appropriate "Really?" and "Wow," and "You don't say," and "Impressive!" responses at all the right places. Sigh. Vampires and their toys.

The back of the car was stuffed full of packages and bags, and it was just Iblis and me for however long this drive would be. Joy.

We left the parking cave and I shortly realized we were leaving a mountain in the midst of mountains. Iblis kept on about the car and I leaned back, tuned him out, and reveled in the landscape around me. "Night in the mountains" was not a theme to waste. The moon was full, and with my am'r-enhanced vision, I could wallow in the loveliness.

Why would they want to rush away from being Children of the Night when the night was this beautiful?

It was late spring, and there were still some day-flowers open. The night-flowers were starting to send out gorgeous scents, plus the resonant smells of pine trees and wet soil wafted to me. After being stifled underground, the smell of the fresh night air was enough to get drunk on.

About an hour later I had to ask him for a "rest break," to my intense mortification. Happily, he waved the others in the convoy along, so I didn't have the whole group waiting on my bladder. He overtook them in no time after I'd finished, his fancy car growling as he passed them all to get to the front again.

I was tired of his fancy car after a few short hours of driving in it. My new am'r-nafsh body did not have the same cramping of muscles or that horrible thing where limbs fell asleep, but an over-eight-hour-drive in a comfortable car will still make you hate it and want to not be in it any longer. The Etox Zafer had not been designed for comfort in the first place. Mostly we were on the open road and the views were amazing, but after the kilometers had rolled by we started passing through small towns, which then became bigger towns. Road signs flashed by with numbers like D950, D955, D080, unpronounceable-looking names like Sarıgöl Caddesi, İnönü Caddesi, Küçükkonak Köyü Yolu, Erzurum Ağrı Yolu. After one of the bigger towns, there was a police checkpoint. Iblis was in the lead and had a friendly chat with the officer; a fat wad of colorful bills changed hands. All the cars in our convoy were waved along. Iblis cheerfully told me this was one of the good things about driving at night: "Many troubles of the day are just not there." We still found ourselves behind the occasional slow trucks that blocked the road, at which Iblis honked profusely until they lurched aside to make room for him to pass. The drivers behind us honked as they passed as well, filling the night with raucous noise until we were in the dark and silence of the open road again. Occasionally, he would precipitously swerve. It made me gasp and think we were going to die the first time and it never got any less disconcerting. Each time it was to avoid an impressive pothole, except the time it was to avoid the cow which had appeared with horrifying suddenness in our headlights.

Iblis was one of those people who liked to talk as he drove, and he spewed a strange travelogue of Turkey that interwove his history of traveling around this part of the world over the ages with the changes he had seen and all the ways that things were exactly the same. It was fascinating; the historian in me thrilled at the details and wished I could take notes. The other parts of me were all too aware I was being driven at about a hundred and forty kilometers an hour (which was what? About ninety miles an hour?) by the maddest of madmen, away from the last place Sandu had seen me. How could Sandu track me? Could he follow my scent as it blew out the open window? Even if I memorized the impossible names of the roads we were traveling, how could I get the information back to him?

The sky started lightening in the east. We were in a part of Turkey with little but desert-like badlands by way of nature to all sides of us, and the sky was a big feature of the view from all directions. Iblis put on sunglasses and indicated I was to search the glove box until I found an extra pair for my use. They didn't compliment my face, but I slid them on gratefully. The higher the sun rose, the less the Mad Genie said, and he soon subsided into scowling silence, the sufferer of a terrible light-hangover.

We reached the cave before the sun was too high or painfully bright in the sky. We'd turned off the main road onto something much like a glorified cattle path, and it was doing the Zafer's undercarriage no favors. We lurched along, turning right and left in interesting switchbacks until we came to a squat hill with high scrub in front of it. I watched in horror as we drove straight at it. We turned sharply at the very last second, and a hidden entrance to a low cave admitted us. We were safely underground, away from the intense daylight. I had to admit I sighed with relief at the same time as Sultan Psycho did.

This cave was not a vampire lair—nor was it Aladdin's cave—but simply an underground road. A *long* underground road. I wondered if there were networks of vampire-gnawed pathways under the whole world and I shyly inquired about it to Iblis, hoping not to be shot down. Unlike Sandu, Iblis was happy to answer any questions I had, often with a far greater depth of information and direction of discourse than I'd anticipated or even wanted. It made me uncomfortable to realize my good guys had left me painfully and dangerously ignorant, while the bad guys were sharing knowledge—even if it was their warped and propagandized version of it—with pleasure and enthusiasm.

This tunnel, it seemed, was even farther "underground" than being under the surface of the earth. It was a border crossing, or rather, a way to get around border crossings with all their tiresome paperwork, passports, and non-optional large amounts of graft. It was also basically a vampire truck stop, giving tired travelers of the night a chance to rest through a too-long, too-bright day. "Every once in a while, the people of clay find our tunnels," Iblis added. "Their outlaws, criminals, terrorists. We do our clay brothers a service then, for once one of them goes in and we find him, well, he does not come back out."

So, basically, the truck stop is sometimes stocked with snacks for the road, I thought. I shocked myself with my callousness. It must be the inferior company I'd been keeping.

We drove for at least an hour before we pulled to the side of the tunnel. Everyone else followed, turned off their ignition, and went to sleep.

Seriously, only *I* could fall into an adventure story where the bad-guy vampires pull over for a nap. In the books and movies, once the action starts, people don't stop for a nap in their car. They are too busy blowing things up or having sex or killing someone at the end of a great fight scene. I tried to stay awake and think of some way to sneak off and get a message to the good guys about where I was, but I just ended up panicking myself. Then I worried about where Sandu was, and how he and the good guys were going to find me, and ruminating upon the fact that Sandu had left me with the bad guys for the ostensible purpose of helping him, but what good had I been? None. Zilch. Zip. Finally, disgusted both with myself, and also with Sandu for leaving me with not even a half-assed plan, I fell asleep, curled up in the stupid sporty leather bucket seat.

I came to with Iblis shaking my shoulder and saying my name. Well, saying "Naz hanım," at any rate. He got us out of the Zafer, and a jinnī to whom I'd not been introduced unpacked the back and got in, turned it around, and headed back the way we'd come. My heart lurched when I saw the Qarînah waiting by the dusty four-wheel-drive vehicle Iblis was leading me to. He called shotgun, and I shared a backseat with a pile of full white sacks.

Al-Jinn Convoys Ltd. was back on the road again.

Thenceforward they talked in languages I couldn't understand. At least, I could just keep to myself in the back seat and not have to engage with Bat-Bitch.

We emerged from the vampire Underground Railroad right after sunset, and I immediately knew we were in another country. The potholes in Turkey had been impressive, but they could not compete with the state of the roads wherever we were now. There were more potholes than road.

Also, the road signs now went from having letters I could read (if not pronounce) to a completely foreign alphabet unlike anything I'd ever seen before. We were on highways the whole way, a journey that seemed to take about three hours. I never got a true sense of the country, a factor both of it being nighttime and the truly distracting state of the roads.

We turned off the highway and found another hidden entrance to the next line in the Vampire Underground Railroad, which categorically killed the sight-seeing. This time we drove for at least two hours and came up in a wild, mountainous region. Never mind road maintenance; here, there was no observable infrastructure. We bumped along what was barely even a path until my teeth felt like they were going to rattle out of my head.

Were the vampire fangs around me feeling any more stable?

Around sunrise, we were hitting wider dirt roads, roughly paved roads, and small villages. Iblis's SUV was leading the convoy, of course, and Bat-Bitch pulled into a decrepit farm. The main farm building was big enough to house all the vehicles. Everyone got out, and we headed *en masse* to the farmhouse, which was far nicer on the inside than the rickety exterior would lead anyone to believe. I had to ask and then make a rush for the lavatory. I savored my first real sit-down toilet in I-don't-know-how-long with an almost embarrassing bliss.

When I came out, Obizuth shooed me to where the other gals were resting, stretching out, and gossiping in a room with six mattresses and blacked-out windows—a room obviously set up solely as a daylight-crash-pad for am'r.

Nadilla shyly handed me some almonds and dried apricots, and I found myself deeply touched by her act of kindness.

She does not need to eat, but she remembered to feed me.

I immediately started worrying about Stockholm syndrome. It had been less than two weeks, and no one had tortured me in the slightest. Well, except for the Mad Genie's endless lectures on his justifications and plans for world domination, but other than that, no traditional torture. How could it *not* upset me to realize how grateful I was for the most basic consideration. I'd always liked to think I was one of those people who would only break after the most gruesome of interrogations. It was upsetting to realize I was not made of even remotely stern stuff.

We slept all day, or at least, I did. When I awoke at twilight, I was alone in the room. I wondered where everyone had gone—and the realization crashed down upon me that this was the first time I'd been left *alone*. Now was the moment to do something. Anything.

OK, then. Of all the anythings, what should I do first?

I found myself frozen into inaction, imagining various options and following through the scenarios until they inevitably went horribly wrong. The worst, but also the most likely of the bunch, was that even if I got far enough away from the Mad Genie Gang, I would find there were no good guys following us just out of sight. No one keeping track of me. And I had chosen, back in that jail cell, to stay and let the bad guys take me off into some senseless, increasingly insane, and perilous future with no hope of rescue or being in Sandu's arms ever again.

I forced myself out of bed and walked as quietly as I could to the door, boots in hand. The hallway was empty, and all doors I could see were closed. The house was quiet, the only sound being a sharp wind outside whipping around the building. I snuck down the hall in my bare feet, carrying my boots.

Still no signs of life. Er, undeath either.

I stood outside on a decrepit porch, pulling my boots onto my feet while looking around, trying to not give in to desperation so soon. The land near the house and barn was clear, growing only patchy grass and weeds. About a hundred yards away, saplings and young trees began the transition into thin woodland, which grew denser the farther it stretched. The trees drew my eyes as the obvious location for anyone who did not want to be seen to be lurking.

I listened behind me but heard no stirring from the house. No shouts of "The captive has escaped!" Since I was still at liberty, I started cautiously towards the woods, looking right and left into the deepening evening shadows. As time stretched, I had plenty of opportunity to range from confident assurance through to irresolute uncertainty.

Yes, this is how the heroine of the story makes her escape. Of course, Sandu is waiting for me just ahead!

But no. What the hell was I doing? No one was out there, and Sultan Psycho would shortly be Quite Displeased.

Just as that unpleasant thought jangled through my brain, I saw movement in the trees—a person. Not Sandu—my heart twanged with disappointment—but it looked like...could it be Dragoș?

He'd be most welcome, despite his lack of Sandu-ness. He waved me to him. I proceeded towards him more quickly and confidently, bursting with gladness and relief that someone was out there for me, after all.

Which was when I heard the most horrible sound in the world: the farmhouse door opening behind me. And managing to be worse than "most horrible," the Qarînah's cold voice stretched out after me across the yard. "Where are you going, Naz hanım?"

"Ah, I needed some air. And to stretch my legs after all that driving." The Dragoș-shaped-person had disappeared. I turned around, feeling terrible despair and depression rushing through me, and walked back to where the Bat-Bitch waited like a disapproving schoolmarm scowling at a misbehaving child. "You *will not* go anywhere by yourself," she informed me, her dislike of me dripping from her every word. "You are not in America anymore, and you should at the very least have the escort of another female. Do you understand?"

"Yes, I am sorry. I do want to fit into my new world," I told her meekly, trying to project the demeanor of a willing and obedient acolyte who just *lived* for instruction and guidance. It made me feel a bit ill. What I found I actually wanted was violent and graphic enough to surprise me, but this repugnant sucking up was required *now* if I ever wanted to have another chance of wandering off alone.

The Qarînah dropped me off in the girls' dormitory and left.

The injunction to always have an escort doesn't seem to apply to her. Bitch.

Obizuth and the others fussed over me, and we took turns using the primitive bathing facilities to get as clean as we could with cold water and a rag. At least there were clean outfits for all of us.

While that was going on, I noticed every face I saw was flushed with health, eyes glinting with satisfied pleasure. I knew that look, having seen it on Sandu after every...well, *session*. And there was a warm, rich perfume rising from all of them which I realized with shock was the sweet smell of fresh kee blood, practically oozing out of their pores. So *that* was what everyone had been doing while I slept in and missed my chance to escape. Where did they get the people, the living, the...the kee? I hadn't smelled anyone in the house who wasn't a known genie. Of course, I'd only been in a few rooms of the rambling building, and I didn't have the sniffer of a fully-fledged am'r.

I wondered if I should be insulted I hadn't been invited to the party, but upon a few seconds of reflection, I realized how good it had been that I wasn't. In the immediate high of blood-drinking, the whole room might have decided they simply *must* have a sip from the one am'r-nafsh in the room, the arch-enemy's frithaputhra at that! I didn't want even *one* of them drinking from me, and I certainly wouldn't survive *all* of them tippling from my veins.

And what else would I have done there if I was not *dessert*? Drink blood from a kee myself?

I shuddered at the thought—and shuddered even harder at the small part of me that considered it might not be a bad idea, certainly more satisfying than a handful of dried fruit and nuts. As an am'r-nafsh, I didn't know if anyone's vhoon but Sandu's was even good for me.

Add that to The Very Long List of Important Things I Don't Know. But, of course, it needed to be well down the list under such action items as "How Do I Get Away From The Bad Guys At The Right Time," followed immediately by "When Is the Right Time?"

While I worked through my useless contemplations, we trouped out to the barn, where Iblis was directing the loading of supplies into the vehicles and redistributing drivers and passengers. I was back in the lead car with him and the Qarînah again, and I had an even bigger pile of white sacks to lean against. I took the time to investigate the words printed on the sack in red and yellow and black: ANFO Patlayıcı. I didn't know what that meant. They were not particularly comfy to lean on at any rate, so I used the door armrest instead and looked out the window.

We finally started hitting civilization and highways and road signs, most in the Latin alphabet again. Villages started flashing past, with names like Sharq, Turklar, İmamverdili. After the sign for Bəhramtəpə, things started getting more modern, with more lights interrupting the night. The last hour was along a coastal highway that ended in a city full of fancy skyscrapers. It was surreal to be back in the kee world, surrounded by innocent people who had no idea a convoy of vampires, albeit ones who thought they were genies, were passing amongst and through their seemingly safe civilization. I stared out of the windows, wondering if things looked strangely foreign because I was in a foreign city, or because I no longer fit in the mortal world at all.

Chapter Nineteen

THE ENDLESS DRIVE ENDED, finally, at the docks. I had to consciously focus on overcoming the stench of rotten old boats and dirty dockside water with every breath. Everyone parked around us, cramming the small area. The biggest boat at the dock was an unpromising ancient ferryboat in all possible shades of rust and decay. It was the only boat with any indication of activity—lights lit and human forms moving within. A man, an actual kee whose aroma had an off-putting top note that indicated a certain lack of personal hygiene but had delightful base notes of warm, delicious kee blood, came over to greet Sultan Psycho and welcome him aboard.

Iblis ordered me to accompany them back to the boat, and we climbed the somewhat dubious gangway. I observed that decrepitude was a ship-wide decorating theme. Discussion between the captain and the Mad Genie had started on the dock and continued as we moved through a narrow corridor to a small cabin.

I stood awkwardly in a corner, wondering why my presence was required, while the captain insisted on what seemed to be terms of his boat's rental with determined vehemence. He had a long list of items, and it was boring to be stuck listening to an unintelligible discussion that probably would've been just as tedious in English. Iblis smiled amiably and seemed to agree easily to every condition.

Finally, the captain held out his hand to shake on an agreement, grinning and obviously certain he'd gotten the best of the deal. As they clasped hands, he was pulled with shocking speed into Iblis's arms and spun as he was pulled, so his arms were trapped back between their bodies. He tried to cry out, but Iblis had his hand over his mouth and his teeth in the man's neck. I watched in frozen disbelief as the man struggled and squawked while his blood was suctioned in great gulps from his jugular. With even more horror, I saw the Mad Genie use his other hand to roughly undo the man's belt, tear open his trousers, press him face-first against the wall, and thrust into him roughly as he continued to guzzle blood. I stood there, immobile, feeling like I was being raped right along with him by being forced to watch this horrifying violation.

The man's stifled cries and futile struggles eventually slackened, and he went totally limp. Iblis dropped the body, adjusted himself back into his suit, and turned to me, smiling. "I am sorry to be such a bore, Naz hanım, but I hungered, and I realized I hungered in more ways than one. It is a compliment to you, *tatlım*. My lust for you is strong, yet I have been denied you for the time being. I must be strong for what comes, and thus must I meet my needs from clay, since I cannot yet have your sweeter *nektar*." I just stared at him and at the blood smeared on one side of his mouth. Iblis seemed to catch that I was not on the same page as him. He shrugged, and tossed out the afterthought, "He had to die anyway."

In all this time being around first the am'r and then the jinn, I had not seen anyone die. No *people* had been harmed in the making of this crazy experience, at least not that I had seen. I stared down at the body and wondered who he'd been, and if he had a family or a pet who would miss him, who would have a hard time without him.

I'd thought things had started getting real when I'd first been am'r-nafsh-napped. I'd been wrong.

"*Shamhurish!*" the Fucking Insane Rapist Genie yelled out of the cabin. A jinnī popped into the cabin. "*Evet, sultanım?*"

"Shamhurish at-Tayyar, has everything been taken care of?"

"Yes, my Sultan! The crew has been disposed of. We are all on board and ready to go."

"Excellent. Take care of this for me," Iblis negligently kicked the corpse, which was lying there obscenely, blood smeared on its neck and the naked buttocks obscenely exposed.

Shamhurish picked up the body with negligent ease, and I averted my eyes from the nameless captain's frontal nakedness as he was hauled out. Someone had to show him some tiny modicum of respect.

"I will leave you here, Naz hanım. Get as comfortable as you can. It will take about seventeen hours to make this crossing."

He turned to leave, and I found myself blurting, "You have a little blood just *there*—" I gestured to the location on my face. I wanted to ask him how he could possibly think he was a genie-of-the-lamp when he was so obviously a *vampire*. The worst sort of a vampire at that—the kind that makes the villagers want to get out the pitchforks and burning torches and do brutal rituals in cemeteries with garlic and long wooden spikes. I looked at The-Genie-Formerly-Known-as-Mehmet with hatred and a desire to start learning how to use a wooden stake and anything good at decapitation.

Just hand me the tools of the trade, even if I'm now half-vampire.

He nonchalantly wiped the blood away and smiled his brilliant smile at me, his metallic eyes glittering with madness, "*Teşekkür ederim, sevgili.*" And then he was gone, and not a moment too soon because I couldn't keep up the pretense any longer. I collapsed onto a lower bunk bed. I didn't want anyone to hear my crying, so I wept noiselessly into a pillow, a pillow that smelled like it had belonged to the dead captain—which made me spasm harder in silent sobs.

I spent the next seventeen and a half hours in that cabin, or so the clock on the desk told me. I didn't want to see anyone, vampire or am'r or jinn or whatever the fuck they wanted to call themselves. Obizuth and Nadilla both tried at separate times to come in, but I opened the door a crack and told them I was seasick and I needed to just be alone. Of course, I was not seasick; I was pretty sure I couldn't get any kind of sick anymore. They had obviously forgotten their own time as am'r-nafsh, for they bought the story and left me alone. I was certain the door was being guarded during the night, but I didn't care as long as I didn't have to see or interact with whichever loathsome creature was on the other side. Happily, the Fucking Insane Rapist Genie did not try to come back in. I don't know what I would have done, but it would not have ended well.

There was a bathroom in the cabin, a small square of space with a filthy shower I had no desire to attempt to use. I *did* need to use the squat toilet, but the less said about it, the better. There was a porthole, and during the daylight hours, I sat atop the desk in front of it and stared out into the headache-inducing glare. Punishing myself didn't do any good, I knew, but it was the only thing that made me feel remotely better about anything. I didn't think there was a guard on my door during the day and I contemplated rushing out, jumping off the ship, and drowning in the sunlit

Caspian Sea. Then I realized I'd probably just come back as a water-logged am'r, and I didn't know how to then kill myself permanently at that point.

Another item to add to my to-do list: "Am'r Suicide, How To Make It Conclusive."

Having given up on the self-torture for a while, I was on the bunk drifting between nightmares and the waking nightmare of reality when I felt the boat thump roughly into something solid. After some shouted directions, we thunked gently into it on a regular beat. We were obviously tying up at a dock, although where in the world that dock was, I could not guess.

Did Sandu know? How was he ever going to find me again? How could I get him information about the Fucking Insane Rapist Genie and his equally insane genie gang? And why hadn't I asked him these questions back in my comfortable dungeon under the mountain? He'd said he would come get me, but *when?* Had I missed my only chance when I missed Dragoș?

I heard a shouted hail from outside the boat, and Iblis called back. Shortly thereafter, Obizuth came into the cabin, gave me more dried fruit and nuts, and helped me put on a headscarf and shades. I silently followed her out of the cabin and disembarked from the vessel of rust and disillusionment to find we had not sailed to another city, but we had come ashore.

It was not a promising shore. The pebbly sand was covered in debris, and the beach smelled strongly of every type of pollution. The sand of the beach turned into hills of the same thirsty shades of tan, khaki, and umber. There was a convoy of utility vehicles in the early evening light, which was still not close enough to sunset to please anyone. No sports cars here, just dusty utilitarian boxes on wheels, a few unremarkable cars with Lada and Opel on them, and an incongruous red Corolla. To make it all-the-more thrilling, the person striding over to me was Bat-Bitch, draped to kill, with humongous eighties blue-blockers over most of the top half of her face.

"Come with me," she snapped, and Obizuth and I exchanged glances that meant, "Damn, but she's a raging bitch, isn't she?" She practically dragged me over to a 4x4, shoved me in the back, and closed the door. I heard discussion outside in one of the myriad languages I couldn't understand, but the voices were all too recognizable as Iblis and the Qarînah. They climbed in the front, and we peeled off in a cloud of fine sand and clanging pebbles in the direction of Who The Fuck Knows, our caravan of grouchy sun-hungover jinn lurching along behind us.

It eventually got better as we drove away from the sunset into the dimming east. After some miles of dispiriting dusty tracks, things began looking greener and more alive. The hills provided some scrubland: grasses, flowering shrubs, and succulents with bright flowers catching the light from behind us. The trees were strange gnarled, twisted things, but there was the yellow-green hint of spring on their limbs. If I'd chosen to be here, walking through these hills, I could have found it beautiful, watching the cool sunlight sliding ever more angled across the alien florae. As it was, it reminded me that every rotation of the tires was taking me to some unknown but undoubtedly disagreeable fate, rolling farther from help, farther from even such dubious allies as the am'r.

Eventually the sun went down, and I watched the landscape change from scrubby hills to outright desert. Strange ghostly trees looking like thin, branchy bushes on drugs occasionally rose in the moonlight to startle me from a near-trance state. We were not on roads, but the desert was a smoother ride than the roads we'd driven on in the past days. The sound of the wheels on the sand and the wind rushing past the windows lulled me into a stupor. Perhaps I'd burnt out my fear and exhausted my adrenaline. Now the road to my doom just anesthetized me.

For hours and hours, we drove. The only break was another humiliating bathroom stop just for me. I huddled behind one of those twisted bush-tree things and saw the droppings of some other living creature, a small one. I hoped it was happily living a good life in the desert and had not been killed by whatever predators lurked out here. I was kind of *over* predators at the moment.

A few times, we drove past little villages: small collections of round, woven huts alongside more modern homes, dead trees and wire used as fencing around them. The road was just a regularly-driven path of tire tracks. Telephone lines strung these villages together. Those and the rubbish that accumulated around the villages were the only things proving we had not driven back in time. No one came out of their homes to watch our convoy sweep past and back out into the empty desert. *Smart people.*

The sun rose. Like the rest of the so-called-jinn, I put on sunglasses as soon as the rays were stretching out from behind us. Behind the glasses, I closed my eyes and wished I was anywhere else in the world, as long as it was not a moving car in a sunny desert.

I was jolted awake when the car abruptly halted. We were in a parking cave again. Had we found another mountain in the middle of this endless desert, or were we just in a pit in the ground? It didn't really matter. Am'r were obviously burrowing creatures.

However, upon inspection, it was not the vampire lair I'd been expecting. We were in a plain old cave that had a sandy floor, with the cars from our convoy unloading various obscure items to join other...well, various obscure items. There were more white bags of ANFO Patlayıcı, whatever that was. There were lots of boxes and crates; as no one was paying attention to me, I wandered over to them. There were what looked like red plastic funnels, only they were seemingly filled with something. Also, boxes filled with long, thin white sausage-like things. They had writing on them, and after a double-take, I realized those words were in English. I sidled closer and peeked in: DYNO and DANGER EXPLOSIVE.

Oh, shit. I sidled away, trying to make it look casual.

What the fuck? Why were al-jinn hoarding explosives? No, rephrase that: just *what* horrible plan did they have? I already knew the answer to "Why?" was: "Not for any good reason."

I looked around. Sacks, crates, and boxes were being moved with eager industry both from car-to-car and from caches that were already here into other vehicles. More items were being added from the back of the cave: large black drums of something and blue plastic containers. The latter I recognized, or I recognized the shape and the smell. I couldn't read ▯▯▯▯▯▯, but I knew a fuel container when I saw it. Upon recognition, the smell hit me like I had run into a wall: oily, acrid, and harsh. I quickly edged out of the way as some jinn came over to start loading the containers into the backs of the 4x4s.

This is profoundly bad. I needed to be away from these D-Day preparations. No one was watching me, being caught up in the nefarious hustle and bustle. I wandered casually and indirectly towards the opening of the cave. Getting lost in the desert and dealing with sunstroke and dehydration sounded vastly preferable to sticking around with the Mad Genie Bomber Corps.

The soft smell of the desert morning wafted into the cave. Even more nonchalantly, I wandered a bit farther towards the entrance. I'd almost made it to the left-hand side of the opening when Bat-Bitch materialized beside me.

"Where are you going, *sevgili?*" she purred with rancid sarcasm.

"I just wanted to get an idea of our surroundings, Shaqîqah," I said, trying to sound oblivious to her scorn. "No one has taken the time to catch me up on our plans. I want to help, but I don't know what to *do*." I put all my frustration at my thwarted escape into my voice, hoping it would be read as the frustration of the fervent convert wanting to be part of all the exciting things.

"Ahhhh. You want to *help*," she spat. Bat-Bitch was not fooled. "Our Sultan wants you with him in this battle. He believes you are true to our cause. I know you to be the whore of Kazıklı bey, but *he* believes in you and wants you by his side for our glorious victory. I know you will eventually expose your deception, and then will come *my* personal victory, when I will help my Sultan drain you dry and leave your body to distress your patar and distract him into a fatal mistake. Or else, if we have killed him first, I may beg to be allowed to drain you to the edge of painful existence, leaving you always on the brink of life. Draining you over and over, never feeding you, but leaving you to fade out slowly in an agony of hunger and impotence. I will not count my work complete until I have helped to destroy you."

I blinked at her. I had always known it was *war* between us—had sensed it from our very first meeting—but I had not expected this outright declaration, this overt defiance of her master in sheer antagonism for lil' ol' me.

"I understand," I told her, meeting her eyes. "And I feel the same."

She nodded. "You will come with me now to Sultan Iblis. If you are to be told anything, he will tell you."

There wasn't much I could say or do, so I followed her back into the cave through the busy hum of bad guys getting ready to do bad things. Iblis waved off the Qarînah's concerns—and me. I was escorted to an area in the back of the cave where the lady jinn had gathered. Of course. Even though it was marginally easier to be around them, I still resented being sent to the harem.

Not that this was a true harem—there being no point in such a thing for either am'r or jinn—but it seemed a lifetime of separation of the sexes had flowed over into unconscious habit after death and rebirth should have removed such kee segregation.

Room was made for me and a few nods and small smiles came my way, but no one drew me into conversation.

All activity was dying down. Jinn were settling on the sandy floor, lounging as bonelessly as cats, and talking and laughing quietly in groups. There was a feeling of killing time.

There was a commotion at the front of the cave. A large vehicle arrived, and I heard an increased babble of voices and boisterous laughter. What seemed to be female voices came from the entrance of the cave, which was strange since I thought all the women in the harem had self-herded to the back. The anticipation I'd been feeling became a current of expectancy.

The Qarînah glided over. Ignoring everyone else, she said to Bghilt, "Take *her* elsewhere." "Her," it seemed, was me, and Bghilt was obviously less than delighted to be my escort away from the fun. She took my hand, not in a friendly way, and led me even farther back in the cave, where the walls seemed to fold in. We went right, then left, in a weird geologic origami. There was a tall, thin crack where the pressure had been too much, and there, morning light and desert air sliced in. Two male jinn waited, obviously both on guard duty, bored and antsy to participate in whatever fun I was about to miss. Bghilt said something to them in the language I was beginning to recognize as Turkish, and they nodded and left us in something only slightly more decorous than an eager rush.

"We wait, now," Bghilt said to me. "Now we guard." Her English wasn't as good as most of the other jinn, but I thought I'd try asking anyway. "Why are we on guard duty, Bghilt?"

"Because now we...is word 'feed?'" I nodded, and she continued, "Not 'we,' for *we* wait...here. Until is done. For you are...not safe...during feed." She was not in a good humor and forcing her to try to stumble through a foreign language was not increasing her cheer, so I didn't ask anything more. We leaned against the rock wall and looked out over the continuingly brightening desert, not companionably.

For all that Bghilt's explanation was terse at best, I got the point. If the jinn were, ahem, having a take-out dinner vampire-style, being the enemy's am'r-nafsh in the room was not an optimal place for me if I wanted *not* to become dessert. If Bghilt had had even a few more words of English, I might have tried to get the answers to more of the questions I'd wanted to ask, like, "How the hell did he sell you on being a jinnī instead of an am'r?" But as that conversation was obviously not going to happen, I looked at the too-bright alien landscape and hoped the breakfast feast would not take too long. I didn't need either a blinding headache or for Bghilt to take *her* blinding headache out on me.

I realized I was worrying more about a photosensitivity-induced headache than I was about the human beings who'd been brought to a cave in the desert to feed a bunch of hungry vampires on the morning before battle. Did that seem like a situation any of them were likely to walk away from?

How had I become so inured to the death of human beings? I mean, sure, I freaked out when it was right in my face, but I seemed to be totally fine with an unknown number of lives being drained away behind my back.

But what could I do to save them?

Bghilt and I continued to lean on the cave wall, thinking our own thoughts, waiting for the vampiric orgy to be over. Each of us was unhappy for her own reasons.

Unexpectedly, I heard a *crunch*. I whipped my head around to see Neplach holding Bghilt up, her head at a terrible angle. She was alive and looking at me with pain and panic in her rich brown eyes. From behind his hand over her mouth, I could hear the drone of pain in her strangled breathing. Standing behind her as he was, Neplach's head sprouted up behind Bghilt's body where her head *should have* been. It was a wrong and terrible sight, which was made even more surreal when he spoke to me.

"*Moje dcera*, we have not much time. I could use the sustenance this am'r would provide, but also I could just end her suffering this moment. Tell me which you would prefer."

Well, shit. For sure, I knew I'd rather not see whatever Neplach was about to do. But this was my ally, and more than my ally, my friend. He would be my teacher in this insane new life or undeath, so I guessed I'd better get over myself.

"Please, sir. Do what you need to do." Moral coward that I was, I looked away.

His teeth, when he pushed them into her neck, were not as silent as I'd have liked. There was an added urgency of pain to her breaths, but both began to fade as he drained her. I couldn't watch, but I made myself listen to every minute of it, a half-assed penance that was all I could give Bghilt's final moments.

At least he didn't rape her.

In my new world, what was the difference between the good guys and the bad guys? "At Least We Won't Rape You As We Suck The Lifeblood From Your Body" was not the best advertising slogan I'd ever heard.

The sucking of said lifeblood continued, followed by the sounds of a body hitting the ground, a knife being drawn, and hacking.

After a while, I realized the only things I *could* hear were the desert birds singing and the wind blowing gently over sand. I turned to Neplach, who'd managed not to have any blood in his beard or even on his hands, for which I was deeply appreciative. I did not look down. "*Moje dcera*, I believe it would be best if I became to you a *bakheb-vhoonho*, a blood-giver. In the coming moments, it might well be vital for you to have added strength and ability, and my vhoon would give you such."

I think my jaw dropped. Neplach continued quickly but calmly, "It will not...disturb the bond with your patar. It will connect us, but I would not suggest it if I thought Wladislaus would be upset."

My first highly emotional thought was: But Sandu might... No, I couldn't let myself think that way.

I needed to step back and consider this unemotionally. Now was not the time for unreasoned decisions. Neplach was an aojysht, an elder of Sandu's, and someone he deeply respected. I hadn't been in the am'r world long, but I had a feeling aojysht, or whatever the word was, didn't go around offering their blood to any ol' person that often. This was probably some sort of honor I couldn't appreciate as fully as I should.

Anyway, this situation pretty well constituted an emergency, and Sandu was not here to ask—and why was *he* not here, but Neplach was?—I had to make up my mind as best I could, based on the limited information Sandu had previously seen fit to share with me. I trusted Neplach implicitly, so there was no point in wasting time debating this issue with my ignorant ass-self.

I looked at Neplach and he read my answer in my face. He took the huge knife he had just used—although I was relieved to see he'd taken the time to wipe it clean—and drew it lightly across his inner wrist, making a fine cut, impressively precise for such an unwieldy blade. Blood spurted out immediately, and I clutched it to my mouth to make sure I did not waste a drop of what he was honoring me with.

Yeah, it's all about honor. Really.

I was shocked to discover his blood tasted wholly different from Vlad's. It was smoother and mellower, with an earthiness to the iron tang. I had not realized just how *hungry* I was—not for food, but for this.

Blood is more than food. More than anything.

I don't know how long I drank, but I felt the wound closing, and I almost tore at it with my teeth for more. Realizing I was about to do that—and to whom I was about to do it—made me pull back and look up at Neplach, hoping I had not committed some grave breach of etiquette in the mindlessness of my drinking. His eyes looked hotly into mine, and the new connection hit me like a punch to the gut.

But it was a *good* punch, or at least now I could take the hit or something, because it was wonderful. I gazed into his eyes, which had previously looked to be a kind, soft brown. Now I realized "brown" had simply meant all the colors of the rainbow were mixed together, and there they were, all around me, all through me, pumping vitality in the form of color into the least of my capillaries. The rainbow was Neplach and it was me and it was our connection as well—our own rainbow bridge between the commonality within him and within me, which was the shared blood, but also so much more.

I loved him, and he loved me, and I would learn from him how to use this gift he'd given me. I felt the changes within me and loved them because they were a splash of his wisdom and courage and serenity, now part of me for always.

"*Moje neteř*, my dear little niece," he said to me and ran a finger along my cheek. I leaned into his hand and rested my face against it. "Call me '*strýc*'—'uncle'—from now on, *moje neteř*."

"Yes, my dear *strýc*," I said, and had to keep from crying rainbow tears.

"We cannot stop to enjoy our vhoon-bond. That is not what it was for, as gratifying as it has been. Now we have many hours of sunlit desert to cross, and news of this coming attack to bring to my lord Bagamil and your patar so they can prepare—" He stopped abruptly and looked around. I had heard nothing, but I also whipped my head around in a flash of panic.

They were on us. I tried to fight, but not only were there arms now holding me, arms more like stone than flesh, but the fabric of my clothing was being used all-too-effectively to bind me. I could not get enough room to tear my way out. In the struggle, my headscarf came down over my face. I could not see to know where to lash out, nor what to do next.

But I could *hear*. Neplach fought like a whole army. There were sounds of blows, sounds of blades going through clothing and skin and bone, cries of pain and shock...and those sounds lasted a long, long time, while hope surged and then slowly died in me. There were just too many of them and only one of him, and despite his blood surging through me, I couldn't do anything to help him.

Oh, I *know* I had no training, no weapons. But I found in myself a desire to inflict as much damage as I could upon a body: eyes, throat, soft places I could rip out or punch into, limbs to be bent the wrong way until they broke. At that moment a longing to inflict violence such as I'd never known before sang through me.

And I could do nothing.

I tried. I kicked until the arms around me loosened a little, and then I elbowed against whatever I could as hard as I could. I felt a little space, and so I lashed out harder in every direction.

And then I was crashing down to the ground, a heavy am'r body landing on top of me. And then more weight, more bodies flattening my legs, mangling my arms, crushing the air from my chest.

I could do nothing but heave in frustration under the bodies piled upon me, holding me down. I could only find the breath to scream until my voice was but a scratchy keen.

After, they let me up. They didn't set me free, nor remove the scarf from over my eyes. I was roughly tugged and shoved around the cave. It felt like it took forever. Then I could tell from sounds and smells that I was back at the front of the cave, and I knew the Mad Genie was by my side from the smell of him. He removed my scarf. There was too much light.

Chapter Twenty

Iblis's mad metallic eyes peered into mine. I once would have shied away, but now I flashed all the violence I'd discovered in myself right back at him. His eyes gleamed with the echoes of it, and a chilling smile flashed between his red mustache and beard.

"What is this, Naz hanım? Did we let you get too thirsty? Is my little scholar also a warrior at heart? Are you so eager to drain our enemies that you started without us? I see the hunger for battle is already awake within you. Could you not wait for me, *tatlım?*"

"*Ya Sultan!* That is not how it was!" Bat-Bitch shoved between us urgently in her eagerness to narc me out. "She was planning to steal away with the infidel and bring news of our plans to your enemies. To betray us all! *Ya Shaykh*, she has uncovered her true self to you! Now is the time to destroy this...*sharmouta ghadira!*"

Iblis looked long at the Qarînah. He turned those glittering eyes to me and gave me the same treatment. I was pretty sure we females were both supposed to look down and be submissive, but our hatred of each other ensured neither of us was willing to look away at this vital moment. We were both pumped too full of adrenalin and animosity.

Finally, the Mad Genie turned back to Bat-Bitch. "*La*. You are mistaken. She is ours and we shall keep her. I can feel the fire in her and see the smokeless shimmer of heat that makes our natures clear. She is still new to our ways, but she will learn. We shall teach her. We shall teach her *now*."

I thought Bat-Bitch was going to argue, but she just deflated. Hah! Take that, you subjugated genie-bitch, I thought, but my victory was fleeting.

I had forgotten Neplach. Even as his blood charged through my veins, I had forgotten him.

Iblis moved away, and the jinn cleared a path...to Neplach, who was in bad, bad shape. All his limbs were at wrong angles, which upset the eyes. They had been staked down that way, so any speed-healing he could do would not yield him working arms or legs. He was sliced terribly: his black robes were nothing but bloody rags over skin carved down to bone, ribbons of flesh mingling with the black tatters. Even with any healing he had already managed, it did not look good. One eye was gone—one beautiful rainbow-brown eye was gone, and nothing but a red puckered eye socket remained—but the other eye, that beautiful and beloved eye, looked right at me, sending me a message to be strong.

So I did not gasp. Honestly, I was too shocked and distraught to make a sound. I might have looked like I was calmly viewing the spectacle, but inside, I was *thoroughly* losing my shit.

Iblis took my arm courteously. "Now, Naz hanım, I shall teach you how we kill infidels who would try to stop the people of the smokeless and scorching fire! In this, our hour of reclaiming our place above the base world of clay, no one, not even such a mighty elder, will hinder our triumph!"

He continued in full tutor-mode, "To kill one of these creatures one must be complete, for they will heal from all but the final annihilation. But, first, there is some good blood left in his clay, for all the taint of grave dust. I know you tried to drain him yourself, my bloodthirsty little warrior, but it is not easy to drain such as he. I have three who have earned his ancient blood for their own healing and their strength in the battle to come. Aşmedai bey, *sadrazam!* Sūt, *oda-bashi!* Danhaş, *sanjak-bey!*"

Three jinn moved up in front of us, standing on the far side of my poor Neplach. He did not look at them. His remaining eye stayed on me, full of desperate message and meaning. My eyes traveled to the three behind him, however, and while they were obviously not staked down, they were not in much better shape. All sported more than one injury too severe to have healed already. Indeed, despite however much blood they'd powered-up with before the fighting began, all three were cut up pretty badly, including no left hand on the third one, and the first missing an ear along with an impressive chunk of scalp. And they were, well, *limping*. One had a *very* broken arm, which hung painfully and awkwardly at his side, bone sticking out of the front. My pride in Neplach knew no bounds.

Iblis did not seem bothered that so many of his proud jinn warriors had been fucked up by one dusty infidel, however. He radiated commanderly pride and spent many words praising each jinnī in turn. I took the time to meet Neplach's eye. Wordlessly, I understood him. He told me he knew it was his time. I must survive and get to Bagamil and Sandu as best I could. And he loved me, for he was my uncle-in-blood and I his dear niece. His blood had changed me forever and made us family for as long as I lived. *That* was another reason I shouldn't do anything stupid and must endure what was to come.

The person I had *been* would have wanted to do something profoundly stupid, but with Neplach's blood in me, I could see how foolish and wasteful it would be. In the core of me, which had previously been entirely in discord and disarray, was now a small piece of stillness, which all the chaos of the world could not penetrate.

Iblis had finally gotten through his speechifying. None too soon for anyone, but especially not for Aşmedai, Sūt, and Danhaş, who, after quick words of thanks—and in Danhaş' case, a quick snap from shoving his jutting arm bone back into place—lowered themselves with somewhat less than the usual supernatural grace around Neplach: one at his neck, one at his chest, and one twisting out Neplach's thigh to get to the femoral. In unison, they threw themselves upon him, the one at the chest ripping with his nails to get under the clavicle. Neplach made not a sound but kept trying to look at me. I stepped to the side so I could see his face around the bodies of his killers. We looked at each other, and he told me things that sank into my heart without waiting for my conscious understanding, things that filled me with a strange awareness, not yet able to fully grasp the knowledge but feeling it on the tip of my mind.

His eye dimmed. He was not all-the-way-dead, so the link between us was not broken. It was like he was asleep, unconscious, maybe comatose. The three stood back, licking their lips. His blood had healed them remarkably fast: no bone or exposed muscle remained to be seen, limbs back in their right alignment, strong and sure, and skin unblemished in the too-bright morning light pouring into the cave.

I must have made some movement or sound because the Mad Genie broke in upon my thoughts. "Ah, but this was the first step only, Naz hanım. Still the infidel could rise from the dust. We must complete what we started with the fire which is our nature and our best weapon. But first—" he gestured to a healed jinnī, "Aşmedai *sadrazam, lütfen!*"

Aşmedai pulled a curved saber from his belt, and then Neplach's head was no longer attached to his body. It rolled to the side, and his eye no longer looked at me. The connection—our connection—being severed was more shocking and violent than the act itself.

The head was taken away, although I didn't see where. I didn't care where. It wasn't Neplach, not anymore. They brought Iblis a flamethrower, which apparently was what those weapon-y-looking things had been. He pulled it on like a backpack and fastened a strap around his waist. He took out the nozzle bit and pressed down on one part, then pressed down on another. A jet of flame shot out at the body that was not Neplach, and the jinn cheered as it burst into flame along its whole length. The harsh reek of the gasoline brought me closer to tears than anything which had come before. The flames rushed as if I were watching them in fast-forward, and the Mad Genie made more inspirational proclamations to his gang. Whether they were in English, Turkish, Arabic, or Martian, I did not know. I watched the flames morph blue, white, and orange as the skin charred. The fire seemed then to find a fuel source within the body and the flames settled into a steady burn, desiccating, shrinking, darkening the flesh such that the fire seemed almost to be mummifying him. After a long while, everyone watching in silence, the flames were little yellow licks along a greasy-looking skeleton. Finally, there was just a somewhat human-shaped pile of smoking charcoal and ash.

That was not a smokeless fire.

"Now, my newest little Janissary, you know how to kill the people of the unclean clay. Now you are blooded in this battle, and you shall fight along with your Sultan, alongside your brothers and sisters, as we remove the infidels and prepare the world for the rule of Jinnestan!" As he spoke, he was less conversing with me and more addressing those around him, his voice rising so everyone could hear and revel as his inspiration washed over them.

We were back to our regularly scheduled programming, and various jinn started coming up to Iblis and getting instructions in various languages. Utility vehicles and trucks headed out of the cave, loaded with sacks and crates and drums—distinctly military shapes, shapes of destruction and death.

Iblis, now sporting his shades in the ever-brightening day, as were all the other jinn, went around directing the distribution and loading, giving off a buzz of supreme purposefulness and contentment. If ever anyone was in his element, it was the Insane Fucking Genie. Indeed, he seemed the least insane I'd ever seen him: focused, attentive, and decisive. Not like some caricature of psychosis, but like a real person, doing real things. Sadly, those things were going to be Really Bad Things.

I stood to the side as the piles of *stuff* in the cave grew less and less. Bat-Bitch had pointedly deputized a babysitter to stand beside me; it was Obizuth, and she did not speak to me, look at me, or even try to sniff me. I realized I had forgotten all about Bghilt. So probably had Iblis, and possibly the Qarînah, but Obizuth had not. She'd lost a friend—possibly a friend of many years, decades, centuries—and it was all my fault. Indeed, I'd been caught conspiring with her killer, the smell of his blood was running through my veins, and while her Sultan might have decided I'd just started the battle early due to over-eagerness for slaughter and mayhem, she either didn't buy it or didn't care. She'd lost her friend.

And right at that moment, I was wearing the clothes Bghilt loaned me. *Oh.*

I looked around uncomfortably. I did *not* like how easygoing about death the New Noosh™ had become. Bghilt had been a person, even if she also was a vampire who had been tricked by a cult of personality into thinking she was a jinnī. And Neplach was...well, my uncle-in-blood, and someone I'd kind of already loved. And here I was, *not* having a screaming meltdown. If you thought about it, having a meltdown would have been proof of good mental health.

I could say I just hadn't had time to process the information, but I'd had more than enough time sitting around twiddling my thumbs during travel or while locked in a cell. I could try to blame Neplach's wise, tranquil blood flowing through me, changing me, but it didn't work well as an excuse for everything that had come before. Maybe Vlad's blood had changed me in deeper ways than I'd realized.

Maybe, maybe. Maybe I just needed to stop looking for excuses.

If I was becoming a monster, well, I was going to be keeping company with monsters from now on. Until it was my cause of death. And then my cause of death a second time.

I realized I'd been staring at something without actually seeing it. Stacked against a cave wall was a pile of bodies. Since they hadn't been decapitated or burned to cinders, they were human bodies. I realized they were the remains of the pre-battle feast: the drumstick bones, the grape stems and pips, the apple cores, the rejected crusts, the empty cups with the dregs dried at the bottom.

I stared at the feet and legs, arms with strangely vulnerable flopped hands, sides of bodies with breasts and genitals carelessly exposed. Just left there, privacy no longer an issue, the way remaining grape stems do not offend.

I felt nothing, just an absence of feeling what-I-ought-to-have-been-feeling.

Maybe someday I'll get time to mourn my humanity.

Obizuth and I continued to stand there and still did not speak.

After a while, the activity started to die down. The Mad Genie worked his way back to me, pep-talking, pressing the flesh, and up-psyching the whole way. Once he got to me he smiled, a terrifying combination of clear focus and glittering madness, and said, "Naz hanım, my savage little warrior, you will bring a thrill to my Shad-u-kam, my kingdom of Pleasure and Delight. I wonder, are we ready for you? As we construct Jinnestan in this world, you will blend the old knowledge with the new. I have remade you from the fuel of my foe into the jewel of my Juherabad! You will provide inspiration to me as I provide the suspiration of the smokeless fire to all my people!" He pulled me over to the bed of a truck, gave me a hand up to join him, and, raising his voice only a little, cried, "*Cinlerim!*"

I always seemed to be his focal point for speechifying, and now was no exception. He was obviously doing it in English to include me. I wished this was a movie and *someone* would use his monologuing to foil Iblis's evil plans and bring closer my happily-ever-after ending, but the oration droned on. I looked around.

And saw a spike attached where the side mirror met the door on the driver's side of the truck. It had a...*head* stuck on the end of it, and even from the back, I knew perfectly well whose head it was—my dear *strýc*, my Neplach. Now that I was looking, I realized the scent of his drying blood had drawn my eyes that way.

Rage rushed through me, but what could I do? If I jumped Iblis with intent to shut him up for all time, he would incapacitate me as easily as Neplach had done to Bghilt. More easily even, for she was full am'r, and I only am'r-nafsh. He would drain me of blood, probably while raping me, and maybe, to add insult to injury, do another damn speech before he chopped off my head and set me alight. If that killed full am'r, it would certainly do the job on me. Anyway, it wasn't the Disney ending I was hoping for, so I set it aside and listened because I had nothing else to do.

"—this is what we have been waiting for! Now we, the people of the fire, will cleanse with fire those unbelievers who would deny us our heritage and our future!

"I say 'our future,' for once we have removed those who would place a block across our path, the world will be ours for the remaking! Allah created the jinn before Adam. In the words of my past self, did I tell Him: 'I am better than Adam: Thou didst create me from fire, and him from clay.' Those who would defy us, who would resist our manifest destiny, they are worse than clay, for they are made of the mud of the mausoleum. They are the dust of the tomb! They think their greater numbers will overwhelm us and end our future before it begins, but as infidels, they do not see the very greatness of the cause. The greatness that derives from following the *truth* will overwhelm their greatness of numbers! Our every jinnī will be as one hundred of their 'am'r!'" He spat to demonstrate how bad the word tasted in his mouth.

"And once they are gone, once we have brought to our side those who would be our brothers and have cut down those who would be our enemies, our next step shall be to take our place over the sons of clay who believe they rule the world. Allah created us *first* of a purer material. How could we *not* be set above creatures of dirt, of flesh that decays, of years so short and meaningless? No, I know I speak to your hearts when I say that Jinnestan is our future, and our future is the future of the whole world!

"We are not only smokeless fire, but we have also hidden from mortal sight! Now, however, there will be much smoke—for clay *does* smoke when you burn it!—and we will be in hiding no longer! We will step forward and take what is ours by right, and our enemies will perish in the fire as we reshape the world!

"And now we go to fight our first battle, *kardeşlerim*. Together, we strike our first blow. I know that each of you has ached for this moment, and it is here! Follow me, my jinn, and with me start the fire. *Our fire!*"

He made a dramatic leap from the back of the truck and raised a chivalrous hand to help me, his trophy, down. That was the moment where it crystallized for me that while I loved the idea of being Super-Librarian to the am'r, I hated every minute of being the Mad Genie's propaganda pin-up.

Not much I can do about it, I thought as I was escorted showily around to the cab of the truck, had the door opened for me, and was given a hand up into my seat.

Yeah, I really, really hate this.

Iblis climbed up on his side, stood looking out over the hood—Ncplach's head beside him—and shouted, "*Cinlerim! Gidelim!*" The jinn cheered, ululated, and chanted things in their various languages, and he slid down bonelessly into his seat, his body almost vibrating with pleasure.

"We go!" he announced with the enthusiasm of a young boy playing his first wargame. Off we went. I saw a pair of sunglasses clipped to the sun visor and scrambled with awkward haste to get them over my eyes. It was only after they were on that I realized what a pounding headache I had.

Well, if anyone ever had an excuse for a headache, I think I did. Unfortunately, it was probably not due so much to grief and unrelenting, impotent rage as it was to the nice sunny day.

Happily, vampires' cars—and jinn vehicles, as well, fancy that!—always had extra shades in them. As I gratefully closed my eyes behind the protective darkening, Iblis pulled out, leading the convoy of jinn-identified am'r heading out to their holy war.

Being the Mad Genie, he was already talking to me again. In annoying contrast to Sandu, he was as always ready and willing to share with me. I tried to push aside the headache and the hatred pounding behind my eyes and listen. "The Gavur, he hides from truth and fire under this desert. We go to burn him and all the unbelievers out like the vermin they are. He is there now. Kazıklı bey also is in the stronghold of his patar, and—"

"They are *here*? How do you know? And *why* are they here?"

"Yes, they are both here, with many blind followers. We bring *illumination* to them!" He paused to laugh uproariously at his own joke. "I know this because not *all* blindly follow the Gavur, and not all are happy to submit to his beloved henchman. As for why they are here, they are here for *you, sevgili!* Kazıklı bey wants you back, and he has brought his patar and many am'r with him to fight to get you back at his side, back believing his lies, using you to sell them to the other am'r. This is the Gavur's oldest stronghold, and they are planning your abduction."

Well, İblis might be your madder sort of hatter, but I had to assume he knew a thing or two about getting intel on his enemies.

It was certainly more than I knew, but then again, when was that anything new?

Sultan Psycho was running off at the mouth again, and I strained to shut off my brain and listen.

"*Sabır acıdır, meyvesi tatlıdır!* That means, 'Patience is bitter, but its fruit is sweet!' He was not the greatest of my enemies, but I have waited a long, long time to end him, that he may never rise again! But first, I hope to destroy the Gavur and see the anguish on Kazıklı bey's face!

"It may take a little while to wipe out all the *gizli yılan*, the snakes in hiding, but tonight is the stroke of their defeat, and if they afterward are like a headless chicken that does not know it is dead, *peki*, hunting them down and killing them all will entertain us. Ah! There goes Aşmedai." A few vehicles had broken off from the convoy and headed off at a right angle. As more did the same in other directions, he continued, "Now, Asoom bin Jan-Tarnushi...and there, Malik al-Sahabi Maimun with his jinn. They go now to the farthest points."

But I wanted to know *details*, in case at the eleventh hour, I could do *something* to help someone somewhere *somehow*.

"So, how will you accomplish our great victory?"

"*Peki*, Naz hanım, it reminds me of my conquest of *Konstantiniye!* But this time, I do not have my Orban with me." He sighed in deep nostalgia. "Indeed, I do not have the full might of the empire behind me this time. I must build Jinnestan from the ground up as they say, and right now, I must start from *under* the ground, hehehe! But times have changed. This time I do not bring great and imposing war machines to batter walls of stone and walls of faith. No, my weapons this time are subtlety, up to a point, hehehe! They will not be at all *subtle* once my battle begins!

"My jinn will go to all the doorways leading to the Gavur's sanctuary, which he thought hidden. They will find the guards killed already by those inside who are loyal to me. As far inside those entrances as is possible, keeping the element of surprise, will be loaded with all the components to create vast destruction: little mountains of high explosives in each location. While our enemy sleeps for the day, we bring our fire to him! Before sunset, all will be ready.

"Then we shall let them know the war has begun: we shall fire our Shmels into each entrance. The initial blasts will be terrible in those confined spaces and will set off more explosives in waves, as far as each team has been able to penetrate. I expect many deaths from this stage of my attack—"

"Wait, just from the explosions, or from the fire?"

"Your thirst for blood and death delights me, *sevgili*." He chuckled in a paternalistic way that made my teeth grate.

Oh, yeah: I did want to know how to kill am'r, but mostly am'r who called themselves genies—and two in particular.

"Explosions alone might not kill them unless you obliterate both the head and the heart within the chest. From that injury, they will not be able to heal. Of course, if you burn him until he is nothing but ash—if you make clay into dust—he will not rise again, as you have seen. But if the injury is not severe enough, they may reform. Regenerate, in time.

"If the blast of my wrath allows any to escape from the exits, there will be jinn waiting with flamethrowers, and of course, their blades!

"My jinn shall go into the caves after it is all over and burn anything not destroyed already—and will look for survivors with some fight in them as well! I do not know how many foes will be left to give my jinn exercise. I hope there will be some, for they are eager for battle, and I would not deny it to them!

"And in the glow of the embers, our enemies burnt to ash and blowing away in the scorching wind of our victory, I shall take you, Naz hanım, and make you mine—one of my people of the fire!"

Ah. So that was the battle plan. Big bada-booms, bonus pyromania, some fun genie-on-vampire violence if enough unbarbecued ambulatory enemies could be found for satisfaction, and then a fiery consummation and embracing of the Dark Side in the smoldering rubble. Good times!

I could tell from the quality of the silence that he was waiting for my response. "It's...almost too much for me to contemplate, my Sultan. This day...um...will change everything."

"That is true, *tatlım*. Today I change the world, and you have the honor to be at my side for it. You will record it all for the archives you shall keep. You are my Kritobulos for these times!"

Whatever that means. Lucky, lucky me.

We arrived at our destination. I didn't want to be there, but I also didn't want to keep listening to Sultan Psycho unceasingly. It was a carefully hidden crack in an outcrop of rock, camouflaged by strategic plantings of those funny bush-trees. I'd never have found it on my own.

A couple jinn came over to Iblis, and after a while, I understood they were doing final testing of communications via satellite phone and handheld transceivers, which included a lot of repetitions of *"Tamam, anlaşıldı!"*

Some vehicles had pulled up around us. Others had broken away and headed out to other entrances to

CHAPTER TWENTY

Bagamil's underground citadel. Here, minion-jinn scurried like ants—deadly, silent ants. First, they checked the entrance, and once it was deemed clear, they lifted and carried their heavy loads without any more sound than the wind across the sand and through the bushy trees, taking the white sacks, the drums of kerosene, and other accessories of mass destruction down into the crack. The only sound I'd heard the whole time was the creak of the tires on sand as we drove up. I hoped they were making more noise putting things down inside the cave. Maybe it might, I dunno, echo a bit? But what good was it hoping?

Maybe now I could make my dramatic escape?

I looked around. No one seemed to be paying any attention to me. Maybe if I picked up one of those smaller blue plastic containers or a box of the white sausages and *helpfully* carried it in, I could manage to get far enough to make a run for it.

I walked over to the next truck; the one we'd arrived in had only the big black drums. Here were a couple perfectly convenient blue cans, and I could totally carry one in each hand—

"What are you doing, Naz hanım?" Only one person could make my genie pet name sound so scornful; only one person could make her hatred of me so pellucid through otherwise innocent words. I turned to face Bat-Bitch.

"I am *helping*, Shaqîqah. I *hope* I am allowed to assist in these final, vital moments?"

"You may *help*, little traitor. You may help indeed! I will set *you* alight and use you to ignite the first fire!"

I started to see red. No, I didn't start to see red: everything *was* boiling red. The anger I'd discovered in myself when Neplach was taken had never left me. It had been simmering inside me, waiting for the right moment. For Bat-Bitch.

"I do not have to take this treatment from you, O Qarînah." I put as much disrespectful mockery into her title as possible. "Your Sultan and master has told you that more than once. Will you disobey him? What does he do to people who disobey him, I wonder? So get out of my way and let me do my part for our cause. Don't you try to hog all the glory! I'm going to prove myself to Iblis. I don't care what you think!" I grabbed both cans and tried to swing them as effortlessly as an am'r would.

I did not see her move, but she was in my face before I could blink. Bad planning on my part; I was committed to holding up heavy oil cans in both hands. I wondered if I could get enough momentum up to smash her head in with them before she killed me painfully. Probably not.

"*Ya sharmouta!*" Bat-Bitch was so livid she forgot English. She followed up the first obvious insult with a flow of what sounded like particularly nasty things in Arabic. Despite the language barrier, I felt I understood her. She didn't care anymore what Iblis wanted. She was going to deal with me here and now, consequences be damned. I understood because I felt the same way. It was the only thing she and I would ever have in common.

It felt like we were locked in a feverish bubble. The rest of the world might still exist, but neither of us cared. Nothing in time or space mattered outside our hate-bubble. I was going to die; I knew it and accepted it because I *finally* could do my best to rip out her heart and bash in her head, if I had to do it with my bare fingers. At that moment, I believed without reservation that I could.

We each drew a breath and knew that after releasing it, it would *start*. Then somehow Sultan Psycho was between us, and insanity made his anger jagged-edged and abruptly sobering. He too lost his English, which was fine by me because what poured out of him sounded like a brutally vicious reaming-out. At some point, he realized I couldn't understand a word and switched mid-sentence, "—and there will be no more of this, or I will teach you submission, and make it a lesson you shall never forget, no matter how long you exist afterward. Do you doubt my ability to do this?" He looked at her, then me. I shook my head, afraid to do anything more. The Qarînah replied, as meekly as I had ever heard her, "*La, ya Sultan.*"

"Then, if you both would not *mind*—" Ouch. He might be insane enough to think he's a fucking genie, but he could still lay down some nastily applied sarcasm. "I would like to begin my war now."

Chapter Twenty-One

So, I did nothing to save the day. Any hopes I had cherished of being the hero of my own story were dashed when Iblis called over a jinnī named Sa'sa'ah—calling him *berat-emini*, whatever that meant—to kneel beside us and shoot the horrifying weapon called a "Shmel," which was basically like shooting a rocket from a tube resting on your shoulder. When he was ready, Iblis took a grand stance, hand resting poetically on his curved saber, and growled, "*Ateş!*"

Sa'sa'ah's aim was inhumanly perfect: with a strangely dull and low-pitched *BOOM*, the rocket-thing shot between the narrow walls of the opening. There was this curious hiatus in breathing and the forward progress of time, then the cave BOOMED into a formless expanding mass of noise and smoke and dirt. And before I could even begin to respond, the *world BOOM-BOOM-BOOMED* into pandemonium, shaking us off our feet, the sound of similar explosions echoing from farther away. Even more detonations shook us, muffled from being underground and possibly

CHAPTER TWENTY-ONE

also because my ears and heart had been deafened by the first explosion and the proof of my complete and utter failure.

Around us, jinn-identified am'r got up and ran around, coming back with flamethrowers. Iblis was checking his sat phone. Underground explosions continued, some closer, some echoing from farther away. To our left, a whole stretch of ground shook like some localized earthquake and fell several feet in. Two vehicles that had been parked nearby slid down and noisily landed inside the crater, adding to the chaos. The Mad Genie was roaring with wild laughter. His minions took their cue, their whooping and shouting lost in the tumult. A few let off celebratory blasts from their flamethrowers.

There were debris clouds and harsh smoke everywhere, the sky apocalyptically fiery-orange in the last of the sunset. Between that and the smell of explosives and burning, it seemed like a reasonably accurate representation of hell.

I stood in the last light of this most terrible day—with the promise of an even more nightmarish night—shivering and wondering how everything could have gone so terribly wrong. *This* was not where I was supposed to end up: watching the bad guys blow up my good guys while I stood by helplessly and uselessly. I contemplated ways to set myself on fire without anyone stopping me. It seemed a preferable option to the upcoming "passion in the embers" with the Fucking Insane Genie.

Who, when I trepidatiously looked around for him, was back to talking on his sat phone, evidently getting reports from the other locations. He didn't speak in English, but I didn't need to try to listen to his plans now. It was all over. The good guys had lost, and I had lost Sandu and Bagamil now, as well as Neplach.

I'd thought I understood shock before, but no. Nope. I hadn't.

How many had been blown apart beyond any supernatural healing? How many had burned to cinders in their agonizing last moments? How many were trapped under fallen rock and rubble, burned and broken?

As I slumped there, viscerally experiencing every possible terrible death, a vise-like grip tightened around my upper arm and the Qarînah hauled me over to one of the remaining vehicles. She shoved me in, and I found myself smushed between her and the Jean(ocidal) Genie, who was talking rapidly into his phone.

Our mini-convoy quickly took us past what was obviously another explosion site. The original entrance was clearly visible, due to the fact it was emitting smoke from under the debris pile it had become. A new hole had chasmed open nearby and we parked by it. While clouds of heavy smoke were roiling out, it clearly was still an area of concern. We joined the minions who were there already. Most were armed with flamethrowers, although Iblis was now armed not with his phone, but with his sword.

"We have exposed one of their bolt holes!" he explained to me, excitement pulsating from him. He looked around at the jinn excitedly hoisting their flamethrowers. "Hürmiz, Nızar, Zalambūr!" They drew to attention; he gave them instructions. They all responded enthusiastically and trooped into the black, smoking hole.

We waited. I waited numbly. Everyone else waited with excitement, which, as time oozed by with no return or responses on the walkie-talkies, became impatience, then frustration, at least for the Jean(ocidal) Genie. He spat orders at the next batch of three jinn and sent them in, I assumed to check up on the first three and report back ASAP. He took to doing warm-up swishes with his blade to pass the time, stopping now and then to call other jinn in different areas before again checking in on the jinn who'd gone inside. Nothing from inside. While the news from the sat phones had started well, over time what he was hearing led to exasperation and pacing, and soon progressed to Iblis swearing under his breath and angrily staring alternately at his devices and the smoking chasm that had swallowed his jinn.

Finally, he lost it. After ordering a few jinn to stay outside with walkie-talkies and flamethrowers at the ready, he turned to the Qarînah and me. "Now, follow closely!" He stopped to think for a moment and turned to a jinnī who was not coming in with us. "Firuz, lend Naz hanım your shamshir." Firuz did not look best pleased about that, but his hand went, albeit reluctantly, to the hilt at his waist.

"*Ya Sultan!*" Bat-Bitch cried, unable to contain herself. "You cannot arm her! What if she turns on us?"

I could have told her it wouldn't end well. Indeed, I had trouble not noticeably smirking as Mehmet turned to her and grabbed her by the neck with such speed there was not even a blur. "I cannot? You *will* learn obedience this night! I have been too lax with you and given you too much power. It has gone to your head, if you think you can question my orders! And so what if she turned on you? Could she chop off your head or cut out your heart before you could stop her? She is a soft *Amerikalı*. And even if she were trained to the sword, could you not disarm her barehanded? She is still of dull, cloddish clay. Insolent fool! You value your hatred of her over your obedience to me!"

The Qarînah had gone limp in his grasp. When he let go of her neck, she dropped—well, not like a stone. She still managed to be beautifully graceful on the way down, landing in a puddle of perfect submission at his feet. Iblis glared at Firuz, who handed me the elegantly curved blade with alacrity. I took it with all the meek compliance I could express through body language, but inside, a little part of me perked back to life. Yes, it was stupid—everything the Jean(ocidal) Genie had said was true. But. There was now a weapon in my hand, and it sparked a pathetic flame of hope inside me.

"*Ayağa kalkın!*" Iblis snapped at the prostrate Qarînah. "Follow!" he snapped at me. And follow him we did, into the black, gaping, smoking maw of the earth.

As we entered, I realized I was still wearing my sunglasses. I pulled them off and wished for a gas mask or something because the air was acrid and choking. It got worse the deeper we went.

It was eerily still in the smoky air. We moved in single file: Iblis taking point, the Qarînah, me, and then a couple of minion-jinn behind me. It was obviously a passageway that had been made by am'r hands, but it had been hidden well enough that it had only been discovered after it started issuing smoke. I wondered if anyone had managed to escape through it before it had been revealed.

We went deeper and deeper in. Iblis checked his walkie-talkie a few times, but finally, we got past the point where it worked. He was pissed.

"They *should* have left transceivers along this way. We should have communications as far along as they have come."

Nobody mentioned aloud the obvious reason for the transceivers having not been set up, although we'd not tripped over any bodies—nor any side passages—yet. I found this cheering, but I was afraid to hope.

We had climbed over varying amounts of rubble as we went, from dirt and pebbles to large rocks. Now we hit a huge mound of collapsed cave, with only enough space to crawl through at the top. Iblis inspected it, but it was unclear if there were jinn on the other side. He waved for the minion-jinn to go on ahead of us. The first called out something that seemed to indicate the way was safe because the second crawled along in a more relaxed way. He also called back, and Iblis waved to the Qarînah to go next. As she managed her skirts—not even a superhuman can crawl gracefully in a long robe—I found that the riddle of the fox, the chicken, and the grain was at the top of my mind. If you don't want the Qarînah and me trying to kill one another while you are busy dealing with a dangerous situation, what is the best order for us to crawl through?

My inappropriate sense of humor was returning. Whether this was a good thing or not was debatable.

It took the Qarînah slightly longer than it had taken the betrousered minions to get to the other side. Abruptly, we heard her urgent hiss for Iblis.

"*Amına koyayım!*" he muttered, and hissed at me, "Follow directly on my heels!"

I did as ordered, beyond intrigued by what awaited us. Any capacity for fear had pretty well been burnt out of me by now, and anything that freaked out Bat-Bitch was good in my book.

The Jean(ocidal) Genie was swearing before he got all the way through. By the time I worked myself through the gap, I found him still swearing and looking desperately around, sword drawn. I tried to memorize the curses, but the only one I caught was "!" since it was repeated frequently. A quick look around showed me why: no minions. Both were gone without a trace in the amount of time it took to get the Qarînah across, which had not been especially long.

That *must* mean some am'r survived! Dared I hope Sandu was one of them?

Iblis certainly thought so since his swearing now included "Kazıklı bey" at regular intervals. Bat-Bitch planted herself beside me and held onto my sword-arm with a circulation-stopping grip. "Where is he?" she snarled at me.

"Who?" I asked in pure and sweet innocence.

"Kazıklı bey. Your master."

"He's not my *master*. And I don't know if he's alive or dead. I didn't even know he was here until Sultan Iblis told me. So I just. Don't. Know."

She turned from me, keeping up the death-grip, and spoke Arabic rapidly to Iblis. He replied to her. No one bothered translating for me.

We moved on, Iblis first, sword at the ready, the Qarînah and I following behind, walking together since she wouldn't let me go. She had a sword too, and she kept me slightly behind her, her left hand gripping me like iron, making me move at her speed and at the distance from her she preferred. My sword was even more useless than it would have been, since not only was she holding the arm which held it, but after a while, I could barely feel anything in my fingers and had to concentrate just to keep a grip on it.

We soon had to either angle off to the right or take a sharp left. Neither passage had anything I could see to recommend it over the other. The Mad Genie and Bat-Bitch had a low-pitched discussion about it, again not in English. My opinion was not required. They sniffed like truffle hogs, but the acrid smoke made smelling anything else impossible. That they had cancelled out one of their own strongest senses made me deeply happy, despite my constantly burning eyes, nose, and throat.

Iblis insisted on the sharp left. Off we went—*Exeunt stage left!*—in our strange, insecure little procession. I realized the Madness of King Genie was getting more pronounced every minute. He was muttering to himself, catching himself, and snaking forward silently, head moving continuously, nostrils twitching, then slowly slouching back into murmuration, catching himself again with a start.

Should I scream? Should I start a fight with Bat-Bitch to distract everyone so the good guys could sneak up on us more readily?

The problem—as the problem had been this whole fucking time—was that I had no clue. Maybe this was the wrong spot, and if I started shit here, it would severely disadvantage the home team? Or maybe they were tracking us, just waiting for me to hit my cue? I couldn't know, and that not-knowing made me wonder if I might end up as stark, raving nutters as Ol' Genie-boy.

With no warning, we came out into a huge space: a natural cavern, now much damaged by fire and explosive-caused earthquakes. And, for the first time, there were bodies. Well, things that had probably once been bodies. Piles of charcoal and ash, and others less perfectly incinerated. After Iblis and the Qarînah went even more rigid, I also started to hear echoes reverberating around the space: distant shouting, fighting, and a couple of times, a *whoosh* sound followed by more active bedlam, which I realized with a nasty start was the sound of flamethrowers in action. This perked my companions up while taking some of the wind out of my sails. There were still bad guys doing bad things to my good guys, dammit!

They used that distraction to hit us. Neither Iblis nor the Qarînah saw it coming. Neither, to be fair, did I.

All I knew was the Qarînah was falling down, hauling me with her. We landed, and I got kicked and punched as she scrabbled with an unknown assailant. Then I understood that her sword was caught in my skirts, and somehow I clamped my legs together around it and felt both cruel edges digging into my inner thighs as she desperately tried to free the blade. I might be a *soft American*, but I did have strong thighs and my desperation was greater than her own.

She gave up on the blade and turned to fight the attacker with her bare hands—not weapons to underestimate by any means. They were fighting on top of me, and I was trying to get out from under them while holding onto my sword *and* trying to deal with the one between my thighs. It cut me more with each movement, but I kept it away from *her*. I caught an elbow or something to my chin, which knocked my head so brutally to the side that I thought for a moment my neck was broken. But no, it was just going to be exceedingly sore if I survived this experience. I took a knee or something to my stomach and nearly vomited. As I lay wheezing for air, they rolled violently off me, and I scrabbled, graceless and gasping, away from their fight.

It was a mostly silent struggle. Neither combatant made a sound except for panting and the occasional low grunt of pain. There was no witty verbal sparring, just a sincere desire by each participant to be the winner of the fight. The air in this larger space was less smoky, and I could almost follow it: there was a man in black leather who had a matte-black blade, I thought, but she wasn't letting him use it. Her death-grip was on his sword-hand, and from my own experience, I was certain she could break bones if given enough motivation. Her robes were ripped, and I could see the light brown skin of her legs kicking and clasping, using her lower-body strength to its best advantage while they were both down.

CHAPTER TWENTY-ONE

He had her pinned. He freed his arm and raised the blade. She punched him in the throat. He was down. *No!*

I don't know what I did. I must have gotten up and run to her. I must have thrown myself upon her, sword first. I had no skill, I could barely see to aim, and I think I remember tripping over *him* on the way down.

But I landed right. Right in her eye, that is. I found myself lying on top of her, awkwardly to the left of the sword, which was sticking straight up out of her left eye. The right eye was looking at me, hate and pain and confusion mingled in a basilisk stare. I know *I* was frozen by it. Even with a sword through her brain, she was one formidable bitch.

Dragoș' dear voice, husky behind me, urged, "Move, Noosh! We finish this!" He hauled me off to the side and I watched as he slammed a long black combat knife into her chest and with powerful rips, cut her heart out. Not neatly, mind you, but it all came out in pieces by the end, and her chest was a gaping hole.

I was not numb anymore. Blood-lust pounded through me like a storm, whipping up my blood to seafoam and roaring waves. Dragoș took a look at me, then pulled my sword out of her eye socket and handed it to me with a proud neatness to the gesture. "Decapitate her, *doamna mea!* It is not easy, you will find, but *do it!*"

No, it was *not* easy, even with a sharp and well balanced sword. The muscles and sinews were tough and rubbery, the spine surprisingly resistant. It took a while, but I had a lot of pent-up aggression, and this was one Bat-Bitch who would not be rising again if *I* had anything to say about it—and I said it with my blade, over and over. Finally, her head was separate from her body, and her eyes no longer froze me.

It was amazing.

After it was done, I thrust my hands down to where the blood had pooled from her neck and rubbed my hands in it, then brought them up to my mouth to taste her blood. It was cold already, congealing, and it was too metallic and strangely bitter, like burned coffee. But there was a sweetness there anyway—the sweet taste of revenge, I realized that and I laughed, and held out my fingers for Dragoș to lick. He grabbed my wrist and sucked my fingers clean, and he laughed with a rough, dark-edged sound that made me all too aware of him in a whole new way. The way he was looking at me, it was clear he felt the same.

He let go of my hand and pushed himself away from me, his dark eyes glinting. "You have changed, Noosh! Grown up a bit, *nu?* We had better go find your patar and help him if he needs it. Best perhaps we not continue this right now."

He was right, I had some very distracting feelings I shouldn't act on without consideration and conversation. To distract myself I looked around. The only things around us were the pleasingly wrecked corpse of Bat-Bitch and the people-shaped charcoal piles.

There were several exits from the cavern, I noticed, and then what Dragoș had said about my patar finally hit. "Sandu was *here*? Was he fighting Iblis? Where is Iblis? Which way did they go?"

Dragoș laughed, "You've been around these *nenorociți nebuni* too long! He's not actually a genie named Iblis. He's delusional, but *we* have not forgotten that he is Mehmet. And shall call him that as we kill him." He wiped his knife on his pant leg and re-sheathed it on a scabbard that hung under his armpit.

"Fine, but which way did they go?"

"Can you not smell him?" he asked. I closed my eyes and took a deep whiff of acrid smoke, explosive chemicals, burned rock, burned flesh, and Bat-Bitch's blood. I could even, since he was next to me, smell Dragoș, but otherwise my senses had been seriously impaired by the smoke. I could get nothing more. I shook my head, ashamed I could not smell my patar.

"You are still am'r-nafsh," Dragoș said kindly. "There is much for you to learn and skills you cannot yet possess. But now, come!" He set off across the cavern at speed—not running, but moving fast in that am'r way. I could barely manage to keep up, but extreme motivation helped.

What was happening with Sandu? What would the Mad Genie do, with his evil plans falling down around him?

Down one passageway we went, then another, and I didn't care that I was utterly lost, as usual. I could hear fighting echoing from various distances, and once, another huge explosion that made the world shake for a long moment. We didn't stop.

Until, that is, we got to a room that was still on fire. There had been a setup much like the Rave Cave; what was left of a long table was still burning. The walls flickered as if illuminated by light through water, except this was more like shadows through fire.

Just ahead of us, larger shadows were flickering as well: Iblis and Sandu, Mehmet and Vlad, old enemies playing out their ancient deadly game.

They were fighting with swords. Mehmet had his long curved one. Sandu had the sword I remembered from the last time I saw him, except now it was out of the scabbard, flashing and glinting in the firelight. They were going at it hard and fast. I could hardly make out the movements until one sword clashed against another, then there was a pause before they sprang apart and started all over again. They were not pressing each other so hard they could not talk, and although it was in Turkish, it had the feel of being the sort of witty insults meant to raise tempers, a sort of foreplay to killing.

"I understand it," Dragoș remarked, reading my mind. "Vlad is asking about Mehmet's leg—I think he said gout?—and the reply is, how is the Impaler's back these days? Is there a knife still in it?

"Now they are speaking of old battles. Vlad has brought up Târgovişte. He mentions forests of Turks. Mehmet says the Impaler failed to kill him then, as he always will. They are now arguing about who won. Vlad says he has a great fondness for ruining the plans of a sultan who relies upon superior numbers; obviously, he is not the superior strategist. Mehmet replies, he always achieved his objectives, no matter how many lives the Impaler wasted to try to stop him; it was Vlad who failed every time. That his every so-called-victory was propaganda to cover defeat.

"Vlad mentions that Mehmet was not the only one who could use gunpowder. He says at Giurgiu, he turned Hamza Pasha and his cavalry into bloody mud. Not one man walked away. He wonders how that could be called defeat?

"Mehmet says that indeed, he must thank the Dracul—that's Vlad's father—for teaching him about gunpowder. In exchange, he says the Ottomans taught Vlad his trademark, didn't they? Where would the Impaler be without what he learned at their hands after his father left him without a backward look? *Băga-mi-aş pula!* And he must thank a Transylvanian, his crafty Master Orban, for the good cannon he used to blow down the walls of Constantinople, and—ah, *nu!*—now Mehmet brings up Poenari—*pizda mă-sii!* He says the impenetrable fortress was not so impenetrable when he, the Conqueror, came to it. He is saying the Impaler was only good at impaling his own people and his enemies had no trouble bringing him down every time."

Mehmet had obviously pissed Sandu off pretty effectively. I knew nothing about sword fighting, but it was clearly not going well for Sandu right now. When I could see his face, he was scowling. Mehmet was not done, either.

"Now he says that Vlad was only ever an *ısrarcı kimse*, a—what do you call it, 'gadfly?' That he was a little insect bloodsucker before he became a ghoul, never more than an annoyance buzzing around battlefields. He says that Vlad only came to power thanks to his—Mehmet's—father. He says when Vlad was cast down by his own people, he ran to the Turks for help. He says that he—Mehmet—took in battle the greatest city of Christendom while Vlad was hiding in the skirts of his teenage cousin, licking the hand of the man who killed his father—*Aoleu!* Now he calls Vlad *sivrisinek*—I think that is 'mosquito'—and it is time for him to finally squash him."

Now I was worried about Sandu. It had never occurred to me that he could not best the Mad Genie without the slightest problem. But he *was* having problems. Mehmet was winning, both the verbal sparring and the sword fighting. I was frozen, watching with mounting anxiety, as Sandu's movements became more frenzied, less graceful and controlled. Mehmet's smile glittered from his mouth and from his eyes, which glowed red as they caught the firelight. He knew he had won. All had not gone according to his plans today, but now...*now* he was winning. I could read it in his every movement as they danced and swung in the flickering light.

Dragoș, however, was not frozen, and he shoved me hard to get my attention. "Over there. Do you see?" I looked and there was a dead jinnī, still strapped into his flamethrower although missing his head. And another beside him, who was just a torso under the backpack frame of the flamethrower. It made sense—this room was not as full of smoke, the walls not blackened, so the fire here must have come from something other than the explosions, and thus the jinn had died by the sword, their flamethrowers unused. "Go get the...the...*aruncătoarea de flăcări*. I'll distract Mehmet. Bring them to Vlad. *Acum! NOW!*" And he was off, yelling as he ran to attack the Mad Genie with his sword, which he pulled from its scabbard as he ran.

I ran to the bodies and started hauling the flamethrowers off them; I had to assume that's what Dragoș wanted. Pulling the one off the torso was easiest. I didn't let myself think about it being a body part that went from neck to belly button; it was simply the easiest to deal with.

Flamethrowers are unwieldy things. I needed both hands to get the second, so I had to drop the first and then detangle the other from the body to which it was strapped at the shoulders and waist. There followed an awkward few minutes while I tried to figure out how to carry both. I could hear a lot of yelling in various languages from the fight. I think Mehmet *and* Sandu were *both* yelling at Dragoș, but I didn't dare take the time to look up. I had figured it out: I strapped myself into the flamethrower that was in my hands, then reached down and grabbed the other one and ran to join the fight.

Dragoș was going at it with Mehmet fast and furious. Sandu was circling with impotent rage—so he *had* been shouting at Dragoș. I ran to Sandu and thrust the flamethrower at him. He glared at me for a second with naked rage on his face, and I knew I was seeing the face of Vlad Țepeș, not the man Sandu said he had become. I recoiled and some change played out inside him, washing outward over his face. While it was still full of fury, in some subtle way, it was the face I knew. He grabbed the flamethrower and pulled it over his shoulders.

This left me with the immediate problem of how I planned to operate *my* flamethrower. I remembered seeing Mehmet working the nozzle over Neplach's headless corpse, and—with an Impaler-like fury in my own breast—I turned the nozzle towards the Jean(ocidal) Genie, pulled one lever with one hand and pulled another lever with the other.

The machine coughed, choked…and died. I stood there in shock. It hadn't occurred to me the damned thing might be damaged or even just out of fuel.

Sandu had his flamethrower aimed, but Mehmet and Dragoș now were dancing around too fast for him to shoot and not end up with *two* charbroiled swordfighters where we wanted only one. Sandu and I shouted his name at the same moment, and his eyes flicked to us. Mehmet took that moment to swing the blade across his neck. Dragoș fell back, a terrible line of red across his throat—but he fell back far enough to be out of the line of fire.

And it was a line of fire. Sandu's flamethrower still had fuel, and it burst out emphatically, as if given extra ferocity by Sandu's hatred of his old enemy, catching Mehmet's head and pouring down his body, in a long, blazing line of flame.

Mehmet turned to face us, and for a brief moment, he *was* Iblis, a perfect being of fire, his eyes glittering madness and reflected flames from his burning body—and something else. Something like completion, or maybe revelation.

But his clothes were on fire, and his skin turned brown and peeled back in black curls like burning paper as the underlying flesh caught. Then it was if he caught from the inside, burning faster and hotter. Right before our eyes, he charred, and his flesh desiccated over his bones. His metallic eyes took longer than his flesh, and he seemed to be watching us right back, until they too—finally, *finally*—seemed to sink into their sockets. By then, the ears and nose had shrunk to half of their size and the lips had somehow expanded around the mouth, exposing the front teeth in a terrible grin. The eyes burned, leaving only small lumps of ashen tissue in each open socket of the wizened skull. The exposed bones turned whitish-gray before they too succumbed to the flame.

Except for the *whoosh* of the flamethrower and then the crackle of the flames consuming the flesh and bone, all had been silent. For some moments after the ashen remains collapsed into an untidy heap on the floor we stayed silent, just staring at the smoking mound of ashes and charred bone.

I had just looked at Sandu and he at me in a wordless outpouring of pure intensity when Dragoș made a sound: a gurgling, desperate sound. Sandu was at his side faster than I could see, and I was not far behind. Sandu was examining Dragoș' neck, which had been...well, half-severed was the best way to describe it. Not a killing wound for an am'r, but not a pleasant or convenient one.

"I *must* attend to this, Noosh," Sandu said. With his words, a flush of resentment coursed through me. I was *not* a squeamish kee anymore who wouldn't understand such things. "Of course!" I replied, trying not to let my peevishness show in my voice. "How can I help?"

It was the right answer because Sandu's face, without noticeably altering expression, looked less tense. "Keep your senses on alert while I am busy," he suggested simply. No pat on the back for being a good little am'r-nafsh, but being someone Sandu and Dragoș could count on was the real reward for me now.

I shed my useless flamethrower and wandered around the periphery, standing in each of the entrances to the room in turn and stretching my senses. They were better than they had been before I'd shared blood with Sandu, but I still understood they were pathetic compared to what an am'r could have perceived, and that frustrated me.

I sensed nothing outside any of the doorways, so as I patrolled between them I risked glances back at the action. Sandu had sliced his wrist open and applied the blood to Dragoș' throat wound. To be honest, I didn't look too closely at that part since it seemed he was, well, really working it in. It looked even less comfortable to endure than to watch, and I was happy to turn away.

The next time I turned around, Sandu had re-slashed his wrist, and Dragoș was drinking thirstily from it. Am'r first aid was all about blood. *That's handy for them.* I found myself idly wondering if, knowing am'r, Dragoș would manage to have an erection at this point, and if Sandu did as well, but put the thought aside and focused all my senses intently out of the entranceway in which I was currently standing.

As I started to do yet another circuit of the room, Sandu called me over. "I've sensed nothing, for what that's worth," I told him.

"Thank you, *draga mea*," he said solemnly, and I knew it was for more than the lookout of doubtful value.

"*Da, surata mea*," Dragoș said in a huskier voice than usual. I couldn't tell if it was from having just had his throat hacked in half and healed, or from arousal from the blood-drinking. Maybe both. "You are my dear sister, and I am proud to be so joined to you."

I looked at Dragoș. His English was usually way less archaic and formally cumbersome than Sandu's. I abruptly understood what was going on. Sandu was his patar, too. How had I *not* noticed that before?

"I am proud to have you as a brother, dear Dragoș," I said, and felt my eyes tearing up. Dragoș put an arm up to Sandu, then more tentatively reached out to me. Suddenly we were all three in an embrace, and I was savoring the connection to people I cared about and trusted—who were *family*. It was needed. It was healing. I sniffed and smelled the scent of Sandu, the scent of Dragoș, and wondered how I had *not* known before.

Never mind. Here in the midst of chaos and terror, flame and destruction, was pure, tangible comfort. I soaked it in and tried to pour it back out to my new family.

I could have stood for a good deal more of it, but Dragoș and Sandu pulled away at the same moment and were abruptly all business again.

Well, we *were* still in the middle of a burning, exploding battlefield.

"You are injured as well, *dragă* Anushka. Your vhoon-smell is filling the air."

Oh. I had totally forgotten about *that*. Now, of course, my thighs started throbbing with pain that seemed to be trying to make up for all the time I'd not paid attention to it. Suddenly, Sandu and Dragoș had sat me down and were pulling apart the shreds of the fabric from my dress and the under-trousers. I suddenly felt strangely shy about the men inspecting my inner thighs.

After some uncomfortable probing, Sandu announced that I was very lucky—just surface lacerations. No deep damage to muscles that would keep me from walking and no sliced veins. "These can heal on their own, *draga mea*. We have much to do without delay." I nodded. These sorts of injuries were paper cuts to the am'r, and Sandu probably shouldn't lose any more blood, and Dragoș definitely couldn't. I just had to pull up my big-girl panties and deal.

Sandu continued, "We must find Bagamil *immediately*. Equally importantly, we need to let the so-called-jinn know their leader is dead, and they have the option of running away and pretending it never happened."

"Or fighting to the death," Dragoș put in, grinning.

"I do not think many will choose that," Sandu replied. "If any do, it will be the ones he has made since he started this madness, who have known no other way."

"Um, why not?" I had to ask. "Didn't we just make a martyr of Mehmet? This might make them fight harder in his memory. They seemed pretty fucking devoted to him."

"They are *am'r*," Sandu said with a smile. "There are a few leaders charismatic enough to bring groups of am'r together for a little while, but without their leader they will wander off. Go lick their wounds somewhere private. They will be embarrassed when they realize how stupid they have been, and they will see his failure as proof that he was a fool—a foolish leader they should never have followed. They will denounce him and pretend they never truly believed they were genies."

"Hmmm," was my reply because that seemed simplistic. But we didn't have time to stand there talking. "Oh! Wait!" I cried out and went back to the bits of ex-jinn.

Rooting around in what I could only call "rather hurriedly tossed-about body parts" was not the most pleasant thing ever, but the way my evening had been going, this was just fine. I was happy that A.) these jinn-identified am'r were no longer a threat, and B.) I didn't have to stand around and watch them burn to death. Focusing on the positive, I found what I'd hoped to find.

For *once* in this whole great clusterfuck of events, I could be useful in a timely manner.

"Here!" I said proudly, handing Sandu a walkie-talkie.

He looked at it. Dragoș looked at it. They both looked at me. Sandu seemed not to be able to process any emotions, so he showed none. Dragoș raised an eyebrow of approval at me. I felt like I had won a medal.

The walkie-talkie came to life with a constant stream of chatter. That stopped immediately when Sandu pressed the button and asked in Arabic for Mehmet's second-in-command. There were some confused replies. Then, after Dragoș told him Bat-Bitch was dead—I got a quick, proud glance from my patar when he gave me the not-entirely-deserved credit for killing her—Sandu got back on the horn and made an announcement, which Dragoș quietly translated for me.

"He's saying that Mehmet was killed by his hand and that the one known as the Qarînah was killed by his fritha-puthıa. Now he says that the choice of those who remain is to die at the hands of Bagamil, Vlad the Impaler, and their...'irate' is I think the best translation, so their itate followers—that's us!—or they can, eh, exit very quickly and hope we do not remember their faces or their scents. There is more in that vein."

After Sandu stopped talking, the walkie-talkie was dead quiet. Maybe he was right and the rest of the genies would magically transform back into am'r—saving their skins, abandoning their supposed brothers and sisters, and running off to sulk and lick their ruffled fur back into place like it had never happened.

At any rate, off we went to find Bagamil. Well, after I admitted to and took care of my humiliating need to use the bathroom and met the funny little rodent-thing.

Chapter Twenty-Two

Sandu spoke very quietly to me as we walked. Dragoș took point, staying a bit ahead of us. He was looking out for any remaining enemies who might still be willing to fight about whether they were jinn or not, and for dangers from the damaged caves we were combing. He scented the air a lot.

Sandu was sniffing too, in between words. "We were in council. We were discussing—"

"Arguing!" floated back from Dragoș.

"*Ei bine, da*, we were arguing about the best way to deal with Mehmet and his followers. Whether they *all* needed to die, or if just killing the leaders was sufficient. There was some…difference of opinion…on the best way to accomplish this. We had just come up with a plan to which all agreed when the explosions began.

"Bagamil and I split up to best deal with the situation. Now, perhaps this is just the worry of a son for a father… Can the old man take care of himself? *E ridicol!* Bagamil outlived his enemies for many centuries before I was born as a kee. But still, I will be happier when we find him."

"Or *he* finds us." This, calmly, from Dragoș, who was around a corner from us.

We walked for what felt like miles. Bagamil's headquarters were truly ancient, and there had been plenty of time to tunnel out in all directions. We explored rooms that were decorated in the most beautiful and exotic ways—or once had been, before fire and earthquake had destroyed them.

We didn't just walk. We edged around huge piles of rubble or gaping pits. We climbed over mounds of debris blocking passageways. We had to—well, Sandu and Dragoș had to—force open doors that were blocked on one side or both with the wreckage Mehmet had inflicted on what had obviously been an exquisitely ornamented place. It had been not just a citadel but a beloved home.

We found bodies along the way. Where they were of Team Mehmet, Sandu and Dragoș would take a moment to ensure they were permanently dead. Where they were Team Bagamil, they would take a moment as well and see if they might be brought back with some TLC and blood. Obviously, piles of charcoal were not coming back, but three bodies could indeed change back into functioning am'r: Răzvan, from the Romanian crew, Zopyros, beloved frithaputhra of Tryphena—and where was *she*? All-the-way-dead? Trapped somewhere else?—and

Llorenç the Catalan. They were noted but left to come back for. Bagamil was of primary importance.

There was one room Sandu did not let me into. He followed Dragoș into it and stopped, barring the way with his arms. He called Dragoș out and then turned to go, not letting me see in. "There is nothing there, *micuțo*."

"Really?"

"Not what you are thinking. Not bodies. Well, not bodies of am'r. There were...*books* in there. Scrolls. Tablets. There might be some that are salvageable, but we do not have time for *you* to enter that room."

He knew me too well. "Yes, my patar." I sighed, trying to keep myself from ducking around him and rushing into the room. Not only could he very easily stop me but finding Bagamil was a higher priority. *Really.*

As we went along, Sandu got more and more agitated. In that way of his where he didn't express any emotion, of course, but both Dragoș and I could read him without anything so crude as a physical display, which meant we both were becoming equally distressed.

Finally, after what seemed an exceedingly long distance and time, Sandu visibly had a light-bulb moment. We turned around, came back down the stretch of passageway we'd been searching, and went down another, one I was pretty sure we'd not been down yet due to its being entirely blocked by debris. I helped them to clear it as best I could, but my "help" was mostly just keeping out of the way of two am'r gone into hyper-speed mode. By the time we could get through, even *they* looked a little ruffled.

We crawled through and I slid down the debris pile on the other side. This area was almost entirely wrecked. One of those rocket-things must have impacted right near here. The walls were cracked and burnt, and the hallway was more of a concept. The air was close and acrid. I was coughing and gasping as we went farther down the tunnel, but Sandu and Dragoș were too absorbed to notice. We stopped at a bit of wall, as charred and damaged as the rest of the hall but otherwise not noticeably a doorway or anything.

"I wonder…" Sandu started with words but continued with action, pulling larger bits of rubble out of the way. Dragoș and I helped him, although it was like he didn't remember we were there. When the blank bit of wall was clear, Sandu felt around on it. If there was a hidden door there, I thought, there's not much chance of getting it open. Just as that thought ran across my mind, Sandu pressed something, and there was a *click,* followed by the sounds of dust and small debris trickling down. Sandu pushed, and then he pushed harder.

The door reluctantly moved. Dragoș and I crowded in after him, and as Sandu rushed forward, we could see two bodies. One was clad in bright, friendly yellow, or what had once been bright, friendly yellow and was now singed and sooty. From what I could see, Mister Sunshine was not seriously injured, but he was not moving.

Neither was the other body. It was one of the jinn, and he wasn't looking all that well. Not horribly burned or anything, just not healthy. And unmoving.

I was unnerved. Seeing Bagamil, who had aspects of, if not total omnipotence, something kind of like it...seeing him lying there so still, as still as death... Well, *I* was rattled.

Sandu, on the other hand, looked almost cheerful. "Dragoș, *fiul meu*, go now. Find our friends and have them take care of Răzvan, Llorenç, and Zopyros. And look for Tryphena. Send everyone else away, but tell them Bagamil has...has met his ending. Let them assume it from what you do *not* say, perhaps. But it is very important you do this perfectly. Send everyone away: those who are damaged to go heal, those who have am'r-nafsh to check on their safety. You know what you must do. Many of our vehicles will be damaged, but I imagine you will find enemy transport parked around various egresses. Then, I need you to find Apolinar and bring him here. Quietly, you understand, *da?*"

Dragoș paused, thinking it through. "*Da, patar*. This will take a while. You will stay...*here?* Do you need anything?"

"Yes, we will remain here. When you return with Apolinar, bring transportation for us all. And kee sustenance for Noosh."

"*Da, domnul meu, inteleg și ascult.*" Dragoș bowed, face serious and humble, but a wicked twinkle in his eyes.

"*Fir-ai al dracului!*" Sandu replied, jokingly annoyed.

"Indeed, I have long since!" Dragoș replied, then turned to me and pulled me into an embrace. "I'll be seeing you soon, sister-mine! Don't do anything I wouldn't do, eh?" With that, he am'r-sped from the room.

"I think I need to learn Romanian," I said to Sandu, who was smirking after him.

"*Da, draga mea*. I will enjoy teaching you. I will enjoy teaching you many other things, too."

"So, Sandu. Are we...um...staying in this place while everyone else goes away for a reason?"

"*Sufleţel*, we are. Come here."

I went to him. He put his arms around me, and we just stood there. He looked down at me. In this underground room, there was no light to catch in his eyes, but I could somehow see the gold-flecked green of them, and they had no less power than they ever did. I breathed in his scent and just melted into his eyes, then softened against his body. It was all *better* than I remembered; just standing here with him now was almost as good as the blood-fueled sex we'd had so many times. I did not want to be apart from him, and if that meant staying in a bombed-out cave in the middle of nowhere, well, okey-dokey.

"There are a few things to do, *draga mea*, and I hope you will help me. And then..." He paused. I waited.

"I know you feel I have been remiss in telling you the things you need to know in this new...*life* which you have begun with me. There may be…some…legitimacy to that point of view.

"Since we have been apart and the risks to you were all too immediate, I have realized how ill-prepared you were. It was my fault, my fault entirely. I was…too eager to bring you to me, to us. And I was…I was fearful that telling you things in the wrong *order* would make you reject us. Reject me.

"But my fears, my…*flaws*, endangered you beyond any other threat we have faced. So. Now, if you will stay with me here, I will begin to make up for the ways I have failed you. I will tell you long and tedious tales of Wladislaus Drăculea. I will tell you the secrets of the am'r. You may ask me all the questions your heart desires, and I will not fail to answer or attempt to entice you away to other matters.

"I will make it up to you. I will make you stronger with knowledge, the way I know my sweet librarian prefers above all."

"Well, Sandu, maybe not above. Maybe equal to? Oh, my love! There are things I have to tell you now, too. I don't know how. I don't even know if what I did was OK, but I must tell you. Neplach and I…well, that is, Neplach said—"

"Hush, *micuţo*. Do you not think I can tell his vhoon has strengthened you? Relax, *dragă* Noosh. All is well. You will tell me all about it. But I have been waiting so long to make things up to you. Let me tell you some things. Let me ease my soul as we work. And then we will have a long time, a good long time, to share...so much more."

And so we turned to do the things that needed to be done, and I listened as the vampire Vlad Dracula began to tell me a story.

Epilogue

"Hewwwo? Wha' timezit?"

"Oh shit, did I do the math wrong? I'm sorry, Zuzu!"

"Noosh? It's you? How are you? *Where* are you? It's been *months*! What the fuck? You've been AWOL way past the end of your vacation leave. I've had to do a whole song-and-dance for Herr Direktor. The Board wants to replace you, and it's only because I've been willing to do your job without a pay raise that you have a job left!"

"Oh, fuck, I'm *really* sorry, Zuz! It's just...well...um...it's really a long story."

"It had better be! You told me some drug-addled bullshit about princes and vampires and saving the world. And orgies. And you promised me some of those *really good drugs*, remember? So, when can I come over and get them? And the whole story!"

"Well...uh...you can't, really. I'm not coming home."

"What? No! Stop playing games, Noosh."

"No, I mean, I'm not even in the country. And I'm not coming back to Centerville or the Haw-Fuck-My-Life. I'll send a formal letter recommending that you be hired for my job. With a retroactive pay raise for all the time you've been unofficially doing it."

"I don't *want* your job! I want you to come back and tell me *everything*."

"Maybe I'll stop by and visit sometime, Zuzu. Just not for a while. Look, it's super-trite and obvious: girl meets boy, girl falls in love with boy, girl and boy go on a bit of an adventure. And then ... um ... after some interesting experiences, they live happily ever after. Boring, really. It's just the boy really is, well...rich. And stuff. I wasn't exaggerating about that. And he has his own personal library, as it were, and I'm in charge of that now. So, it was just a move to the private sphere, really."

"With a random strange guy in a random strange country. Which you won't even tell me about."

"Well, we got...um...married. If that helps."

"*What*? And you didn't invite me?"

"It was a very small ceremony. Just the paperwork. Sort of."

"Noosh."

"I am really, *really* sorry, Zuz. Please, just accept this for now."

"Well, are you happy?"

"Really, *really* happy. I didn't know I could be so happy. It's...I'm... it's just, well...indescribable."

"I'm getting that. Well, as long as you are happy, Noosh. But I miss you."

"I miss you, too, Zuz! And someday, you'll get the whole story."

"There weren't ever any drugs, were there?"

"No. Not...not in the way you're thinking, anyway."

"OK. That's comforting. I think. When you are ready to come back and tell me the story. I'll be here. Doing your job, getting your paycheck."

"I'm glad. No one better!"

"I won't tell Dre you said that. Hey, Dre will be *my* minion, now! I like that!"

"Poor Dre! Don't be too cruel."

"Oh, he likes it. Maybe there will be a wedding to invite you to, someday. If he behaves. And if you'll come?"

"I'll do my best! Look, I should let you get back to sleep."

"Whatever. Like I'm going back to sleep now. Maybe I'll call Dre and share the pain."

"You do that. Love you, Zuzu."

"Yeah, right. If you loved me, you'd have invited me to the wedding. But I love you, despite your running off and not telling me about your adventures. So, stay happily ever after, wherever you are."

"I'll do the best I can. I mean, you never know how the story ends. And you just can't trust writers with your favorite characters, can you?"

"Well, besides *me*, you're my favorite character in this story. And if the writer fucks with us, I think we can take 'em!"

"Oh, yes. I think we could deal with *anything* now. I have some *resources*, let's just say. Anyway, since we have that settled, I'll say bye for now."

"Take care of yourself, Noosh. *Seriously*. But bye for now."

Index of Non-English Phrases

PHRASE • TRANSLATION • LANGUAGE

A trebuit să soseşti de dimineață? • Did you have to arrive in the morning? • Romanian

aceasta este • this is • Romanian

Acum! • Now! • Romanian

Amerikalı • American • Turkish

amına koyayım • Literally "let me stick it in your pussy" but it's also "fuck / fuck you / fucking X" • Turkish

ANFO Patlayıcı • ammonium nitrate/fuel oil, explosive • Turkish

Aoleu! • Ouch! • Romanian

aruncătoarea de flăcări • flamethrower • Romanian

Aşmedai bey, sadrazam • Mr. Asmodeus, grand vizier • Turkish

Ateş! • Fire! • Turkish

Ayağa kalkın! • Stand up! • Turkish

INDEX OF NON-ENGLISH PHRASES

Băga-mi-aş pula! • Fuck! (literally, "I would stick my dick into") • Romanian

berat-emini • a distributor of ordinances • Turkish

biliyorum • I know • Turkish

biz cinler • us (we) jinn • Turkish

ca un lup • (hungry) like a wolf • Romanian

çay • tea • Turkish

Ce nu te omoară, te face mai puternic • What does not kill you, makes you stronger • Romanian

chamuda • cutie • Hebrew

cinler • Genie • Turkish

cinlerim • Genies • Turkish

cogito ergo sum • I think, therefore I am • Latin

creatură senzuală • sensual creature • Romanian

da • Yes • Romanian

Da, domnul meu, inteleg şi ascult! • Yes, my lord, I understand and I listen! • Romanian

De ce ai adus un am'r-nafsh aici? • Why did you bring your am'r-nafsh here? • Romanian

devşirme • "child levy" or "blood tax" • Turkish

Dinle! • Listen! • Turkish

Dobryj vyechyer • Good evening • Russian

domnişoara • Miss • Romanian

domnul şi Stăpinul meu • my Lord and Master • Romanian

domnule Pricolici—prostuţule • Mr. Pricolici—you silly boy • Romanian

draga mea • my darling, my sweetheart • Romanian
dragă Noosh • dear Noosh • Romanian
dragonul meu • my dragon/demon • Romanian
E ridicol! • It's ridiculous! • Romanian
ei bine … • well … • Romanian
Enchanté, ma belle mademoiselle • Delighted, my beautiful girl • French
esti a mea • you are mine • Romanian
evet • yes • Turkish
Fātiḥ • Conqueror • Turkish
Fātiḥ, gel! Yanlış bir şey! • Conqueror, come! Something's wrong! • Turkish
Fir-ai al dracului! • Go to hell!, literally, "you should belong to the devil."
Fir-ar să fie! • Mild curse, like "Damn it," untranslatable to English • Romanian
fiul meu • My son • Romanian
Frenk • Foreign(er), Western(er), from "Frankish." Not a polite term. • Turkish
Frøken • Miss • Norwegian
gavur • infidel, foreigner, worshiper of fire, non-believer • Turkish
Gidelim! • Let's go! • Turkish
gizli yılan • snakes in hiding • Turkish
grande petite mort • big little death ("little death" is term for orgasm) • French
gulyabani • ghoul • Turkish

INDEX OF NON-ENGLISH PHRASES

güzel danışman • beautiful advisor • Turkish
güzelim • beautiful • Turkish
hadaka no tsukiai • naked friendship (platonic bathing together) • Japanese
hader, ya Sultan • Yes, Sultan • Arabic
hai să nu dezgropăm morţii • Let sleeping dogs lie, literally, "Let's not disturb the dead" • Romanian
hammam • Turkish baths • Turkish
hanım • Miss, Lady, term of respect • Turkish
Intră! Fii binevent! Bine ai venit! Intră, tatăl meu, și tu, și tu, noua mea prietenă! • Enter! Welcome! You are welcome! Come, my father, and you, and you, my new friend! • Romanian
ısrarcı kimse • gadfly • Turkish
jinnī / jinn • genie / genies • Arabic
□□□□□□ • kerosene • Russian
kalba • Bitch, literally "female dog" • Arabic
kardeşlerim • my brothers • Turkish
Kazıklı bey • Sir Impaler • Turkish
Konbanwa • Good evening • Japanese
kumandan muavini • deputy commander • Turkish
kütüphaneci • librarian • Turkish
l'universelle araignée • the universal spider, a nickname for Louis XI • French
la • no • Arabic
Liniștește-te, te rog. • Calm down, please. • Romanian
lütfen • please • Turkish

masīHī • Christian • Arabic

Merhaba, benim adım Iblis • Hello, my name is Iblis • Turkish

micuţo • little one • Romanian

moje neteř • my niece • Czech

mon petite chou • my little cabbage (endearment) • French

mulţumesc • thank you • Romanian

nenorociţi nebuni • crazy bastards • Romanian

Noroc! • Cheers!/Good Luck!/More power to you! • Romanian

nu • No • Romanian

O Quam Misericors est Deus, Pius et Justus • O how Merciful is God, Faithful and Just • Latin

oda-bashi • "head of chamber," a corporal of the Janissaries • Turkish

onsen • hot spring • Japanese

opat • abbot • Czech

Öyle değil mi? • Is it not? / Eh? • Turkish

peki ... • well ... • Turkish

Pizda mă-sii! • Fuck me! literally, "Fuck his mother's cunt." • Romanian

poreclă pentru • nickname for • Romanian

Sabır acıdır, meyvesi tatlıdır. • Patience is bitter, but its fruit is sweet. • Turkish

sanjak-bey • a high officer of feudal cavalry and governor of a district • Turkish

INDEX OF NON-ENGLISH PHRASES

Sevgili kızım • My dear girl • Turkish
Shalom • Hello/Goodbye/Peace • Hebrew
Shaqîqah • Sister • Arabic
sharmouta ghadira • treacherous bitch • Arabic
Siktir! • Fuck!/Fuck you!/Get fucked! • Turkish
sincer îmi cer scuze • honestly I can apologize • Romanian
sivrisinek • mosquito • Turkish
Somn uşor, vise plăcute. • Sleep well, sweet dreams. • Romanian
ştii • you know • Romanian
strýc • uncle • Czech
sufleţel • my soul • Romanian
sultanım • my sultan • Turkish
surata mea • my sister • Romanian
taci • Hush • Romanian
Tamam, anlaşıldı! • Roger, over! • Turkish
tatlım • sweetie • Turkish
te rog • please • Romanian
te rog, săruta-mă • Please, kiss me • Romanian
Teşekkür ederim, sevgili. • Thank you, dear. • Turkish
toată • all (a inventat toată = making up whole cloth) • Romanian
tribut de sânge • Blood tax • Romanian
Voivode • Warlord, medieval title used in Wallachia & Transylvania • Old Slavic

Voivode, domnul meu Drăculea, tatăl meu iubit • Voivode, my lord Dracula, my beloved father • Romanian

ya sharmouta • Oh, bitch/slut, literally "dirty washrag" • Arabic

ya Shaykh • my Lord • Arabic

Glossary of the Am'r Language

AM'R WORD • DEFINITION

adharmhem • one who endangers am'r as a whole, or the act of endangering the am'r as whole

ahstha • coma am'r fall into when deprived off too much blood and/or oxygen

am'r *(sing. & pl.)* • commonly known as a "vampire"

am'r-nafsh *(sing. & pl.)* • A living human being who shared blood with an am'r three times, but not yet died.

Aojasc' am'ratv! • "Strength and immortality!"

aojysht *(sing.)*, **aojyshtaish** *(pl.)* • am'r elder, am'r elders

bakheb-vhoonho • giver of blood, used for am'r who give blood to other am'r or kee; used for the stronger blood going to the weaker, whether am'r or kee

cinyaa • my lover

esteshcinast • *verb:* to know by smell, specifically to recognize the vhoon-anghyaa of other am'r *(Present tense: "I esteshcinasti", past tense "I have esteshcinastii")*

fraheshteshnesh • first blood meal as a newly awoken am'r

frangkhilaat • to feed / take nutrition from a kee

frithaputhra *(sing.)*, **-ish** *(pl.)* • "beloved child", title used by a am'r for an am'r / am'r-nafsh made with the former's blood

gharpatar • grandfather, maker of my maker

izchha *(sing.)*, **-ish** *(pl.)* • a "sacrifice", a mortal who is selected to donate blood (with or without sex)

kee *(sing. & pl.)* • mortal, non-vampire, living human being

maadak • intoxicating drink; effects am'r like strong hallucinogen / tranquilizer

maadakyo • corrupted with maadak, a mortal who has drunk maadak

pat'rkosh • patar-killer

patar • "parent" or "maker"; title used by a am'r or am'r-nafsh for the am'r who made them

tokhmarenc • dying the final death; "giving the tokhmarenc" is killing another am'r so they cannot rise again

vhoon • blood

vhoon-anghyaa • blood influence, blood-line, the traits that come down from your patar; also the smell of your patar in your blood

vhoon-berefteh • to be bled

vhoon-vaa • am'r-style healing with blood

vhoon-vayon • am'r love making, with other am'r or am'r-nafsh

vistarascha • dying the mortal death; becoming am'r

Acknowledgments

I've always planned, since I was seventeen and decided I'd be an author someday, to thank the two authors who first made me want to write novels: Robert A. Heinlein and Samuel R. Delaney. They are the best influences a writer could hope for.

Professor David Lenson: thank you for personally encouraging me to write about vampires back when I was supposed to be writing, you know, non-fiction papers for your class!

Beatrice: Thank you for all the wonderful phone calls working out how mythical creatures might really biologically function.

Anne-Marie: Thank you for being my on-call archivist, and thanks for marrying into my crazy family and making it even crazier!

Lauren: You went from being the bestest fan anyone could hope for to being an integral part of this whole thing. I never anticipated needing a business partner, but I'm so glad when I needed one that you were willing to come on this crazy ride with me. Thank you, and I hope we ride on together for a satisfying and rewarding time.

Tiffany: I'm so lucky to finally have an editor like you. Thank you for all the support and enthusiasm from day one of working together.

Kwasi: I'm so grateful you were available to redo the covers, as we moved to the new editions. Your art takes the whole package up a serious notch!

Saraphina Churchill: Your patience in teaching me InDesign will never cease to amaze me. Thank you so much for your valuable time and all the laughs.

Mark Cotton: I simply could not do an LLC without you, knowing you are there to advise me makes me feel braver.

Lars Hedbor: From the very beginning, you have provided such sustaining support that I honestly do not know how to thank you. Sometime we shall wear tricorn hats together and share drinks and good food.

Chaz Brenchley: A better mentor a girl could not ask. Many hugs until I can be hanging out with you and Karen again in person.

Dr. Charles Moser: thanks for help with anatomy of the circulatory system and for the tip about Turkish tea. Dinners with you are missed.

Dr. Elayne Pope: thank you so much for patiently answered some very strange questions about burning corpses from a complete (and completely strange) stranger.

Ligia Buzan & Elijah Zarwan: I don't even know how to thank you enough for the language guidance and education. Thanks for helping me play in sandboxes which I don't really know enough to play in! Any mistakes in languages in this novel are my fault, not theirs!

Sheeba Arif: I sent along to you an almost impossible job, where I'd chosen Vlad's old enemy from history to be the bad guy in this book, without realizing what a mess that would make for me as a writer, trying not to perpetuate anti-Turkish and anti-Arab sentiments. I cannot thank you enough for helping me sort through the mess with such patience and care for the story I was trying to tell. After your suggestions, this is a much better book.

Debbie Notkin: Thank you for coming up with the title over tacos with me. I miss regular meals with you.

My life underwent a lot of changes during the writing and the quest to (re)publish this book. At the time of publication, the people most immediately supporting me as a writer and human every day are Trent and Bethany and Krissy. Thank you all for putting up with how weird and probably annoying it is to live with a writer. (And especially, thank you Bethany for the support when numbers come into play and I become a wobbly mess.)

Also, I'd like to thank Robert Lebling for gathering so much jinn information in one handy and enjoyably readable place: *Legends of the Fire Spirits: Jinn and Genies from*

Arabia to Zanzibar is recommended to anyone who wants to know more about that fascinating race.

I recommend *In the Shadows of Empires* by Sir Jens to anyone who loves history.

I also need to thank all the people who have posted so much random information on the internet. From devoted Wikipedia editors (the unsung heroes of the internet, unless you chance to sit next to one in a pub, in which case their praise cannot be sung for long enough, and preferably in more rounds of beer) and also the somewhat crusty users of intravenous-drug-use forums, which are surprisingly handy sources of information when you are writing a book such as this.

Thank you to all the fans of the Blood & Ancient Scrolls series, for supporting me during their first publication, and for sticking around while the books needed to be republished. Everyone who has bought a second copy of this book, just to support this whole endeavour, you are showing the world what true fandom means, and I appreciate you a thousand thousand times over!

Finally, to that guy in the bathroom at ManRay club, who, after my first performance there, burst in on me in the ladies' room cleaning up the blood (mostly fake—long story!) and delightedly announced, "You guys really ARE vampires!" Don't stop believing, my man.

About Raven Belasco

Raven Belasco has been fascinated by vampires since she was 12 years old. You probably shouldn't let 12-year-olds read Stoker's Dracula, but Raven grew up in a house where, if she could get the book off the shelf, she could read it. Anyway, the bloody seeds were planted both for her to become a fan of horror, and a verbose writer.

Raven writes not just for her own pleasure, but to make books that give any-and-everybody an enjoyable escape, and to delight fellow geeks with weird historical details and multi-level puns. She wants to pay forward the joy that books have brought her through tough times or otherwise boring waiting-rooms.

To keep up with the Blood & Ancient Scrolls series, you can sign up for Raven's Newsletter at https://ancientscrolls.beehiiv.com/subscribe

Or find her online: https://ravenbelas.co/